ECHOES OF

EMBER & EFFIGY

This is a work of fiction. Similarities to real people, places, or events are entirely coincidental.

ECHOES OF EMBER & EFFIGY

First edition. October 13, 2024.

Written by Vana Elaire.

Edited by Maryssa Gordon.

Cover design by Shai Premades.

To the gentle souls who brighten our realm.
Don't let them steal your light.

Chapter 1

MY FATHER IS THE DEVIL, and my mother, the High Priestess. But I was born the Fool—a lesser god, with not even the powers of a rose quartz. And crystals are only as formidable as the mind of the mortal who wields them. Or so I am told.

Most hate my father, a trickster god of temptation. My mother they revere.

Sometimes, I think I would like to be hated. It is a strong emotion with many attachments. Not at all like indifference, which takes no effort to feel. It is how I am used to being regarded by Celestials and mortals alike. I receive their prayers by chance only. Never am I venerated in earnest.

It is a dispiriting existence. To be always starved of the worship that others receive freely. They are drunk on it. Robust and overflowing. *Jovial.* And out of pity, they bestow upon me their scraps, like the hurried orisons one offers for good weather or safe travels. They are better than nothing.

I could speak forever of grievances. But I must begin this testimony in the place where all motives originate. Youth.

My childhood came and went in a flash. They are the only pleasant memories I have of my parents.

For those precious few years, Father and Mother doted on me. "A boy!" they rejoiced upon my birth. "He will be a god among gods!" Such is what they believed, till my period of Celestial growing ended. My amber eyes remained fixed, always the color of tide-dampened sands. They did not change with my emotions or expel the white light needed to manifest the wishes of mortals. And if I could not gain their reverence, I could not be worthy. I could not be a god.

What I remember most vividly from those early years is the singed smell of offerings. Of how the scent of charred animal flesh burned through my nose. Of how I wished those beasts had been slain for me.

I would linger about the Aries Court for hours at a time, sequestering myself in the Hall of Effigies. My own sculpture, newly forged, remained bare. Smokeless and dim. While that of my father, in his horned form, glowed bright from the scales of the Emros—a snake whose skin is said to be made of diamonds. The highest offering a mortal can give. And alongside it stood my mother's carved likeness, blazing and gloried. I leaned to her and caught the sweet fragrance of the rose oil worn by the priest who had sacrificed to her in the mortal realm. And with it came the whispered pleas and orisons. The wishes and prayers, wants and desires. A request for a healing here, a miracle there. This is what they longed for. Most of it would go ignored. The Celestials did not have much care for pleasures or comforts not their own. On occasion, they answered, but this was only to secure further veneration, for a thread of hope is more valuable than a cord of certainty.

"Keep them in lack, and they'll forever want. Forever look to you, hoping for a recurrence of that one time you answered and met the need of some distant ancestor. Grant too often or too abundantly, and they'll forget your grace. Forget what it is to be without it. Forget the importance of the divinity that elevates you above them." My uncle, the Magician, had said this to me, eyes still glowing white from a Granting. He did not often Grant. He had no need of it. There were songs about him. His divine status had held high for centuries, like that of my parents. Mortals *believed* in them. Exalted them without doubt—as assuredly as they trusted our great Moon of the High Nine to sway the tides of her oceans or of the Sun to bathe us with light day after day. I had not heard him enter. I was too young to notice that he was always creeping, always lurking. Back then, I had not the language to describe the way he made me feel. I only knew that I did not like it. This advice was in answer to a remark. I had made it to my cousin, his daughter, Arcana, born a mere twelve seasons after myself.

"If mine burned like Father's, I would give them whatever they asked of me," I said as we sat, legs crossed, before my marble twin. It would be reshaped when I was of an age and height—a man. For now, it was only a boy of six that we gazed upon. "When they begin to ask, I will Grant every wish. I want to help them. All of them." Arcana smiled at this.

"They will love you," she said, the ghost of a sleepy smile forming on her lips; it fell away when Uncle came in. She ran to him, little body clinging to his waist. He scooped her up and together they looked down at me. Arcana's face as she stared was cute and round and in those days, still pleasant. I touched her vacated spot on the cold granite, wishing my uncle would leave so we could be alone again.

"Ah, Magi! If I were searching for you, which I was not, this would be the last place I'd think to look."

The fringe of my uncle's crimson robes brushed against me as he turned to regard Father. Uncle did not return the Devil's smile. I would not have either. It was of the disingenuous sort, the one he brought out when annoyed. And anyway, the Magician was not known for his kindness. That was reserved for his precious Arcana. "Don't tell me you've Granted," continued Father, "that's twice in the span of a decade! It's no wonder you cannot keep your effigy lit. I scarcely remember the last time mine was without smoke or at the very least, a faint glow."

"Who says that I have?" replied Uncle.

"Your eyes were gleaming with the white light a moment ago. It has faded away now. But they were," I said. I heard my Father chuckle above me. He was in his handsome, male form, but he had forgotten to do away with his hooves. They clicked atop the granite near my fingers. I touched one, and instantly, they were feet again, bony with long tendons, like mine.

"Your boy seeks to Grant every mortal whim," said Uncle.

"No son of mine would be so daft."

"See it with your own eyes, then."

I had heard the Magician could share his sight, show a person a vision of the past, or sometimes, rarely, the future. Most Celestials could perform basic charms, little spells of convenience. Or curses, if the occasion called for it. Even mortals had their crystals and Astrologers. But Uncle was a true sorcerer, born to it by divine right—by the will of the higher gods, the planets. It is said that Mercury gave him the gift to bend all magic in the Celestial realm to his will. He exercised such abilities now.

The levity fell from Father's face as the illusion overtook him, and when it was finished, I could scarcely meet his gaze. He leered down at me in that way that was his alone, and I longed to be anywhere but under his eyes.

"I am hungry, Father; I want a sweet." Arcana's voice rang clear as a bell in the hall, breaking that awful, stifled silence. I was grateful for it.

"Come then. Let's see if we can fetch a honey cake. The Cancerian Court always has treats at this hour."

I watched them go. Arcana spared me a glance and half of a smile, and then it was just me and Father.

"Stop slouching. Get off the floor. Stand upright and behave in the manner befitting one such as you—like the divine Celestial you were bred to be. I would have taken you for a mortal if I didn't know you to be otherwise." I rose at my father's command, though I was confused and did not know what he meant by likening me to them.

"I have never seen a mortal," I said.

"They are not much."

My confusion vanished, and with it went much of my confidence. I had been imagining myself a god. Had pictured my effigy in the eye of my mind, brightly burning with offering. I had almost believed it. It seemed an absurdity to think of such things now. I saw myself reflected in the mirror of my father's eyes, and the delusion of my grandeur faded like a flame doused with water. My shoulders slumped of their own volition, and this only served to make everything worse. If I had blinked, I might have missed the swift shift of shades within his eyes. Their fixed, calm brown switched to fierce cerulean. For a moment, I thought he would strike me.

"Sorry," I muttered, attempting to get ahead of the scolding I knew was sure to follow for the disgrace of my poor bearing. His severe expression eased at this, and through the modulation, I regained some of the self-assurance I had lost.

"Conduct yourself in accordance with your rank and you will have nothing to apologize for."

I nodded, but he took little heed of me as he spoke. After all, he had not come to the Hall of Effigies to seek me out. He had come to indulge his hubris. My small frame stood beside his, dwarfed by his enormity. We were bathed in the light that emanated from his carving. Smoke wafted around us from a fresh slaughter, and the Devil received it with a grin, one which stretched so wide I was certain his flesh would tear from the tension. He placed his hand on the marble of his head. This was always my favorite thing to see. I had only witnessed Mother perform the action just once before, when I had been too little to speak. Celestials had no need to physically absorb their venerations, just the essence of them, the mere knowledge of the adulation was enough to sustain. We were tethered to our effigies and forthwith imbued with whatever was offered to them in the mortal realm. But to take it corporeally was to experience every pleasure that exists in the world at once.

Father went limp under its influence, like a kitten lifted by the scruff. He levitated above his duplicate—above *me*, and though I could not see his face, I knew that it was painted in rapture. It was some time before he descended, and when he collected himself, he turned to me.

"After your trials, this is what your godhead will be." He sealed the declaration with a touch upon my forehead, just between my eyes. His two fingers glowed with the transference. He had given me a small portion of his veneration, a single drop from his ocean of obeisance. Not enough to sustain but enough to inspire. "What is mine shall be yours, so long as you prove yourself worthy of it. Your preeminence shall bring to my altars more glory, and more deference, just as a divine son should."

He left me then, and I was alone, with only my thoughts and the inebriation of his gift for company. I swayed with it, relishing the way it lifted my spirits and clouded my head. I was once again envisioning myself an exalted Celestial. But this musing soon dwindled with the waning of Father's boon and I was left with the weight of expectations: my performance at the looming trials.

I had not considered them in all my days spent wandering the halls of the Zodiac Courts, mingling with my distant cousins—the Cups, Swords, Pentacles, and other lesser gods. My head in those years was filled with trivial, childish whimsy. I should have been preparing myself. In a mere six seasons, I would be tasked with a staging of my divinity before the twelve courts and the planets. The latter wanted to make certain the offspring of the Celestial coupling they permitted was journeying along the path of greatness—that I was not engendered in vain. Arcana and I were the final divinities allowed to spawn from a Celestial pairing of the major gods. The last were the Lovers, born to the Emperor and Empress. I had heard stories about the miracles they each Granted in their youth trials. Of how their effigies shone with the laurels of their merit. And when it came time for their second trial, the truly important one that occurs after a Celestial reaches maturity, the halls were alight for decades from the festivals held in their honor. They flickered even now, centuries later.

In this evocation, I stand before them and admire the fruits of those trials. None in the hall shone so bright as my father's, but theirs is still a grand sight to behold. Second brightest is Mother, and then Uncle. I scan them all and take in the varying degrees of mortal adulation. My eyes jump from the Emperor to the Hanged Man, to the Hierophant, and so on, till they land on the weakest of us. Temperance is the least revered and I shudder at the prospect of becoming the new owner of that title. I shake off the terror and move to stand before my likeness, thinking of the Astrologers who will read the skies and make predictions about which days are better than others to offer to me. About how much blood should be spilled in my name. I do not remember it, but on the day of my birth, the mortals held a festival. My parentage alone had secured me that reverence. When I learned of this, I remember thinking how easy a thing it must be to win their favor, their love, their worship.

I lingered there, regarding that hardened replica, unmoving save for the steady rise and fall of my chest. It was not till my face began to ache that I realized, I had been smiling like a fool.

Chapter 2

THE BRIGHT AMETHYST OF ARCANA'S EYES begins to vary a mere week ahead of our youth trials. As we stand in the Gemini courtyard gardens, she presses her little nose against mine, then widens them, emphasizing the dazzling display of her budding maturity. Her breaths are hot on me, and laced with the smell of the sweets she ate a moment ago.

"Do you see?" she asks, still wide-eyed.

"Yes, they are different," I say, biting back my jealousy as I watch the slow change. They shift and settle on a shade of green as vibrant as the grass in Leo season. The memory of that morning always burns me.

"Can yours change yet?"

They could not.

"I think so," I lied.

"Let me see."

There was nothing to behold, but I made a show of it anyway, blinking rapidly and raising my dark brows. Arcana turned the corners of her lips down and the expression made her look wise beyond the five years I knew her to be.

"No, it is not like that. You cannot make it so by force. It just comes."

"What do you mean, *comes*?"

"You know, like a feeling does. You cannot make yourself be happy when really, you are sad. You can pretend that you are but it is not the same. It is not real. You are pretending."

From anyone else it would have been a jeer. But there was no malice behind the accusation. And moreover, it was true. I had nothing to say for myself in the way of refutation and so I stood there, and let the silence grow between us. The tears would have begun to well in my treasonous, unchanging eyes were it not for the tiny fingers that slipped around my hand.

"It's alright, cousin. They will change soon enough."

"Will they? I rather think they'll stay fixed in that sallow shade of mud for all eternity. In fact, I've wagered my veneration reserves on as much." This was Tiberias, one of the minor deities belonging to the Suit of Swords. He towered over us at ten, but he looked to be twice that as he sneered, hands on hips and nose upturned. I wondered how long he had been there without my noticing his presence.

"Well, you haven't wagered much then. Minor as you are," came Arcana's reply, clever and cutting as quartz, even at that age. "I've visited the Hall of Effigies for your lot of deities nearly every day. Nothing is ever lit. That is why I hate the Gemini Court. It is so dull and cold here."

I think this last is what set him off—he plucked her, hard and swift against the shell of her ear. His eyes were slow to shift through the colors, which was indicative of his lesser divinity. But even so, we were young children and could be easily bested in any Celestial duel, despite hierarchy. Except...

Arcana's eyes dart through an array of colors in an instant.

It is a dusky sienna that stares up at Tiberias. Later, I would learn to steer clear of her whenever she was seen bearing this hue.

The radiance that pours from her sockets shocks me. A rich gold, gleaming so bright I am forced to squint—to shield my eyes from the sheer magnitude of its effulgence. It blasts Tiberias backward, sending him skidding across the soft earth in the courtyard.

Arcana goes to stand over him when she is finished, sprinting to close the gap on little legs. She turns to look at me but I am a statue stunned to stiffness. I would not have moved even if beckoned. I glimpse the sight from a distance with a note of detached horror.

The flesh on one side of his body had been seared.

"You...little...b-bitch." Tiberias's voice is dreadful and thin.

"Father said if someone ever called me that, I should kick them."

I looked away as she did it. The sound of that wretched, gurgling cough that followed. I will never forget it. Arcana pranced over to me and took me by the hand, tugging me along. Over my shoulder, I looked timorously at him, sprawled in the dirt on his back. His tortured gaze hooked into mine. We did not yet know what Arcana truly was. But even so, I did not pity him. He should never have laid hands on her.

She tightens her grip on me and I quicken my pace.

"Let us leave the Air Wing and not see it again until our trials," she said.

I let her guide me along, past the two-headed bronze statue and the fountain of honey wine. We trekked on till we reached the Fire Wing, and this is when I turned to her.

"How long have you been able to do magic?" I asked. She wrinkled her nose at this.

"That was not magic. It is just godhead. You have it too."

"No, I do not."

"Not yet. But you will."

I shook my head.

"You *will*," she said again. "It is already living inside here," she touched my chest with her pointing finger. "You just have to learn how to pull it out."

"And how did you learn to do it?"

"Father. He gives me some of his veneration to practice."

I wondered why my father had not done as much.

"Will he be alright?" I asked.

"Who?"

"Tiberias."

Arcana shrugged, the action a quick and careless blur on her tiny frame. "He has divine blood. He will heal."

"And do you think he will tell the others?"

"Tell them what?"

"That my eyes still cannot change. That yours can."

"Maybe. If he does, he will have to tell them it was I who burned him. And I do not think he would want to admit that."

I had not considered this.

"But who cares," she continued. "You will show everyone you can at the trials."

This also I had not considered—had not *believed*.

"Will you teach me some of what you know? Like how to *pull it out*?" I asked.

She smiled and draped an arm round me, tucking her brown coils behind her ear.

"Sure, but first, I want something to eat."

·······»·) ✷ (·«········

I imagined that dueling on borrowed veneration took a lot out of a Celestial, not that I knew from experience at that period of my life. But I assumed it had done, judging by the way Arcana all but inhaled the pot of Angel's Stew we came by in the Cancerian Court. I offered her the rest of mine and she devoured it as quickly as if it were a cure for some rare malady with which she had been afflicted.

The realm was ever-replenishing and alive. There was always ample food in the dining hall, always warm and always delicious. Though we did not have any true need of it. It was just another pleasure, like bathing or sleeping. A comfort. I managed to secure us some honey cakes and Arcana's eyes lit up at this—those delightful confections were always the quickest to go and the slowest to materialize. The gods loved their sweets.

When she was good and sated, Arcana licked her sticky lips and carried me off and away from prying eyes, where she taught me everything she knew about godhead.

From her earlier performance in the courtyard, I had presumed her to be some all-knowing prodigy. That she would somehow bestow upon me the ability to achieve feats of wonder at the heights of my divinity. Only the former was true. Hours passed and I had not been able to attain even a modicum of progress. Of improvement. But Arcana did not lose patience with me.

"I think you are one of those gods that need coaxing in order to bring it out, like the Chariot."

My brow furrowed in beaten astonishment. "Your mother needs that? Are you sure?"

"Yes, long ago. At her trials. But not anymore. I think it will be the same with you. Once you are under the pressure, it will just *come out.*"

When she saw that I had not been assuaged, she looped her arm in mine and rested her head on my shoulder.

14

"You are a major divinity. A High Celestial, like me. We were born of greatness. Born to be great."

This at last comforted me, and I let my head loll atop hers. We stood like that for a length of time, still and content in the secluded corridor, watching from the archway as the stars shimmered in the night sky. We separated after some moments and Arcana looked at me, smiling faintly before pressing two glowing fingers to my temple.

"It is not much. Store it away."

"How?"

"Don't let the pleasure overtake you. Fight it off and it will be saved for later use."

I did as she said and fought against the bliss. I felt the veneration slip into my being. Felt it swell and then settle in my chest. A new sensation unleashed itself inside me. How had I not known I could do this? Why had I been left to discover it on my own? I felt the weight of my inadequacies upon me as Arcana's hand slid from my face.

"Archie, dear. What are you doing?" Our heads whipped around in unison at the sound of the stern voice.

"Nothing, Father," said Arcana, making her way over to the Magician.

"It did not look like nothing." Arcana ignores this and leaps into Uncle's arms. One peck on his cheek from her and it is forgotten. He aims a glare at me that could cut glass and then it is his back that I see, and Arcana waving at me from behind it. I watch her fade down the corridor till it is just me, alone under the archway. Staring, staring, staring. At the black expanse. At nothing and at everything. Till I grow weary of it and meander to my quarters.

The Moon spills her light inside my chamber, silver-smooth and just as luminous. I have always loved our Moon. I was born under her—a child of the Cancer constellation. I had been trying to stave off the weight of my eyelids, but her soft light lulled me to slumber. I wanted to wait up for Father, but on this night, he was taking too long with his gallivanting in the mortal realm. I think there is a village he has taken to terrorizing. They believe him a demon or an unfettered spirit—one who has lingered in the Parallel Dimension of dead mortals too long and is hence unable to transcend beyond the veil to their afterlife. He comes to them in the guise of such a shape. Whispers to them his plans of unspeakable horrors. Then after some days or weeks, when they are scared beyond reason, he assumes another shape. A mortal one. He is a learned man and most knowledgeable in the subject of banishing ghouls. He advises them to sacrifice to the Devil, highest of Celestials. This, among other trickery, is how Father came to be the most venerated.

After a few short hours in repose, I am jolted awake by the distant sound of his laughter. It is mingled with Mother's. When I enter their bedchamber, they are both high-colored and glistening and I am certain they have just finished engaging in acts that I am too young to understand. Father still has horns, leftover from whatever form he had been wearing. Mother does not seem to mind.

"What do you want?" she asks, beckoning me forward with a gesture. When I stand before her, she inspects me, frowning.

"I wanted to ask Father something."

"Why not ask me? You are mine as much as his."

I swallow the bitter words I want to say. *Because you never listen to comprehend. Only to reply. Only to hear yourself speak because you so love the sound of your own voice.*

Father had been busying himself near the window. I think he was searching the sable heavens for High Goddess Venus. But he turned round upon the mention and fixed a pointed look at me.

"Tess is right. But I have an ear to lend. So come. Ask it of me."

I always hated dealing with the pair of them. Interactions were tolerable, to a degree, when they were separate. I could handle Mother's silent stares on their own, each charged with her obvious and growing resentment of me. Father hid his suspicions better. Or perhaps he truly thought my lack to be a passing phase. It does not matter now, after everything. After the truth of it. Only...let it be known that enduring their shared regard at that crucial point of my youth, their sidelong glares and whispered slights, was like being slowly suffocated and crushed by some invisible mass.

Mother sighs at my back while I shuffle toward the Devil. I do not like his mood tonight, the energy of it is strange. But I ask my question anyway, taking care not to let my voice tremble too much in the delivery.

"May I have some of your...veneration?" I cringe at my cadence and Father tries to pretend he is not doing the same, though I glimpse the glint of burgundy that flashes in his eyes. It is only there for an instant but I know it well, the shade of his shame.

"Give you my stores? Why should I?"

"For practice."

"*Practice?*"

"Yes, so that I may learn how to *pull it out.* Arcana says I need instruction. That her father gives—"

"Enough!" His voice was thunder and his expression the raging storm to which it belonged. "I'll not be given a lecture about the way that mimicking Magi rears his progeny. Least of all by my own son. And as for *instruction.* Do you think I was given as much when the planets shaped me? You have no need of such banal cajoling. You are a Celestial, born of highest divinity. I petitioned the Moon herself to grant us your conception. The twelve courts will marvel at your trials and seek to emulate all that you are."

He had convinced himself of this and so I allowed myself to believe it as well. I left them then, and we saw nothing of each other again. Till the day of my trials.

Chapter 3

THERE ARE MANY FACES GATHERED inside the arena of the Aquarius Court. Major and minor deities alike. Some I recognize, others I do not. There are even mortals, but they are kept so far away I cannot see. They are meant to relay the tales of our feats, to inspire in their kind the desire to honor us. My gaze, when I venture to peer into the crowd, lands on Tiberias. A week later and his burns still have not completely healed. And I still do not feel sorry for him.

The Oracle and the Magician have their heads together. They look like scheming cohorts from the angle in which I view them.

I turned away swiftly before they could notice me watching. I would soon have many eyes on me, and I hated the thought of it.

It is rumored the planets themselves shall be watching, attending silently from the heavens.

"Can you feel them?" asked Arcana.

"Feel who?"

"The High Nine."

"Oh. Yes. I can." A lie. I felt nothing and was glad of it.

"May Saturn be pleased with me."

This was the ruler of her sign, Capricorn. I think she was waiting for me to say something in the same vein about the Moon. I made an attempt at feigning sentiment and was certain she saw through it, but I could not be bothered to care. I just wanted this day over with and behind me.

"Is it you first or me?" I asked her.

I did not have to wait for her to answer. She was announced and walked proudly out from behind our nook in the wings. The sea of onlookers parted for her. She disappeared into the throng of them and I found myself alone. Waiting.

It is not advised to watch the trials of another Celestial before you have had your own. Each of us gods is different, and some better than others. I should have stayed put.

It is expected of a Celestial to possess at least one perfect quality. Be it controlling the elements or curing poor health. Creating something from nothing. The gift of transmutation or telepathy. Arcana, in her trials, had mastered them all. She would have gone on demonstrating her abilities but I think my presence is what brings about the end of her performance.

"Ah, step forward, young Celestial. It is time to win your adulations." The Star beckons me to the center, and when I pass Arcana, she beams at me. She has done well and has much to be pleased about. I hear the fawning *oohs* and *ahs* as she joins the horde of spectators. And hear also, the beat of my pulse roaring in my ears.

The obsidian floor has been polished so thoroughly that it serves as a mirror. I do my best to ignore the frazzled reflection that peers at me from within it.

The Star says, "I present the Fool. Highest of divinities. Son of the Devil and the High Priestess."

A rumble of cheers erupts.

"Let us start with the rudiments. Show us a quick procession of your shades. How many do you have?"

Nothing, nothing, and more nothing. Only that familiar, perpetual amber. My default. My constant.

But the Star is not fazed, and her smile is still wide. If it is contrived, then she is the maven of posturing.

"No matter. You are still young. Sometimes these things come later. Much later. Right, Temperance?" This is the lowest of jeers and I know that he is somewhere, seated among the many in the crowd, seething. When I hear the first murmurs of their incredulity, I swallow the lump in my throat. *Can he really not change them yet? With such parentage?* I know this to be what they are saying in their heads and I dare not glance around, dare not be confronted by their multitude of censorious eyes.

"Let us come to another trial then." Something appears behind the Star. I cannot yet see what it is, but a collective gasp resounds throughout the arena. The Star has intentionally obscured it from my view, but when she steps aside, I find myself stifling gasps of my own.

A fire rages before me, smoke billowing up to spear the high-domed ceiling. Near it, peculiar little structures have been erected. "This mortal village is but an illusion, but the fire and the crops it burns are quite real. Vanquish these destructive flames and save the livelihood of the poor mortals they threaten. Recultivate their harvest. Let all witness the glory of your godhead."

I had not a clue how I was meant to go about achieving this.

Then I remember what Arcana told me. *Let it come out. Let it come out. Let it come out.* I search the droves for her, search for a hint. For something. For anything. But I am only met with the hardened expressions of lesser deities unknown.

The fire grows.

The Star's smile is not so wide as it once was.

I stare at the scorching flames at length. They spread beyond the circle in which I stand. Tiberias is the first to flee, and I do not blame him. Though I hate the satisfied smirk he wears. More of them disperse, and I try desperately to hone the abilities I am not sure I possess. Try to command this elusive force that lives within me. The one that is mine by right of birth. *Please, if you are there. Come out. COME OUT.*

"Is there another? May—may I have…something different?" I ask, raising my voice to ensure it carries over the cacophony of mass exodus. The bottom of the Star's flowing, white garment has somehow caught fire, and she answers me with divided attention.

"Well, yes, but. This is the least of your trials. The next will be much more—Oh, Jupiter in heaven! Oh great benefic, this is ridiculous!" The blaze began to travel up the length of her gown. Uncle appears by her side the next instant. A beat later, and the flames have vanished.

"I quite had it under control, Magi. But thank you nonetheless."

"Nonsense. You would have combusted and our dear little Fool would have joined you in your celestial inferno." The smile he flashes is smug and unnerving and…empty, like the arena. Only a few remain. So little in number I can count them on one hand. Beside Uncle is Arcana, and her expression is like a knife in me. *I was wrong about you.* It says.

I was wrong about it all. I cannot bear to look at her. And so I made to leave, lumbering away toward the dreadful sight of my parents. As I walk, the Magician speaks behind my back. "Pity, it seems godhead has skipped over you." It is barely louder than a whisper but Father closes the space between them in a blur of colorful movement, and though I cannot see his eyes, I am certain they are a crazed cerulean. Certain he will win the duel which Uncle's words have initiated. The Devil is full of pride. That is why the High Priestess chose *him* for a husband and not Uncle.

I do not think she ever wanted *me,* however. As they spar, a scowl twists upon my mother's face, etching it with the lines and wrinkles of dissatisfaction. She regards me a moment.

"At least you are not ugly," she says. And this was true. I am not. My lips are a bow, plump and pink. Hair dark and curly. Skin a polished bronze. I am fine-featured and beautiful, almost girlishly so for a male. But despite this, there is a sadness behind my eyes. A hollow. I sometimes stare at it in the mirror, pulling faces, willing it away. Yet it remains, peeking stubbornly from the dark amber of my gaze. It is there even when I smile—which is not often.

Together, we watched Father get the best of the Magician. A part of me feels vindicated, though I cannot say why. I know it is not me he is fighting for—not my honor—not *me* as an individual, but *me* as the extension of *him.* He is merely defending his hubris.

After a while, Mother said, "Look closely. This entire arena yields to him. See how skillfully he maneuvers it to his advantage? There is not a single surface of it upon which your uncle has not been thrashed. Do you see how glorious he is?"

"Yes."

"That is sheer godhead, unleashed and unadulterated. Nothing of that lives inside you—nothing divine."

I was too numb to feel the sting of her assessment. I think I must have scurried off after hearing it. I do not remember much of what happened that day, when the trials were over. Only that I found my way to the Hall of Effigies. It is no surprise that mine remained unvenerated. But what I do not expect are the faint embers that emerge upon Arcana's. Next come the orisons. Then soon after, the unmistakable bright shimmer—someone, some *mortal,* has paid her the highest deference. The Emros.

Envy and indignation mix to form a knot in my stomach. The feeling drives me to tears.

I might have stayed there, crying all night. Only when evening fell, Father arrived, wearing the pale body of a muscled youth, and the head of a horned bull. A monstrosity that would frighten any man. But I was a child, and the son of Celestials, and not frightened at all. This was normal for him, these hideous shapes. He never stayed long in an ordinary form. Most Celestials craved beauty. It was odd if you did not. Perhaps that is why he was largely avoided in our realm. His appearance may not have scared me, but his presence was unsettling. I did not know what cruel things he might have said. I ran off and hid so as not to hear them.

And that is the story of my trials.

·········)·) ◆ (·(·········

As I grew older, whispers of disappointment began to taint the air around me. Hitherto my trials, I was used to a level of respect in all my dealings with the major and minor deities of the twelve courts. There was a certain regard that my esteemed parentage bore me. I had never noticed it before, and only in its absence did I learn the significance of its presence. Gone were the pleasantries I used to come by in the halls, the small gestures of recognition or the odd offer of a sweet and a little wave to go along with it. Now there was only disregard and, if the atmosphere of planetary retrograde called for it, contempt. I had only known pats on the head. The best seats in the dining hall. Smiles.

Increasingly, I found the gods would exchange knowing glances whenever my name was mentioned or my presence announced. Divine eyes filled with a mix of pity and disdain. I was an anomaly—an aberration that challenged their expectations. A mockery of Celestial lineage.

Once, not long after my trials, a minor deity threw a crystal at my feet. They were mortal things—instruments that guided them or provided a small taste of power if the one to which it belonged was versed in such applications. But they meant nothing to a Celestial.

"I think you'll be needing this," she said after tossing it. I did not know her name but she donned robes of silk and crimson, which were the common fashion worn by those divinities belonging to the Suit of

Cups. She walked away chortling and fell in with a group of other sneering cousins. I stared down at it, confused at first and not understanding what was meant by it. It took a while for the claws of the insult to grip me. *Mortals have no powers. They need these devices. They are saying, "You have no power."*

Fury rose in me like the tide. I snatched it up and reared back my fist to throw it with all my might. But thought better of it at the last moment. It was smooth in the center of my palm, and pretty—the dark facet of it streaked with deepest ruby. Bloodstone, I later came to know it as. I liked the feel of it in my hand, and so I kept it, stowing it away in my cloak and wondering for the first time about the mortals, about the happenings in their realm and—

About their fleeting lives.

Chapter 4

SOON AFTER I TURNED SEVEN, I overheard a conversation that was not meant for my ears. It is a difficult thing to maintain neutrality when someone is speaking ill of you. Worse when you know the person doing it.

I was often in the Cosmic Library of the Scorpio Court, where all Celestial events and knowledge are recorded. The restricted section of it was the Oracle's domain, but she was rarely there and never guarded it, not even with defensive charms that would do her bidding in her absence. I think she assumed that with all of eternity before us, no one would care about the past.

I did.

With the trials of my youth done and failed, I took an interest in those who came before me. I spent hours studying each one, searching for a Celestial that shared my shortcomings. Not a single trial concluded in the manner in which mine had. I watched them all, the entirety of those precursory ones that occur in youth, and had been about to start on the second round, which takes place after maturity when I heard voices in the distance.

The halls of the Water Wing were scarcely without noise. I waited for them to fade.

They did not. Only grew nearer, louder.

I seized the crystal tablet from the Oracle's seeing water. If I could wield my abilities, I might have been able to command it dry before filing it away again. But they remained as nonexistent as they were in my trials. I pressed the tablet against me and wiped the moisture onto my cloak, then, in a rush, returned it to its place on the shelves.

I scurried around the bend and that is when I saw them. Father and Mother and the Oracle. Highest praise to Jupiter. They did not see me. I may have been without abilities, but I was not without speed. I weaved myself into a clearing and was shielded by a large pillar at the end of it. I took a gander from behind it and caught the sight of them as they passed by. I could tell from the range of their voices they had stopped near the area I vacated not long ago.

"I think someone has been in here. The waters are not as still as they should be and—"

"Who cares? They are likely long gone by now. Do what I asked and quickly. We have other matters to attend to." The sound of Father's voice raised the hair of my flesh.

I heard the Oracle expel an exasperated breath. Then,

"I cannot see anything."

"And? What does that mean?" asked Mother.

"Disaster, usually," replied the Oracle.

"Curse the heavens. Is one wastrel not enough? Must the planets see fit to strap us with another?"

"What makes you think they would give you another? You know well what the heavens ordained after Arcana and even her conception was never meant to—"

The blood beat loudly in my ears, drowning out their words. Had they truly sought out the Oracle to consult her on the birth of a second child? I pictured my replacement, improbable as they may be, shining and glorious and ready to redeem them from the failure of all that was my being.

All at once it dawns on me. This measure—this seeking of counsel. They had foregone it during the long seasons of my stay in the womb. For they never doubted I would be anything other than exceptional and peerless. The shame of this awareness speared through me like a fowl on a roasting spit, piercing what little dignity I maintained.

I stood there at length, insensible to all but the feeling of the weight of this realization.

It is only the strident sound of Father's voice that pulls me from my visceral haze.

"What of prophecy? Will he never be—"

"There aren't any I can see." The Oracle spat. "Though one may arise in the future, as paths diverge and it is always changing and…"

They turned away from the Oracle and left. I waited till the heavy thud of their footsteps receded down the aisles. I crept from the cover of the pillar and dashed away, taking no great care to be discreet in my flight. Nothing mattered to me in that moment save for the desperate need to flee from the confines of those halls. From everything. Running, running, running away. It seems this is all I was born for.

I burst out of the library and collided with Arcana. The force of impact sends us both toppling over on the cool floor. I had not seen or spoken to her in the seasons since my trials and this was intentional. I avoided her at every turn. I knew she must have hated me after witnessing the humiliating spectacle of that day. Knew that she detested having ever been affiliated with me. And when her eyes grew alight with that familiar and terrible sienna, I froze, bracing myself for what was to come.

On the floor I wait for the blast and

wait and wait. Till I—

"Are you alright? I did not see you and thought you were someone else for a moment," she said, rising.

She has matured so much since last I saw her. I remember thinking this. Remember marveling at it. At her. That tenebrous sienna is gone and she stares at me with orbs of brightest amethyst.

"Yes. I am fine. And sorry. I did not see you either. I was trying to—"

"Keep away from me?"

"What?" I feigned ignorance but forgot how easily she saw through these things.

"You know what I mean," she replied.

"I thought…you—would not want to…I thought you… *hated me.*"

She lifted one of her brows. "Hated you? What for?"

I felt rueful and stupid in the face of my presumptions, but for no reason I can name, began to laugh. She laughed too. And with that, our kinship was rekindled.

·········ᐅ·) ◉ (·ᐸ·········

I am nearly twelve when I first cross paths with a mortal.

In a way, it all came about because of Arcana. She may not have hated me but that knowledge did little to lessen the overwhelm of my negligible divinity. As her veneration increased, I found her less and less by my side. She was a favorite, well-known and wanted in every court. Every season there was a new gala to which she was invited, a new feast.

I leaned against one of the ivory columns in the Floating Ballroom of the Libra Court and watched her dance with ugly Tiberias. I had only come at her insistence and had not been formally invited. I am never invited.

She had promised to stay near me all night if I turned up but I knew from the moment it left her lips it was a lie. She adored being adored and fawned over. She was something new, and the gods loved whatever was both novel and promising. Years later, there was still talk of her trials. High praises and admiration. For none so young as her in the history of Celestials had performed as well. They all wanted her attention. The lesser divinities craved a touch and taste of power they would never hold for themselves, and the higher desired a chance to forge an alliance with the strongest of us, one to last through the centuries of our eternity. I wanted it because she and loneliness were my only companions.

I cradled a crystal chalice of Stars Brew and sipped slowly, more for the show of occupying myself with an action than for want of tasting or savoring it. But that is not to say it was not delightful and cool on my tongue. When I peer over the rim, Arcana is before me, prying it from my hands and gulping till it is almost empty.

"How did you do that?" I asked. For merely a moment ago, she was at the other end of the ballroom, dancing circles around Death and the Tower.

"How do you think I did it?"

"If I knew, I would not have asked."

She beamed at me with ink-black eyes, and this is when I knew she was truly enjoying herself.

"I can be everywhere at once."

I stared at her, perplexed. "What?"

"Look over there." She pointed toward the far end of the ballroom, and I saw her dancing with Death and the Tower as I had a moment ago. Only she was still by my side while I watched her twirling. I had not the words to express my astonishment and so I let my gaping mouth speak for me. I think I must have managed a half-whispered query or frazzled plea of explanation because the next moment, she began giggling and thrust the chalice into my hand, urging me to drink. I downed a mouthful and cleared my throat.

"I do not...how did you—"

"I am not sure yet, the name for it. But the one that is speaking to you now is the real me. That one dancing is the copy. But I have to concentrate hard to make her speak and act in a nature that is not odd. It's like I am split in half, and this is the better portion. I must get back in before they notice I am strange. It's happened once before with the Hanged Man. No one knows apart from him, and well, now you. But do come over and dance when I am in again."

She was gone the next instant, a gust of cool air against my cheek the only evidence of her departure. A new weed of jealousy sprouted within me then, thorny and indignant. I tried my best to cut it down. To remind the nasty little voice that blared denigrations in my head that they were not her fault, my shortcomings. They were mine alone, and I would see them accounted for. Arcana was the strong wind, and I, a mild breeze, and though the awareness of that pained me, it was alright. So long as she did not hate me as thoroughly as I hated myself. The burden of my lowly divinity was lessened in her company, and when we were alone together, I tended to forget it. But it was all I could think of here, in the ballroom, among the lot of deities from every wing and court.

Still clutching my nearly empty chalice, I stared in her direction, trailing her whirling form across the distance and waiting for the right moment to join as she had asked. I did not like dancing. It left room for further scrutiny, and I had endured more than enough of it over the years. But perhaps this night, I could be brave. Perhaps being in proximity to Arcana's brilliance would make me gallant and bright. These were the sorts of lies I often told myself.

When her eyes meet mine, I take in a deep breath and step forward.

A firm hand on my shoulder gives me pause. I tear my attention away from her and turn it on the Celestial standing at my side.

"Going somewhere?" asked Uncle. I could never get a veritable feel of his emotions—he always made certain to cast an illusion on his shades. An assortment of them leered down at me. I remember loathing this about him, among many other things.

"To dance," I said, draining the last of my Stars Brew and setting the empty container aside.

"With whom? Who here would have you?"

"Cousin."

He suppressed a strangled laugh, that for a moment, made him appear as if he were retching. "I do not think so," he said.

"She asked it of me."

"Perhaps you imagined she did."

When I did not reply, he leaned down so that his lips were level with my ear. "You are a stain on her. If you cared for her in the slightest then you would not sully her so. It would be better if you left. Besides, I am about to propose that all of us guests engage in a tournament to entertain ourselves. But if you insist and would rather stay and have your dance, then you are free to join the game but know that it requires...divinity. A great deal of it."

He waited for my answer. Long seconds ticked by. It did not come. He straightened and, with his magic, produced a pitch that drew the eyes of every Celestial in the ballroom.

"Celestials, deities, major and minor alike, shall we play a game of Astral—"

I fled and was gone from the ballroom before he finished the sentence.

Inside my chamber, I snatched off the emerald green cape Arcana had fashioned for me. It was beautiful against my skin and eyes, but in that moment, I hated it—it did nothing but remind me of her excellence. Made certain that I would not forget the lack of mine. I threw it onto the floor and flung myself across the bed.

I wanted nothing more than to sink into sleep. To lose all awareness. But the screeching sounds of Father and Mother's coupling carried through the halls of our palace and sang into my unwilling ears—preventing even the slightest chance of respite.

With a huff I sprang up and left our dwelling and was utterly confounded when I crossed Mother in the corridors. I turned back without her ever noticing me and made for the Fire Wing, hoping whichever deity Father was bedding knew the arts of defense.

It had been some time since last I visited the Aries Court. The Hall of Effigies no longer held the same appeal. My trials were behind me, and so were my dreams of conquering them—of garnering droves of adulation.

I find despicable, the familiar singed smell I once delighted in, as it wafts under my nose—an odor. It is not for me.

I looked to Arcana's effigy and wondered if she had yet Granted. It smoked and glowed with prayers and hopes. *Reverence.* She might answer them at least once, they deserved as much. I do not know what I will tell her when she asks why I did not come to dance. I do not know if she has noticed my absence. If she cares that I am gone. If she is sweeping the ballroom for me and saying to herself, where are you? *Your father said there would be games, and so I ran.* I feel stupid even thinking these words.

And worse when I glance at my sculpted double, bare and dim and unacknowledged. I am taller now, than I was at six, and it is dwarfed by me. I place a hand on my marble head, running it along the winding shape of my curls. *At least you are not ugly. Nothing of that lives inside you, nothing divine.* These unbidden words come and more, and I crouch at the feet of myself, despondent.

The silence of the hall is so loud that when I hear the faint whisper, I convince myself it is merely the workings of my imagination.

When it comes again, I leap backward startled and gaping. I whip my head in every direction, certain I am no longer alone. I search for the figure of some jeering Celestial. But around me, I find the same solitude. The same silence. Another whisper.

I press my ear to the stone of me and hear it clear as streaming water:

"Fool, Fool, Fool, please help me. Someone, anyone, help me."

Chapter 5

A CENTURY MIGHT HAVE COME AND GONE while I knelt at the feet of my effigy, examining it in disbelief. I would not have noticed the years passing. That is how intently I stared at it, listening, waiting. After the third whisper, I closed my eyes and heard only the sound of my own shallow breaths.

I am met with the sight of a miracle when I open them.

I should clarify. It was not truly anything miraculous. Only I had never known settings other than the opulent halls and palaces of the Zodiac Courts in our realm.

Night had reigned in full glory when I abandoned the Floating Ballroom for my chambers, the sky black and filled with stars. But now the sun's rays beamed down on me from above, where clouds as white as bone drifted and danced. I knelt in an unending bed of soft grass and found its thin blades between my fingers. It stretched as far as my eyes could see in every direction, and all around me were many trees and stones and

Where am I?

I thought I had merely pondered these words from the confines of my mind but—

"Crescent Forest. Please, will you help me? I'm such a fool, I should have known I couldn't have...Ouch! Mercy upon me, hurry, please. I would be grateful for your efforts, even if it's hopeless. I know I'm a fool I know it, but..."

A forest? I had never seen one. Never heard of them. I knew only winsome gardens; there existed a multitude of them in the Celestial realm. But I was far from there now.

I am embarrassed by how long it takes me to realize just how far from it I am. I think it is because no one ever told me what the mortal realm was like. Or how easy a thing it is to find yourself transported to it.

Reflecting back on that day, I do not know how I could have overlooked him. He sat slumped against the trunk of a large tree not far from where I knelt, ringlets of fiery copper hair cascading over his shoulders. He does not look at me as I approach him. He only has eyes for his leg. And when he speaks, it is just to say, "Fool, such a fool I am. Fool, fool, fool". He continues admonishing himself in this vein, and slowly, I begin to understand.

When I reach him, I see that he is only a boy, likely of my age and height though I cannot attest to the latter with any certainty. Not yet.

The sight of his leg elicits a gasp from my lips, and I huddle beside it to get a closer look. It is swollen and blotched with welts of blue and purple, a sharp and ugly contrast to the uniform golden hue of the rest of his complexion. Something slithers around the bruising extremity, coiling tighter with every blink I take. It is beautiful and shimmers with the brilliance of a thousand jewels, and I have seen it somewhere before. Though never alive.

"It hurts. Please can you help me? Do something, anything. I have a small blade in my satchel, but I don't trust my hands to be steady. I can't even stand to look at it crushing me for longer than a few moments at a time."

His voice shook and trembled with every word. The terror that poured from him infected me, and I began to quiver too, but even so, I said, "Yes, give me the blade, and I will help." This was beyond absurd of me, for I had not the slightest idea what I would do once he handed it over.

He fumbled with his belongings while I hovered over the creature, gawking as it steadily wound itself to the brink of taut—till it could twist no further. The boy winced and pressed the knife into my palm. Without thinking, I raised it over my head, preparing to stab, but the boy yelled,

"Stop! You must strike out its eyes. The blade is not strong enough to penetrate the skin of Emros. It's a blessing it hasn't bitten me yet. Then, I would be dead and have no need of aid. You will only anger it to retaliation by striking its head."

I paused to consider its eyes, large and red as rubies. I felt my nerve leaving me and quickly stabbed at one but drew back as the snake hissed and snapped. It almost sank its pointed fangs into the flesh of my wrist. This infuriated me and so much of what happened next is a blur. I remember a white light flashing in front of me. No, not in front of me. Out of me. Out of my eyes. I do not know when I cast the blade aside, but it lay in the grass and squeezed between my palm and fingers, where it had once been, was the Emros—limp and lifeless in my hand. I dropped it, and it fell to the ground with a soft thud.

I stared down at his mangled limb with a combination of horror and pity. I wanted so badly to rid him of the pain. It must have been agony to endure that slow torture.

As if in reply to this longing, the injury began to heal, gradually mending till the dark and discolored skin was smooth and unblemished. I remember this part with perfect clarity because it is the first time I felt an inkling of something divine moving through me.

A swelling silence, stretching on and on and on and

A cry of relief from the mortal I have saved.

I have *saved. I have healed.*

I would have crouched there, gaping and marveling at this triumph indefinitely, but the boy leaps to his feet and pulls me to mine, gripping me in an embrace of gratitude that is so tight it drains me of air and leaves me gasping. I pry myself free of it.

When we break from one another, it is his turn to gasp.

"Your eyes! How can they be…They are glowing white. Are you—"

I turn my back on him, swift and abrupt, and I do not understand why I want to run and hide and... *White, he said. Glowing white.* Visions come; Uncle leering over me in the Hall of Effigies. Father mocking him. A boy of six prattling on about the glow he has seen looking out at him. About the Granting he bore witness to and

I have Granted. I do not know why it took me so long to come to this realization. But armed with it, I found the strength to steel myself—to turn back around.

"It is nothing. I am fine. Your leg, how does it feel?" I said.

"It is not nothing. I saw the light in your eyes, the Emros. You killed it with your bare hands. You—"

The line of our gaze connects.

He pauses.

I think it was the first time we truly registered one another. Any chance of an ordinary greeting had been lost amidst the frenzy, but now, there was no urgent peril to distract me from him. Or him from me.

Did all mortals look like this? Father once told me they were not much. However, while I looked upon his face, I found myself questioning the validity of this judgment. His eyes were a bright hazel, rich and warm as honey. I stared into them and felt something stirring inside me, like the envy that bubbled in the halls of the twelve courts whenever I stood in the presence of betters. A mortal only. Who was he to possess such elegant features? They rivaled my own—eclipsed them. I want to hate him for this. I mean to.

But the smile that spreads across his face disarms me, quelling my jealousy and offering in its place something I cannot describe. It is like a warmth of sorts—the feeling so unfamiliar that I am rooted in stiffness and struck dumb by it. My scalp prickles with it, and I can think of nothing else but the pleasure.

"I know what you are."

The sound of his voice startled me, and sheepishly, I became aware of my half-open mouth. "Do you?" I asked in reply. He nodded, copper curls catching the sunlight, glistening under it.

"You are a Celestial. A god."

I had never thought of myself as such. "And who are you? What is your name?" I asked.

He grew flustered at this and rubbed his hands together as if I had reprimanded him. "Sorry. I am Varyn Carnelian. Son of the nobleman, Vedlan Carnelian, an Aurora Priest and devotee of the great Celestial, Justice."

Varyn. I tasted the name—found its flavor pleasing. He carried about him a certain grace and I was not at all surprised to learn that he was descended from nobility. "Ah, so that is why you smell so strongly of rose oil," I said.

I smelled like it too, because of the manner in which he held me to him in that crushing embrace.

His smile as it grows is a beautiful thing, and I cannot help the slow spread of my own. "Yes, I was scolded, harshly, by my Father for spilling it on myself during the offering today, so much wasted and—oh," he paused and prostrated at my feet. "How ungrateful you must think me, going on about offerings when I haven't even said a word of thanks and…which deity are you?"

If this is what worship truly felt like, then I did not want it. It was foreign, and ungainly. And what had I done to earn it? I scarcely remember being an active participant in that burst of…It had been as if I were unconscious.

I reached for him and drew him up, so that we were level again. Nearly level. He stood taller than me, but only just.

"You do not need to venerate me," I said.

"My worship...you do not want it?"

I do not deserve it.

I keep this thought in my head and then shake it. "No, it is a waste." I had not meant to say this. He had not been prepared to hear it.

Bemusement was something rare to him, I think. The expression of it seemed an unwelcome guest among his countenance, his brows reluctant to draw near. "But, how else am I meant to honor you?" The intense furrowing looked harsh among his smooth features.

"You need not. I am just a minor deity, from the Suit of Pentacles."

I do not know what moved me to lie. Or if he believed it. I fixed my attention on the dead Emros to distract from my dishonesty. "What were you trying to do here? How did it get you?" I asked, picking it up and inspecting it. The weight of it shocked me, and I found myself struggling with its density.

"Careful, their venom is deadly. If you hold it so close to its mouth, it could get on your skin. It only takes a little."

"Nothing is deadly to me."

Varyn laughed and took the Emros from my hands, cautious as he set it down, belly up. "Right, you are a god; of course you cannot perish, least of all from the bite of such a creature. What is your name, please? I would see this beast burned at your altar. I wish to give you the reverence you are owed."

"I do not have one. And that is not necessary."

More of that reluctant furrowing. "But you must have something for it…I must speak your name in prayer, I must call you…*something.*"

"Call me whatever you like."

"You mean—choose a name for you?" he asked, indignant and incredulous and…offended, I think.

"Yes. Let it serve as your offering."

"But I…I—"

"You have not answered my question. How did it find itself around your leg?"

I wished to draw his attention away from the subject of names and divinity, but wished also, truly, to know the reason behind his misfortune.

He glanced over at the dead serpent, lying in the grass like a glittering ornament. In all my years spent admiring their glow in the Hall of Effigies, I had not once imagined or considered the mortal's place in all of it—the danger they put themselves in to secure these pretty things. There was so much I did not know. So much I would rather not know, now, after everything that has passed.

Varyn lifted his white, knee-length garment and touched the place on his leg where the Emros had coiled itself. He massaged circles around the area, a faint smile pulling at the corners of his lips. Which were, like mine, a perfect bow, though slightly fuller and impossibly pink and symmetrical. I felt a surge of that former resentment coming on again, but it left me as soon as his eyes—tinged with a kind of humorous chagrin—met mine.

"If you did not think me a fool already, then you will when I have finished. By the stars, my younger sister, Celine, has more sense than to do what I have—nevermind. I will tell you, but only on the condition that you spare your ridicule of me until the end."

I would not have mocked him even if it were warranted. I knew the sting of jeers and derision too well. There existed in me no desire to replicate it. But he could not have known this, for Celestials were not renowned for their civility. "You will hear no ridicule from me," I said. He smiled and took a seat in the grass. I followed him.

"I should have taken more heed of my horoscope. Father draws them up for us by the week. He is not an Astrologer but he knows his way around the lunars and cards and, anyway—I suppose that's when the trouble began. I was to *stay away from temptation*. That is what was ordained for us Pisceans and—what? What is it?"

I must have been pulling some sort of face, though in my mind I believed myself stoic.

I was not and, in fact, had been grinning rather stupidly at the mention of his sign. This manner of conversing would take some getting used to. I knew my way around hostility. It was the language spoken to me all my life. But navigating an exchange that consisted purely of cordial genteel was a different story.

"I am of the water element, too," I said, taking back control of my features and rearranging them into a more dignified bearing—like the one Varyn wore. Even in distress he had maintained some amount of princely decorum.

"Ah, what sign?"

"Cancer."

Again that slow-spreading smile. I keep a handle on my own this time.

"Celine is a Cancerian. We get on well. I find both water and earth agreeable. All of my favorite people are Taureans. My mother is..." He trailed off and glanced at the Emros beside us. His smile dwindled a small measure, and he shook his head. "Sorry," he continued, "I am—where was I?"

"It is my fault. I distracted you with talk of signs," I said. "You were speaking of your horoscope before that."

"Yes, right. Temptation. I was meant to steer clear of it, is what was advised. I came here to clear my head. It's been a trying morning. And week. The whole season and year, really, but that is beside the point. I wanted to go for a swim in the river after helping Father with the ceremony. I left the temple and made my way here. Usually, I would not wear a plain offering smock outside like a commoner. I would not have bare legs. But as the cloth is light and so easy to slip in and out of, I considered it a fitting garment for my leisure. I left the city walls and took the path of a shortcut that, I will admit, is not well traveled by me. And that is when I caught sight of the Emros. It was slithering, facing north, toward the river, the perfect position for capture. It would not even see me. It did of course, cunning little miscreant. I was not quiet enough. Nor quick enough in getting my blade, as you saw. I should have left it. But they're rare to come by these days, and I thought...my mother, she...is very ill. I thought perhaps they would be more keen to listen if I had that to decorate my prayers. Everyone says their beauty makes them more fruitful and that its shimmer can transcend the heavens and—can it?"

He stared at me, sanguine, hazel eyes as wide as the green expanse stretching before us. I had not the heart to tell him the nature of our ways. That sort of candor should not be heard by mortal ears. I thought of all the occasions I sat idolizing those orisons—of the disregard most were met with. A quiet gloom began to well in me. I pushed it down and said,

"Yes, it is beautiful."

"You have seen it?"

"Not often."

"So it's true. What's it like there, I wonder, to live among only gods and divinity?"

It is lonely.

I want to say this, but of course, I do not. Instead, I rise and look over my shoulder in search of the river he spoke of and ask,

"Do you still wish to go for a swim?"

Chapter 6

I LET VARYN LEAD ME THROUGH THE FOREST. Walking, walking, walking. Watching the Emros sparkle and catch light as he drags the dead thing behind him. A prize. It is as much his as it is mine. Though I have no need or want of it. The knowledge of my part in its death is tribute enough for me.

More walking. On and on, till the trees grow less dense.

I hear the river before I see it, sitting just beyond the clearing like a rare jewel nestled among common treasures.

Varyn ran ahead, and I watched him plunge his foot into the water.

"It's perfect. Come, I'll take your garments with mine and place them away where nothing wet can touch them." He said this as he stripped off his thin smock and sandals, eyes scanning the area for a suitable spot. Quickly, he found one—a thick branch on a nearby tree. I peeled off my robes, feeling somewhat silly as I handed them over to him. If he noticed this, I could not tell. He had busied himself with the chore of flinging the Emros atop the branch, balancing on the tips of his toes to reach it. When he had positioned it just right, he set his smock beside it. Then mine.

"Oh, what's this?" he asked, looking down at his feet where something had fallen from my robes during the transfer. He picked it up and smoothed a thumb over it. "Bloodstone," he said in a half-whisper.

"You know it?" I asked.

"It's a crystal of prosperity for the Pisces. Well, it can be, if you are skilled enough to draw out its power. I didn't know Celestials had any use for them."

"We do not. I…found it, lying abandoned in a garden one day. I thought it looked charming, and so I kept it."

The far-off recollection of a minor deity tossing it at my feet, sneering, drifted into my head, and I grew hot. That was two lies told. I do not know why I felt moved to such artifice.

Varyn appeared convinced and unsuspecting of any deceit on my part. If nothing else, I could be a decent liar, at least. He nodded, still studying the facet of the stone. In a way, I had not been entirely duplicitous. I did find it charming and took to carrying it around the halls with me as a sort of trinket to toy with—to busy idle hands and distract me from my solitude. "It is yours, keep it," I said.

"Really? Are you sure?"

"Yes, quite. I have no use for it, as you said. It was just something pretty that I liked. Take it."

"Well, if you insist—"

"I do."

He laughed, and the sound was like the ambient melody of birdsong, high and bright. "Thank you. I'm the grateful recipient of many blessings it seems. What a day. My horoscope said nothing of this." Another high-colored laugh, fading as he turns and runs toward the water. Jumps. The resounding splash pierces the serene silence of the atmosphere around us. "What are you waiting for? Get in. Come and race me!"

I ran.

In the water, he is infuriatingly fast, and it is not till he wins three races that I finally realize I am not a good swimmer. Or at least not good enough to beat him. But it is the first time I do not mind losing—failing.

I was used to taunting ridicule in the face of my losses and lack, but Varyn, after winning five times in a row, bobbed in the water and said,

"It's alright, no one ever beats me. I'm like a fish."

He laughed and disappeared under the surface, where I felt him swimming circles round my legs. Round and round and round and round till at last he came back up, wearing a cunning smile, and declared,

"I have an idea. Let's play a game."

"What sort of game?" I asked, intrigued and amused.

"Try and guess."

I stared at him and tried to predict the secrets he withheld, searching for them among the giddy lines around his smile, in the half-crescent moons that looked out at me.

"I give up. Tell me," I said after studying him at length.

"I'll offer you a hint. We are each doing it right now."

Silence and staring. Staring and silence, spreading to fill the space between us.

I had never felt more empty-headed than I did in that moment. Still, he did not mock me for it.

"Another hint then," he said and placed his hand over my nose and mouth. "Now, it is only me who is doing it."

Moments passed, and my chest grew tight from the lack of air and...

and...

"Oh, you mean breathing?" I asked, peeling his hands away. He nodded, triumphant and gleeful.

"Very good! Now think, what kind of game can be had of that, here on the water? What kind of competition?"

"Ah," I said, the pieces clicking into place as comprehension dawned, "You want to see which of us can hold our breath underwater for the longest."

He threw his fists into the air and shook them. "Yes, that's it! Do you want to play?"

It seemed an easy enough game, and at least I did not have to be fast to win it. "Yes, alright."

"Brilliant. On the count of three, take a deep breath, and then we go under together."

I nodded. He counted.

We watched each other, squinting through slits at first, till we sank to a comfortable level beneath the surface. He stuck his tongue out at me, and I let out a small laugh, losing some of my air because of it. The tiny bubbles of held breath left me, and with their departure, he smirked. Slowly, I came to understand the logic behind his playful gesture. I resolved to be more strategic and thought a while. Hard. Feeling for an advantage. Pondering. Mulling and musing in the depths of both mind and water, trying to think up a trick clever enough to ensnare this cunning mortal boy. This Varyn. But I was not guileful or wily like some gods—like most gods.

And yet, a god, I was.

A Celestial, minor or major. It did not matter, for I needed no great feats of divinity for this. I could not lose even if I wanted to. I stared at him through the blurry blue and wondered if he had yet realized it. Or if he knew it already and still believed himself capable of outlasting me. This made me laugh, and I did not care that it hurt or that so many of my bubbles were leaving me. I swam to Varyn, closing the bit of distance that was between us, and stuck my tongue out. He was reluctant, at first, to let the smirk fade from his lips. His eyes were trained on me, and I saw the moment in which the understanding struck him. Saw him digest it.

I thought he would be stubborn and make a challenge of it anyway, but he conceded with a smile, reluctant and slow-spreading but charming all the same.

He swam up first, then me.

When we reach the surface, he is breathless and panting but somehow, laughing his musical laugh and it is so infectious that we share it, belting it out together as we swim back to land. I cannot remember ever laughing so hard or so long.

"Well, I am a complete buffoon," said Varyn as we sat panting on the riverbank, watching the river run.

"If you are, then so too am I." I said it without thinking and felt the shock of it settle over us like morning mist. He regarded me with raised brows and a half-open mouth.

"What do you mean?"

"I did not know it till we were under. I realized it when you made me lose my air. I wanted to get back at you, and when I tried to think of a way, it came to me."

I do not remember who started laughing first, only that we each ended up bowled over, clutching the ache in our abdomens. The fit was slow to pass, and when it was done, tears rolled from his eyes.

"I don't know which is worse. That I challenged a Celestial incapable of suffocation to a match of holding breath, or that I managed to stumble upon a Celestial unaware of owning such capabilities. By the stars, how do you forget something like that?"

I had not forgotten it but, rather, never considered it—all the aspects of my invulnerability, that is. Eternity did not feel like a reality to me. I was not yet a man and could not fathom the passage of centuries and centuries. The mere idea of it was something distant, if not intangible, to me. But we were children, and this was nothing I knew how to put in words for Varyn or myself, and so I simply shrugged and said,

"I am young."

"How old are you?" he asked, jocular expression turning quizzical.

"Nearly twelve."

"I am...older than you." He sounded incredulous and stared at me as if seeing me for the first time, pausing, considering. Holding me under that honeyed gaze that I both envied and admired.

"How much older?"

"Guess."

"Not this again."

A smile. Friendly. Mischievous. I do not bother trying to hide my own anymore.

"Come on, it'll be fun. And besides I am owed another game. Seeing as the last one doesn't count."

I can tell he is a boy who is used to getting his way. That is adored by mothers and cousins and never told, *no*. I have known him short hours and already want to indulge every silly little whim.

"Fine. But what will I have for my victory, if I guess correctly?" I asked.

He leaned back to consider it, one hand stroking his chin. "Anything you like."

I studied him, scrutinizing every facet of his being. We were each of us in boyhood. This much I knew with absolute certainty from the look of our scrawny arms and legs. Our narrow chests and the absence of muscle. But his face was sharp with angles in a way mine was not.

"I think you are twelve. Or nearly thirteen."

"Pick one."

I looked him over again, with narrowed eyes. Contemplating which age he most closely resembled.

"Twelve."

He clapped. "How did you know?"

"Just a guess."

"Well, soon, we will both be twelve for a time."

We were nearing the Cancerian season of my birth. I was not looking forward to it. I would not have celebrations like most other divinities. I was nothing to celebrate.

"What's the matter?" he asked. I had not noticed the frown as it formed on my lips. I had not noticed him watching me think.

"Nothing, I am fine," I said, trying to pretend these words were true—to convince myself they were.

We fell into a silence that I might have found uncomfortable had it happened any earlier—before the matches and games. Before the laughter and the smiles and the sharing of them both.

The sun's rays would soon be gone, but for now they painted us, warming our skin and casting shadows behind our lazing forms.

Around us, the tranquil sounds of the forest.

Between us, a calming quiet, thriving in the blank space, seeking to fill the whole of it. Spreading, spreading, till Varyn broke it.

"Your name," he said.

My heart quickened at this but steadied when he added, "May I still choose one to call you by? I have the perfect one."

"Oh," I said, raising one of my brows in mild surprise. "Yes, if you wish. Will you make a game of that too? Will you force me to guess?"

He shook his head and pinched my arm. "No, I will not make you guess."

"Well then, let me hear this name you have chosen for me."

Chapter 7

"WILL YOU TELL ME IF YOU DO NOT LIKE IT?" asked Varyn.

"Do you think I will not like it?"

"No."

"Then tell me."

We sat peering at one another in anxious observation. Him smirking. And me, watching. I may not have been made to guess but he was still making a game of it. The waiting. The anticipation. I do not think he could help it. For him, it seemed there need be gaiety and entertainment in everything—even the mundane. I did not mind.

"I think you should be called Ambroz."

In our language this meant undying and *eternal*—in the formal, High Celestian used by us gods and by the priests when delivering their orisons. It could also mean *bright*.

"So, what do you think?" he asked.

Now it was my turn to play at having him guess—to make him wait. But I was not good at these sorts of things. I could not hide my pleased approval, much as I tried. Could not stop him from reading my expression. I knew I had failed the second he smiled at me, and so resigned my pretense with a nod.

"I like it. You are good at choosing names."

He beamed. They were the kind of words he loved to hear, I think. Praise and flattery seemed nothing foreign or strange to him—came often and freely to him, as easily as sleep comes to the weary. I tried to imagine how it must feel to be always on the receiving end of that approbation. Found that I could not.

"And you, Ambroz, are good at holding your breath." He stretched, yawning as his limbs lengthened till they were lax and he was resting, laying on his back with both hands tucked under his head. I did the same. "Tell me about your parents, your life—the gods," he said with another cracking yawn. "I've always loved the gods, the stories. The Lovers and their meddling, the Hermit and her wisdom."

There was nothing to love. And I had nothing to tell.

"You first," I said.

"What would you know?"

"About life here, in the mortal realm. About how you pass your days."

He told me, eagerly, of the goings on in Ethelia, the region of his birth. Of his family and noble parentage—the expectations of his status as the son of a learned and esteemed Aurora Priest. Of his dreams of becoming a merchant and leaving it all behind to sail the Scorpion Sea. He spoke very briefly, though fondly, of his ailing mother and of his sister Celine who was showing early signs of a rare aptitude for Nerosi—a kind of communication with mortal souls stuck at the veil. He sounded proud of this and said that he would make certain she was schooled in the art despite his father's objection to it. He regaled me with tales of his mischief, his disobedience of the mortal directives expected of his title. He told me of the tedium of education. The endless lessons and preparations for exams. As a noble, he was required to have a talent for a wide range of things: languages, arts, alchemy, crystals and the skill of drawing out their energy for the use of both personal and communal application. He possessed the ingenuity to excel at all of it, he professed. But was excited by none of it.

"I want to conquer beasts and make art," he said, sighing into the sky. "To see the world and know adventure. Not take up some stuffy clergy post and stay in one place for all my days."

"You do not like Ethelia?" I asked.

"I like it just fine. I simply don't wish to be confined to it. It is expected of me to take over my father's mantle. To spend my life—*here*."

His face was tilted upward so that it was showered by the sunlight. He closed his eyes to shield them from the golden rays that poured over him, setting the vibrant, copper-red of his curly hair ablaze. I closed mine too, and imagined all that Varyn told me of his life, his dreams. I wondered about his home, about how it all looked. About his family and the adoration they held for him. I gathered he loved them very much and wondered too about that—how it must feel, being wanted.

I am not sure when it happened, but we drifted off to sleep. Perhaps we did not notice how tired we were from swimming so many races. Or how soft the earth was beneath our limbs.

When I wake, it is to the sound of shouting.

"Varyn," I whispered, gently shaking him by the shoulder. "Someone is calling your name."

He is slow to stir, but when he finally comes to, he jolts upright, blinking in the sight of the setting sun.

"Lord Varyn, are you here? Your father sent me for you," a voice shouted in the distance.

"Mercy me, this will be the scolding of the century," said Varyn. He rushed over to the branch where we left our things and pulled on his smock.

"Are you in trouble?" I asked. He shook his head and handed me my robes, slipping on his sandals while I dressed.

"Not trouble exactly, no. I'm expected back by a certain hour every day and Father doesn't like it when I don't return on time. He will just be cross with me, that's all."

"I am sorry. If I kept you from it I am—"

"You have nothing to be sorry for. It was me who fell asleep. And besides, it's not as if you knew of my obligations." He turned and collected the Emros. "Add to that, I have this to bargain with. No way he can be harsh with me once he sees it. So don't worry, I'll be fine."

"Lord Varyn! Where are you?"

I peered in the direction of the voice. It sounded nearer to us than it had been.

"Who is he?" I asked, straining to see through the thick of the forest in the fading light.

"Just one of the serving boys. Father always sends him. I reckon he's annoyed—to have been pulled from his other duties for this."

"I see. Well, I will not keep you from him any longer then. You had best be off."

"You haven't kept me from anything, I told you. By the stars, are you always this stubborn?" he said this last with a chuckle, shaking his head and waving goodbye as he walked away from me. He took only a few steps before he stopped and turned back. "Oh, I almost forgot. I owe you something for earlier. What would you have?"

"I thought we agreed upon it already—I need no offering or veneration for—"

"No," he swatted a hand through the air, dismissive, "not that."

I looked blankly at him, unsure of what to think or why he believed himself beholden to me.

"What then?"

He moved closer to me, ignoring the shouts of his serving boy, which were getting progressively louder.

"For your victory. Earlier, you guessed my age correctly. And wanted to know what you would have if you did. Remember?"

"Oh, right."

I had been joking, trying my hand at teasing, trying to be like him. I did not truly wish for any rewards, but...

how uncompromising, this Varyn. How persuasive. A mortal, I kept reminding myself. Just a mortal. He stood across from me, smiling his wily smile, and I did not try to argue against it. I did not want to.

"And I said you could have whatever you liked," he continued, "so, what would you have for your prize?"

What I wanted more than anything was for him to stay, so that we might play again. To swim and swim. Race till sunrise and do it all again the next morning, the next evening. I had never had a day such as this—so entirely filled with mirth and levity.

"That you come again and play. That we be...*friends*," I said.

I had hoped he had not heard the tremble in my voice—the uncertainty. But his eyes bore a look I knew well. I had seen it often, staring out at me in the twelve courts, burning me. The disappointed expression cut through my layers, sharp and cold. Of course he did not want more of my company. No one wanted it. Why had I ever thought this would be any different?

I waited for the ugly words to follow. Expected to hear the derision come pouring out as he opened his mouth but,

laughter. I hear laughter. The same kind we had been sharing all afternoon.

"You wasted it! I would have done anything. Stand on my head. Run errands. Be your servant for a week or, oh! Even buy you meals, meat, as much as you wanted, with the crescents Father gives me for my allowance. You needn't have won any guessing games for a friendship. We are already friends." He shook his head again, like he had earlier when he called me stubborn. I felt daft. And happy.

"Lord Varyn! I cannot bring the carriage through the trees. They are too dense. I beg you, stop ignoring me, for I know you are there. I see your bright, flame head, even in the darkness. Come, please! Let us journey back before the transport crystal loses power."

We both laughed at this.

"I'm going to tell Father you called me flame head! And that I ran off crying because of it. And that is what kept me so long," shouted Varyn.

"My lord, please. I would appreciate it if you did not."

"Apologize then!"

"I am...sorry." It sounded as if he were speaking through clenched teeth, and this only made us laugh even harder.

"You must go," I said.

"Fine. But will you come and see me again?"

"When?"

"Whenever you like," said Varyn. "The day after your birthday, perhaps? Since it is so near the season for it. I have a break from my lessons. What day is it? I will bring you a gift."

When I told him the date, he nodded and said, "Right. We'll meet at the tree then. Where you found me. How did you find me, by the way?"

"Lord Varyn, please hurry!"

I urged him to go, waving him away and feeling grateful for the serving boy's interruption. I had not the faintest idea how to answer.

"I will tell you when I see you again. Now go on," I said.

He smirked and ran off toward the trees.

"Goodbye, Ambroz," he said, turning back to wave at me.

"Goodbye, Varyn."

·········∙)·) ◉ (·(∙·········

The river ran behind me, loud and not as calm as it had been when I lay beside it with Varyn. My new friend. How had I gotten here? How would I get back? Did I even want to go back?

No. I did not.

Even so, I envisioned myself in the Celestial realm, roaming the halls of the twelve courts aimlessly. Visualized my chamber in the palace I shared with my parents, my plush bed and

I found its downy pillows under my head. Found myself staring around, blinking in the familiar sight of my bedchamber. Crescent Forest and the mortal realm had disappeared without my noticing. I had not so much as blinked and

gone. As if it never were. As if I were never there. But how?

I rolled over and looked down at the floor. Stared at the emerald cape I had flung there.

Arcana.

Perhaps she could give me answers. It was well past morning. I had been away long hours, not that it mattered. My presence or absence was scarcely noticed by anyone. Save for Arcana, on a good day. I wondered if she was upset with me for dashing off without giving her the dance she had asked for. Hoped she would not be. I needed her to tell me how to get back to Varyn.

Chapter 8

I HAD OFTEN STUDIED MY REFLECTION IN THE MIRROR. A habit formed shortly after my youth trials that years later, at nearly twelve, I struggled to let go of. Struggled to stop checking. Incessantly. Compulsively. Waiting, waiting for that special day to arrive. I stared and watched, watched and stared—kept telling myself they would change. Lingered there for long periods—hours at a time, some days.

Nothing. Never. Always dark and always amber.

Glowing white. Varyn had said that.

I leap from my bed as the words circle inside my mind:

*glowingglowingglowingglowing*white*glowingwhite*

When I reach the tall mirror, I do not confront myself. Not right away. I shut my eyes, squeezing them tight till they ache from the pressure. I do not care if it brings me discomfort. I cannot meet my reflection just yet. First, I must imagine. And hope. And ponder upon what my shades will be now that my godhead has finally *come out.*

I open them, peeling them one by one. Slow and assiduous, wanting to savor every drop of this hopeful suspense. Stars explode in my vision from the prolonged force of holding them shut, and when they clear,

still dark, still amber. A flare of anger. Surely this will make them change

still dark, still amber

Tears well and

still dark

still amber

I want to scream, but I do not. I do not even let the tears spill. I stare at myself till they recede and dry up, then replace them with iron determination. There is power in me. I know there is. I have healed. I have Granted.

My feet move of their own volition and I let them. I do not protest, even as they carry me into Father and Mother's bedchamber. I do not know why I have come.

Perhaps it is because a large part of me yearned for their approval, their validation. No matter how much I disliked them. They bore me, and I would see myself accepted by them. I would prove that I am the Celestial they asked for. This is what I thought as I stepped over the threshold.

Inside their chamber, the silver blood of a deity is painted on nearly every surface. Some of it has dried and caked under Mother's fingernails. Her palms are stained with it. I am careful not to slip on the pools of silvery slick that line the floors—liquid starlight.

"Where is Father?"

"Who cares? What do you want?" replies Mother. She sits in the center of the bed, toying with a floating orb of yellow light, watching it rotate as it hovers just above the center of her palm.

"What happened here? And what is that?"

"Veneration stores. I ripped them out of a minor deity of the Cups that your father saw fit enough to lay with, the filthy little bitch. He might as well have bedded a mortal. They are just as lowly." Her voice was flat and void of all but spite. In our realm, there are few things worse than being thought of as weak. There are few things worse than being born, the Fool. Whatever deity Mother had done this to would now fare far worse among the twelve courts, worse even than I had in the years since my trials. Wounded *and* without veneration. Bare.

"Is Father alright?"

This was a stupid question. I do not know why I asked it. Of course he was alright. He is the Devil, the most venerated among major divinities. Mother stared daggers at me. For once, I did not fault her for it.

"He blames me."

"What?"

"For you. For your...deficiency. He thinks it is my womb that tainted you so. Seeks to prove it by coupling with wenches in the very bed we share!" Her shrill voice rang loud enough to shatter glass. I winced, and had to force myself not to drive my fingers in my ears to blot it out. I might have run from this tirade at six, but I am nearly twelve, nearly a young man and I have Granted.

It is this knowledge that lends me the courage to contest her. To defend myself for once.

"I am not deficient. I am a Celestial, same as you, I have godhead."

Narrowed eyes and a scoff. Her face is bronze and beautiful as mine but I hate it.

"You are nothing like me."

"I have Granted! I have been venerated, handsomely, and I healed a mortal of injury," I do not add that Varyn's summoning and my Granting happened unintentionally. If I must argue with a half-truth, then let it be the better half.

"I do not believe you."

"I have done it!"

She closed her hand into a fist and absorbed the glowing yellow orb she had been fiddling with, then rose and glided toward me.

"If you have done what you claim and believe yourself a Celestial equal to me then ward off this blow."

She waved her hand and I went flying across the room, skidding hard from the force of her assault.

"Come on then, wage your counterattack. Let it be a duel since you are possessed of godhead!"

Again, she waved, and again, I went flying, crashing into a wall behind her.

"I will even make it easy for you. I will stand still and let you have your go at me. Come on."

I staggered to my feet, burning with anger. This would be the moment I would prove myself, I thought. Let it be this moment, this instance. *Now!* I waved my hand as she had done.

Nothing.

Why could I not draw it out as I had done in the forest?

Once more I waved it, willing her to fly. But she remained. Steady and unmovable. I cannot stand the look on her face. Within it lives a thousand taunts, and I want nothing more than to see them erased. To have her regard me as worthy of something other than her malice.

These are the sorts of wishful things I yearned for as a boy, soon to be twelve. I know better now.

I lingered there, enduring her glares and letting that smothering tension grow till I could bear it no longer. I stalked off on stiff legs, chest tight and sore from the strength of her blows. The sound of her final strike trailed behind me as I left.

"Nothing divine lives inside you. Remember that the next time you feel moved to challenge a Celestial."

I had grown immune to hearing this and ignored the dull pang of indignation that sought to see me retort.

I shuffled through the halls of our palace and wandered into the dining quarters of the Cancerian Court, where the scent of roasted fowl enticed me to stay. I needed something to distract me from myself. Few things in this realm gave me pleasure, and food was among them.

I sat eating in a corner and tuned out my surroundings so thoroughly that I did not notice Arcana had joined me till she poked my arm with a rigid finger. She chuckled when I finally met her gaze.

"That is how my copies behave when I split."

"Oh? And how is that?"

"Slack and slow to respond."

"Well," I said around a large bite of meat, "I have had an eventful morning. Evening too."

"Is that why you left the ballroom without a word?"

I wanted to tell her about Uncle, but instead, I merely huffed and took another bite. I did not know how hungry I had been till I stared down at my nearly empty plate. Arcana eyed the dwindling contents with her inquiring hue of dark sapphire.

"And that is how hastily I eat when I use too much of my veneration stores too quickly," she said.

I paused in rumination, conjuring that fleeting spark of godhead to the forefront of my mind, living it again.

"I…have Granted."

Her dark sapphire morphed into the silver of surprise. "Really?"

I nodded, waiting for her colors to change again. To settle on gray incredulity. But instead, they fade to her steady amethyst.

"You, *believe me*?" I asked, trying not to sound as shocked as I felt.

"Why would I not? What reason have you to lie? And when did it happen?"

"I—"

"Wait, I want to eat while I hear it. Shall I get you more as well?"

I nodded, grateful and eager to share the tale without fear of it being received by skeptical ears.

There weren't any eyes present in our corner of the hall to witness Arcana make a copy of herself and send it off to collect our meals. I gawked, flummoxed and speechless during the whole of the scene.

"It is done now. I am back. Tell me everything."

I told her. And left no detail from the story. She listened, intent and engaged through the entirety.

"Flame head? That is funny," she said when I had come to the end of it. "But why did you not tell him who you truly were? If he spreads the tale, it could bring your effigy veneration. Mortals love a healing, they would put your name in a verse of song for it."

I shrugged. I had not the courage to tell her that I did not want Varyn to think of me as I had been thought of all my life. Better to be Ambroz than the Fool.

"Well, at least you know there is godhead in you."

"Is there? I cannot make it come again, no matter how hard I try."

"Maybe it will come all at once, when it is time for our second trials."

"That is a terrible thought. Six years of waiting to see if your theory is correct—what torment."

"It is something."

A bitter truth I would rather not confront.

"What about my eyes?" I asked. "Why will they not change? Even after having Granted?"

She sighed. "I am not sure. It's certainly out of the ordinary. All Celestials possess shades, even if they possess nothing else. It is odd, I admit, and having them makes divinity easier. It feels good. I remember what it was like when I was little and could not—"

She had the compassion to stop herself there. It was not my intention to sulk but I could not be bothered to pretend as though I did not begrudge her divinity.

We filled the awkward silence with chews and swallows. Losing our thoughts in the savory flavors till the tension of the quiet dulled. She resumed and this time, with caution.

"It is not..." she looked around at nothing in particular, searching the air for the rest of her sentence.

"It is not what?"

"Our shades drive our emotion, and emotion drives our light, But It is not always ideal—having the shades."

"What do you mean?"

She leaned forward. "How would you describe my disposition, now, as we sit here talking?"

"Neutral, perhaps. No wait. Content?"

"And now?"

I struggled not to flinch at the abrupt change. The sienna came and went in a flash but the beat of my heart took its time in finding a normal rhythm again.

"You were...angry?"

"Right. Do you see what I am getting at?"

"That I know your shades?"

"Yes. And I know nothing of yours. You haven't any with which I may judge you by. Is it not a kind of power to not be read by those around you?"

"I suppose," I said, thinking of Uncle and his multi-colored illusion. Of how irritating I found it.

"It is only you and Father I cannot read. I asked him to teach me."

"And did he?"

"He refused."

"Why?"

"He said it could be dangerous, and they may become stuck. If the illusion does not come naturally, it should not be tried."

She leaned back in her chair, letting out a restless sigh. I had been about to suggest we leave for another court when it occurred to me.

"Oh," I said, "I meant to ask you. How do I get back?"

"Get back where?"

"The mortal realm."

Chapter 9

"THAT IS EASY. The same way that you came, of course."

"But that is the thing. I do not even know how I came to be there. Or how I managed to arrive back here in the realm. One moment, I am standing in one place. The next, I am in another," I said, looking at her, wide-eyed and expectant.

"Yes, that is how it goes. It's different for every Celestial. Some must summon portals, others fashion wings. For you it seems a mere thought is all that is needed. It's easier for some than it is others and what works for this deity may not work for another. You are lucky. And," she leaned closer to me, "I think it is a good sign."

"A good sign of what?"

"Your godhead. Tell me again how you found yourself in the forest."

"I heard my name, whispered over and over in orison, coming faintly from my effigy."

"And you focused on it?"

"Yes, it was all I could do. All I could think of."

Arcana smirked, and slowly, the events began to make sense. I had believed everything that had occurred to be out of my control. But all along, I had been the cause. I had done it on my own. Twice.

Arcana's tiny smirk crept away—transferred itself onto my lips. "Here, have a bit of mine just in case," she said as she rose from her seat and touched two fingers to my temple.

"In case of what? And where are you going?"

"In case it should return. You can practice trying to pull it out while you wait for another burst, like I used to when we were little."

"Practice with you?"

"If you want. But not now. I'm tired and wish to sleep. I spent the whole night dancing."

I watched her as she walked away, staring till she disappeared out of sight. I wondered if she knew how great a gift she had given me—what she had *returned* to me. I had all but lost it in my duel with Mother if it could even be called that, for I had not the ability to defend against a single one of her attacks. She had torn what little hope I had within me to shreds, but now Arcana offered it to me anew, whole and intact.

Something of divinity lived inside me, weak and capricious as it may be, and I would not be convinced otherwise again, not by any deity, be they major or minor.

Armed with this rare conviction, I rose and strode out of the halls of the Cancerian Court, marching through them till I reached the Cosmic Library of our Water Wing in the Scorpio Court.

The texts and scrolls were a comfort to me, a place where I could forget the realm and my place in it. Ordinarily.

Though when I drifted inside, I was met not with the serenity I so sought, but instead the sight of Uncle, conversing with the Oracle in my favorite section of columns. Their eyes fell on me in unison, almost as if it were a choreographed effort. I froze, unsure what to make of their regard. Unsure how to proceed. I became a solid figure, and was both too late to pretend I had not seen them and too stubborn to flee as I had done in the ballroom.

Whatever they were doing, they could do it while ignoring my presence. This I decided as I walked past them to find a book of charms. I used to read them all the time in the year after my trials, hoping some spark of it would flare in me. It took seasons for me to give up the aspiration. Though now, I had new incentives to revisit that longing. I scanned the selection for an old favorite, thinking perhaps I would practice one or two as Arcana had suggested.

But I struggled to immerse myself in the materials as the feeling of being watched overwhelmed me. I stole a quick glance at them and regretted it straight away. It fell on me once more, that jointly organized stare, ogling me from a distance.

"Is it charms you're looking at?" asked the Magician, lips curling into a pernicious smirk.

I did not answer. He appeared beside me in a flash. One of his tricks.

"I can't see why you would waste your time on it," he said.

"It is not a waste." His face bore shock enough for the two of us. The words spilled from my lips in a volley, tumbling from them without a second's thought spared for consequence.

Dark brows lifted above mercurial eyes. I wished I could read those shades—decipher the meaning that lay within them.

"Of course it is."

"I can Grant."

"Please." He scoffed.

"I have done."

He glared at me through narrowed slits, and for the first time in my life, I felt triumphant, even as I stood under him, slight and puny as I was.

"You are mistaken."

"He is telling the truth," said the Oracle. I did not like the sound of her voice, the tone of it was wrong—nonplussed and colored with a touch of irritation. Uncle peeled his glare off me and fixed it on her.

"What?" he asked.

"I saw it. I...*see* it."

"You saw him Grant? To whom? Who would venerate," he paused and made a limp gesture of disgust in my direction, "*this*?"

The Oracle expelled a sigh of exasperation. "No, you misunderstand. I mean his—"

"My path," I said, blurting it out—the bits of aspersions I overheard as a boy of seven came rushing back to me, too hard and fast to be contained. They had stayed with me through the years, and I would remember the lurching feeling in the pit of my stomach whenever I revisited that day—which was often. Despite the haunting taint that Father and Mother's inquiry left on my existence, I still looked upon their meeting with slight favor. The Oracle had not given them anything definite, though they regarded it as such. I did too, for a time. But now, a certain clarity emerged within me. A fact. The future is always changing. She had once said. And what had I experienced these last few hours if not profound change?

I realized too late that I stood ruminating over this notion and had been standing stiff in a trance while contemplating it. I should never have said anything, for it was an inadvertent confession of my eavesdropping. I do wonder, now in hindsight and after all that has happened, if things might have turned out differently for me had I been a little wiser this day. Had I never said a word to either of them? But I am getting too far ahead of events.

"And what could you know of that?" asked the Oracle. I did not know her well enough to derive meaning from the pale maroon shade that peered out at me. She shifted her gaze between Uncle and I. Something in the mannerism unsettled me. I was too naive to understand the importance of this moment—of these shared looks and glares. And so I answered honestly.

"I heard you speak of it here, to Father."

The Oracle made to answer, but the Magician's tongue was quicker.

"Yes, of course. That is so like him, denial. Why should he accept what is clear to all? Well, tell your father that no grand fate awaits you, nephew. He need not pester the Oracle for matters so trivial."

"And what do you know of my fate?" I demanded.

"That it is meager, same as—"

"You cannot know that." This bold temerity infuriated him. I could tell even without knowledge of his shades.

"Oh?" he sneered, eyes darting to the Oracle, a malign half-grin on his lips.

Perhaps they thought me too young to infer anything from the exchange. I did, however—though what it was exactly, I had not the awareness of, but the glower the Oracle cast in my direction unnerved me, and I wondered what she and the Magician gained from this joint harassment. I knew well why Uncle disliked me. I am the son of my Father. That was enough. He and the Devil had been at odds for centuries. All Celestials are covetous of reverence to varying degrees. The Magician especially so. He had been most venerated till Saturn bore my father. His hatred of me, I understood. With my birth and lesser divinity, he is, in a sense, avenged of his displacement.

Though I had built a kind of tolerance to ill-treatment, I did not wish to stay and hear their petty discourse any longer. I took the book of charms and made to leave.

"Keep away from my darling Archie."

I ignored this.

"She shall be exalted to heights you cannot fathom, and I'll not have you holding her back with your mediocrity."

This last I may have imagined, for I could barely hear anything over the roaring tumult of my own indignant thoughts as I stormed away. But I am sure something to the effect was said. Uncle always had to have the last word.

I let my troubled feelings guide me as I drifted down the halls and in doing so, discovered that I yearned to go and study my charms in seclusion. My bedchamber would have been the most ideal setting, but I could not bear the thought of going back there till I knew for certain the blood of that poor deity had been scoured from the palace. And what is more, I did not wish to share the dwelling with Mother again, not yet. I needed space away for a time.

I considered the Nebula Gardens but too many deities were abound, scattered here and there, soaking up the intoxicants of various florals. I had narrowly avoided being cornered by Tiberias, though a part of me was mildly eager to test a theory of divinity on him. Better to have not. I had endured enough unpleasantness for a single morning.

The enchanted fountains and terraces were favored by the Pentacles and as such, I shunned those also.

What I really wanted was to visit the Galaxy Baths and immerse myself in the rejuvenating pools of liquid stardust. The waters held a calm which I longed to be bathed in, but the hour was unfortunate and I found them to be bustling with arguing deities, castigating one another for lingering too long as afforded by their rank in veneration. The more revered a Celestial, the more entitled they were to scarce pleasures.

In the end I settled for the Hall of Effigies. If nothing else, it offered seclusion to an extent. Though inside, I found an unfamiliar Celestial. The Hermit stood studying her effigy. I had never seen her in the twelve courts before. It was rumored that she stayed often in the mortal realm. I turned to leave.

"You needn't abandon on my account, son of the Devil. Come."

I had not expected her to acknowledge me. I had not expected to be recognized.

"How…do you know who I am?"

"I know many things. I know that you came to this hall wishing to find it empty. And so shall it be," said the Hermit. She turned and made to depart, ivory robe fanning out behind her. There existed something appealing about her presence. I, who had been accustomed to spiteful exchanges and rancor, felt the need to extend myself in a manner that lay outside of my usual withdrawn tendencies.

"No, wait!" I had not meant to shout and hoped she did not take offense. I corrected myself and tried again in a softer tone of voice. "I do not mind if I am not alone."

She stopped and focused her attention on me, sweeping her long, coarse locs aside. "Perhaps, I am the one who minds. Solitude is superior to company."

I had not the words to counter her—in fact, I rather agreed and thought of telling her so. Instead, I remained quiet as she observed me.

"Tell me, young Fool, what all do you know of me?"

"I know only what I have been told. I am not certain which stories, if any, are true."

I had heard snatches of the various tales from the mouths of other divinities. She was not often seen among the twelve courts, and this only aided in lending legitimacy to the lore surrounding her. Upon her birth, they say our elder god, the reasoning Mercury, imbued her with the knowledge of all events. And that she has chosen to dwell among mortals to forget all that she knows. It is said she is possessed of every occurrence, past, present, and future. And that she avoids our kind because of it.

"Some tales are. Some are not. Do you wish to know something of your future?" she asked.

It is believed that Celestial hearts are quiet, that they must sustain us for eternity and do so with minimal detection, nothing above a subdued hum. I had no such heart and wondered if she could hear the intensely beating drum punching against my chest.

If I accepted this augur, the awareness of it might haunt me or drive me to madness. And if I declined, so too would I be consumed by the brooding of regret. Each option carried with it consequences too complex for a child yet to enter their twelfth year to truly grasp, and so I did what any youth would do. I shrugged and said, "Yes, if you feel inclined to tell me. I would be glad to know of it."

She drank from the air, long and deep. "A day will come when you will seek me out for guidance and for counsel and knowledge of that which is forbidden. I will not refuse you."

"You will not refuse me?" I repeated the words, slow and trance-like, absorbing the declaration as I stared into her marigold eyes—the hue of wisdom. I would see that shade again, much later as a man, and be comforted by that which they impart me with.

The Hermit shook her head. "No, Ambroz. I will not."

Chapter 10

I DID NOT HAVE TO ASK HER HOW SHE LEARNED THIS NAME. The inquiry—and shock—was apparent in my features, I think. She gave a low, quiet laugh, a deep hum of a sound that I found oddly pleasant.

"Some of it is true," she said with a half-smile, "But I need no foretelling to know of it. Can you not hear it?"

"Hear what?" I asked, brows drawn. She pointed, motioning to my effigy. When I turned to look, it was all I could do not to gasp. *Smoke.*

There was

smoke. Thin

thin ribbons

of it. I ran to it, kneeling at its feet as I had done that first time. A faint glow of embers shone around the marble of me. And from it came an echo of a whisper. I could hardly hear it. I pressed my ear against the stone and closed my eyes, willing the other sense to amplify—to compensate. Listening, listening till,

"Thank you, Ambroz. Thank you."

I knew his voice. *You did not have to.* I thought. But I was glad that he did. I had never known veneration. Had never seen my effigy lit. I did not care that it was the dullest glow in the hall. That Arcana's light could rival the stars. That my Father was a sun in the room. It did not matter. It was enough.

When I opened my eyes, I saw the Hermit standing near her effigy, eyes glowing white. I wondered if mine would ever glow again.

After she had finished Granting, she turned to me, offered a nod of farewell, and left.

Only Saturn knows for how long I stayed there, taking in the sight of those embers. Inhaling the redolent aroma of offering. It was not mine any longer; the glow and smoke had long faded, but the memory and the feeling of veneration remained. The experience was not at all the same as receiving the borrowed stores of another Celestial. I felt light as a breeze—felt as if I would float and float and never come down from the heights I attained.

I understand in this moment, I think, the boasting and petty nature of Celestials. Understand the reason they fight and strive to be highest revered. The reason my Father does not care that he is hated for hatred and fear begets worship. The high of this worship is worth fighting for. It is an intoxicant like no other and

No.

I should not be like them. I forced myself free of the haze of reverence, that inebriating cloud of delight. It was not an easy thing. I remembered that feeling which coursed through me when my mortal friend prostrated himself.

Do not bow to me.

I thought of his ailing mother and the peril he put himself in the way of to secure a fruitful offering for her. The sight of that twisted and bruised leg. I thought of Father and Uncle's leering looks when they learned of my grand plans of Granting. Of how stupid they thought me—of how lowly a thing it was to them, my yearning to appease a mortal's orison. *I will not be like them.* It was the first time I felt as such. The first time I did not wish to be revered. If it would drive me to callousness, I did not want it. I left the hall, and saw little of it in the years that would follow.

·········)·) ◉ (·(·········

Divinities of all twelve courts began preparations for the Cancerian season. Each sign was shown special favor in the realm during the season of their birth. It was custom for Celestials to bestow gifts of veneration and starlight upon those born under the sign that was being celebrated, and dedicated galas were thrown in honor of major divinities during their season. The last of these I can remember attending was that of my mother. I was five, and it went on for days, an endless festivity that spanned the course of many nights. I remember enjoying it, but I think that is only because I possessed little

65

knowledge of most matters, let alone my place in them. And I had not the stain of public humiliation upon me from the foundering spectacle of my trials.

This season, I would attend no balls and receive no benefactions. The same as last season and the one before it. And all others in the time since my trials. The day of my birth would come and go, and there would be no acknowledgment of it. No grand event held like those in honor of Mother or Arcana to mark my entry into a new year. I had grown to accept this and even adapted to the occasion, becoming intensely withdrawn and finding new ways to make myself indistinguishable from the scenery. Wasted efforts. I need not have gone to any lengths to be invisible—in this realm, to see me was to see nothing.

My birthday meant little to anyone—meant little to *me*. Merely the marking of another year in which I spent the duration wishing I was anyone other than the middling son of two major deities. I would have paid little heed to the season, to the *day*, were it not for the reunion I had secured with my friend. I counted down the days so as not to forget. And when the date arrived, I lay in bed, staring up at nothing till the hour became appropriate. In the darkness behind my eyes, I conjured the place called Crescent Forest. Saw its trees and felt its warmth. I imagined myself standing in the center of its green expanse. Smelled the grass and heard the chirping of birds, the running river the...

I am there.

I am...*here*.

I almost cannot believe that it has worked, and nearly convince myself it is merely a dream. But none of my dreams are as pleasant as this.

"You came!"

I turn and look for him. Smile broadly when I see the vibrant, auburn curls bouncing in the distance as he runs to me. I run, too. We collide into one another, and I am embraced, lifted, then spun round once in the air, and we are sharing the same high laughter. We have shared it before, and it is no less jubilant.

"Of course I came," I said as he planted me back on the ground. "Why would I not?"

"I don't know. I thought perhaps you would forget," said Varyn, still gathering his breath from the sprint. He was dressed more smartly than last time, and wore an elegant navy garment embroidered with gold around the seams. And his legs were not bare as they had been but covered in a smooth brown material that was drawn tight against the flesh. I had not known mortals owned attire as fine as this. "You showed at the perfect time. I arrived just moments ago and expected not to see you so soon. I'm glad you came."

"I am glad too. How is your mother?"

His wide smile shrank a small measure, and this made me wish I had not asked. "Some days are better than others."

I nodded, glancing at a small box he produced from his person. "What is that?" I asked.

He smirked. "Guess."

I made a sound that was part sigh, part laugh, and said, "This again!"

"Fine then, I take it back. I won't make you guess. But only because it's your birthday, and teasing someone on their birthday is quite mean. Here, open it."

The box was no bigger than my palm and was plain and black. I unlatched it and looked inside to find a delicate gold pendant fashioned in the shape of the Moon when she is in her crescent form.

"Well, do you like it?" asked Varyn.

I smoothed my thumb over the tiny moon, watching it glint in the sunlight.

"It is the best gift I have ever been given," I say.

It is the only gift I have ever been given, I think.

Varyn stood smiling. "Good. I wasn't sure if I'd made the right decision. I was going to get you the crab but thought this one would be better suited to you."

He was right. I loved our Moon. I fastened it round my neck. "Thank you. When the Piscean season comes, I will get you something, too."

He scoffed, but it was not like the scoffs I grew up hearing. His was a light and amused sound. I wanted to hear it again.

"Don't trouble yourself with it. You've already saved my skin, I think that is gift enough for all my years."

"I will get you something anyway. Then we shall be even, and I will have gotten my revenge," I said.

This scoff was better than the last, for there came along with it a snort of contrived indignation.

"*Revenge*?" he drew the word out, folding his arms across his chest in mock anger. "What for?"

"Think long and hard," I said, poking him on the shoulder, "oh noble son of a noble Aurora Priest."

His mind went to work while the honeyed hazel of his eyes scanned me, humoring my feigned tantrum. His warm, golden cheeks flushed pink when it finally dawned on him.

"Ah," he said, tossing his bright-colored head back, "you mean the offering?"

"Yes, that. I told you there was no need of it, but—"

"I know, I know. But I still thought you should have something for it. It was only a small one. I might have died that day, were it not for you. I was raised to honor the gods. And when one has shown me favor such as you did, well I can't help it. It felt wrong not to. I feared bad omens. And anyway, friends should thank one another."

He had a manner of speaking, this Varyn. He could convince me of anything, it seemed. If he thought the sun was blue, and told me as such with enough conviction, I might be inclined to believe him, I think, even against better judgment. I tilted my head to one side and regarded him, eyes narrowed in jest. He smiled at this.

"Fine," I said, "I shall not seek reprisal. But tell me something, have I gone out of my head, or have you gotten taller?"

His eyes lit up like stars.

"I have in fact. By an inch. Father says I am sprouting up like a weed. And will be taller than most boys and even him. It is all the better it's happening so fast—I bet I can beat you in a footrace. First one to that tree is a golden honey cake. Last is spoiled, smelly, week-old fowl!"

I dashed off before he finished this speech of prizes and penalty, leaving him behind to spew his curses and laughter as he raced at my back.

For all my cheating, I still lost. He was even faster on land than he was in the water.

And in the river, I lost more races, except for one where he had given me an advantage by swimming with his eyes closed. I insisted it did not count, for it was a victory born of pity, and he splashed me with water and said, "Fine, another game then. Come onto the riverbank and wrestle me."

Of course I lost those matches, too, all five of them. When he had defeated me a sixth time I collapsed onto my back, panting up at the sky as he lay beside me.

"How is it that you are so strong? We are both twelve and skinny as twigs."

"Skinny as twigs? Speak for yourself, Ambroz. I am no twig." He sprang up and ran to one of the trees, testing each of its branches for sturdiness till he found one that did not spring when tugged. "Can a twig do this?" Varyn gripped the branch with both hands, hung from it, and lifted his weight till his chest became level with the tree limb. He repeated the action, and I counted his repetitions in my head. After twenty of them, I rose and walked to the tree.

"Where did you learn how to do that?"

"This is what the common boys do. It's how you become strong for the Quartz Games."

"I have never heard of those games."

"They are for common boys. A test of endurance and wits. It is like a show of manhood, and many get their wives and suitors from their performance in them. The next games are not for another four years. I keep begging Father to let me compete in them, but they are not meant for the sons of noblemen. I don't care, I still want to do it. Do you want to have a go at curling on the tree?"

I had little confidence in my strength, but I nodded anyway, and he came down. I had to jump to reach the branch and even then, all I could do was dangle there. Varyn teased me and said my arms were thin as pins. He grabbed hold of my legs and took up my weight so that the pulling was not so hard and impossible a task. We practiced this way for I know not how long but in the end, I managed two lifts unaided and felt like a champion.

"There is hope for you yet. Soon those pins will be proper arms, and then we can make a game of it and see who can do the most lifts."

"Soon? Why not now?"

This was a truly ridiculous invitation, for I was already panting and near the point of collapse, but my accomplishing two lifts unsupported swelled my head with the pride of delusion. He humored me, and I lost within the first second, dropping to the grass in exhaustion after half a pull. Varyn laughed himself pink, and the exuberant sound filled the forest. I did not mind losing.

"I will beat you at something one day," I said, collecting my breaths on the forest floor. Varyn sat beside me.

"I do not doubt it. But that day is not today, dearest Ambroz." He took pleasure in gloating, and I took pleasure in the sight of him, giddy and gleaming with triumph. It was nice to have a friend.

"This is the best Cancerian season I have ever had," I said.

"Really? Do the gods not celebrate in a grander fashion?"

"They do. Only not for me."

Something in the calm of the environment spurred me to this confession. I do not think I would have made it otherwise. I studied the distance between his brows, watched it become shorter.

"Why?"

"I am not a deity worthy of celebration in my realm."

He tipped his head back, chin jutting out as if affronted. "Of course you are. Whoever says you're not is stupid. They are wrong."

His conviction in this was stronger than the whole of me, and for a moment, I believed him.

"My divinity. It is weak, inconstant, and erratic. Others in my realm are greater. I am lowly in comparison."

"So lowly as to have saved a boy from greatest danger? To kill a beast in half a blink, then heal the wound it left behind?" To hear him say it while speaking in that way of his, which left no room for doubt, I felt for the first time a rare faith in myself. But I, being the child that I was, raised among titans of divinity like Arcana and the Devil, pushed it down and cast it off. Deprecation was better known to me and far more reliable a credence than the grandeur Varyn sought to persuade me of. I stared at a spot of welted grass on the ground. Picked at it.

"You cannot know, for you are not versed in the way of our realm. I am the weakest among them. That day with the Emros, it was the first time I had ever used my divinity. Till then, I thought myself lame in it. And was shocked it came forth. I have not managed to bring it out since."

"So what? They are still stupid and wrong. You deserve as much as any other deity."

"Do I?" I had been so used to scorn and contempt from others, and now, when there were no others of my kind to ridicule me, had taken up the vacancy myself. An abrupt sadness overwhelmed me and I could not meet his eyes.

"I thought you were merely being pious or humble that day you asked me not to bow to you, which is odd for your lot, but—you truly *believe* it? That you are not worthy?"

"You don't?" I asked in reply, still picking at the patch of grass. "You are a mortal, and I a Celestial, yet you have bested me in every way there is. I do not mind it. It is fun, our games and matches. But the fact remains. I cannot beat you. Because I am weak."

"No one can beat me. It is not just you." He did not say this to boast. He spoke plainly, as if he were telling me the weather or the position of the sun in the sky. This factuality of tone made me laugh. Though for what reason, I cannot name. He laughed, too, and I lifted my head so as not to miss the sight of his smile. So few people ever smiled at me.

"No one?" I sounded dubious, but I believed his claims. I knew of his skill—knew well that it was the master of mine.

"Not a single boy at our academy, not even Jayce, and he is the oldest of us. Do not let me be the standard you judge yourself against. You may be weak in some things, yes. But you are strong in others."

These words hung between us, and I found that I did not wish to raise an argument against them. Even if I tried, I would have lost to him.

Chapter 11

VARYN TAUGHT ME HOW TO SKIP STONES. To climb a tree without losing my footing. To swim through the water on my back so that the sun bathed our chests and faces with its light. We played as only children can, like there exists nothing but the moment and its mirth. Like there is no time or obligation beyond the day but merely the next pleasure awaiting indulgence.

"Will your serving boy come and collect you again?" I asked as we sat cooling on the riverbank after a swimming match. Varyn looked up at the sun, still high and a long way off from disappearing under the horizon.

"No. I will be back before supper this time, as is expected. But do you think that…"

I waited for the rest of his sentence, but he did not finish it.

"Do I think what?" I asked.

"That you would like to come home with me later for supper?"

I gazed out at the river and considered my answer. I did not know mortals, their customs. I only knew Varyn. A part of me was reluctant, but another, much stronger part was excitedly delighted.

"Yes, but…only…I—" I struggled to find the right words.

"You don't have to, I just thought it would give us more time to spend before we have to part."

"No, it is not that. I want to. It is only. Well, your family."

"What of them?"

"Will they not think it strange, my being there?"

"Because you are a Celestial?"

This was not what I meant but his mentioning of it caused me to begin considering it. I was merely shy of them and had set about implying it, but his question gave me pause.

"That is not strange," he continued, "and anyway, how would they know unless told?"

"You knew," I said.

"That's because you saved me. I wouldn't have known otherwise. You look like any other boy my age, just more beautiful. But the same is often said of me so there is nothing strange in that."

An odd feeling took root within me, and there was a momentary quickening in the beat of my heart. Perhaps it is because I was seldom complimented that the words affected me so.

"Nothing strange in that," I reiterated, the statement falling from numb lips—it was the only articulate sentence I could manage. With effort, I shook myself out of that peculiar haze, hoping he had not noticed anything odd in me.

"Yes, nothing at all. And anyway, minor deities are regularly in Ethelia. Cups and Pentacles, Swords, and Wands. They make themselves known here and there. It is nothing out of the way to make an acquaintance of one. The women in the lower villages sometimes couple with them. They think it's lucky to carry the babe of a Celestial, good for health and fortune."

"Is it the same for the major divinities? Are they often seen here?"

"I don't think so, though I cannot say with certainty. I have heard rumor of the Hermit's many dwellings but this could just be old merchant's tales."

I nodded. I was glad to hear it and wished not to cross paths with any of them save for the Hermit. I did not mind her, for she had shown me a kindness in the realm I would not soon forget.

"So, you will come then?" asked Varyn.

"Yes."

He lifted a hand to his brow, leaning back to shield his honey eyes from the sun. "Good. We can play longer."

"How will we get there?"

"By walking, of course. Father doesn't let me have the carriage for leisure. Only errands. But don't worry. It's not too far."

I came to learn that he and I shared differing opinions on what is considered far. I had expended myself in the forest, swimming endlessly in the river, chasing after him through the trees in many games of hide and fetch. Racing and climbing. We spent the day on such activities, carrying on till the light of the sun began to fade. And that is when we began our journey through Ethelia.

For me, it felt as such, though to Varyn, it was merely an ordinary walk in a familiar region. I had never seen anything like the place. We strolled beside one another down winding, narrow paths he called streets. They were cramped and busy, yet a part of me was charmed by them. Along these streets, I came to understand what Father meant when he said the mortals were not much. I had imagined them all to be like Varyn: vibrant, full of varied shades, bright-tempered, gentle, and golden. I was wrong. We came upon quarreling men, angry drunkards. People of glum and dull disposition. I felt some stares on me; I did not like them.

"I thought you said I would not be noticed. They are all looking at me strangely."

"They are looking at the both of us. Nobleman's sons aren't often in the common villages. I don't usually take this route. It's a shortcut. You seemed tired, and I wanted to get us there quicker."

"Oh, I thought perhaps they found me peculiar."

"No, it's nothing like that. If you like, we can double back and take the main roads, leaving the village and going the long way around. We won't come into contact with many others, but it will take longer to get back."

I looked about us, and saw many churlish faces. Some regarded us for only a moment before turning their attention elsewhere. Others lingered, as if establishing in us an insanity we were not yet aware we possessed.

"Have you taken this way before?" I asked.

"Yes, once."

"Well, we have come this far. Let us not begin another route."

Varyn nodded, and we continued down a small street. When we reached the end of it, he steered me to the right, where we turned into a corner that led down a smaller, darker street, leaving the sundry of villagers behind. We had looked out of sorts among the throngs of them, dressed in graying, tattered smocks. I thought of the one Varyn wore the day I came upon him and the Emros, and took a glance at him as he walked beside me in the cramped passageway, donned in his smart, pretty garments. A stark contrast against our somber surroundings. If I had not taken this sidelong peek at him, I might never have noticed the vagrant in the periphery of my vision.

He was so quiet in his approach, and must have been trailing us in this veiled and slinking way for many streets. The knife was at Varyn's throat the very instant I became aware of his presence. I had not even time enough to gasp.

"You will empty your pockets, or I will empty you of all the blood within your veins."

His voice—the timbre of it. Grating like metal scraped against a stone. He pressed the blade to the column of Varyn's throat—my friend's face, painted in terror as he looked at me, was not a face that I knew. It enraged me to see that distress.

I do not remember how I managed it with such precision. Time and the mutable lens of memory have made a blur of it all. But here and now, I will try to recount it as accurately as my twelve-year-old mind had perceived it:

The light was beautiful as it left me, warm as honey, the whole long burst of it like a stretch of sunset pouring out from behind my eyes. The sound of the blade clanking to the ground is what brought me back to myself. Varyn, quick thinking as he was, kicked it away from the vagrant's reach just as he made to lunge for it. This angered me further, and another hot flash of that effulgence spewed out from within me.

Afterward, it was like looking at Tiberias, cowering in the gardens of the Gemini Court. The vagrant pleaded, I think, seared limbs raised to shield his face.

"Gods help me. I did not know. Forgive me. You looked like ordinary children, stupid nobleman's offspring prancing the alleys, rich without a care. Easy marks. I did not know. Stars believe me. I am sorry."

"The gods will not help you," I said, with a fury I had not summoned.

"Of course, of course. I know it, not when I have sought to harm one of their Celestial fledglings, but please, mercy," he cried, "It was not by intention. High Priestess as my witness."

I flinched involuntarily upon hearing it and the man feared I meant him further harm. He shut his eyes as if bracing for another blast, but it did not come. I did not wish to injure him again, as I had moments ago.

And even if I had, I do not think it would have come out. Godhead in me was fickle and sporadic. In one minute, I governed it, and in the next, called it forth with all the impetus of my will, only to be met with nothing. A fleeting moment this was, same as it had been with the Emros.

Yet I still found a certain glee in the instance, transient as it may be. My whole being tingled when that power had poured from me, and unlike my previous brush with it, I had possessed some modicum of control over the ability.

The vagrant sat whimpering on the ground, cowering there like a wounded animal. I might have pitied him had he not attempted to harm us—to harm Varyn. I tore my gaze away from the man and searched for him. He stood behind me, shaken and trembling slightly but otherwise unscathed. His eyes were fixed on the man, and he stared at him somewhat vacantly. I was not sure if he had awareness of me.

"You...*burned* him," Varyn whispered, still peering intensely at our assailant. I could not read his expression.

Please, I thought, *let him not be frightened of me.* Or angry. I do not know which would have been worse. I feared them both.

"I am sorry. It was all I could think to do. Had I better control of my divinity, I would not have—"

"For me. Burned him for me," said Varyn, cutting in, muttering the words to himself as if in a stupor. I do not think he heard me speaking. "Saved me from a blade across my throat."

"I would do it again," I said. "I would do it a thousand times... for a friend."

This he heard, for he turned to look at me after I said it. He brought out that slow-spreading smile I so admired, though behind it lay an uncharacteristic hint of melancholy. I thought he might have made some reply, but he turned away from me and marched toward the vagrant.

"You are badly injured. I do not feel sorry for you, sir. Had you simply asked without threat of violence, I would have given. Here—" Varyn plunged a hand into his breast pocket and pulled from there a quantity of gold crescents. He tossed them into the man's lap and strode back to me, taking me firmly by the hand and tugging me along back the way we came.

Behind us, the man cried pleas of thanks. I tried to turn and look at him once more, but Varyn rushed me out of that dark passage with an authority I had not yet known of him. With it, he carried me out into the streets, hand still fiercely gripping me. Together, we trudged through the place, retracing paths already walked upon. Varyn was swift-footed, I had to trot to keep pace with him. We went some distance like this, and when it was clear he would not slow down for me, I gave up trying to match his speed and let myself fall back somewhat. I could not see his face, and had only the sight of his curly red hair to stare at as I lumbered behind him.

"Are you angry with me?"

He did not answer and kept pulling me on with the tenacity of one leading a charge. We kept on that way till we were cleared of the village, and at last, he turned to me, breaking that nimble stride to throw his arms around me.

I held him.

Most people are ashamed of their tears and Varyn was no different. I let him hide his face from me as he wept silently over my shoulder. The only indication of his sobs was the sound of his breaths, heavy and long. I knew the feeling.

"It is alright," I said, "We are safe now."

He gave no reply but to tighten the embrace. He must have been so afraid, and I saw now that his pride had not allowed him free expression of that fear when we stood with the vagrant in the dark passage. I put a hand on his head, stroked the length of his hair, still damp in some parts from the river. The quiet weeping lessened after some time, and he revealed himself to me, wiping away the remnants from his cheeks.

"Will you forgive me, Ambroz?"

"Forgive you for what?"

"For this."

He prostrated himself at my feet as he had done that very first day we met. Or, he tried to—I did not let him get that far. I snatched him by the arm just as he made to kneel.

"Stop that. There is no need to…I have no need of it. Your worship. I told you, I do not want it."

"But you saved me. Again. I foolishly put you in the way of danger and you saved me. Saved me from having a knife open my throat, saved my life. What would you have me give for that? Nothing? Truly?"

"Just your friendship is enough."

"But you already have that! You are already my friend, the best one I've ever had. Let me give you something please. You are owed more than that for what all you have done for me."

"If I am owed something then you have already given it."

"When have I given it?"

"Right this moment. You called me best. I have never been best at anything. Now I can say that I am."

I have always found the greatest laughter comes after tears. It is sweeter—that happiness. Sweeter because of the bitterness which preceded it. Varyn was tasting that sweetness now, letting it fill him. We shared it and then it was me who was crying, though my tears were born of silly joy and hilarity.

"You are mad, do you know that? An utter lunatic. I am glad to have you by my side," said Varyn and after having informed me of my insanity, there was more laughter, deep and resounding. We clapped our hands over our mouths to stifle the sound of it.

When it had passed I urged us on, draping my arm round him and guiding us toward the forest for we had reached it again in our retreat. Though now it was cloaked in darkness—the sun having long disappeared.

"Now you have made me save your life *and* walk for ages after doing it. You are lucky we are friends. I despise journeying by foot."

"Then I shall carry you on my back."

He did, despite my giggling protests. But he only made it a few steps before pausing and setting me down. I thought it must have been because he found me too heavy but that was not it.

"By the stars," said Varyn, looking beyond at something I could not see. "He sent the serving boy after me again."

"The one who called you flame head?"

We laughed.

Chapter 12

MORTAL CARRIAGES ARE STRANGE AND WONDERFUL FEATS OF INGENUITY. I sat beside Varyn as it glided down the quaint roads of his village. I caught glimpses of them outside the small windows. The area was leagues better than the gloom from which we had just escaped. I call it an escape for I felt captive to that dull and dreary setting. I was pleased to be free of it.

"How does it work?" I asked Varyn, taking appraisal of the elegant interior. It was small without being cramped, firm yet not uncomfortable. There was room enough for a third and fourth, but the serving boy sat apart from us, in the front compartment so that we only saw his back.

"How does what work?"

"This carriage, is your serving boy making it go?"

"Ah, no—he is just steering it. It is powered by a transport crystal. That is what makes it go, as you say. The crystal is Father's."

"A crystal? Like the bloodstone I gave you?"

Varyn chuckled at this. "No, no. Those cannot give that sort of energy, they are just for people, their moods or prosperity or protection, things like that. The ones for the carriages are different, they are mined from the Aetherium mountains deep within the earth, then their energy is harnessed with Luminary Lumes. It runs on a charge from them."

I waited for him to continue with further explanation but he said nothing more on the subject. I pretended to understand, nodding and lifting my brow as if I had received some profound bit of information.

"I see. Will your father be angry? You have no Emros to assuage him this time. Only me."

"Not angry, no. Disappointed perhaps, which is sometimes worse. But all will be well. I'll ask forgiveness of him and vow to refill the rose oil of the altars in the temple for a week straight. That is like a penance to me, the smell stays on you for ages."

"What will you tell him when he asks what kept you?"

Varyn shrugged. "I don't know, certainly not the truth, he'll have me sequestered in the manor until I am a man if he ever learns I was in the lower villages. He thinks ill of them, that they are godless. He is wrong. But I cannot argue with Father on some things, you know how parents can be. What is your father like?"

I looked blankly ahead, stared at nothing.

He is like a tempest, the Devil. I think into that void. *One who rages and gales simply for the sake of showing that he can, with no care for those who might be dispossessed by the blowing of his winds.*

I prised my focus off that emptiness and endeavored to give an honest reply.

"You would not like him," I said.

"Is he unkind to you?"

A long pause.

"Yes," I whispered, hating the sound of that admission.

"You are right. I do not like him."

He said it in the same manner in which he told me of my worthiness back in the forest. I smiled. I was always smiling around him.

I wore the expression for much of the remainder of our travel.

After a short while, the smooth ride of the carriage came to a stop and Varyn opened the door. He stepped down and held it ajar for me. When I came out, the serving boy drove away—I watched as he departed out of sight, down a long pathway lit by dim and yellow light, contained within objects which Varyn called lanterns. We had something like them in the Celestial realm, though far brighter.

"Where is he going?" I asked.

"To park the carriage in its place, and then to retire to the servants quarters. Come on, the entrance is this way." He motioned for me and I came to walk by his side, advancing toward what reminded me of a little palace.

Inside we were greeted by another serving boy, pinch-faced, tall and thin. He carried with him a silver tray and looked to be in the middle of something but he paused at the sight of us.

"Lord Varyn," he said, inclining his head slightly downward, he turned to me and repeated the gesture.

"Where is Father?" asked Varyn.

"In the elm study, I believe he is waiting for you, so that you might all dine together seeing as your mother feels well enough to take her meals in the main hall tonight."

"Thank you," said Varyn, turning and making for what I presumed to be the elm study. I watched him disappear into the curve of a corridor. A second later he reemerged, poking his head round the bend.

"What are you doing still standing there? Come on, I thought you were following me."

"You want me to go with you?" I asked, entirely perplexed. I thought he would have liked me to wait while he spoke to his father. I was not yet ready to meet the man, nor to be scolded if he was of an ill temperament.

"Of course I do. I'm not going alone. Besides, you must be introduced."

I came as I was bid, feeling awkward as I hastened to close the gap between us.

"I am nervous, what if he does not like me?" I asked in a whisper.

"There is nothing for you to be nervous of. You are not his son. He will not be harsh with you. Only me. Don't worry."

I do not know why the idea of meeting his father intimidated me so. Perhaps it was because my own was the single example I had to measure all fathers against. I had learned all the tricks of avoiding the Devil. Knew when to speak and in which tone of voice to do it in. Knew how to make myself invisible even in his presence. Knew how to weather the storms of his mercurial temperament.

I knew nothing of *this* father, except that he had helped to create the boy I was most fond of.

We came at length to a tall wooden door and after a deep breath, Varyn gave it three firm knocks. I imagined a scenario of it swinging violently open. Saw within the frame an angry form, leering down at us in preparation to spew a torrent of furious denigrations.

"You may enter," answered a soft voice behind the door. The sound of it did not align with the shadowed version of him I had conjured in the eye of my mind. Beside me Varyn straightened his posture, drawing himself up to be the tallest I had ever seen him. He slipped a hand over the clear crystal doorknob. Twisted once. Pushed it open.

Varyn stepped over the threshold first. He had to beckon me to do the same with a glance thrown over his shoulder. I had been afflicted with momentary paralysis brought on by my imagined musings of a thundering verbal assault.

Inside of the elm study, the light fixture radiated a soft yellow warmth, much like the tones I had spotted in the lanterns outside. His father sat writing behind a wide desk, stacks of papers strewn across it every which way. I had expected a tumble of fiery copper curls and a delicate boyish face to go along with them. I had expected another Varyn. One that was more worn—older and broader perhaps, but no less bright.

But the face before me was stern and solemn and void of youth, though not yet aged enough to be lined with wrinkles. He paused in his writing, running thin fingers through short raven hair, streaked in some areas with silver. A glass of water stood beside his quill and he sipped it, eyes downcast as he studied his paper.

"You have gone over curfew...again, Varyn," he said, taking up the quill once more to resume his writing. He kept on without looking up.

His cadence surprised me. It was gentle—measured and even. No sign of the anger or irritation I had ascribed to the one I pictured hearing in my invented sequence.

"Forgive me, Father."

"What kept you?"

Varyn ambled over to the desk, leaving me standing in the center of the study. He went behind it and stood at his father's side, looking down at him.

"Nothing kept me. I neglected to keep awareness of the time as it passed. I crossed paths with a friend and we played all day without a care for anything but our enjoyment. He is here with me now, for supper."

"Oh?" His father looked up from his materials and took notice of me. I felt betrayed, and wondered why Varyn had implicated me in the tale—named me as the cause for his violation of the agreement established between him and his father. "Hello. And who might you be?" He smiled at me, and at once the feeling of betrayal was replaced by a sense of ease. It was Varyn's smile, and briefly I saw a flash of my friend reflected in this strange man's face. I made to reply but Varyn knelt before his father and took hold of his hand.

"He is called Ambroz and we have only known each other for a short while but he is my best friend. As dear to me as water and sunlight are to crops."

His father gave a low chuckle—a rich, deep sound. "Are you a poet now?"

Varyn ignored this and pressed a kiss into his father's hand, then brought it to his forehead. In answer, his father placed that same hand on top of Varyn's head, resting it in the soft bed of his curls.

"I am sorry," Varyn continued, "I did not mean to ignore your commands."

"Yet still, they went ignored. Intent does not negate outcome. It does not always matter what one *meant* to do, Varyn. You may harm someone without intention to, yet they are still harmed."

"I know, Father. That is why I shall atone. The rose oil, I will see to it that the bottles remain full. In all Aurora Temples of your jurisdiction for a week. And I will make offering on your behalf."

His father raised a brow and put a hand on Varyn's chin, tilting his face upward by it. "That is a serious obligation. I pay an Aurora understudy a handsome stipend for that post."

"I know it, Father."

He paused to consider the offer. "Very well," he said, motioning for Varyn to rise and turning his attention to me. "Come here, Ambroz is it? Let me have a proper look at you."

I lumbered over to him, and Varyn made room, stepping aside so that I stood directly in front of his father. He held out a hand to me. I took it and was enveloped by his large, calloused grip. "I am Lord Vedlan Carnelian. Is it true what my son says? That you two are dearest of friends?"

"Yes, s-sir. Lord Vedlan." My voice trembled, and I tried to correct the modulation by clearing my throat, "Varyn is my closest friend. The best friend I have ever known."

I looked surreptitiously at Varyn and glimpsed his small, diffident smile from the corner of my eye. Lord Vedlan nodded—he seemed pleased with my answer. Pleased with the pair of us, despite his earlier reprimands. He studied me, my features, as if searching for something within them. His eyes were brown as earth. And they were kind in their assessment of me. I wondered why I had ever feared the man—felt foolish and daft for it.

"Any friend of Varyn's is a friend of this household and welcome in it for as long as they wish."

"I thank you, Lord Vedlan," I said, inclining my head in the same manner as the serving boys. Lord Vedlan nodded, and beside me, Varyn suppressed a snicker. I thought it might have been a silly thing to do even as I acted out the gesture, and this confirmed it. But there was something courtly and majestic about Lord Vedlan's presence that prompted me to perform the action. He shifted his brown eyes to Varyn, and I almost missed having their attention focused on me.

"I would like to put forth an addendum to the arrangement you proposed."

"Father?"

"It is to do with your sinecure. A portion of it shall go to the understudy's stipend, as she will be displaced for the week."

I felt Varyn deflate a little, but he was quick to regain his composure.

"Yes, Father."

"Do you feel this is fair recompense for your act of negligence?"

"I leave it to your judgment, Father."

He chuckled again, as he had done when Varyn knelt and kissed the back of his hand and told him of our friendship.

"I think a bit of consequence is needed to sharpen your mind so that next time, you will not be so lax in your regard of what I have prescribed," he gave Varyn's shoulder a light squeeze, "It is done out of love and for the purpose of teaching you a valuable lesson, not spite or malice. You understand?"

"I do."

"Good. Now go and wash yourselves for supper. And quickly."

We scurried away at our dismissal, each of us unburdened and light of gait. When we were no longer at a distance of being overheard, Varyn turned to me.

"Do you see? I told you there wasn't anything to fret about. He quite likes you. He likes most people but I think he likes you a little more."

"Really? I think you are just saying that to say it. To make me feel better."

"I am not," he fired back.

"Alright, alright. Well, for what it is worth, I like him too. He seems like a very nice father. Though I am sorry about your allowance."

"Me too. But I won't miss it terribly. I've been saving quite a lot, and I don't spend what crescents I have on much."

"How many crescents did you spend on my gift?" I asked, fingering the half-moon around my neck. He smirked and folded his arms across his chest.

"It's a secret. And anyway, it's poor luck to ask the price of a gift. Five years of it."

"Five years of poor luck? Mercy, I did not know."

"Yes, that is what everyone says, especially if it's a birthday gift that is in question. But you can reverse it if the person you asked gets to ask a question of their own. Though you must answer honestly, it doesn't count otherwise, and you'll be stuck with poor luck for all those years."

"What would you know? Ask anything."

I hoped it would be something I could answer. He took his time pondering, hand on chin, the whole agonizing while.

"Now that you are twelve, what do you like most about it?"

He could be so simple at times. I adored this about him.

"What I like most about being twelve is that you are also twelve. That we get to be twelve together."

His lips started on their slow, upward curve. He flung an arm round my shoulder, pulled me near. We walked together, both of us twelve. Both of us happy.

Chapter 13

THE LABYRINTHINE HALLS OF VARYN'S HOME reminded me somewhat of the Sagittarius Court. I scarcely ever visited those winding corridors but always managed to lose my way once inside. I followed him till we reached the washroom. We splashed our faces and quickly cleansed for supper, hurrying along to the main hall afterward.

When we entered, a young girl sat waiting at the long rectangular dining table.

"Hello, Celine," said Varyn, ruffling her volume of copper curls as he took the seat opposite her. She huffed and shoved him away.

"Stop teasing. Your hands are all wet."

"That's what that mop of hair is for. To dry them."

Celine punched his arm.

"What did you do that for?" Varyn whined, massaging the area. She had been about to answer with another hard blow when she caught my eye. She lowered her fist and smiled. There was something of Varyn in her, but not much. Like him, she was pretty, though with vastly different features. A broader nose and fuller lips. Her eyes were dark where his were light, and although their hair shared the same bright hue, the nature of their curls differed. Celine's were tightly coiled, but Varyn's hung in loose spirals. I leaned forward to better observe her.

"I am Ambroz," I said as I sat beside Varyn. "It is nice to meet you."

"And you. I am Celine."

"He knows. I have told him all about you. Sang your praises."

She raised her copper brows, their height painting her expression with incredulity.

"He is telling the truth," I said to her.

Varyn gave her cheek an affectionate pinch, and she smiled, smoothing down the coarse hair he had disheveled.

"He is a Cancerian, like you. His birthday has just passed."

"Happy birthday," said Celine.

"Thank you."

"A birthday? Varyn, you should have told us, we could have prepared a cake for your guest."

We three whipped our heads up in unison to greet the sound of her voice—for it reached us before the sight of her did. She walked in slowly, leaning against the support of two serving girls on either side of her. They eased her into the seat and she adjusted herself, taking deep breaths, each one of them a labor. Varyn rose and crossed the table, planting a kiss on his mother's cheek.

"It's fine, Mother. He doesn't want a cake, right Ambroz?"

"That is right," I said, "It is enough that I am here with my friend."

"What a sweet boy. You remind me of my Varyn—too humble for your own good." She waved away one of the serving girls and placed a hand on the other. "Go and have the cook prepare a little sweet for him anyway. Bring it out at the end of the meal."

"Yes, Lady Elayne," she replied.

"*Mother*," Varyn opposed.

"Hush, go and sit down. Birthdays are special. Another year to share with the ones you love. They should be observed and treated as such, marked with something delightful. And what is more delightful than a sweet?"

I would have protested against this along with Varyn if I were not so endeared by her sentiment. And I did cherish a good sweet.

Varyn plopped back down by my side with a shake of his head. Across the table, I met his mother's tired eyes and gave a shy nod of thanks.

Soon after, Lord Vedlan entered and greeted his wife before taking his place at the table. Lady Elayne began to cough as the servers set out the meal. A few of them sounded painful and were expelled from her with a violent, heaving force. She stifled them with a cloth.

"You forgot to take your medicines again?" said Lord Vedlan. He had a servant bring it round without waiting for her answer, then supervised the dose.

"Yes, well, I slept for quite a while and hadn't realized." The words sounded harsh and ragged, like the chore of her breaths. She brought the cloth to her mouth at the onset of another cough, and when she pulled it away, the white material was flecked with crimson.

"I'll send for the physician."

"You needn't. I'm fine. It's no more than usual."

"Tomorrow then, first thing. And the healer in the interim, her tonics and crystals did you well last time."

"Yes, fine."

Throughout the remainder of our meal, Varyn, Celine, and Lord Vedlan took turns eyeing her furtively. The intervals of her choking fits grew longer and longer as the remedy began to take effect till they altogether disappeared. Her spirits lightened, and we were all of us more genial by the end of the meal—Lord Vedlan in particular when the sweet which was earlier insisted upon arrived.

"I am surrounded by water and earth, it seems," he said after learning of my birthday.

"The best elements," boasted Varyn.

I sat drinking in this amiable atmosphere. I had never known one like it. Is this what parents were meant to be? Talkative and lively? They spoke of every subject and listened in turn. Varyn spoke the most, making everyone laugh with his clever quips. Celine seemed always dreaming and I recognized much of myself in her. Lord Vedlan and Lady Elayne were well suited to one another, each the owner of a leveled disposition that complimented the other. Why had I not inherited such parents? They regaled on and on, and I lost myself in the listening.

"The hour is late for a carriage. You are welcome, should you like, to stay the night."

I heard the clear, distinct voice but it took quite a while for me to realize this statement had been directed at me. Lord Vedlan peered at me over the rim of his glass, and his solemn regard left me scrambling for a satisfactory answer.

"Sleep here?" I asked, certain I must have looked childish and daft and wanting to kick myself for being caught so entirely off guard.

"Yes, I hope I am correct in assuming you are here visiting from the northern region. You have the accent. Your High Celestian is extraordinary. I hear the noble ones up north send their sons and daughters away to learn of the world quite young but I didn't imagine they did it at so early an age as you are. I must admit, I find it a rather strange practice. But your parents must think very highly of you to send you off, and rightfully so. Where are you staying?"

I had not the slightest idea what to say and Varyn knew it. He cleared his throat, readying himself to save me the humiliation of bumbling through an unconvincing reply.

"He hasn't sorted it yet. I was going to help him find a suitable arrangement. His possessions are still in transport."

"Ah, quite the inconvenience. Well, you are more than welcome here," said Lord Vedlan. "Varyn can make a space for you in his chamber and lend you some items. Right?" He gestured expectantly toward Varyn.

"Yes, of course."

"So, what do you say, Ambroz?" asked Lord Vedlan.

I looked at Varyn. He looked back, eyes silently pleading for a swift answer. I searched my mind for one.

There would be no deities awaiting my return in the Celestial realm. I was not bound by any curfew like Varyn. My presence or absence did not matter—no one ever took notice of me, and if I stayed here, perhaps the day would not have to end. Varyn and I could spend the night on quiet games, exchanging whispered stories in the dark till we grew too tired to converse. *Yes.*

"If it is no trouble then—"

Lady Elayne swiped her hand through the air before I could finish. "Of course it is no trouble, darling," she said.

"No trouble at all, don't be ridiculous," Lord Vedlan added.

"Thank you," I said. "It is much appreciated."

"You are quite welcome."

Varyn and I shared a glance. It held a dozen words and the promise of gleeful rejoicing once we were away from everyone—alone together where we could speak freely. The servants came in, and things shifted around us. Seats were vacated as they bustled about, clearing away trays, plates, and glasses. Meanwhile, I sat in awe of Varyn. Of his astute mind and how easily ploys and ideas poured into it. Of how he made things so simple.

Later, after we had washed and played ourselves weary, I lay staring at him in my threadbare cot on the floor across from his bed.

He had made it for me out of heavy quilts and pillows. Now he sat before a mirror. I watched his hands working, fingers dancing over one another as they weaved his curls into a neat braid. He caught my eye in the reflection and chuckled.

"I already know what you are thinking. Go on, say it."

"Say what?"

"That I look like a girl with my long braid."

He did rather look like one, but this was not why I had been staring. I jeered at him anyway, finding the invitation too tempting to pass over.

"Well, since you are giving me permission: you look like a girl with your long, pretty braid."

He snorted. "If I don't tuck them away, my head will be a nest in the morning—all tangled. It is a trick Celine taught me."

"Ah," I said, nodding and thinking of her. I pictured her somewhere in her chamber, braiding her hair in the same manner. She had been so quiet during supper, only chiming in with a laugh here and there. I thought of her features. Of how different they were from Varyn's. "Celine is—" I had been about to make mention of them but stopped myself for fear of overspeaking.

"Celine is what?"

"Nothing. Nevermind."

"No, please, go on."

"It is just. Well, I was curious why…" I trailed off again. I did not want to say the wrong thing.

"You are wondering why Celine looks so different. From Father and I?"

"Yes," I said, relieved not to have offended him.

"Celine is not Father's—not born of his body. Only Mother's. Her birth father is a foreigner. Over a decade ago, he passed through our land with some merchants and courted Mother when Father was being a difficult husband. I was too young to remember, but apparently, I lived abroad with them for some time. That's what Father tells me. He traveled there and fought the man and won Mother back, promising he would be a better husband for her. She did not know she was with child when she left. Father didn't care when he learned of it. He said he wanted Mother and would take her back however she came. I am happy he did. And I am happy she came back."

His words hung thick in the air. It was funny. I had been so thoroughly frightened of his father earlier. But now, having met him, it was hard to imagine Lord Vedlan being anything other than the even-tempered man I had dined with hours ago. I attempted to envision him as the difficult husband of Varyn's story, and try as I might, could not see him cast in that role. Could not so much as picture him raising his voice, let alone trekking to a foreign land and wrangling a man into submission with words or fists, or both.

"Does Celine know? Of her birth father?" I asked.

"Yes, of course."

"And he knows of Celine?"

Varyn frowned. "Yes, Father allowed them to begin corresponding through letters some seasons ago."

"Does that mean he is going to come and see her—take her?"

"Take her? No, he cannot. Let him try. I will box him myself. She is Mother's. By right of body. That is how it is in Ethelia."

"And where he is from—his land, is it like that there too?"

"Why should I care if it is or isn't? He did not grow her for long seasons inside his belly. Celine is Mother's to claim, and Father's by right of that."

I found myself infected with his bitterness.

"I think Celine should not send him letters," I said.

Varyn grinned. "You are just like me. I wanted to tear the first letter he sent back to shreds, but Father said that jealousy was impious. And that Celine should have this right of communication if she wanted it. I thought she would want to go and visit him, but when I asked her about it, she said no. And that she only loves Father. That she only wants our family. That made me feel better, and now I don't care about the letters anymore."

"Good."

Hearing it satisfied me too, and I burrowed into my bed of quilts on the floor. Varyn opened the window and a breeze floated in over our heads, carrying with it the scent of grass and flowers. He yawned and stretched and tossed his braid over his shoulder—peeled back his thin bed sheets, and climbed in. The weight of my eyelids grew heavy while I watched him settle between the fabric. I let them close.

"Oh, I almost forgot to show you." They flew open at the sound of his voice, and I watched him again. He rose from the bed, tiptoed to his dressing table. I waited as he rummaged through his possessions.

"What is it?" I asked as he handed me a blank sheet of parchment.

He slipped into the bed again. "Flip it around and look at the other side."

I sat atop the quilts, legs crossed. I had not been prepared to see what awaited me and met the sight of it with a slight jolt which I tried to pretend was a hiccup. I had not succeeded in convincing anyone other than myself of this, for Varyn had been observing me the whole while. Waiting for this very reaction, I think—his soft giggles indicated as much. I studied what I held between my fingers.

My likeness stared out at me from within those borders, and I was a

> bright
> vivid
> medley of shades.

Chapter 14

HE HAD DRAWN ME WITH THE GLOWING WHITE EYES of one who has Granted. I traced a finger over them, looped it round the dark color of my curls. It was strange to see myself through the lens of another. But I sat transfixed. I had not believed myself so prestigious. So fierce. Was this truly the way he viewed me? What he saw whenever he conjured me up in his head? I wondered what other beautiful things he kept locked there—in the cellar of his mind. Wondered if he might be convinced to lend me the key.

"This is...I have never..." I could not find the words. My thoughts were lost, swimming somewhere in that picture. I stared at it till I found them. "I look...divine."

I tore my eyes away from the drawing in time to see the smile bloom across his face.

"I sketched it right after we met. I couldn't stop thinking of what happened. I was having nightmares about it. And would sometimes wake to find myself clutching my leg. Putting you on the parchment helped me to forget the terror. And instead, remember the blessing."

Now the smile was blossoming across my features.

"I did not know you had such talent."

"It is just a hobby. My mother is better. I get it from her. Celine envies me. She can barely manage a circle."

"I do not blame her. I would, too. Even my reflection is not as lively as this. I used to imagine myself this way when I was a small child. I look like a true and proper deity."

"That's because you are. Have you forgotten already what you did today, in the villages?"

I had not forgotten it, though I had been trying to make sense of its reoccurrence. I was no closer to reigning my elusive divinity than I had been that first time.

"No," I said. "But…"

"But what? Do not tell me you still have a low opinion of your divinity. You cannot possibly. Not after that. You should have seen yourself, that light. I have never witnessed anything like it, even before, in the forest. It was not like that."

I shook my head. "You do not understand. It was no different than the forest. I cannot make it come back at my will the way everyone else can. The way I am meant to."

"Are you sure?"

"Yes."

"Try it. Right now. See if you can make a little of the light pour out."

"But I cannot."

"That is why you must try. Stare at the parchment, the edge of it. Try to char it with your light, just at the corners. Come on."

I sighed in frustration. Now I would not only disappoint myself, but him too. I knew it would not work, but I made an attempt anyway, for Varyn's sake. So that he might see me for what I truly was. Lesser. The Fool. I sat concentrating on the fringe of the image, feeling his hopeful eyes on me. I did what I had done in Mother's chamber—willed it to come out. I held my breath. Trying.

tryingtryingtryingtryingtryingtry

Nothing. I set the illustration aside.

"Do it again. Your eyes, they were lighting up. Or just beginning to. I know they were."

"No, Varyn, they were not. You wanted them to, but they were not."

"How do you know? You can't even see yourself. I'm the one staring."

He was becoming indignant, agitated.

"Because I know it—within me. When it happens, there is a feeling. I did not have it. It is useless. It will not come out. I told you."

Some of the fight went out of him. I hated to see it. That slump of the shoulders. We were silent a while. The pair of us staring past one another in the dim light.

"We'll practice," he said.

"What?"

"Every night. You and I will practice. Your imaginary belongings that are in transport. The arrangement you're still sorting out. It will take some time and you'll be spending it here, to keep up the ruse. So, every night we will practice. We'll make a game of it."

This relentless Varyn. Could there be any refusing him when he was like this? When he was so determined? He seemed an unmovable mountain from where he sat on his bed.

I drew in a deep breath, expelled it, and conceded.

"Fine. If that is your wish."

"It very well is."

A part of me wanted to throttle him for being so obstinate. Another wanted to embrace him, as I had when he cried over my shoulder. The latter urge was stronger. I chuckled.

"What is so funny?" He was smirking.

"Nothing. It is nothing. But tell me. How long will I be bound to this game of practicing? What is the acceptable time frame of transporting possessions and securing lodgings?"

He thought a moment, head lolling to the side. "Let's give it one week. Then we'll tell him we've found a place, an inn or boarding house."

I pondered it. A week with Varyn. A week of his games. A week of smiles.

"Fine, agreed. But I do feel poorly about it all you know?"

"Poorly about what all?"

"Deceiving your father."

"Well," he lengthened this word as if it were a verse of song, "it's not all lies."

"How do you figure?"

"Father is the one who made the assumption. We just didn't correct him. And you *are* from up north, in a sense."

"Varyn, you know well that I am not from any of your regions."

"Yes, but north is north. It's always up. Is the Celestial realm not above us?"

I could not resist snorting at this. He exercised slyness like it was a sport or another one of his games. I shook my head, amused. From the

95

margins of sight, the drawing caught my attention once more, and I surveyed it. Marveled at it.

"May I keep it?" I asked.

Varyn opened his mouth merely to shut it a moment later. Again he repeated it. Then,

"I can draw you another one. I only wanted to show it to you. Sometimes I still like to look at it when I am feeling unsettled from a night terror."

"Oh, right, of course." He had told me as much already. It was silly of me to ask, and my cheeks grew warm. I handed it back to him and sheepishly watched as he returned it to the compartment of his dressing table.

"You can have a look at it anytime you like," he said, yawning through the offer as he climbed into bed. I did the same and lay on my side, peering at him. "Or I can draw another—make you a copy of your own."

"No, that is quite alright. I will not soon forget it, and can see it whenever I wish through recollection."

He yawned again. "You will tell me if you change your mind?"

His yawns now plagued me, and my reply took the form of a wordless mewl. I put a hand over my mouth to muffle the noise. My watery eyes transformed him into a bleary splotch of gold and copper—when the tears cleared, we studied one another, exchanging drowsy gazes. I had been drifting when the sound of his voice drew me from the beckoning reaches of slumber.

"Say it again," I mumbled, having only heard the shape and tone of his sentence instead of the words that formed it.

"Your eyes are always dark. Like a deep shade of amber."

"Yes, and what of it?"

"The other Celestials. They all have changing shades."

"How do you know of that?"

"From lessons. We must study the major and minor divinities in our courses on offerings and Astrology. I realized it just as I was falling asleep. Yours never changes. They are supposed to. I think that is why you cannot get a handle on your light."

"They teach you of our light in the lessons?"

"Yes, and other things."

"What other things? What all do you know?"

"Lots of things. Years of learning. I would be here all night babbling on about it. But I'm sure I cannot tell you anything which you do not yet know."

Already he had told me something I did not know. I did not know mortals had knowledge of our shades. I did not know we were a subject of study, here, among them.

"Our shades. What have you been taught about our shades? About what it is they do?" I asked.

"That is easy. It was one of my examination questions a few years ago. I memorized this word for it, *facilitate*. It means to make something less difficult. That is what the shades do—help with the transition between the two natures."

"Two natures?"

"Yes, dictated by the planets—the Upright and the Reversed. Each deity is born in either of those, but the shades are what makes it easier to move between the two energies and get your light, something like that. Which one are you? Oh, wait let me have a guess at it. Upright? You must be, for you are more benevolent, like Justice and the Hermit."

How could a mortal boy have known more about these sorts of things than I? It had been as if I were a mystery to myself all these years. I did not know of any natures, of which of them I had inherited. But I did not want to seem witless to him, and so I affirmed his guess, and claimed Upright.

"I knew it," he said, stretching a little and suppressing a yawn. "So, your shades. That seems to be what is the matter. Not enough changing. But they *have* changed, haven't they?"

"No," I confessed. I saw no reason to lie. He already knew of my deficiency.

"But...should it not have happened already?"

"It should have, yes. But it did not." I felt ashamed to admit this, as if it were something within my control.

"No matter, It will happen soon, I'm sure. It must."

"And if it does not?"

He shrugged. "We'll figure it out—together. It's not as if you have no ability at all. There is something strong in you, Ambroz. And it can't stay locked inside there forever. It must come forth eventually. Perhaps you just have to grow a bit more. You are only twelve, after all."

I said nothing, and simply let the words settle over me. Let them fill my mind. I had learned more about my godhead in a single day spent with Varyn than I had in my twelve years living in the Celestial realm. The halls and deities of the Zodiac Courts taught me nothing of my being, save for how to disdain it. Did Arcana know this? My mother and father? Uncle? They had imparted me nothing. Was I not even worthy enough to them to know of myself?

I had not realized how tightly my fists were clenched till the burst of pain surged through me. I opened my palms to find them stained silver. I had never seen my own blood, never had my flesh torn open. I remembered Tiberias and his burns and wondered how long it had taken him to heal. Wondered how long it would take me, if at all.

That last was a pitying sort of thought, born of my discontent. I shook it off, for the pain of injury had left as quickly as it came. I smoothed a hand over the thin skin of my palm, searching for the slit. Nothing. It had sealed with the swiftness of a blink. *If that is the very least I can do, perhaps all is not lost.* It was a needed consolation, and I allowed myself to sink into the soothing chasm of that solace.

I neglected all awareness in the retreat, staring out at nothing with unseeing eyes. When at last I returned, it was to sticky hands and a snoring Varyn. I left the comfort of my cot on the floor in search of a cloth, wishing to liberate my palms from the evidence of the quiet war that had waged within me. I spotted a little basin at the far end of the chamber, near the door. In the dim light, I crept over to it, taking care to remain light on my feet so as not to wake Varyn.

The basin held a small quantity of water, and beside it lay two folded cloths stacked atop one another. I half submerged it, then took the damp material back to my cot and started scrubbing at the remnants of my wounds.

After some minutes, the creaking of wood drew my concentration away from the task. I jerked my head up and found Celine standing across from me, one hand on Varyn's shoulder. If she noticed the stained cloth in the dim light, she did not make mention of it, and merely stared at me with her large brown eyes.

Chapter 15

"OH, PARDON. I FORGOT YOU WERE IN HERE," Celine said. Varyn stirred at the sound of her voice as I made to answer. He inched himself away from her, eyes still closed, and threw the covers partially off his body. Celine climbed into the gap he had created and huddled beside him.

"Are they frightening you again?" asked Varyn in a hoarse mumble. He rolled onto his back, and I noted that he still had not opened his eyes. It seemed as if he were accustomed to the maneuver—accustomed to the interruption of his rest, tuned to the practice of communicating while still very much asleep despite it.

"Not this time, but I don't want to listen to them. Their sounds won't follow me in here, with you. They don't want to be around others. Just me," replied Celine.

"Is it the same little girl from last time?"

"Yes, she misses her mother and doesn't understand why she didn't come with her. That's what I gather from all her weeping. She won't stop. I tried to help her, talk to her and explain what's happened but she doesn't listen. She thinks she's still here and that others can talk to her too. That she might be with her mother again."

"Well, tomorrow I will cleanse your bedroom with Luminaris root, for now, try and fall back asleep."

"Alright."

She closed her eyes and fell into slumber shortly thereafter. I stared at their sleeping forms, utterly bemused by the exchange. I lay across from them, trying to make sense of it for five, ten, nearly twenty minutes, till I gave up and resolved to ask Varyn for an explanation in the morning.

No sooner had I relinquished my efforts did I recall something Varyn had told me in the forest. A word came to me: *Nerosi.* He had spoken of her aptitude for it—had almost gloated about it. He believed it to be a talent, though now, having witnessed it in part, it seemed more of an irritant to Celine than anything. Some poor mortal soul, lingering in that parallel dimension, confused and weeping, calling out to her in the middle of the night. I wondered how such a thing did not frighten her. But she was used to it, I suppose. So long as there was a Varyn to turn to—a routine of sharing beds and sleepily conversing. I glanced at them, lying beside one another, two bright heads in the darkness, and smiled a little.

············>·) ◉ (·(············

The dawn light is what woke me, pouring in through the open window, slowly coaxing me to rise and meet the day. Celine was gone from the chamber, along with Varyn. But he came barreling in as I made up my cot and boasted of how much longer he had been awake than I. In answer, I threw pillows at his head and told him he snored like a wild beast, and we laughed and wrestled till Celine came in and bid us to ready ourselves for the morning meal. He somehow managed to make a game of that, too, racing and hurrying along to see which one of us was quickest to wash and dress.

After having eaten, I sat beside Celine in her chamber, watching him perform the task he had promised her the night before.

"Tell me again what he is doing," I said to Celine. We each sat on the end of her bed, looking at Varyn move from corner to corner, distributing ribbons of smoke that swirled into the air from a thick log of some sweet-smelling herb. He was muttering to himself the whole while in tones too low for me to hear.

"He is cleansing the energy of the room, banishing that which is not wanted or welcome here. So that I might have some peace and quiet tonight."

It amazed me, to hear her speak about the affair with such composure. "It does not frighten you? To hear them?" I asked.

She shook her head. "It used to in the beginning. Until I realized they were mostly more terrified of me and what I represented than I was of them. Varyn was there the first time it happened. I was seven, and it scared me terribly but he knew all about it from lessons and told me I was lucky. That is what took away my fear. Now I just want to help them sort out their troubles so they can pass on and get to the other side. Father doesn't like it so we keep it a secret. But one day I will be famous and rich for it. That's what Varyn says."

"That's right," said Varyn, looking over his shoulder at us to flash a wink at Celine. He was balancing on the ledge of her window now, directing his swirls of smoke toward the corner of the ceiling. "People will come from all over to see you and get a reading. They'll cross the Scorpion Sea just for a few moments of your time. Wait and see." Celine beamed, tucking her hands between her legs. Varyn turned back round and kept on. I leaned closer to her.

"But why does your father dislike it?" Instinct drew my eyes to the half-open door of her bedroom, as if merely uttering the question would summon Lord Vedlan to appear behind it.

"I don't really know. I think he is just angry still—about the time one of them broke his favorite lantern."

"They didn't just break it, they shattered it. A hundred tiny pieces all over the common room floor," said Varyn. He was down from the window now, and working on the crevices of the wood flooring.

"He must think them capable of harming you then," I said, imagining the scene of them all huddled round the broken thing. I could not blame him, I too would be angry to have my belongings destroyed by some invisible intruder. "Are they? If they can smash objects, then what is to stop them hurting you or anyone else?"

Celine shook her head, vehement and assured. "No, they wouldn't. That one was just confused by everything. It was my fault."

I wrinkled my brow. "*Your* fault?"

"It was an old man. I couldn't understand his accent. I had been trying at first to communicate with him, but then I got annoyed by it all and started ignoring him. He was just trying to get my attention again."

"Can you see them?"

"Just once I was able to, and not very well. Varyn says in order to see them clearly I must be taught. There is an institute for girls like me which has lessons. It's a day's journey from our home. I want to attend, if only Father would let me. I want to perceive them. See their faces."

She was staring out the window, only half aware of me I think. The clouds parted and sunlight flooded through. It danced across her smooth brown skin, illuminating her expression, which bore a wisdom beyond her years. They regathered and the light faded, but she still shone.

"Don't worry about Father, I have already convinced Mother to talk to him about it. She will sway his opinion any day now."

Celine beamed again. "Really?" she asked, abandoning the view outside her window and capturing Varyn's eyes instead. He nodded and came to stand over us.

"Your turn."

Celine rose and let him make circles of smoke above her head and round her body.

"Thank you Vary," she said when he was finished, pressing her face against his chest in a tight embrace. He held her to him, patted her on the back. She slipped out from under his clutches and skipped to the window, eager to open it and let the clouds of suffocating smoke waft outside.

Varyn turned to me. "Do you want to go and play?" he asked.

We played.

........⦁·⦁ ✹ ⦁·⦁........

Every day there was a new game. He took me exploring, and showed me the way round his village under the guise of scouting accommodations. We spent our days seeing this place and that. Going here and there. He was well known among many of the mortals and it was hard to go about without drawing the eye of some or all of them. They would ask after his father or inquire about the health of Lady Elayne. I did not like the latter, and I do not think Varyn did either. But always he would answer them politely. He knew the right thing to say to everyone, and had a clever reply waiting and ready on his tongue whenever someone wanted to know of me or my northern origins. I do not know how he made space in his head for so many stories—how one never contradicted the other. They flowed from him, quick and fluid as the river. I was someone of importance in them, and my cheeks grew warm to hear him speak of me in that vein.

In the evenings, we stayed awake well past midnight hours and practiced our game of pulling out my godhead. It never made an appearance, though Varyn would swear he saw a hint of a white glow in my eyes each time I was near to giving up. It took me longer than I care to admit—the catching on that it was just another one of his wily tricks to keep me trying despite the futility of it all. Some nights I did not mind it, I liked to see that sanguine glint in his eye, even if only for a moment.

Soon it came time for him to fulfill his promise of duty to Lord Vedlan.

I accompanied him.

I had never seen one of our temples. I knew Father had the most, he boasted often of them. Whenever a new one had been erected, he would make it known throughout the halls of our twelve courts. "Did you hear about my new temple? It is decorated and lavish—the skin of Emros adorns the entrance, and the mortals keep a sacrifice burning at my altar." He loved their envied expressions, and Mother too. In the time before my trials, I dreamed of the day when I would make such grand declarations of my own divinity. But that is all behind me now.

In the temple, the sculpture of Justice looks nearly identical to her carving in the Hall of Effigies. I put a hand on the stone of her head, lifting myself on the tips of my toes to be of a height to reach it. I wanted to know how the marble of mortals felt, and if it differed from that which existed in our realm. It did not, and if I were Justice, I would be pleased with it.

Her altar still smokes with offering, though Varyn and I are the only ones present. I remember being fascinated by this, and wondered aloud how it was possible, thinking some trick or divinity must have been employed.

"Someone came in before us and paid reverence," said Varyn. "Father manages this temple and leads the worship ceremonies on offering day but some like to come on non ceremony days and give on their own."

He was rushing about, busy with tasks and responsibilities beyond my comprehension. This was but one of many temples his father presided over and he seemed in a hurry to be done so that we might begin our travel to the next.

"Is there something I can assist with?" I asked, watching him tinker with a large vessel, filled with some amber liquid, face set in a fierce scowl.

"No, I can manage it."

"What is that you are holding?"

"The last of the rose oil stores. Remind me to tell Father we must order more for the Fairhill temple."

He answered without looking up at me, and his scowl deepened as he continued to struggle with it.

"Are you sure I cannot help?"

"I'm sure. It's just stuck for some reason, the seal of it won't come off. It's fastened too tight I think."

"Here, let me have a go," I said. He was reluctant to step aside and even more wary when I began twisting the stopper. It remained stiff no matter how much force I applied in the turning.

"I suppose you were right about my arms then."

"What?"

"Thin as pins and weaker still."

He shook his head, chuckling. "No, it's not that. It's not you. Something is wrong with this one. They are never so stubborn." He took it over again, gripping the little glass ball with all his might. He gave it several seconds of ardent pressure. A loud crack echoed through the temple and he released the vessel with a jolting scream.

I remember the deep slice in his cupped hand and the blood which pooled there. What I do not remember is mending both his flesh, and the large vessel of rose oil. A repeat of Crescent Forest—of our brush with the Emros. It had been as if I were experiencing it anew. Varyn stared at me with that same astonished expression. But I did not wish to run and hide as I had longed to that day.

"Your light. It...came...again." He was gaping at me, smoothing his hand over the healed cut without bothering to look down at it.

"I did not make it come."

"Yes you did. You grabbed hold of the rose oil, blasted it. Then looked at my hand and did it once more, only softer, without the full amount of the light you used on the glass."

Upon hearing these words, I became aware of something in my grip, and with a shock, discovered my fingers wrapped round the stout neck of the vessel. I peeled them off, eyes wide.

"But…I do not remember it—any of it. How—"

"It was all the work of seconds, half-seconds really. One for each. You are certain you felt nothing as you did it? *Saw* nothing?"

"Yes…no wait," I said, a small flash of it returning to me—blood and a grimace of pain. "I did see something."

"And what was it? What did you see?"

"You."

Chapter 16

WE CARRIED ON VISITING TEMPLES FOR THE REMAINDER OF that day. Varyn would rub circles over his hand every so often, and cast a furtive look in my direction. He wanted to discuss it further, hoping my answers would help him to solve the riddle within me. But I refused to speak any more on the subject. That was three times now that the light had come forth unbidden, vanishing back to nothing, leaving me swift as it came and with not even the memory of my feat. Varyn and I spent night after night playing our game of practice and at the end of each one, met our rest with disappointment. The erratic nature of my divinity was beginning to infuriate me.

I settled down on my cot feeling much the same as I had during all the previous nights, but for a new stinging sense of being disillusioned.

"I think it is a sign that something great is soon to come," said Varyn. He had just finished securing the end of his braid and this is when we usually took up our game.

"Is it alright if we do not play tonight?" I asked.

"I thought you might say that." He rose and went to his dressing table. "How about we do something different then?"

"Yes, I would like it if we did."

"Come and sit on the bed."

I shuffled over to it and plopped down as he rummaged about with his things. Some minutes passed and he returned with a number of materials, blank parchment being one among them.

"You are going to draw me?" I asked.

"Yes." He sat across from me and began arranging his tools. "This one is for you to keep."

"You do not have to, I told you."

"I want to." He reached, slowly, and placed his hand on my chin, angled my face upward, slight and gentle. I stared at him, pulse quickening, as if seeing him for the first time. His thumb slid softly across my chin as he adjusted my face, I had never been so thoroughly aware of sensation as I found myself to be in that moment. Again he adjusted me, brushing his thumb along my chin with the action. He was looking at me, appraising me and pleased with the assessment, watching without seeing. Still I felt shy under that gaze, in a manner I had not been on any other occasion. His hand fell away and I found that I could breathe again. Did not know when I had stopped.

"I must stay still the entire time?" I asked, more so to hear something other than the sound of my own breaths than for want of an answer.

"Yes, if you find it possible. I can draw from memory of course but I want to make this one as accurate as can be, since it is for you to keep. Whenever you look at it, it should be as if you're seeing yourself in the mirror, with each feature in its rightful place."

"I will pretend I am made of stone then."

I was trying to make him laugh but he only shook his head, half smiling with divided attention. He took it seriously—the creation of this image. His hands had already begun their work, outlining the shape of me. They moved across that blank space as if dancing. The lines and curves came out with the ease of breathing. For a long while I sat staring at the inverted beginnings of the illustration in his lap, watching his tools drift along the parchment every which way.

"You must look up at me, Ambroz. I need to see your eyes."

That shyness returned and I narrowly managed to suppress flinching at the request. His voice had come like a soft breeze against sweltering skin, timid and lax but still demanding of attention. I had not been aware of myself peeking down at the progression. I had been too mesmerized by the movement of his hands.

"Sorry," I muttered, getting back into position.

"I thought you were pretending to be made of stone. Stones do not let their gazes wander." He was grinning.

"I suppose I am not a very good stone."

"No, not at all. But you are a very fetching one."

I would have laughed at this if I were not trying so desperately to remain still as he had asked. Instead I let my eyes rest on him, watching, admiring. Rain pattered against the window behind him, the lulling sound of it the only thing which could be heard between us. I listened at length to the ever changing rhythm of its fall. My thoughts, drifting somewhat, found their way to that other drawing he had fashioned. Through musing I began to recreate it, and once formed, a yearning welled within me. I ignored it and listened again to the drops of rain. But quickly it made itself known for a second time, refusing disregard.

"Varyn?"

"Hmm?" His brow was set in stern concentration.

"Can you leave my eyes as they are? Without the light?"

He broke from his artist's trance and studied me. "You do not like it with the light?"

"I like it well enough. But did you not say you wished for it to be a mirror of me?"

"Well, yes but—"

"Then leave it, please. Draw me as I am here, now."

He did not protest, merely fell back into that severe and assiduous bearing.

Without pause he worked, etching me till the sound of the rain diminished and was no longer a third presence among us. We sat inches from one another yet I could not reach him. He may well have been the sea and I the distant shore. I would have given anything to know what was in his head. The silence blared. At last, Varyn looked up and broke it.

"I am sorry if..." he hesitated, flung his braid over his shoulder with a soft huff. "I am sorry if today was upsetting for you. It is not an easy thing, I think. To have an ability you cannot control."

It was not till he spoke these words that I realized I had been longing to hear them. Yearning to have this understanding be shared by another.

"I did not think you knew of it."

"I didn't, not at first. I couldn't make sense of it—of why it did not please you to have such power hidden away within yourself. I thought: at least he has the light, control over it or not. But I see now, after today. It comes through you without care of your consent. You are the tool and not the craftsmen, and this is what upsets you."

"Yes," I said, leaning forward as if there were a hook in me, of which Varyn tugged. "That is exactly it."

He nodded. "If you don't want to practice with our game any longer…if it upsets you, then let's not continue with it."

"You do not think it necessary? To keep trying at it so that one day I might truly be able to call myself a divinity?"

"It only matters what you think of it."

"I…I think…" What did I think? I was so unsure of myself. "What do *you* think?" I asked.

"I think it does not matter if you have any light or divinity. You are still *Ambroz*, you are still bright."

I beamed at this. I had never beamed. I never had reason to, and so I did not know how silly I looked—how close to tears the expression seemed to the one perceiving it. Varyn set the drawing face down and came to put his arms round me. Water signs cry easily and he thought little of it. Though I was not crying, I still let him hold me.

The skin of his neck brushes against my cheek in the embrace, soft and warm. He smells sweet, like a meadow of flowers. He often smells this way at night, and a faint whisper of it wafts about as I sleep. But our nearness has amplified the scent of him. I want to linger there, breathe it in and have it fill me. The intensity of this urge startles me and I pull back from him, hiding my face away, turning it aside under the pretense of wiping tears.

He let me compose myself without a word, and waited till I turned back round.

"You're better now?" he asked.

"Yes," I glanced at the parchment by his side. "Is it finished?"

"Nearly, just a few more touches and it will be done."

I learned that night, how critical artists can be of their craft, even young ones still honing their developing skill. His few touches morphed into a multitude of additions and revision. I thought they might never end. Whenever it appeared as if he would relent, he picked out some other aspect which displeased him and occupied himself with its correction. I think the one who creates perceives their art differently than the one who is meant to inherit it. He kept frowning down at his lap and the longer he stared, the deeper his scowl. I feared he might tear it to shreds if he sat glowering for a second longer. I slipped it from his hands and was taken aback by my twin—a shining, bronzed, winsome boy. I have said before that I often gazed at myself in the mirror, at my eyes, willing that dispirited youth within them to disappear. There is not a trace of him in Varyn's illustration. He captured me, as I had always dreamed of being, yet never was.

"It's a bit lopsided, just here," he was referencing the shaded corner of my rosy lips. "I can make it better, just give me some more time with it and—"

"No," I said, shielding it from him. "It is already the perfect reflection of me."

I could not stop myself gaping at it and walked back to my little threadbare bed on the floor without cautioning to look anywhere else except down at my hands. I sat taking in those shades a while, captivated by them. I think Varyn said a word or two but I was not listening. He grew impatient and took it from me. I might have tugged it back from him were it not such a thin, fragile thing, but instead, I let it escape my grasp, though not without reluctance.

"Where was that stiffness when you were pretending to be a stone? By the stars, it was like I was all alone in here, talking to the air and furniture."

"I could not help it, sorry," I said. But my eyes still lingered on it even as I gave the apology. He stood over me, the parchment hanging by his side. Peeved, he removed it from my view altogether, hiding it behind his back. His grin bore a hint of petulance. "But…I thought you said it was mine."

He inclined his head laterally. "Are you… *pouting?*"

I was and laughed at the childish absurdity. "Give it back. I want to look at it again."

"It's not going anywhere. It can't get up and walk away if that's what you're worried about. It also cannot speak to you, which is what I have been trying to do for the last—"

"It was rude of me, I know. I did apologize, however."

"Yes, you did. But my acceptance of it, that is another story." He was looking at me in that way of his—the mischievous one. I rolled my eyes and readied myself to hear the instructions of whatever match or contest he intended I overcome to win his forgiveness.

"And what, Varyn, must I do to be forgiven?"

He backed away, slow and measured, narrowed smirking eyes fixed on me till he reached his dressing table.

"It will be nice and safe here until you leave," he said, stowing it in one of his compartments. "Which is soon. One day from now."

I trailed him as he ambled to his bed, waiting for the conditions of my pardon. He burrowed under the covers and propped himself up on an elbow, looking at me as he lay there resting on his side.

"I will forgive you if you stay here with us for a little longer."

"But we have already told Lord Vedlan I would only need board for a week."

"Yes, yes, I know. But it flew by like hours, and now we are at the end of it. These days have been so fun. I want more of them. Tomorrow will be here before long, and I don't want you to leave so soon."

"In truth, nor do I."

"So that is why we must tell Father there has been some trouble with sorting your living arrangement."

"I do not wish to lie to him further."

"You will not have to. I will do it for you."

"But what if he discovers our scheme? Or worse, is fooled by it and still rejects me?"

"You worry too much. He will not refuse you. He likes you—more than most. I told him you have been helping me in the temples, and he was very pleased. He will think of the extension of your stay as a favor returned."

"Are you certain?"

"Yes, entirely."

"And how long will you ask for this time? Another week?"

"Guess."

"*Varyn*," I said, groaning.

"Come on, just one guess."

I thought on it a while. "Another week, I think that is the most reasonable amount."

He shook his head. "No, that would fly and be gone in a wink, just as the last one was."

"So how long then?"

"A season."

Chapter 17

I ASKED HIM TO REPEAT IT SEVERAL TIMES FOR FEAR I HAD misheard the answer. It remained the same, the only variant being the tone of delivery, which suggested mild annoyance at the repetition. When I asked a final time, he clapped a hand to his forehead, as if something which was forgotten had just returned to him.

"I am so dimwitted," he said. "I did not even bother asking if you had obligations to which you must return to in your realm."

"No, no. I do not. It is nothing of the sort."

I could disappear for a century, and they would not notice so long as I appeared for my second trials.

"Then what is it? Why are you hesitant?"

"Well, apart from lying to your father, there is the matter of..." I paused, for I had lost whatever reasoning I believed I possessed. What *was* the matter? I was happy here. There existed not a single day of this short week which I did not spend in either leisure or gaiety. Even the labor of tidying the temples had been enjoyable, for I had endured it in the company of Varyn. Lord Vedlan and Lady Elayne were kind to me and little Celine, too, with all her wits. She taught me something new about mortals every day—like their practice of adorning themselves with jewelry made of crystals to ward off misfortune and protect against those with negative energy or intentions. She had given me a ring to wear, made of moonstone. I had no need of it, of course, but wore it anyway and was reminded of her dreamy charm each time I looked upon the opalescent band wrapped round my finger.

I thought hard, and kept on searching for fault or reason to deny him but could find none. I had not once felt unwelcome among them. Even the servants had taken care to know of me and learn my name. I was wanted here, I think. My presence not tolerated or endured, but *wanted*.

"There is the matter of what? By the stars, have you become a stone again? Where did you go?" asked Varyn.

"Sorry," I said, gathering my thoughts, forcing myself to swim up and leave the depths of my musing. "I was thinking."

"Thinking of what? Excuses for why you cannot stay?" He was fidgeting with his braid, picking at it and ruining the neat weave. "So, let me hear it then. What reason have you come up with?"

I did not have one and said the first silly thing that came to mind.

"A season is quite a long while for mortals, is it not?"

"It is. But you're not a mortal. And anyway, we will hardly spend it here. We don't have to stay lingering around the manor now that I've fulfilled my promise to Father. We can go to Crescent Forest nearly every day. Come on, it will be fun. It's my last free season before lessons resume. After that, I will be lucky if I can play once in a week."

"Lessons?" I had forgotten about these. Mortals had so many cumbersome obligations. "You will have them every day?"

"Yes."

"Can we not play after them?"

"No, there won't be time. I'm starting Alchemy this year. I hear it's difficult and requires hours of night study. Transmutation of elements is among the curriculum too."

I nodded as if I knew what this meant.

"I see," I said, imagining the pair of us together, day after day, running wildly through the forest. "I shall spend the season here then."

In the dim light, I can make out his burgeoning smile. We share it, though the curve is prettiest on him.

"It will be the best season you have ever had," said Varyn. "Wait and see."

He was right.

·········)·) ● (·(·········

I had learned every facet of that forest almost by memory when we came to the end of our season. Even now, after all the time that has passed, I can still see it. Every tall tree and branch. If I concentrate, I can conjure the sound of the river, the woody scent of the air.

We explored the whole of the landscape that season, I think. Climbing, running, jumping and hiding. The length of our races on earth and water grew and grew till they spanned so far we became lost in the vast tangle of our tracks.

Sometimes Celine would join us and pick pretty flowers for her mother. I liked the way Lady Elayne seemed to come alive at the sight of them and how she hugged Celine and smoothed a hand over my hair in thanks.

My favorite days were when it was just Varyn and I, lying by the riverbank as the sun bathed us. Talking under it for hours. His mind was endless as the sea. There was little I knew that he did not know more of, be it the arts or culture, Astrology, or even the gods themselves. With him, I was not a deity—he expected nothing of me but games and boisterous laughter. I felt alive in his presence and bright, like the name he had given me. But he was brighter still. Just being near him was reason enough to smile. To see him as he ran or swam or jumped, beating me at everything. If there were such a thing as perfection, then he was the brother of it. Even so, around him, I did not feel lesser, instead, I was like the god others had always thought I should be. If I had something to say, he listened and told me my ideas were clever. If there was something I was not good at, he offered advice and encouragement and praised me for attempting it.

On the last night of that season, I lay on my cot, watching him tame his fiery curls into his braid. His hair had gotten longer and the thick rope hung almost past his chest, the tail of it nearly touching the beginning of his lower ribs. He finished and tossed it over his shoulder, meeting my gaze in the action.

"I have told Father that we found a boarding house for you in Fairhill."

"Oh," I said. "Good." I did not think it was good. I did not want to leave.

"Fairhill is close enough to visit by carriage, but far enough to keep up our ruse so that you may call on us often. You *will* come back and visit, right?"

"Yes, of course, if I am welcome."

Varyn glowered at me and folded his arms across his chest. "You know that you are. One full season, and you still doubt it. You will always be welcome. What will it take to convince you of that? And why do you act as if we will turn you out on the streets at any moment? Why still, have you this persistent wariness?"

I shrugged and sighed. "It is just a habit, I suppose."

"Well, you would do well to rid yourself of it." He spoke tersely but no anger hid behind those words. I had been with him long enough to know the meaning of his tones. This one was born from the tedium of repetition. He had told me of my perpetual acceptance here in a dozen different ways, but I was the unavailing son of major divinities and struggled to quell that inner voice which declared them all untruths.

He flung himself onto his bed, expelling a heavy sigh. He was weary, for earlier in the forest, we played a game of chase which lasted hours. "I meant to ask you," he said through a series of yawns. "How will you get back to your realm?"

"With a thought."

His brows soared. "Really?"

"Yes, I was as surprised to learn it as you are. It is the one divine thing that is entirely within my control."

He stared at me a while, taking me in. I stared back, feeling in my chest a slight tug of sorrow. I would miss these nights. Miss our sleepy exchanges, the silly, half-formed bedtime thoughts we shared. Miss the cool breeze which floated in from the window and carried his scent to me.

"I think you are going to be a deity of great power and influence one day, Ambroz."

Those words never left me. I wondered if he knew the weight of them. I wondered if he knew how much they meant to me.

·········⟩⟩ ◉ ⟨⟨·········

The following evening, I bid farewell to everyone, with the promise of return. This Lord Vedlan had made me swear to, giving my shoulder a firm squeeze in the agreement. He sent me off with praises in regards to my High Celestian and some writing materials, in case I ever wanted to send correspondence to my northern region of birth. A twinge of guilt welled in me as I accepted them but Varyn had assuaged me of it with one of his sly little phrases—some guileful line of reasoning which I have since forgotten.

As I walked behind Varyn, I looked back at the charming abode I had called home for the last season, and bid it a silent farewell too. We were on our way to the carriages. The area was secluded enough for me to vanish without anyone's attention on me. I stood before him when we reached it, each of us silent as our eyes rested on one another.

"I will miss you," he said.

"And I you. But I will return soon enough."

"I will think of a new story to tell Father to make you stay longer."

He granted me one of his smiles and I wondered how long it would be till I saw it again. I put my arms round him, he squeezed first, holding me as tight as he had that day I banished the Emros from him. He smelled like flowers and the river. I closed my eyes and inhaled the redolence of him.

"Can I watch as you do it?" he asked after we broke from one another.

"Sure, though I do not know what you might see. I have only ever done it in private."

"When you come and visit again, I will tell you what I saw."

I nodded. "Stand a little further off from me in case something unpredictable occurs, then I shall begin," I said.

He took a few steps in retreat, steadily gazing at me. I had not thought of my chamber in weeks. Now I summoned forth the image of it, envisioning all my chattels and the spaces in which they occupied. I thought of the glow from our Moon as she bestows her silver radiance upon the realm, and saw it come down in fine streaks across my bed. Varyn began to look a long distance from me, as if disappearing down a tunnel. I waved at him, and thought of my tall mirror as he waved back, and the next instant, I met with my reflection.

I had vanished from the mortal realm and been returned to my...what?

Home?

I scoffed at the sentiment. A home is where one belongs and feels wanted. I had known neither of those states here.

In the mirror, my reflection is much the same as it has always been, though it stares back at me with a touch less dejection. But despite the lack of variance, I know something has shifted within me. I am not the same Fool I had been upon my departure. I am not the Fool at all, I think. I am Ambroz. I am Varyn's best friend, and he is mine.

I sighed and clutched the writing materials Lord Vedlan had given me to my chest. Varyn had slipped his illustration of me inside one of the journals. I opened it and admired the drawing, looping my fingers round each of my pretty features. I stood in the center of my chamber, transfixed, just as I had been the first time I laid eyes on the creation. But there is no Varyn to come and tear it from my hands in a huff. I am both pleased and saddened by this.

I studied it for I know not how long, ages perhaps.

Instead of stowing it away with the other materials, I fixed it upon my mirror, up high in the corner, so that I may look upon it often and be reminded of the jovial boy who I might one day become.

It stared down at me from the glass.

I think I might have stayed captive to the beauty of those curves and shades were it not for the sound of distant voices in our palace. There had once been a period when Father and Mother often had guests, while I was a small child, before my trials. These occasions did not cease, but rather became less and less over the years. Now it was preferential to them to spend time away from the confines of the palace halls we shared. They graced other courts and were visitants to feasts of which I was never invited. I did not care, as most of these occasions were little more than boasting competitions. Who had the biggest temple built in their honor or which of us is most popular among the mortals? How many festivals have been held for you in the last few decades? There is almost always a duel, and the loser of it, always indignant and ready to raze down a court or two to redeem their pride. Senseless destruction, for the realm replenishes itself in days but the inconvenience of broken pillars and marble is a bother to navigate in the interim. I remember hating the last time our home was host to one of these celebrations, so thoroughly that I blocked it from the records of memory. But now I am reminded of such times by the faint sound of those voices, growing louder with every second. Was it the Hanged Man who was speaking? And the Emperor too? Each of them had booming timbres. It would have been a struggle for most to differentiate. I could not tell as I listened and did not want to stay and find out.

Our palace was no mystery to me, I knew all the crevices and hidden passageways. I knew how to vanish within it, vanish from it. I crept from the sanctitude of my chamber, out into the halls and down a path I often traveled. It led to an alcove and through it lay a garden. I had begun to make my way to it when the sound of more voices came, and with them, the realization that I was getting closer rather than farther away from their owners.

Turning back would have been simpler than continuing on in that slinking, crouching manner of mine which sought to avoid notice but I did it anyway. By the time I was clear of the palace I was sweating and spent. The Galaxy Baths seemed an appealing solution and I set about a course there, readying myself to face the clamoring deities I would meet inside, all vying for a pool of that intoxicating stardust.

Though when I entered, I was shocked by what I saw.

Chapter 18

EMPTY. No Pentacles, Cups, Swords, or Wands. Not a single divinity anywhere, major or minor. I kicked off my sandals and ran through the vast space, bare feet pounding against the obsidian floors. There were only thin strips of surface between each of the immense, square baths, and I was so overcome with bliss, I forgot to take care to balance. Twice I nearly slipped and fell in, fully clothed. The third time I sobered myself and adopted a brisk, measured stride. I ambled down row after row, surveying the options.

I had my pick of them and took my time on the selection. They were each grand and offered much the same luxury but for the view that swirled above; an enchanting dance of stars and their light, swimming in patterns made to lull one to the state of trance. It was everything I needed.

The stardust of my bath glowed a deep amethyst. It rested beneath a cluster of shining orbs. I stripped off my clothing and stepped in and was at once submerged, encompassed by the balmy equanimity of those infused waters. I floated on my back, mind blank, eyes filled with stars and the sight of our shifting sky. Sailing on that liquid was like being embraced by the softest touch. There existed no sound or distraction as I drifted, weightless body swaying on the surface. The scent of the baths differs from deity to deity. On one occasion it might smell of offering, on another, like warm cakes from the dining hall.

Varyn's smell is what fills my senses, the one he has at night: clean skin, flowers, and the earth-scented breeze.

I lifted a hand to my face, the left, where Celine's moonstone ring still rested on my small finger. I twirled the circle round and round, feeling content. I have never been content in the Celestial realm. After this day, I will never be so again, not here, and yet I neglect to value the moment. A part of me was present, but the other lived somewhere else, experiencing things only half as important as this contentment.

But I am being too harsh on myself, for it is hard to be wholly aware of anything while in the Galaxy Baths, that is why we Celestials loved them after all.

I stayed suspended there till the noise of some divinities filtering in drew me out from the quiet recesses of thought. I could have remained and let the intoxicant of stardust overtake me once more, but I did not want to be among them, even if the knowledge of their presence could be dismissed and forgotten, washed away by the spell of the pool like sand on the shore.

I pulled myself out from the soothing caress of the glowing waters and stood atop the cool obsidian. I was at once dried and dressed, for that is the charm of the baths.

Like our palace, I knew the ways of the space and slipped away without notice of those who had entered while I lazed. But I did not take enough care in my retreat once I made it into the corridors.

Among our Zodiac, the Leo Court held the least appeal to me of all, and aside from the Galaxy Baths, I had no need or want to be about the halls; they were not as familiar to me as some others. I was traveling the length of them, along a path that would lead me out to the gardens of the main Fire Wing, when I came to a corner. Around it, I found myself almost face to face with Tiberias.

He had not grown much taller since my trials, but I had. I think he hated this, being nearly level with me when I was younger than him by four years. I tried to step past him but he mimicked me, moving in the same pace and direction. My counter had been to motion on the opposite side of him, but once more, he mirrored me.

"Let me through," I said.

He sneered. "Or what? Will you blast me? Try it, I would very much like to see you flounder with it again the way you did at your trials."

His eyes flit from their normal, hideous chartreuse to a deep violet. I recognized this shade. He wore it as he lay garbling and squirming in the dirt with his burns when I was six.

"I said or what?" With this, he shoved me, *hard*. Tight fist knocking against my shoulder and throwing me off my center of balance. He may not have been much taller than me, but he was broader. Any blows I delivered in retaliation would have been useless.

Till then, that was what I thought.

"Or nothing, move aside," I demanded. If I could do nothing else, I could at least stand my ground.

In reply, another fist came crashing upon me, then a third, quick and forceful. I blocked the fourth, and this enraged him. His eyes began to glow. He was middling even among lower deities, so his light was slow to come. If I ran, I could likely escape him. A season racing against Varyn had sharpened me—he was river-quick, and the speed of my own sprint was hastened because of it. But if I stayed and challenged him, perhaps my godhead would present itself through will at last.

I had but a moment to come to a decision on this. Without thinking, I slammed both my palms into his chest, and his glow dwindled. Like me, his handle on it was weak.

I am not sure what drove me to do this. I would not have dared it in the past—before having experienced the force of divinity move through me.

I thought of the vagrant in that mortal village, the feeling I had when the light burst from my eyes. The rush.

Tiberias was not used to defending himself from me; I had never struck back in all the occasions in which he tormented me, and there had been many.

Disgust and disbelief mingled to form his indignant expression. I went flying as his blow connected, back colliding with a column behind me. His hands were around my throat the next instant. He had abandoned his light, I suppose he had decided I was not worth it. He strangled me a while, fingers digging into my neck. The pain of it was near the brink of intolerable but I needed to endure it for as long as I could to achieve my goal.

Here I should like to mention that Tiberias is quite stupid, all anger and reaction. I do not know what he was hoping to achieve aside from inflicting pain. Neither of us could perish, and so why he bothered with this intensive strangulation was beyond me.

My back was still braced against the column, and as he was exerting all his force upon my neck, I levied it, feigning collapse and using the energy to help propel me forward.

When there came a break in his effort, I raised my knee, chest high, and kicked him.

He tumbled backward, falling into a roll, heels over head. I almost laughed. If I had any sense, I would have taken this opportunity and fled as quickly as my legs would carry me. But as it turns out, I was quite stupid too.

I had not thought beyond this moment, and in it, I was the Fool, full of all the Devil's pride and with none of his power.

That tumble I sent Tiberias on fueled him to a frenzy of ferocity. His eyes glowed, the deep violet becoming brighter each second. I refused to run, for a fury had been ignited within me also. I took advantage of his slow-coursing light and used the long seconds to gather up a few stones. I hurled them at his head—one or two of them fell short, but the largest bounced off his brow and drew out a streak of silver. I am lucky that his aim was not a fraction as good as mine.

The beam of his effulgence cracked the column behind me and was just shy of scorching off a portion of my ear. I ducked at the blast of the second and charged at him while he was summoning the third, knocking him through an archway. I landed on top of him and thrust my hand to his head, pressing it firmly to the side so that his eyes saw nothing but the stretch of grass. We struggled there, I to keep him pinned beneath me, and he to wrangle himself free of my straddle. He somehow got his hands around my throat again, but without clear sight of me, the effect was lessened. I pressed the side of his face down harder, and his grip on me grew slightly lax.

"Get off me, you weak, cowardly disgrace of a Celestial," he hissed.

"If I am as weak as you say, then prove it."

He proved it. But to my credit, it was not without great effort on his part.

We tussled there for Jupiter knows how long till he eventually got the better of me and threw me off. He quickly climbed on top of me. The reversal of positions was unbearable. I was crushed under the weight of him without any hope of escape. He restrained me by the wrists, and no matter how intensely I writhed, I could not break free of his grip. I hated looking up at his self-satisfied face and squirmed while taking in the ugly sight of it, desperate to be out from under him. I kicked and flailed, but he remained a mountain on top of me.

"No point trying that, now I've got you. Wait until you feel the heat of my divinity melting your skin, you worthless little—"

"Tiberias!"

I knew that voice, and thanked the Moon for the sound of it. He froze upon hearing it, his shades going a dull gray. He was afraid of her. Since that day, if ever he was near her, he showed her the utmost deference, sometimes to the point of fawning. I did not like her tolerance of him—her kindness. I wanted her to disdain him as much as I did.

Behind him, the pattering of her footsteps grew nearer, and I saw the slow change of his expression. The fire within it had been doused. He withdrew his hands and got to his feet, but not before dealing me a sneaky blow between the legs with his knee. I winced and rolled onto my side, groaning as I absorbed that sharp pain.

Arcana helped me off the ground, and the moment I was upright, I lunged for Tiberias, burning for my strike of revenge. But she intercepted.

"How you can even find it in yourself to quarrel after what we learned today is astounding," she spat the words at Tiberias. She had her back to me and so I was left to imagine what her shades were as she delivered them. If his stammering reaction was to be any indication, I am sure they were sienna. He scurried off, and she fixed them on me. I flinched and, in so doing, noticed the abrupt change in them. They flitted from the sienna I had suspected to silver, lingering on me as she gaped.

"Your eyes, they are glowing," she said.

"Really?"

"Y-yes. Well, they were, for a moment. Now they are back the way they always are."

I was still hot with anger and tried to calm myself, to think and process her assertion. But any triumph I might have felt about the re-emergence of my light was compressed by the ache in my groin. I wanted so badly to thrash Tiberias for it.

"What on Saturn's rings were the pair of you doing? What happened?" she asked.

I told her everything, and by the end of it, I thought I might see the glow of her sienna once more. I tried to distract her and prevent that possibility from becoming a reality.

"What did you mean earlier?" I asked.

She wrinkled her brow. "What?"

"You said you had learned something."

"Yes, we all did. Save for you. I was searching for you but could not find you anywhere."

Searching for how long, I wondered. Just this hour? Days? The whole season?

"Has something happened?" I asked.

"There has been a prophecy. We all learned of it when the Oracle gathered us in the arena of the Aquarius Court. It is all anyone can talk about. Where have you been?"

"The Galaxy Baths," I said, motioning vaguely off to the side.

"Ah, I suppose their spell is what caused you to miss the summons then."

"Yes, that is right," I lied. I had not been aware of any summons, though now it became clearer to me why the baths had been so deserted and why there were so many voices in our palace. "What does the prophecy regard?"

"The realm," replied Arcana. "The Oracle's waters made known to her a possible fate of peril. She claims one among us may bring about great devastation. And that if it came to pass, the realm would be as it was in the time before the creation of mortals when we were without veneration and quarreled until the skies bled."

"And the waters divulged nothing more?"

Arcana shook her head. "That is all she was shown. When we inquired of any indication as to who it might be that is responsible for this supposed upheaval, she said the waters gave no answers and that the whole of the picture was vague."

"So nothing is certain then?" I asked.

"No, but it is wonderful gossip and good reason to be wary of one another. And to avoid squabbling. It draws attention." With this, she narrowed her eyes, glaring at me through them. She was the youngest between us and still a child, but at times, in her presence, I felt she was so much more, even then.

"Yes, well, I did not start it."

"And you were doing little to end it by the looks of it."

I thought she would continue with her scolding disapproval of my actions, but she began to drift and focused her attention elsewhere, gaze hovering just beyond my shoulder. She furrowed her brow, twisting her features as if she had discovered something which displeased her.

"Father, what are you doing here?" she asked.

I turned and looked, dreading the sight of him. Yet when I searched the area behind me, I found nothing.

There came a deep, resounding laugh. "My clever girl, how did you spot me?"

I stood bemused, staring in the direction from which Uncle's voice had come. Still, I saw nothing.

"I could tell you, but then you would know my secret and correct yourself in the future," replied Arcana. He laughed again, and slowly, his form materialized, flickering into existence before us.

Chapter 19

THE MAGICIAN SAT PERCHED IN AN ARCHWAY, a wide grin plastered on his lips. He rose, silken garment fluttering out behind him like the wings of bats as he strode over to us.

How long had he been there, watching?

I wondered this, observing him through slits as he draped an arm around Arcana, drawing her near. I disliked the way he always clung to her. When she was smaller, he carried her nearly everywhere. If she were not almost as tall as I, he would be carrying her still. Anything to have his hands on her—to claim some bit of her. She seemed a prized possession to him like something won and earned instead of his begotten offspring. It was unclear to me then why I harbored that judgment, those feelings. I felt ashamed for having them and chided myself for the immature, bitter jealousy of it all, reminding that inner voice to stop pretending as if being the recipient of a parent's doting is not every child's wish.

Though now, in this recounting, as I see these recollections anew with wiser eyes, it was a sensible assessment. But I have yet again strayed ahead of events.

Uncle drew her even nearer to his side, rubbing a hand up and down the length of her arm. In turn, she looked up at him with an adoring smile.

"Will you really keep it from me, darling?" he asked, cooing at her. She tipped her head to one side.

"You have many secrets from me. Surely you can endure it if I had one or two of my own."

He clapped his hands together, tossing his head back and laughing as if this were the most amusing thing he ever heard.

"Too true, too true, darling Archie. I cannot argue. Well, shall I tell you one of them now?"

"Yes, please," she said and glanced at me. Uncle leaned to her ear, but she pulled away. "And cousin, too, he won't tell anyone, right?"

I nodded, though Uncle did not look at me. He had yet to acknowledge my presence among them. His wide grin faltered the slightest amount, and he straightened, large hand still rubbing that linear pattern the length of her arm, clinging, clinging, ever tighter.

"Oh, fine then, darling. If you insist."

"I do!"

A deep chuckle. Contrived.

"It took me a century or more, I cannot recall precisely, to master the spell of concealment. I am the only Celestial who can vanish to nothing at will. Even the Devil cannot do it, he relies on the shroud of shapeshifting, which I can do as well, expertly. That you were able to spot me, Archie, given all my decades perfecting it," he clicked his tongue, "it is astonishing."

She drank in this praise, undisguised glee enveloping her features.

"Will you tell me another?" she asked.

"Greedy greedy, No I shall not. But go and find your mother. Perhaps she can be persuaded to tell you of the time I—" Arcana darted off, giggling, and was gone in seconds.

His wide grin had run off with her. He looked down at me in his usual way.

"I did not take you for a fighter," he said.

"How long were you there, watching?"

"Long enough."

"You saw what Tiberias meant to do? And you did nothing to help?"

"Help *you*? Whatever for? It was perfectly good entertainment. And it seemed quite under control, what with your stones and throwing arm."

"He was going to burn me."

"You would have healed. Or are you lame in that, too?"

"If Arcana had not—"

"Yes, yes, if she had not. If if if, your existence is predicated on *ifs*, isn't it? Well, *if*—"

"I would not be surprised if that prophecy has something to do with you. If anyone would destroy our realm, it is you. I hate you."

127

My tongue had gotten ahead of my mind. It was the petty retort of a child exhausted with the cruelty of adults. Uncle struck me for it. I held the stinging spot on the side of my head, ears ringing, rage building inside me.

He grit his teeth. "You will mind your tone and tongue."

I felt the heat rising in my eyes, along with something else—some other sensation I could not name. It left me before I had the chance to recognize what it was, and by the time I did, it had been too late.

It was merely a short burst but this was enough to make Uncle gasp. The atmosphere between us shifted. He had been leering, ready to reprimand me with another blow. Now he stood aghast. I did not burn him; he had his tricks and warded off my light, but he acted as if I had. I waited for him to counter me, bracing myself, but he did nothing and merely stayed still, regarding me with a look of incredulous...what? Contempt? I could not place the expression.

He muttered words under his breath. Till now, I still do not know what he said as he backed away from me. It was not a retreat brought forth by fear, yet he hastened to leave the area.

Whatever serenity I had gained in the Galaxy Baths was gone now.

I took my time trudging back to our palace, going about the halls in a sort of daze. Too many events had unfurled in too short a span of time. It was as if they had happened around me instead of *to* me. I needed to take them all in, to sort through and dissect each one, but scarcely knew where to begin. So much of it would have been inconceivable to me a mere season ago. Had I changed so much since then?

In my chamber I sink to the floor and study my reflection inside the tall mirror.

I stare at it and
a voice inside my head chants, *glow glow glow*
a gasp escapes me
a faint light kindles in my eyes

·······⋅⋅⟫ ● ⟪⋅⋅·······

I began to gain a handle on my light at last.

For days, I sat within the confines of my chamber and worked at it. It was a strange thing, divinity. At times it felt as though a pressure was

128

mounting within me and would spring out like a great burst of energy. Others it was weak and took some coaxing. But one thing became clear: that godhead in me was no longer wholly inconstant as it had been.

If I sat in front of my reflection and called it forth, it would come—shakily and feeble on one occasion, forcefully on another, but always it came.

This minor control felt a small victory. The only thing that dampened it was my shades. They remained fixed and would change for nothing, it seemed. I tried to imagine the color of my happiness, anger, fear. Would some hues be brighter or duller than others? Would the depth of my emotions be amplified by them? These hopeful musings were the closest I came to seeing them vary from the dark amber I had experienced all my life.

Weeks of fantasizing about them had led me to seek answers. I found nothing in the Cosmic Library on the subject of shades and a Celestial's Upright or Reversed nature. I wanted badly to know which of the two I had inherited ever since I learned of them and thought if I knew, then surely something could be done in the way of getting my eyes to behave as they were meant to. But this ambition proved fruitless, for I did not know where to begin my inquiries and to whom they should even be addressed. I would sooner be kicked between the legs a second time than to ask Father or Mother. They had mended things in my absence and were united again in their hostility. And I had not the courage to seek out Arcana's council since my scrimmage with Uncle, for fear he would be lurking about as he often was. I did not want to face him. I did not want to face anyone and seldom wanted to be here at all. I had been feeling out of sorts since the day I arrived back from the mortal realm. It had been weeks since I left, and yet I still struggled to settle once more into my old way of things, to go about the wings and courts as I used to. I was out of place here.

This dawned on me as I sat gazing at our Moon. She shone full and spread her silver luster across the ink sky in generous proportion. It streamed into my chamber, illuminating all in its path, all that was dark within me.

I thought again of my shades. Perhaps they would turn up on their own, as my divinity had. Time may yet give rise to them. *You are only twelve, after all.* This was Varyn's voice in my head. I smiled at the remembrance of it, glancing toward the corner of my mirror to find his drawing staring boldly down at me.

Thoughts of my shades dwindled and turned into thoughts of him, his hands, working to etch me in their elegant dance of curves and lines.

The view of his chamber filled my mind, broadening to include its soft yellow light and the window near his bed.

I had closed my eyes for but a moment when it happened. It was without intention. Or was it? I cannot recall. Everything has become so muddled now. Though, what is clear is the sight of him through that window.

I stood below it, having been transported during my rumination. From that day on, I was more careful with my thoughts.

The stagnant air of our palace was gone, and now, outside, a breeze ruffled my hair. Its wind flowed into his chamber and might have ruffled that long, bright mane of his also, were it not weaved into a neat braid. He sat at a small table near the end of his bed, chin on fist, looking out at nothing in particular, for it faced an empty wall.

I had not meant to intrude upon him this way and thought at once of my realm, my chamber. But the visions waned to nothing. The desire to have his eyes looking out at me instead of that bare wall was stronger than my will to leave.

"Varyn," I whispered in a harsh cadence which scratched my throat, so that the sound of it would carry. He started and whipped his head round this way and that in search of it but discovered nothing. He did not look to the window and must have thought he was going mad.

I tried again, keeping my voice low. It was a quiet night and the manor grounds seemed empty, but I did not wish to draw attention to myself. Still, he did not think to turn his attention outdoors and kept looking left and right without seeing me.

On the third try, I waved my arms in the air above my head. He caught sight of the wild movement finally and rose from his seat with wide eyes, a hand pressed against his chest.

"By the stars, is that you, Ambroz? I thought I was hearing spirits like Celine. What are you doing out there?"

He came and stuck his head out, chuckling down at me.

"It was an accident," I said, spotting a quill in his hand and feeling a touch daft for disturbing him, for not leaving when I had the chance.

"Well, praise whatever caused the mishap. I am happy to see you again."

Chapter 20

A WARMTH SPREAD THROUGH ME AS I STARED UP AT HIM, watching the braid fall over his shoulder while he looked down at me from that great height.

"I'm afraid the heavy latch has been placed on the main door already. And the servant's entrance is guarded by loud bells. I would tell you to make use of it, but I do not wish to wake anyone with that chiming racket. Can you manage the climb up here? I should think so. I've seen you get up trees that were taller in height," said Varyn, flashing me a grin. "I can help you if need be. Make a rope of cloth and toss it down, perhaps."

I assessed the bricks on the side of the house, squinting through the darkness of night in search of a ledge or spur where I might establish my footing to begin the climb. There weren't any I could see, and so for some time, I stood flummoxed, gaping as I pondered a solution.

This is a testament to my stupidity, for the answer was obvious and involved not an ounce of physical exertion. I shook my head at the realization, clapping a hand to it and chortling.

"What is so funny?" asked Varyn.

"A climb is not necessary. I can just…close my eyes and—"

"Ah yes," he interjected, "Of course, why didn't I think of that?"

I did not tell him I had not thought of it at first, either. I felt silly enough as it were.

"I can do it now, with your permission."

He rolled his eyes. "You make it seem as though I am some dignitary. Stop being so formal and come up here so I can pummel that stuffiness out of you. It's been weeks since I've had a good jostling match."

In a joking manner, he puffed out his chest. As I smiled up at the window, I pictured myself standing behind him, and the next moment, I was there in his chamber, taking in his half-bent form.

"Let us have our match then," I said.

Varyn turned round with a gasp. "That was brilliant. Even more than the last time."

"Oh, right, what did it look like from your end when I left? I have been longing to know."

"As though you vanished. One moment, you were there, and with a blink, you were gone."

"For me, it was different, strange. You seemed a long way off, then you became smaller and smaller, till you faded away and..." I paused and narrowed my eyes. "You must promise to stop getting taller, Varyn, or at least wait for me to catch up till you sprout again."

He laughed and made his way to me, pulling me into an embrace.

"I will do no such thing," he said.

The difference in his height became more apparent once the distance between us was no more. It had been weeks since last we saw each other, a little under two seasons, and yet he stood taller than me by almost a head.

"Envious, are you?" he asked, drawing back and ruffling my hair. "But you have changed too."

"Have I?"

"Yes, you are wearing different garments."

He took pleasure in teasing me this way. We both laughed, and I glanced over at the materials strewn about his little desk. It had not been there before.

"I'm studying for an Alchemy examination that is to be taken in the coming weeks. Father let me borrow the desk from his study," he said when I asked him about it. He went and sat behind it.

"And I have interrupted," I said. "I do not wish to keep you from it. Let me leave you and—"

"No, don't go. I'm glad of the distraction, believe me. Everything was beginning to look the same. I could hardly keep focused. All day, I've been at it. Come and sit near me."

I took up a place on the end of his bed and peered down at his open books. Across the pages were strange symbols and characters I did not understand. But some I did.

"Your handwriting is exquisite. I can never make the vowels so neat," I said.

"Celestian is an easy language to make pretty. You should see my writing in Haneshi or Dorst. Then you would not think me so talented." I knew High Celestian and nothing more. If the mortals wished for us to hear their orisons, they must ask in the language of the stars.

I continued staring at all his pretty words and found in them some of those same curves that were present in the illustrations I became so lost in. I could feel myself drifting into a trance and tore my eyes away, looking instead at Varyn, mouth forming the dark oval of a yawn.

"Tell me of what you've been doing in our time apart," he said, wiping at his teary eyes.

I told him of everything, tongue running away from me as if in a race. The sentences came one after another: the prophecy, my tackling Tiberias, the Magician's retreat—my governance of the godhead within me; he was overjoyed to learn of this and demanded a demonstration.

He gave me some parchment to char, and in seconds, I seared the edges. His eyes were the widest I had ever seen them as he pinched the burned fringe between his fingers.

"I knew it would come! And your shades? What of those?"

"They do not change for anything. I have tried and tried."

"Don't worry, they will, I know they will. Just as I knew your light would come. How does it feel when it leaves you?"

"It is different each time. I cannot describe it but...the sensation is...pleasant."

"And can you use your light for other things?"

"What do you mean?"

"Apart from burning. The way you did in the temple."

"I do not think so."

"Of course you can. Have you tried it?"

"Well...no. I have only been trying to make it come forth. It is still quite weak, and I do not yet know which—"

"Nonsense. Let's try it. Come on."

"But...how?"

He held up the parchment I had partially burned. "With this."

"I am not sure I know what it is you mean for me to do."

"Make it whole again."

"But Varyn I—"

"*Try.* I know that you can."

I stared at it, becoming unsure of my light again for the first time in weeks. I had been solely focused on calling it forth—on getting it out of me. It came when bid, and thus, I had believed myself somewhat in control of it. Though, now I realized I knew nothing of mastery, of guiding it to a specific purpose.

It is said our light is the source of life and capable of creation or destruction, of healing or of injury, like the great sun.

I possessed this light. I was certain of it. Only I did not know how I was meant to assemble it for something such as what Varyn was asking of me.

He sat holding up the partly incinerated parchment. His expression bright and expectant. I glared at the singed edge and called upon my godhead. Promptly, the delightful pressure of it ascended. My breath quickened, heart racing faster and faster, till the delicious feel of that heat...

My light broke free in a swift burst. Varyn and I stared at the mark, both of us frowning at the newly diminished bit on the margin. The more I gazed upon the failure of my attempt, the deeper my frown became, though Varyn's had transformed into something strange and mischievous. Wearing this peculiar expression, he inspected the parchment a long moment. He had been holding it at a distance, away from his person—now he adjusted his grip, lowering the shape till it rested on his chest, near his heart.

"Again," he said, resolute.

I shook my head fiercely. "Not like that. Not there. Hold it up like you were before. Then I will try."

"No."

"Varyn I will not—"

"Again, do not make me repeat it."

His honeyed, hazel eyes bore into me, challenging me, commanding me.

"Do you understand what will happen if I cannot do it? If the wrong light comes? You will be burned, Varyn. *Burned.* I would never forgive myself if I burned you."

"Then don't. Come on. Try."

"*Varyn.*"

"Ambroz."

I sighed a long, frustrated exhalation. He was impossible to reason with when he was like this—so utterly unyielding and obstinate.

"You once called me stubborn," I said, crossing my arms. "But there is none more stubborn than you."

He lifted a brow. "You are angry."

"Yes."

"Good. Let it drive you. Come on, again."

I let out an indignant huff and dropped my arms. He smirked upon realizing I meant to make another attempt.

Defeated and despite my fear of hurting him, I looked intently at the parchment and began to gather my godhead, telling myself it would be alright, that I would not wound my friend. After seconds, I felt the heat of it rushing within me and knew the fire in my eyes began to kindle when

"Wait!"

"What? Did I hurt you?" I asked, pulse hastening.

"No, I am fine. I think I know of something that may help."

"You might have told me sooner."

"I only just realized."

"Well?"

"When you do it…what are you thinking of?"

"I think of the light, of getting it out."

"That is all?"

"Yes."

"And when you came here to my room, what were you thinking of then?"

"Your chamber, of course. Your things, the light, the floors. You."

"This time, when you ask your light to come, ask it to make the parchment whole again as well. Don't think only of getting it out. Think beyond that. Think also of an edge which is unburned."

Why had I not thought of this? It seemed obvious now he said it. I had not yet realized it, but he had always been the wiser of us.

Accepting this advice with a nod, I concentrated again on that edge, acutely aware of the rise and fall of his chest behind it. If I failed, he would be hurt, and this knowledge is what fueled my precision. I did as he had suggested and made use of my thoughts, crafting visions and realities of a parchment never touched by light. These images came easily to me. With them, I called upon my divinity.

In the past, when the light of my godhead left me, I seldom knew how it came to be that it did. Now, I perceive each function of the ability. My breaths, my sight, every beat of blood within me. All were working alongside one another for this single undertaking.

The brief stream of my effulgence blasted a portion of the scorched fringe. I gaped at it and saw that a bit of that blackened edge was revived. I had not managed to make it whole, but in spite of this, Varyn thrust a fist into the air.

"What did I tell you?" he asked, flushed and triumphant. I rose and took it from his hands, feeling equal parts astonished and disappointed.

"But...it is not...I had intended to mend it entirely," I said.

Varyn dismissed this with a wave. "It's still a success. Your light did not burn it further. That's all that matters."

He was right, and I looked at him with new eyes, my previous anger having fallen away.

"You are as stubborn as you are clever," I said.

He awarded me that slow-spreading smile, which I loved to see.

"What will you give me for my cleverness?"

"What would you have?"

We were always exchanging these silly, arbitrary prizes. It was one of my favorite things about our friendship.

"Let us start our game again. You need practice."

"But—"

"No buts, you asked me what I would have. This is it. You don't have to come every night if you do not wish to, although I think this would be of benefit to you."

"What of your studies?"

He shrugged. "I will make some other time for them, and anyway, it doesn't matter. You will master this before long. Wait and see." This seemed a treasured phrase of his.

I waited, eager for what I would see.

Chapter 21

AS VARYN HAD PREDICTED, it was not long before I learned how to make proper use of my light. I took to spending long nights with him, staying up past twilight hours and calling forth my divinity in a thousand different ways. It did not always behave in accordance with my intention and was mostly weak and sometimes altogether ineffective. But Varyn had convinced me this was something I could overcome. I did not believe him and knew well that a Celestial needed veneration to supplement their inherent abilities. And despite the strong Celestial coupling that bore me, mine had always been lowly, and were lower still without reverence. I did not tell this to Varyn. I did not want him getting ideas about making offerings to me as a possible remedy.

Instead, I came down to the mortal realm, nightly, and passed the hours with him.

When we were not taking up our game, we spoke together of everything till our yawns overwhelmed us and our minds clouded with weariness. I was never so lively as I was with him. In the mornings, he left for his studies, and I vanished back to the realm and counted down the hours till I saw him again, sometimes writing out my thoughts or the progress we had made in the journals given to me by his father. I sought solace in them, pouring my feelings onto the blank pages, filling them with talk of prophecy, divinity, anything that plagued or weighed on me. I wrote to furnish the dull and empty stretches of time that were my convention in the absence of Varyn.

One night, just after I had managed to douse a small flame with my light, he turned to me, a look of familiar mischief in his eyes.

"Come with me tomorrow," he said, collecting the matches he had used to make the little fire and stowing them away in one of his dressing table compartments.

"Come with you where?"

"To the academy. I get into the carriage right after the morning meal. Since you are joining us for it, come, spend the day with me."

I had entered and stayed as a guest the proper way this night, not by appearing in his chamber, without the knowledge of my presence shared by anyone else save for he and I, but instead by arriving at the front door of the manor. Lord Vedlan had invited me to stay for the evening, and I obliged him.

"I think it would be odd if I came. I know nothing of your studies. I do not wish to be a nuisance there."

"You won't be. My instructors would be eager to learn about you, if anything. They like to think their teaching customs superior to that of the ones in the north and will probably ask you to compare them with ours. Just make up something if they do. Our Divination's preceptor will be especially curious about you, I think."

"Why do you want me to come?"

He shrugged, contemplating a while and staring blankly ahead.

"I like our nights together. And I think I would like them better if I came to them after having shared the day with you so that you can put faces to the names and places we discuss."

Often he spoke to me of his long days spent at the academy, of his toils with Maths, Alchemy, Astrology, Instrumentation, and others I have forgotten the names of. He would tell me of various mortals he knew and liked or disliked. I would picture it all and color in the details with the ink of my mind, crafting them into figures or shapes that suited me. Though he did not know it, he was asking me to abandon and forget all I knew—to leave the safety of my imagination. It frightened me. I was shy and unsure of myself with everyone but him.

He gazed at me with expectant eyes, for I had been long inside my head.

"Yes," I said. "I will go with you."

This won me a smile, and the next morning, I accompanied him to his studies.

We piled into the carriage, Celine, Varyn, and I, all of us in high spirits, Celine especially. She stroked my hand the whole way, sleepily fondling the moonstone ring she had given me. She liked to see me wearing it, I think. When it came time to step out and enter through the tall doors of their building, she clung to me.

"Come and see me to the premises. Escort me inside," she said, pulling me from Varyn. I looked to him for guidance, and he leaned to my ear.

"She wants to show you off to her friends. They think northern boys are prettier than the ones here," he whispered, following us and shaking his head.

I have never had the eyes of so many girls on me, nor the hands.

"He is staying with us from the north," boasted Celine as one of her friends sampled the feel of my hair. She seemed pleased with the texture and, despite touching me, was hesitant to speak to me directly, and instead exchanged inquiries with Celine about me as if I had not been standing there. I let Celine parade me round till Varyn intervened and ushered me off.

We walked together through the corridors and came to a room with many tall windows.

Inside, others already sat waiting, some with their faces buried between the pages of books, others writing, and a few, staring—at me.

"Who is this?" asked a hulking boy. He rose from his desk and came to stand over Varyn and I as we settled into our seats.

Many eyes were on me now and I felt each individual pair, prodding me with their curiosity. This was what I had feared. I went rigid with nerves and looked to Varyn, pleading silently for his intervention. He granted it.

"Mind your own nose, Jayce. What's it burning you for?" said Varyn.

Jayce, I had heard of the name in many of those nightly stories. He sneered, this Jayce, and had been about to make his retort when another of the staring lot rose from her seat, giggling.

"Everything burns Jayce. If a bird landed just outside the window, he'd go and inquire about its flight path here," she said and came to inspect me, standing near my side.

Laughter spread through the room and everyone decided to turn back round and stop looking at me, save for her and Jayce. She waved at me and tucked a stray coil of her coarse bushel of hair back into the rest, all piled high on top of her head like a cloud.

"I'm Pella."

"Ambroz," I said.

"The northerner," she and Jayce said in unison. They knew me already? I did not know Varyn spoke of me among them. He had never made mention of it in any of the tales he brought to me.

I think I smiled at this revelation, for Pella smiled too, then Jayce, and finally, Varyn. The next moment, we were all of us talking, the conversation spreading to reach and include nearly everyone in the room. Even here, among the diverse sea of them all, Varyn shined brightest. When he spoke, others listened. His words were honey, and they were like bees around them, drawn in by their sweet, golden allure. I withdrew into myself and watched him spin tale after tale, entertaining them till their instructor came and called for attention.

The lessons all went above my comprehension, but we were given small breaks between each, and during the intervals, groups of the students would flock to where Varyn and I sat, asking him for advice or further instruction.

"Did I do this right?" one would say, or "Can you take a look at my equation?"

When they broke for a meal, our bench—Varyn's bench—was the liveliest, crowded with a half-dozen or two energetic bodies all clamoring for his ear.

The lessons continued to be a confusing blur to me. All except the one which followed the afternoon meal: instruments. I liked the room in which the course was being conducted, open and with a flood of sunlight pouring in through arched windows of ivory.

Everyone was practicing the same melody. I watched Varyn's fingers strumming the rhythmic chords of the song. I had known only the verses and was hearing their accompanying tune for the first time. Varyn played his Lerawyn with closed eyes, holding the little gold circle to his chest. His hair hung loose, cascading down almost to the middle of his back. The sun gleamed on him, lighting that vivid copper to fire. He arrived at the conclusion, and his eyes opened slowly. Found me staring.

"You know it?" he asked with a drowsy half-smile.

"The song?"

He nodded. "Mm, the words."

"Yes," I said. It was the song of the Hierophant and well-known in the realm, he would not let us forget it.

"Will you sing them?"

I tensed and looked about the room, aware and timorous. I had been happy in Varyn's shadow, fading into the surroundings.

"But I…I have never—"

He silenced me, placing a hand over mine. "Don't worry. No one will hear you but me if you keep your voice low enough. All Celestials sing well and I…wanted to hear you, even if just for a moment."

It was true; we did all have the voices of stars, but I had never used mine for this—and was partly incredulous as to whether it even existed within me. But weary of lack, I did not allow myself to dwell on it, and decided it had.

"Go on," I said, resistant to the idea of disappointing him.

He played. I sang.

I kept quiet at first, then grew slightly louder when I saw how Varyn liked the sound of me. I closed my eyes, as he had done while playing, and let the chords in, swaying with them, humming during some sections, and feeling the vibration move through me.

Eventually, he drew to a close, and the music stopped. I stopped with it, opening my eyes.

A crowd of onlookers stood huddled round Varyn and me, gaping. His face was the only one I cared to see.

"You sing beautifully," he said. A hum of assent rippled throughout the collection of them. I was too shy to respond and sat wilting under Varyn's brilliant smile.

"You're good. But I can do better," said Jayce. I was relieved when they turned to focus on him. "Play for me, Pella," he added. She snorted but took up her Lerawyn and started on the melody.

Jayce began singing. His voice broke on the first note. Everyone laughed, and he laughed, too, clearing his throat. "That doesn't count," he said. "Let me have another go!" But they had lost interest, filing back to their seats for independent study.

"Will you play again?" I asked Varyn. I wanted to fall under the trance of that spell once more. He lifted the Lerawyn and strummed the delicate strings. I smiled.

The rest of the afternoon was filled with the lessons of many other subjects and when we reached the final one, I wondered how he managed this every day.

"You get used to it," he said when I had asked him. The Astrology and Divination instructor had overheard this and laughed.

"Do they do things differently up there? So that there is less time spent on learning?" she asked.

"Yes," I replied, unsure if this contradicted one of the other lies I had given someone earlier.

"Well, we have the best practices here in Ethelia. It is why so many of your lot come to visit. I hear they don't even make use of the cards up there. How you people draw up a horoscope without the energies of them is beyond me. Truly archaic. Have you ever even seen a deck?"

I shook my head, wishing she would go away. Instead, she placed a stack of cards onto the desk.

"Have a look," she said.

I peered down at them, and the first card I spotted…was the Fool.

Chapter 22

THE INSTRUCTOR STRUGGLED TO SUPPRESS A CHORTLE. I must have been gaping as I sorted through them, finding one after the other of those familiar, divine faces gazing vacantly out at me. They were not particularly accurate, nor did they mirror any of those fine, empyrean features I knew so well from the many instances I endured as the subject of their leering, but the essence of their being was captured—preserved, here on these strange little cards. An impressive imitation.

I stuffed my square to the back, and the instructor let out a faint scoff.

It did not appear very much like me, but even so, I could not bear looking at it.

Almost instantly, I regretted it, for Father's menacing aura greeted me underneath, his resemblance inverted.

I turned it right side up and pushed the stack away.

"Do you not wish to know how they work?" asked the instructor. She did not wait for my answer. "The Fool is a good card, one of the major deities, recently added, though when paired with that next you've drawn…well. It could spell problems if this were a proper reading."

"A reading?" I asked. "What could be read from an image of Celestials?"

"Lots. The energies, their position. All of it is interpreted. Of course, only one skilled in the complex art of divination may decipher them. But as I understand it, most of your kind see foretelling with them as an affront to the gods. Very narrow view. These have little to do with the Celestials, really. It is merely their being and traits we use. They are divorced from their role as revered deities in the deck. We still revere them. Make the offerings and what have you. I don't know why that is so difficult a notion to contend with for some. I once had a priest from Karlindé toss them overboard during my visit back. All of them floating across the waters of the Scorpion Sea. Wasted. I wanted to knock him overboard to join them."

She carried on explaining, but a great deal of it was lost on me. I could not make proper sense of it. I did not have an Astrologer's mind.

When she presented me with another deck, I became further bemused, for they contained the minor deities. But the number of them in our realm far surpassed the little quantity she introduced. Her endless prattling confused me to the point of frustration, and at last—when I could endure no more—I smiled a wide smile and said,

"I like them. When I return, I will tell all those I know in Karlindé to open their minds to the idea of them."

Beside me, Varyn smirked, and a bearing of satisfaction replaced the instructor's incessant lecturing.

"I thought that would never end," Varyn whispered to me after she had left us. We kept our giggling low.

"I am glad this is your final lesson of the day. I do not want to come back here and pity you for the obligation."

He did not bother trying to stifle the sound of his laughter now. Perhaps because he knew I would return, and often, for always, he could convince me of anything.

··········)·) ● (·((·········

At fourteen, I realized my shades would likely never come. Something was broken in me. Or missing. All afternoon, I had felt out of sorts, but now, sitting in the Nebula Gardens beside Arcana and other deities, the epiphany came crashing over my head.

"Here, try this combination," said Arcana, offering me some sap on her finger. I waved it away. I was meeting Varyn later in the forest and did not want to arrive there any more intoxicated than I already was. The floating petals alone were making my head swirl. "What's the matter?" she asked.

"I am fine. Merely thinking."

"Of what? The prophecy? There are hundreds of male Celestials; no use trying to guess which one, it is impossible. And anyway, I bet it won't ever come to pass. Most that grand don't."

The Oracle's news of an amended augury had been rippling throughout the courts but I cared nothing of it. If one of the male deities wanted to bring about the realm's destruction, then let it be.

I sighed and swatted away a petal.

"I am not thinking of the prophecy."

"Then what is it that bothers you?"

"Presently, the sight of that boorish, lumbering oaf of a minor deity, Tiberias, come to find you. Stay still; perhaps he will scurry off if he does not spot you."

"Oh come, he is not so bad, cousin."

I hated to hear that doting tone in her voice. Why she did not outright reject his courting was a mystery to me. I found his pursuit of her disgusting. Arcana was a jewel, adored by all, well venerated for one so young and rising higher each moment. I had not been to the Hall of Effigies since I was a boy but rumor of her brightly burning double was abundant in every court. She had distinguished herself in a way I used to dream of when such things seemed still within my reach. I was a lesser god—insignificant, I knew it well and paid for it often, but Tiberias was not worth her air, her attention.

"Make a copy of yourself, send it to him so that he leaves."

Arcana giggled, reaching for me and tucking a wayward lock of my hair behind my ear, her eyes glossy and black. The sap had gotten to her. She was not usually so silly.

"That requires an amount of effort which I cannot be bothered to give at the moment. Why will you not have any sap? It is sublime today—star-infused in greater concentrations than normal."

"I am not in the mood."

She poked her lip out. "Always brooding you are. You are too handsome to wear such long faces all the time," she said, grabbing me by the chin and giving my head a shake. "Here, have some of my light to lift your spirits." Before I could protest, she transferred a portion of her stores to me. It was an exceptional feeling. I will not pretend otherwise. But always, I was wary of her generosity with veneration, for I knew it drew envious glares and negative attention. I threw glances about the gardens in search of it. Lesser gods always wanted a

146

share of what could not be attained through any merit of their own. And I was the last Celestial deserving of Arcana's charity in their eyes. After all, I did not lavish her with praise and gifts as they had. I did nothing to earn her company.

"Your father," I said, looking over my shoulder. "By chance, is he here? Veiled by some trick of his divinity perhaps?"

"No, I do not sense him. He never comes here anyway. He likes to be of sound mind always. I cannot understand why. It's wonderful to leave your own head sometimes."

I relaxed upon hearing it. Our confrontation that day had left a lasting stain on me, and since then, I made every effort to avoid him. And Tiberias, too, but my streak of good fortune was nearing its end—he was looking in our direction.

I did not fear Tiberias. I was no longer a child and that nasty quarrel had put us on equal footing. But I still detested him. He came strolling over, pretending not to see me as he sat at Arcana's feet. He brought with him talk of prophecy and galas. Arcana was hosting one soon in honor of the erection of her first temple in the mortal realm.

As they conversed, I slipped away and left the gardens—altogether vanishing once I reached the corridor.

I had missed the woody smell of the air in Crescent Forest.

Varyn had not yet arrived. It would be some time before he did since our agreed-upon arrangement was for much later, but I could not endure another moment among Celestials.

Over the years, I had come to prefer the company of mortals. I sought solace here and grew more familiar with the ways of them. The gods believed themselves so different by comparison. But the mortals were similar to us, in a way, only they were ordinary—less beautiful and without divinity. I did not think it an offense anymore, to be likened to them. They had great histories and vast seas. The volume of their peoples and countries a magnificent intrigue. Some of their clever inventions were as good as magic—as good as godhead. The longer I was among them, the more I struggled to understand what reason they deigned to venerate us.

I thought about this as I lay sprawled under the shining sun, listening to the running river. It had been a long while since last I swam in its waters. The academy and other responsibilities kept Varyn busy. But now there was a break in his lessons, he said, something to do with the festival season in honor of the gods. I was glad to spend some days in leisure here. Often I accompanied him in duties and would frequent his academy, lingering for a moment or two. Lord Vedlan said I was one of the family for the way I had attached myself to Varyn. He took to calling me their northern relative. I found it endearing.

The sounds of the water stirred me from my lounging place near the riverbank. The sun had warmed me, and now I wished to be cool. I left my garments at the usual spot and jumped into that enticing blue.

By the time Varyn arrived, I was breathless from so many laps and at a greater disadvantage of winning our races than normal. He liked to make a great show of his victories whenever he won against Jayce or other mortals, but with me, he would simply flash his wily smile and say, "Next time."

I could fill a book with *next-times*.

He won every match and I stared at him as I sat collecting my breaths on the riverbank, watching him wring out his long curls. And watching also the way his muscles shifted beneath his skin.

He was fifteen now—soon I would be too.

I cannot feign as if I do not envy the way his chest has broadened or how much taller than me he has become. How his voice has deepened. Even his hands are larger, the veins in them prominent and beautiful as feathers. I had changed as well, though marginally in contrast. My arms were no longer thin as pins but they were only half as brawny as Varyn's. And I had gotten somewhat taller, though not by much.

I could not name it, but something else, too, had changed—a fluttering inside me and a quickening of my breaths at times when our eyes met. Not always, but enough to note.

I do not understand the feeling. There is a want behind it. Or a need, perhaps. I cannot describe it. It welled in me now as he stood twisting the water from his hair. I watched for as long as I dared. Till he took notice of me. My eyes flitted to the damp ground, focused intensely on it.

"Do you want to wrestle?" he asked.

The fluttering amplified. I kept my gaze averted but felt his steps as he neared me. I willed the feeling away and looked up to find him grinning, hands on hips.

"That is a disingenuous question."

He wrinkled his brow. "What? How?"

I said, "You should have asked: do you want to lose another match?"

He tossed his head back, laughing, exposing the smooth column of his throat. I looked away again.

"Come, I will only use half my strength on you."

I shook my head, but he pulled me to my feet anyway.

"No," I said, chuckling despite myself. "I will not wrestle you."

He looked at me with pleading eyes and slowly began to kneel till he rested in a supplicant's pose below me. I yanked on his arm, but he ignored me, bowing his head in deference. However jest-like, he knew I hated this. It was one of his tricks. He used it whenever he wanted to persuade me of something—or coerce me to acquiesce to his whims.

"My dearest Ambroz, I am your humble servant, and I solemnly request—"

"Stop that. And get up!" My voice was shrill with annoyance but this only made him laugh. "Fine," I said, seizing him by the arm and wrangling it till he rose.

"You never believe me when I say it, but you are a skilled component." He squeezed my upper arm.

"Evidently not skilled enough to win a single match."

"No, but skilled enough to keep me strong and sharp."

"Strong and sharp for what?"

He smirked at me as though he had been waiting to hear this question all his life.

"The Quartz Games. I have two years to shape myself for them."

"But, you do not qualify."

"Who says? Nobles are allowed to compete with the commoners, it is simply outside of convention."

"That is not what I meant. Jayce told me there are rules. You must be of an age."

Varyn shrugged. "So, I will say that I am."

"You mean you intend to lie?"

"Well, I'm certainly not going to wait another four years for the next one. Why must I miss it for being only a single year under eighteen?"

"And what of your father? If you enter and do well, he will hear of it. Will he not be angry with you for both competing *and* lying to meet the qualifications?"

"It's a wonder your face has not transformed into one large and wrinkled worry line from all your fretting."

I shoved him for this. He was so solid it did not even sway him. He merely snorted in amusement.

"It is a valid concern!"

"You overestimate him. He doesn't bother himself with the practices of commoners. He wouldn't know the rules of entry for the Quartz Games if they were staring him in the face."

I folded my arms across my chest. "And let us imagine you are able to compete and you perform so well, your name is mentioned in every village, common or otherwise. Is that not the draw of the games? The glory? You have told me as much. So what then? When he hears talk of it, Lord Vedlan will be furious."

He narrowed his eyes. "Actually, I think all your pretty features are disappearing as you speak. By the stars, the worry creases! They are overtaking the whole of your face."

"Varyn!"

"Ambroz!"

"Can you take nothing seriously?" I asked, huffing and brushing past him. He trailed after me, sighing at my retreating form. I walked on till I found my favorite tree, its branches were rough and bristly, but I liked it for its sturdiness. I leaped up to reach one and tested my weight.

"Yes, fine then. I admit it was a valid concern," said Varyn. He watched me from below as I did slow and continuous repetitions on the branch. I could tell by his expression he was keeping count.

"So, how will you remedy it?"

For a moment he was too distracted with his tally to answer. He would likely make a game of it and try to beat the sum of my lifts.

"Mother likes the idea of the games. I have been talking with her about them since I was ten. Perhaps she could be convinced to sway Father's opinion, like we did with Celine. Would that please you, oh mighty and pious Ambroz?"

I smiled at the mention of Celine. She had been away at the institute for long seasons. In her last letter to Varyn, she spoke of how impressed her preceptors were with the level of her skill and the speed at which her ability to visually perceive the deceased was growing.

"Yes, it does, in fact. So when will you present him with the idea then?

More silent counting.

"Soon." He inclined his head. "You have gotten quite good at that."

I tried to keep from grinning. "How good?"

As he made to respond, my hand slipped. My hold had been too careless. I dangled, one-armed, and struggled to re-establish my grip. When at last I wrapped by hand round the bark, a shooting pain pierced the flesh of my palm. I dropped from the tree, shrieking. Varyn rushed to my side.

"Are you alright?" he asked. I nodded. The fall was short and I was not injured by it, but the pain in my palm persisted. I looked down at it and was met with the sight of torn flesh and a long piece of wood jutting from the opening.

Varyn gasped and took my hand in his, cradling it from the underside. Streaks of silver flowed from the wound and dripped onto his skin. He looked to be in awe of it, staring at the steadily growing pool with his mouth half-open.

"Will you take it out? I do not think I can manage it on my own."

The tear in his attention mended, and he focused it on me.

"Yes, of course. But it might hurt."

"It already hurts," I said.

"I will do it quickly then. On three. One..." I turned my face away. "Two..." Held my breath. "Three."

I tensed, and another blast of pain pulsed in my hand. When I gathered the strength to look at it again, the long piece of wood was gone. But my wound remained open.

Varyn examined the bit of bark and cast it aside, throwing it to the ground with vitriolic force.

"If that tree were a living thing, I would box its head in for you."

I would have laughed were it not for the pain. I looked at him, and tried to keep the strain of it from seeping into my voice, from making it tremble. But despite my efforts, I think he could see the shock in my eyes.

"What's the matter?"

"The cut," I said. "It is not healing."

Chapter 23

WE EACH GAPED AT THE LEAKING SLASH. I had been injured or scraped this way but a few times throughout my life, and always the abrasion sealed within seconds. My light was unpredictable, but healing was the one ability I knew for certain my divinity had secured me. I did not even need to put forth any effort, for it was something guaranteed.

The foundation of this certitude began to crumble as I stood observing my torn flesh.

In the face of this loss, I tried to keep the heat from rising—tried to prevent it blurring my vision, but the more I resisted, the stronger the force with which it rose, on and on, till a pool had welled within my dark and unchanging eyes.

"They are all right about me," I said, my voice weak and thin.

"Who is right about you?"

"The Celestials. My uncle, my f-f-father…" I fought to speak through the rolling tears. "All the things they say behind my back. My weakness in godhead, my inadequacy. *My shades.* They are not coming because I am not worthy of them. I am not divine—not in the way they are. Godhead should be wholly within a deity's control. Anything less means nothing. I am nothing. That is what they say of me and—"

"Enough." Varyn put a hand on my shoulder and silenced me. "You believe every criticism you hear of yourself no matter how absurd—you accept it as an irrefutable fact. When will you learn that the only opinion that matters is the one you hold of yourself? They are wrong and blind if they cannot see the strength in you. The power you have."

I swallowed the lump in my throat, mouth dry as sand. I could not speak even if I wanted to. Varyn sensed this, I think. He took me gently by the hand—the one free of injury—and led me toward the river. He knelt by the edge and began rinsing my blood from his wrists and hands. When he was cleansed of it, he turned to me, motioned me forward.

"Come, we must wash away all your pretty blood so I may get a proper look at that wound," he said, grinning.

His smile spreads, and the warmth of it is like sunlight on my skin. I go to him. He is gentle as he washes me, careful. The sting of the water on my open flesh is blunted by his delicate handling. When it is done, he looks at the cut, eyes widening at something I cannot see.

"Ah, there is a splinter of wood stuck inside, just here," he says.

He points at the ugly shred of bark till my gaze finds it there, resting incongruously among my sterling matter. I try to pick it out, but it is nestled too deep, and the pain of the effort makes me wince. Varyn takes my hand, brings it to his lips. He covers my wound with his mouth. I am sitting, but it feels as though the ground has fallen out from under me. He sucks the tender flesh of my palm, and a shiver runs through me as his tongue works to free the splinter. He misses several times and his wet muscle swirls against me. I am aware of myself in a way I have never been. Every breath, every beat of blood sings. I burn as if on fire…Varyn holds the match which has set me blazing. I wonder if he feels the warmth of it emanating from me. His eyes rest on me, sending more shivers rippling down the length of my spine. I tear mine away from his, and they roam the golden expanse of his bare chest. I do not realize how near to him I have drawn till his scent fills me. I feel as if I may faint under his ministrations when, at last, I am released from the intense heat of his mouth. Between his teeth rests the splinter of bark. He bares them at me, a look of triumph sparkling in his hazel eyes. Of course he has done it. He never loses at anything. His lips are stained with the silver of me, the bow of them plump and flushed from the exertion. Our eyes meet, linger. The look in his—I have never seen it. We are close, so close I feel the warmth of his breath against my face.

"Lord Varyn, I have arrived. Come at your leisure when you are ready." His serving boy called out to us in the distance. Abruptly, we pulled back from one another. I think I was panting.

Varyn spat the piece of branch on the ground.

"Yes, thank you. We'll come out shortly," he said. He rose and bent over the river, rinsing his mouth. I looked down at my palm and found the wound had closed. Varyn turned back round, wiping his lips with the back of his hand. He came and smoothed the pad of his thumb over my newly mended skin.

"Do you see now, Ambroz, how you worried for nothing?"

This small contact gave rise to that fluttering sensation deep within me. Other feelings, too, arose, and I slipped my hand from his delicate grip so as not to feel them, impelling the confusing cluster of emotions to disperse.

"How did you know that would work?"

"I didn't. Not really. I merely guessed it might. From now on, will you stop?"

"Stop what?"

"Doubting yourself."

"If I answered 'yes', I would be lying."

"Then lie to me. Lie to yourself. Over and over. Until you believe it. You are not weak. Let me hear you say it." Some of his damp curls fell into his face, covering part of it from me. He swept them aside and pinned me with his gaze. "I want to hear you tell me of your strength. Say it."

I hesitated, thumbing circles over the previously injured spot on my palm. "I am…" I drew in a deep breath. "I want to be—"

"No. Do not tell me what you want to be. Tell me what you are."

Another breath, deeper than the last. I sucked it in as if it would give me courage.

"I am…strong, I am…a…I am…not nothing…." My mind went momentarily blank as I searched and searched, and: "I am not weak," I professed.

I thought these words would leave upon my tongue the bitter taste of artifice, but a strange calm settled over me instead. Varyn nodded and looked at me as though he were expecting further declarations.

"You do not believe it. Not entirely. Not yet. But you will." He turned and fetched our garments. We dressed in silence—the whispering winds filling the spaces left by words unsaid. It was a restive sort of quiet.

"Varyn," I said, holding up my palm till he took notice. "Thank you."

"You have done the same for me a dozen times or more."

"And I would do it again. Countless times."

"That is why you do not owe me any thanks." He smirked and was about to say something more but stopped himself.

"What is it?" I asked. "What were you going to say?"

He shook his head. "No, you will laugh or think me insane."

"I already think that about you." He poked me hard on the shoulder.

"It's your blood," he said. "It tastes rather sweet, and now I want to have cake with my supper."

I laughed at him like he said I would.

Chapter 24

THE SEASONS TURNED LIKE THE SPINNING OF A WHEEL, one after another, and soon, Varyn and I were sixteen. I remember this year with such vivid clarity and know its details better than any of the others before or since.

I had been so seldom in the Celestial realm that I knew little of its events and heard no talk of matters regarding prophecy or other affairs. I had found a small inn near Varyn's manor, which gave me board in exchange for small favors performed around the establishment. I could fix nearly anything with my light now, and if a task was outside of my abilities, I called on Varyn. The matron believed me to be a northern mortal, as everyone else had. We spoke little, and when I was not needed for aid, she gave me privacy.

I liked my little room and passed much of my time surrounded by its quaint walls. So when I learned upon my return that every divinity in the twelve courts had suspected my father of being the Celestial fated to bring about the destruction of our realm, I was entirely bemused.

I had heard this latest development by chance in the dining hall. Two minor deities of the Cups spoke in hushed tones behind me. I waited a long while for them to leave, then went in search of Arcana. It did not take long to find her. She lazed among some golden vines in one of the courtyard gardens.

"Why do you think?" she said when I questioned her about what I overheard. The tone of her voice was like being doused with freezing water. The look she regarded me with, I recognized it. It was Uncle's leer staring out at me from within Arcana's formidable sienna. It was only there a moment, but under it I felt like the insect Uncle had always treated me as.

"If I knew, I would not be asking you."

"No, merely avoiding me."

"Not only you. Everyone. The whole of the realm. You know well how it is for me here."

"And where is it you disappear to for so many seasons?"

"That is none of your concern." I did not want her to know of my affinity for the mortals and their realm. "What is wrong with you?" I asked. "You are all thorny and cruel like—"

"You would be too if the Devil tried to have your Effigy destroyed!"

"What?"

"He's jealous. I'm near to being brightest burning in the hall. I can summon the winds, sway opinions, Grant thousands of orisions in a blink, and it is all the least of my divinity."

"You need not boast to me."

"I'm not boasting! I did not ask for such power, just as you did not ask for its deficit. It is innate in me. Your father acts as if I have no right to my godhead. As if I should shrink myself so as not to exceed him. I will not."

I stepped away from her, reeling in the face of her tirade.

"I am not the one who needs to hear it, cousin." My voice trembled. I steeled myself and tried again. "You speak as if I am the one that has oppressed you. I did nothing to your Effigy."

"You are the son of your father."

"And you are the daughter of yours. I see that now. Go and drink the rest of his poison, then."

I turned and left her, fists clenched at my sides. I had come back to wish her well—it was the Capricorn season of her birth. I did not know till then how strong an influence parents could have on their children. It was a lesson learned—the seasons change, and with them, people, for the better or for worse.

Chapter 25

THE PISCEAN SEASON WOULD SOON BE UPON US. Varyn was looking forward to it. He would be seventeen—older, yet still one year too young for the Quartz Games he so adamantly set out to compete in. I felt as if I were taking part in some betrayal as we stood outside in the city square, waiting for our turn in the line of would-be contestants.

"Will you stop all your fidgeting? People will think you're ill with shaking fever. No one wants to catch sickness. They'll toss us out before I even have a chance to put my name on the list," Varyn whispered, bending a little to compensate for the difference in our height. I glared up at him.

"I am not fidgeting," I hissed. "I do not see why you could not have gotten permission from Lord Vedlan first. It has been nearly two years, you promised."

"And it is a promise I intend to keep. It's better this way, you'll see."

"How is it better to journey with no direction? To sail the seas with no vessel? What if he says no?"

He smirked. "Then it is for the best that we have come today and entered my name. He cannot prevent me doing something which has already happened."

"When will you tell him then? Will you be so stubborn as to wait till the morning of?"

Varyn snorted. "Be calm. We have until Libra season. That's plenty of time."

I scowled at him as we inched forward in line. "Stars, fine then, later. I will do it later today," he said with a note of exasperation. My expression softened, and I peered over the pair of broad shoulders in front of me, watching as two girls approached the game's official. She reviewed their materials, then directed them to enter a tent positioned behind her seat. When I asked Varyn how he intended to pass this assessment of materials, he presented me with his forgery.

"*You* may look your age. But I don't. I'm the tallest one here. By the stars, do you ever run out of questions?" he said after I asked what he planned to do if this elaborate deceit were to be discovered.

This, at least, was true. I could not deny it. I seemed on the precipice of manhood but Varyn had already arrived. He was not yet through with his transition, and would likely grow taller still, broader. But to look at him was to look at a young man, not a boy. I should add that I speak in terms of appearance only, for at times, he still behaved as immaturely as if he were twelve.

And I should add again that on this day especially we were each on the other's nerves, so take also with these slights the consideration of my nettled temperament.

The line advanced in small measures. We shuffled onward gradually till, at last, Varyn and I were next to be called. I had been standing in front of him the whole while and had been about to trade our position when the official launched a nod of acknowledgment at me.

"Let me see your papers, lad," she said.

"Oh-I-I am not here for entry. It is my friend." Varyn stepped forward and placed his materials into her outstretched hand. Her eyes glazed over them.

"Carnelian is it? A nobleman then."

"Yes," replied Varyn.

"And only eighteen, eh? You look a few years older than that."

I pretended not to see the look of vindication on Varyn's face as he glanced at me.

"Yes, just eighteen. For now."

She appeared charmed by his smile and flashed him one of her own, eyes lingering on his, then trailing slowly over the rest of him. They held one another's gaze, and a springing wave of envy struck me.

I had never felt anything like it and separated myself from the strange emotion at once.

"Right then, Lord Varyn, You're cleared. You may enter just through there, behind me, and find the physician for your physical assessment. I have no doubt you'll pass."

I realized too late I had been glaring at her. Varyn tugged me hard by the arm.

"What's the matter with you?" he asked, half muttering.

"Nothing, sorry."

"Well, come on then, just a bit longer, and we can leave. Did you see how that pretty official was looking at me?"

Once more, that springing resentment blanketed me. It was harder this time to rid myself of it.

"Yes, I...noticed."

"And do you see? It is just as I said it would be. She suspected nothing."

I nodded, not trusting myself to speak as we walked the short distance to the tent.

Inside, a woman greeted us, her dark hair streaked with silver.

"Which of you would like to go first?" she asked.

Varyn explained to her everything and she began kneading her hands over his body, running them along his chest and arms. She prodded him with strange instruments—looked inside every orifice on his face. He was made to perform a number of odd actions, and by the end of them, he was half-dressed, face somewhat flushed from all the activity.

"You're in excellent health. Best of luck at the games." The physician dismissed us with a wave.

Varyn kept on grinning the whole way back to the manor.

"Do you want to know a secret?" he asked. His pleasant moods always affected me, and now I was grinning too, all of that earlier bitterness forgotten.

"Yes, what?"

"Whenever I set out to do something—take examinations or that sort of thing. I always bring this along with me for luck." He slipped a hand into his breast pocket and held his closed fist before me. I already knew what he was going to say. "What are you smirking about?" he asked.

I covered my mouth with my hand and shook my head. "I am waiting to hear you say it," I said. "Go on, tell me to guess what is in your hand."

He regarded me through narrowed, smiling eyes and let out an indignant snort. "Is that your way of calling me predictable then? You know, you're not all that mysterious yourself dearest Ambroz, my virtuous, most honorable friend who cannot bear to tell a—"

"Oh, quiet you. What will I get when I have guessed correctly?"

"That confident are you?"

I scoffed. "Well?"

He draped his arm round my shoulder and the light, floral scent of him surrounded me. I fought hard against the urge to close my eyes and take it in.

"If your guess is accurate. I will ask Father about the games, tonight, during supper. But if you are wrong, you must help me shape myself for the competition."

"I will do that anyway. You know I will."

Many things had changed about Varyn as we grew older, but his smile remained as it always was, slow-spreading and beautiful as the dawn. He presented me with one. I never tired of seeing it.

Alongside this pretty curve, he gave my shoulder an affectionate squeeze and I drew to mind those emotions which overcame me some years ago in the forest. For weeks, I dreamt of the soft feel of his lips against my palm. At times, I could not concentrate on anything else when I was near him. My pulse would soar, and my heart drummed loudly.

Though quieted now, the years have not dulled the intensity of that memory. I had not words for it then, but slowly I came to learn what it was that had changed in me, and was no less confused by it than I had been. I knew what caused the yearning ache deep within me, but what good was the knowledge of illness without remedy?

I looked down at his fist, still clenched tight to conceal his secret. "How many guesses will I have?" I asked.

He withdrew his arm from round me and contemplated. "Just one. But I will give you a hint. What I hold is dear to me."

I thought hard, staring at his hand as if my eyes could see through to its center. What was both dear to Varyn and capable of fitting inside his palm? He liked sweets and always carried one or two but I was much the same and so decided that was not it. Any number of things could be hidden there, yet nothing came to mind and…luck. He said luck. All at once it dawned on me, the vision of it clear as water.

"You know it then?" asked Varyn, taking my silly grin as confirmation.

"Bloodstone," I said.

He nodded and slowly opened his hand, fingers uncurling like a flower in bloom. "It's the very same one you gave me when we were children."

"I know," I said. "You kept it all these years?"

"Of course. I will never let go of it."

I plucked it from his palm, warmed by the heat of his touch, and smoothed my thumb over the facet. For some reason I cannot name, the sight of it moved me so strongly and unexpectedly that I lied and said it was the frigid air that stung my eyes to tears when Varyn asked why they were glistening.

"But the breeze is mild," he said, chuckling. "Come, you don't need to hide your tears from me, Ambroz, I know how intensely you Cancerians are affected by sentiment."

I let the few that had welled drop to my cheeks. Varyn wiped them away.

Chapter 26

AS PROMISED, VARYN BROACHED THE MATTER OF THE GAMES that night at supper. I was often a guest at the manor and so accompanied him there for support. Celine was away at the institute, and Lady Elayne's condition had worsened. She rarely left her bedchamber. I longed for her presence as I sat across from Lord Vedlan. He sat stabbing at his fowl as if it had offended him.

"You are the son of a nobleman. Not some common village boy in rags, Varyn. You have no need to compete for status or wealth. My blood has afforded you both. What do you think they will say when they see you jostling in the mud with low-borns for coins and titles? People will think this family has fallen under the wrath of the gods. I'll not have you inciting that sort of talk."

Varyn huffed. "Is that not already what they say?"

"I beg your pardon?"

"Of Mother! Since I was a child, it is all they—"

Lord Vedlan brought his fist down hard on the table. One of the glasses toppled over and fell to the floor. I winced at the sound of it shattering, stunned by this outward display of emotion. It was the first time I ever saw him abandon his stoic composure. I remembered Varyn's story about him from all those years ago. His actions in the tale seemed unfathomable to me then but now I glimpsed the ire for myself. Even so, I could scarcely believe it.

"Forgive me. I spoke without thinking," said Varyn, the words a low rumble in his throat.

"You very well did," clipped his father. Varyn tensed beside me. A charged silence permeated the air surrounding us.

"Mother would let me," Varyn said, voice soft as silk. "She says it is a good thing to show the world your strength and valor no matter the forum of display."

"Your mother has been delirious with fever half your life."

Why was he being so cruel? I made to speak in her defense, but Varyn rose, scowling. I was relieved to discover a look of remorse slowly replacing Lord Vedlan's stern expression.

"Varyn, I am…"

But he had already stormed out of the dining hall, leaving me alone with his father till a serving boy came and swept away the shards of broken glass. He left promptly, and we were alone again, stewing in the awkward silence.

"I did not mean it," said Lord Vedlan, sighing and smoothing a hand over his face. "Go and tell him that for me, please."

He kept his eyes lowered as he spoke, pushing his half-eaten meal around the plate. I, too, had lost my appetite. I stood and walked to the doorway, pausing at the threshold in an effort to summon all the courage available to me.

"Perhaps it is not my place, though I will say it still: However displeased you are with him, Varyn is my dearest friend. I cannot help wanting to see his desires met. Already he honors you in every way there is. He is the best of his peers—unparalleled in matters of intellect and talent. His reputation is brighter even than his hair. Please. Will you not reconsider your stance?"

He listened with his back to me for the length of my little lecture, and when it was done, turned the slightest measure so that I saw the contour of his bearded jaw. A severe sigh escaped him.

"You are as good as family, but you are right—it is not your place. He has my apology, provided you carry it to him. He will not have my permission to partake in that barbarism. I would sooner turn him out onto the streets than see him lower himself to that."

The harsh shock of those words stirred up an anger in me, but I did not wish to argue with him and took my leave after hearing them.

I searched the manor for Varyn to no avail. By chance a serving girl noticed me inquiring of his whereabouts and pointed me in the direction she last saw him.

If it were not for his striking auburn hair, I would never have spotted him amidst the vast quantity of other mortals as he charged down the village streets. I rushed in pursuit of him, sprinting to keep up with his brisk stride. A single one of his steps equaled two of mine. It was like our races in the forest, always, he was ahead of me. I willed him to lessen his speed, but even the dense crowd could not slow him. The town was busiest at this hour—throngs of patrons coming and going from the shops or their work, visiting the temples or taverns.

After a time, he adopted a more leisurely pace, and I lingered behind him, turning whereupon he turned and mirroring his pauses. By the end of it, we had come to the town square, and I waited for him to decide on a resting place.

A pretty, tiered fountain of ivory lay within the center of the area, spouting streams of water. Varyn stood watching it all collect in the large, round base. I slipped beside him, and together we stared ahead.

His cheeks were streaked with dried tears. I hoped not to see them replaced with fresh ones.

"There is a bench, just there." I pointed to the right of him. "Will you come and sit with me?"

He answered in movement, walking in languid treads till we reached it.

"I didn't know you were following me," he said. "You must be tired. It was a long way."

"Not really. I am alright. I have exerted myself far worse in our matches."

A lazy half-smile curled upon the border of his lips. "Did Father send you?"

"Yes, but I would have come after you even if he had not."

He nodded, blinking sleepily. "Sometimes I hate him. What he said about Mother…" His voice broke, and I placed my hand on his back, rubbing circles against it.

"He did not mean it, Varyn. He is sorry. That is why he sent me—to tell you of how he regrets his words. I am sorry, too, for urging you along so relentlessly. I thought he could be reasoned with on this. I was wrong."

"You needn't apologize. You were just staying true to your sweet, righteous, and good, insufferable self." He nudged me with his shoulder. Even in sadness, he could make me smile. "What is better, do you think: To be virtuous and miserable or wicked and joyous?"

The strumming of a Lerawyn could be heard in the distance. The soft sound of it had carried over to us from a nearby tavern. I listened a moment before answering. "I think it is not so simple as that. Each, at times, may act as the other. One is not wholly virtuous or wholly wicked. Do you think yourself the latter? Is that why you are asking?"

"I must be. I can imagine no other reason why the gods should ignore my prayers and offerings. Why my mother grows weaker year after year."

"Do not put your faith in the gods. They care nothing for virtue only—" I stopped myself, swiping my hand through the air as if to erase what I had spoken. "You are not wicked," I said. "Never think of yourself as such again. You are possessed of the best character I have ever known, among both gods and mortals. If I had power enough to heal Lady Elayne I would in an instant. You are the reason I know godhead—what little of it that lives in me. Till you, I was nothing, merely the F—"

Again, I stopped myself. I had been speaking in a rapid stream, spewing my half-formed thoughts into the empty night and staring out at the fountain as they flowed from me. I looked at Varyn and did not know his expression.

"Merely the Fool. Is that what you were going to say?" he asked.

My breath caught in my throat. "H-how… when did you…"

"I have known all along you were not a minor deity of the Pentacles as you claimed."

"You *knew*? But why did you never say anything?"

"Because you hid it from me. I thought in time you might one day tell me. I didn't want to force you to anything which you were not inclined to give of your own volition."

I stared as I had the first time I ever saw him, stunned to stiffness. "And you call me the righteous one…but how did you learn the truth of my identity?"

He drew in a deep breath as if preparing to hold it for a swim. "I figured it out that very night. I was restless. Though you had healed it, my leg still bore the memory of the wound. It was a strange, phantom sort of ache. It kept me up thinking. I went over the events again and again, trying to find some explanation as to why you appeared before me at such a crucial moment. Then I remembered something I'd heard one day in the village, some years ago at seven, about the trials of two newer Celestials. A temple elder and former Aurora Priest had been chosen as one of the mortal audience. She gave her account of the ceremony when she returned. I did not like how she spoke of one Celestial in particular." Varyn paused, and the distant melody of two Lerawyns filled the silence between us.

"It was me. You did not like how she spoke of *me*, right?" He nodded. "What did she say?" I asked softly.

"It's not important. She was wrong about you anyway. But you asked how I learned the truth of your identity and that is how I came to know it. I put her story of you together with my encounter—as that day I had been calling myself by your name, praying for help, and...you answered me."

"All these years—I thought I was being so clever."

"You were, and careful. I used to wish, at times, your memory would falter or that you would grow weary of keeping it from me. But not once did you come even the slightest bit close to any of this, and so I left it."

I could not look at him and became intensely occupied with studying a spot on the ground. My voice had disappeared to some faraway place. When it returned, I said, "Yours is a remarkable constraint. Are you not angry with me?"

He furrowed his brow. "Whatever for?"

I still could not look at him. "My keeping this part of myself from you. We say each of us is dearest to the other and yet I have not been forthcoming where it matters most."

"Then let us make a promise to one another."

"Yes," I said, finally able to meet his gaze. "I will vow to anything you want."

"Let there be no secrets between us ever again." He placed his hand in mine to seal the agreement. I felt a liar as I held it, for within me lived a well of things still hidden. I feared what he might say or do if he ever learned of the way I longed to feel his breath on me. Or knew of how I sometimes imagined him in my arms with his hair between my fingers. I could not tell him these things. Instead I offered other parts of me in their place. Around us, the night grew lively with tavern goers and Lerawyn songs. And in the midst of it all, I told him everything I had withheld about my life in the Celestial realm. When I had finished we sat a while, exchanging no words or glances but merely listening to the noise of the square.

"Will you still call me…will you still think of me as Ambroz?"

"Yes. I knew you to be the Fool for all our years together—still—you were always Ambroz to me. But it doesn't matter what name I know you by, so long as I can call you my best friend."

I wanted to put my arms round him—to feel the heat of him against me. Instead, I rose and pointed in the direction of one boisterous tavern, asking if he might want to go inside and have another go at the supper we had abandoned.

Chapter 27

I DID NOT CARE FOR THE TASTE OF MEAD. It was like Stars Brew but with none of the sweet, pleasant flavor nor the airy sensation it left inside the body. Varyn finished his with three heaping swallows. I slid the remainder of mine across the table for him, spearing a portion of his fowl. I devoured it before he could protest and looked up at him. At first glance I thought he was scowling at me, for there was not light enough to see very well inside the tavern. But upon further scrutiny, I realized his eyes were merely narrowed and focused elsewhere rather than on me.

"Jayce," said Varyn. "Is that you?" I turned in time to see him, to see both of them. Pella was the first to spot us. She waved, eyes wide, and tugged on Jayce's arm, bringing his attention to our table. He smiled upon taking notice of us. They made their way through the multitude of inebriated patrons to greet us. "What are you doing here?" asked Varyn.

"What's it look like? We've come to have a meal, same as you. For such a bright head, you are quite dim-witted," said Jayce. Varyn smirked as Pella punched Jayce in the arm.

"Oh, shut up," she said, taking a seat. "Go and order us something, will you—be useful for once." Jayce walked away, muttering curses under his breath. "We always come here during season's break. Never knew you came here too. How's yours going, by the way? Ready to take up lessons again?" she asked.

Varyn answered each of her questions. She smiled the whole while he spoke and kept on twirling a stray coil of her hair round her finger.

The years had sharpened her features, giving her a charming sort of beauty that made her look slightly older than Varyn and I.

As they conversed, she stared at him in much the same manner as the game's official had. And I noted that so too had he, gazing back at her with a peculiar sort of fondness. He caught me observing this. I am not sure what expression had been dancing across my features, but when he looked at her again, it was through different eyes. I tried not to watch them so intently thereafter.

A short while later, Jayce returned carrying two plates, and we shuffled round the table to make room for him. As they ate, Varyn waved down a serving boy to supply them mead and once provided, Jayce raised his cup to me, inclining his head.

"Good to see you around again, Ambroz. You've not paid us many visits at the academy this year. What's the matter, Ethelian studies getting too hard for that airy, northern head of yours?" asked Jayce. He sipped his mead, then grinned at me, revealing all the meat that had gotten stuck between his teeth. Varyn and I snorted.

"He's busy with more important things," said Varyn, sneering.

"What is more important than the last years of education? All the best lessons are taught then. I've taken up a course in the etiquette of courting," he chewed a while, then grinned again, all traces of meat gone. "Speaking of, when is your sweet sister Celine coming back from the institute? Surely she will be home in time for the festival, yes?"

Varyn scoffed. "Celine is many things but sweet is not one of them." Pella giggled.

"And how would you know? Of course you cannot see her charms. You are related to her! Now is she coming back or not? I have something special for her."

"What makes you think she'll accept anything from *you*?" asked Varyn.

"Oh, come off it. You know as well as I that any girl in her right mind would leap at my attentions."

Pella's giggling infected Varyn and me. "Please. Celine doesn't want a muscled oaf like you. I've seen enough of the sort she fancies—she likes slight, clever boys, so that's your chances ruined," said Varyn.

"Put a word in for me then."

"What sane person would do that?" Varyn looked on the verge of bursting into laughter.

"It's no matter. Once I'm near her, she won't be able to resist me and will likely fantasize about our future on the spot. I hope she wants children. I want a fire-headed boy to carry on my name."

I had been trying hard to maintain a bearing of indifference, but at this, I let out a snort.

"You said you had something special for her," said Pella. "What is it?"

Jayce cleared his throat. "A song."

"Oh, is it that piece you've been playing all year on the Lerawyn? That one is quite nice, actually," said Pella, brows raised.

"Yes, but that's only the melody. The verses are far better."

"Sing them for us," she urged, taking a sip of her mead.

Varyn folded his arms across his chest and glanced at me from the corner of his eye, amused. We watched as Jayce cleared his throat a second time. He placed a hand over his chest and closed his eyes.

"Celine, Celine, woman of my dreams. Hair soft as wool, those coils, oh how I'd love to pull—"

"I think I am going to be ill," said Varyn. "If you sing another word, I'll bring up my supper all over this table."

Jayce opened his eyes and scowled. "You still haven't answered me. Will she be at this year's festival?"

"Not if I can help it. Are you trying to make her ears bleed? They will once she hears that."

"Nonsense, I have the voice of a Celestial! Everyone agrees, and so will she."

I put my hand on Varyn's shoulder. "Perhaps he is right. Why not let Celine judge for herself?"

Jayce leaned to me, grinning. "I have always liked you, Ambroz. Those rumors I started about you two years ago were merely jokes, you see."

"What rumors?" I asked.

He widened his eyes. "That was a joke, too, ha. Pay it no attention."

"Fine," said Varyn. "She'll be home for the festival. I won't stop her going. I'll be there anyway, in case she needs saving." He turned to me, shoving a finger into my chest. "And you're coming along with me."

"Fair enough," I said. "When is it?"

"Soon, some days after my birthday."

I nodded, wondering if Celine would hate me for this.

We returned to the manor quite late that night. I was glad for that meant Lord Vedlan had already retired to bed.

"Will you still participate in the games?" I asked Varyn as he sat across from me, making his braid. He had trimmed a little of his hair off, as was his habit before the approaching season of his birth. It hung slightly past his chest. When we were younger, the roundness of his face, coupled with the length and mass of his auburn curls, made him appear pretty as a maiden.

But much of that plumpness has fallen away now, and he is all sharp lines and angles.

He secured the end of his braid and sighed. "I don't know. What do you think?" he asked.

"Will it make you happy?"

"More than anything."

"Then I think you should do whatever makes you happy."

He raised a brow. "Do my ears deceive me? Is the principled Ambroz advising me of disobedience?" I tossed a cushion at his head. He caught it.

"I used to think your father was perfect. That he could do no wrong. I saw some of the Devil in him tonight, and I did not like it."

"You mean…he reminded you of *your* father?"

I nodded. "Parents are all alike, it seems. Some lesser in their imposing than others, but always, our ability to meet their expectations rules the measure of love they give us. If they can be so self-serving, then so should you. If you desire it. Do what it is that pleases you, righteous or not, for there is no righteousness in conditional affection. It only breeds estrangement in the end."

He sat with his brows drawn together, lost in the labyrinth of contemplation. His awareness of me seemed non-existent, and he was silent so long, I thought he had forgotten my presence. But I knew it well, that deep musing. I let him be till he came back to himself.

"He expects so much of me," said Varyn, eyes wandering as he spoke. "Sometimes I feel I am drowning beneath the weight of his wants. I am the best at so many things because he accepts nothing less. Because he was the best and his father before him. It's tiring." He reined in his roaming gaze and fixed it on me. "Do you know, when we were younger, I sometimes wished I was you?"

I could not help the chuckle that escaped me. As it did, bemusement enveloped Varyn's features.

"What?" he asked, drawing his brows together once more.

"Every night of my twelfth year, I laid awake thinking...*longing* to switch places with you—wanting nothing more than to be your father's bright son," I said.

Now it was he who chuckled.

We soon fell into the river of conversation. It flowed from us, quick and changing like the tide. So many matters we discussed, one after another. I spoke more on the topic of my realm and him, of his conflicted feelings about his father's plans for his future. I saw each of them now through new eyes.

There was much I learned that night, and at times, I felt we were one as the stories poured from us. The evening stretched on and still we conversed, past twilight, till the soft, pink light of dawn painted the sky.

"I do not know anyone as well as I know you," said Varyn. He yawned and I told him to lay beneath his covers. I sat across from him on the floor as he settled into the bed.

"What about Celine? You know her well."

"She is gone most of the year, and I find her greatly changed with each reunion. Celine is dear to me of course, but you are much more by my side." He yawned again, struggling to keep his eyes open.

"You are best known to me, too."

"Do you like Celine?" he asked.

"Of course. I am looking forward to seeing her again."

"No, I mean in the way Jayce does. Do you dream of having her in that fashion?"

I laughed. "No, not at all. She is as much a sister to me as she is to you."

"Good." He stopped fighting against the weight of his eyelids and let them close.

"Why did you ask?"

I waited for his reply, but it did not come. He had fallen asleep, a faint smile resting on his lips. He looked a delicate youth as he slept. I could not resist watching a while and found myself mesmerized by the slow rise and fall of his chest. Some moments passed, and I pried my attention from that trance and left for my little inn.

Chapter 28

VARYN TURNED SEVENTEEN AND WOULD NOT LET ME FORGET IT. At every opportunity available to him, he established reason to boast about his age. I think he found it exciting to be in his final year of lessons, his last year of adolescence. In Ethelia, youths begin their transition into adulthood from the ages of eighteen to twenty. I reminded him that I, too, would soon be seventeen and that there was nothing special in this but he would not be convinced. He seemed pleased to be in the lead. Everything now was a competition for him. The impending Quartz Games had heightened his already robust, competitive nature. In preparation, we raced and swam, climbed and jostled. The games were seasons away but he wanted to ready himself as much as possible.

I made him take a day of rest when it came time for the festival. Though it was my first instance of attending mortal celebrations, I had been told they were known to be taxing, for the excessive merriment could render one weary.

It was strange to see the effigies of so many Celestials scattered about. They were not the grand and solid sculptures that existed in the Hall of Effigies or even in the mortal temples. Rather, each of them was made of some fragile material of which I was not familiar. There was a certain charm to them, however. I spotted Father and Mother a dozen times over. And Arcana, twice that. When had she become so staunchly revered, I wondered? Many in the crowd wore headdresses of her face. Everywhere I looked, her likeness stared out at me.

The smell of sweet herbs burned in the streets, and hordes of mortals lined them, some giving offerings to their favored Celestial, others chanting orisons. But most were engaged in the attractions of the festival. I could not keep count of how many there were. In one stretch of the way, they were casting lunars. In another, telling fortunes. Alchemists boasted claims of blessed elixirs that would imbue anyone who drank them with the strength of whichever deity they served. Jayce leaped at this. For all his confidence in the tavern, he behaved like a shy child near Celine. He had not said so much as a word to her since we arrived. I kept casting furtive glances in his direction, all of which he ignored. Then, once Celine, Varyn, and Pella had gone off in search of festival cake, Jayce urged me to join him at an Alchemist's elixir table. I went with reluctance, for I had been eyeing a little stand of games and their prizes.

"What brew are you searching for, boy?" asked the tall woman, flicking a hand over her spread of tinctures.

I knew his tone would be indignant before he opened his mouth to answer. "I'm no boy. I'm nearly eighteen," he replied.

'Well, ya look like one to me. Course I can remedy that, plenty of essences here to give you the strength of ten men and courage enough to conquer anything."

"Courage?" asked Jayce, raising a curious brow. I had suspected all along he was in lack of it. Why else had he not yet spoken to Celine? There had been plenty of opportunities as we wandered about the festival.

The woman, who called herself Mistress Dalmaa, plucked one of her vials from the table and held it at eye level. It rested between her thumb and pointing finger. She twirled her other hand around it, the gesture a mesmerizing ebb of movement, like new waves on an old shore.

"This here is the brew you want for that. It is the Empress's Valiance Draught. You'll not find a more efficient concoction, the very best ingredients I use. It is lightning in a bottle, this. One drop under the tongue will give you valor enough to fight a sea scorpion and win."

I looked at Jayce as he eyed the amber liquid, his expression one of both intrigue and uncertainty.

"How much do you want for it?"

"Three gold crescents."

"Three! That's nearly all twelve seasons worth of my sinecure. There's barely three swallows in that!"

"It is worth it, I assure you. The very best ingredients, I said. And I serve the great Magician, it is his Reversed energy I channel when brewing. I have not known failure with it. Not even once."

The mention of my uncle sent a quiver through me.

"What could possibly be in that bottle that is worth three gold crescents?" asked Jayce.

She set the elixir down on the table with a huff. "The ingredients are only half as important as the one who prepares them. It takes a skilled alchemist to achieve vials as potent as mine—one who understands the subtle workings of each component, one who knows how each might interact with the other. I doubt you're familiar with any of them but if you must know, there are high concentrations of three main substances: Solar Nectar, Astral Fire Sparks, and Serpentine Scale Extract."

Jayce narrowed his eyes as if weighing each ingredient. I do not think he knew what any of them were. Already the short list had gone out of my head. As he considered them, I turned and spotted Varyn's bright hair in the distance—Celine and Pella on either side of him.

"They are headed our way. Best make your decision before they join us," I whispered.

Jayce shifted his weight from one foot to the other, chewing on the inside of his cheek. "Will you not accept any less? How about one gold crescent and twenty silver?"

She crossed her arms. "I will accept three gold crescents or nothing."

Jayce made to protest, but I seized him by the arm and looked at Mistress Dalmaa.

"He will need only one drop of this essence to get its effect, yes?" I asked.

She nodded. "Mmhmm, but it will wane before the end of the evening." She swept her heavy-lidded gaze over me and tucked some of her long braids behind her ear, smiling. It was the same sort of smile Pella had given Varyn at the tavern. I smiled back and said,

"Perhaps you will be kind enough to offer a single drop then instead of the whole vial? How many crescents will you accept for that?"

She pursed her lips. "I don't sell by the drop. But for you and your pretty face, I'll make an exception. Three silver crescents, and I'll give the boy his drop."

She kept on smiling at me as Jayce counted his crescents. Her skin was dark and smooth as marble. I liked the way it felt to have her eyes on me.

"Ambroz, you are clever as a god," I heard Jayce whisper beside me as he placed his crescents on the table.

"Handsome as one, too," she said. I grinned at this, rather sheepishly, I am sure, if her pleased expression was to be any indication. Jayce took his drop, and we carried on smiling at one another till I felt a tap on my shoulder. I turned and found Varyn, vibrant hair wind-blown. It took me several moments to notice his outstretched hand offering me a piece of festival cake. He divided his gaze between Mistress Dalmaa and me as I took it from him—I spotted Celine and Pella walking close behind him.

"Thank you," I said to Varyn. I looked once more at Mistress Dalmaa. "And thank *you*," I added as I walked away from her table. She inclined her head and imparted me a small wave.

Varyn trailed after me, tossing a glance over his shoulder.

"Who was she? And why is she staring at you still?" he asked. There was something strange in his tone.

"She is an Alchemist." I took a bite of the festival cake. I had never tasted anything like it—rich and soft, with a layer of some impossibly sweet glaze the color of clouds in the morning sky spread across its brown surface. I lost myself in the flavor and had not bothered to answer the rest of Varyn's question.

"Why was she looking at you like that?" he asked.

"Like what?" I stuffed the remainder of the cake in my mouth.

"Like..." He paused and watched as I licked the sweet remnants from my fingers. "Nevermind. If I'd known you would enjoy that so thoroughly, I would have brought along another."

"I wish you had. It was very nice." We both laughed, and I remembered the table of games I had been eyeing before Jayce dragged me from it. I proposed to Varyn we go and play. He loved games and readily agreed. We made our way to the table, eyes roaming over each of the prizes. One, above all others, stood out to me. It was a colorless little orb and reminded me of our Moon when she is full. The man on the other side of the table plucked it from where it rested on the display behind him.

"You like it?" he asked, holding it before me. I marveled at the sudden change in its color. The orb had taken on a warm, golden glow, beautiful as the sun at dusk. "Color of circle change. Depend on mood. How you feel. You understand?" Before I could answer, he turned and began rummaging through an assortment of his belongings. When he faced me again, he handed me a little square that contained a number of words and colors. I was familiar with the latter but could not read the words.

Varyn peered down at it alongside me. "It is written in Haneshi," he said, then looked up and spoke to the man, but it was all strange sounds and tones which I did not understand. When the man answered, Varyn took the square from me and flipped it over. At last I found words I understood: angry, happy, sad, excited. There were ten words and colors in total. "It's a bit like your shades," Varyn whispered.

He was right. I smiled down at the words and colors. How stinging that this man's inanimate little orb had shades when I did not. I reached for it, but the man held it away from me and took back the square.

"You want touch—you want *have*, you win. You play. Game for this is: find the lume," he said.

"Alright," I mumbled, chastised.

"How many game you take? Two crescents, silver, for each."

I owned no crescents and had been about to take my leave when Varyn placed something in the man's palm.

"I'll take two games," said Varyn.

The man counted the crescents and smiled. He cleared the table and placed a large, red cloth over its surface. Varyn and I watched him prepare the game. The man brought forth three ornately decorated chalices and put them upside down on the table. He lifted one and placed a tiny lume inscribed with the maiden symbol of Virgo underneath.

"To win prize, you must follow lume, understand?"

I nodded, and he began shifting the position of the chalices. I was not prepared for how swiftly his hands arranged them. I lost its original position in the tangle of his movements and stood puzzled when he asked me to point to which chalice I believed the lume was hidden under. I resorted to guessing and grimaced when he lifted the chalice to reveal nothing but empty space beneath it. The man seemed amused by my loss.

But Varyn had paid for two games, I remembered, and I resolved to win the second. I drew in a deep breath to ready myself for another round, this time eyeing the little lume more keenly.

Again the man moved the chalices around—faster than before. I did not take my eyes off the one that had the lume inside. By the end of his lengthy rotations, I felt certain I knew which of them held the lume. I made my choice, holding my breath as he slowly lifted the chalice.

Chapter 29

IT WAS EMPTY. I sighed and looked away from the table, dismayed. The game seemed simple enough, yet I lost each of them.

"Another," said Varyn. He placed two more silver crescents in the man's palm, then slid his hand onto the small of my back. "Let me have a go this time," he said. I stepped aside and let him take my place.

As Varyn stood watching the man make his chalice's orbit in the center of the table, I stood watching him. His brow was set in that same severe and assiduous manner he bore whenever drawing. Now that he was older, and larger, it looked intimidating. He hovered over the table, narrowed, hazel eyes flitting in this direction and that. I had long since lost its placement and wondered if Varyn might have as well, for they moved across the table swift as the wind.

After what seemed an endless number of revolutions, the man and his chalices finally went still. Without a moment's hesitation, Varyn tapped the one in the center. The man flipped it over and beneath it lay the lume. I clapped my hands together without realizing—excitement coursing through me.

"I'll have that little orb for my prize," said Varyn. The man looked confused, and Varyn spoke again in those unfamiliar tones till he procured the orb and its accompanying square of colors.

As we walked away from the table, Varyn placed the little moon in my palm.

"His hands were so fast. How did you manage it?" I asked.

"I knew you wanted that orb, and so losing was not an option." He grinned and draped his arm round my shoulder. "Also, it helped that the chalice he put the lume under had a little dent on it, which neither of the others did."

I burst out laughing. Why had I not thought to look about them for something like that? I wanted to pull him into an embrace and tell him of his brilliance. Instead I held tight to the prize he won for me.

We strolled together as I clutched it, wading through the throngs of mortals dressed as gods: the smoke of offerings, the merchants, the earnest worshippers, the strum of songs, the young, the old.

"Let's see what color it's turned," said Varyn, looking at my fist. I opened it, and together we observed a deep cerulean, vibrant as the skies, blooming inside the tiny sphere. "It says here that one means you are elated. Is that true?" He held the square before me so that I could read for myself the words which corresponded to the shade inside my orb.

"Yes," I said, feeling somewhat shy and exposed. Was this what it was like to have shades? "It is."

He raised a brow. "Haneshi merchants always have such impressive things," he said. "Here, let me have a go."

I gave him my little moon and we waited for the gradual change, each studying our surroundings in anticipation. A group of mortals passed us by, two of them plucking chords on their Lerawyns. The others were singing the song of the Hierophant, all of them high-colored and of a jovial spirit. Slowly, we prised our attention from their revelry and turned it on the orb. Its shade now was a deep green, like the forest after rain. I searched for its meaning on the square and fought to keep from grinning.

"Tell me how I feel," said Varyn, a half-smile tugging at his lips.

"It says you are content." His smile broadened. "Are you?" I asked.

He nodded, and I saw some of my own shyness in his eyes, reflecting back at me, flitting across his features like a glint of moonlight dancing on black waters. It quickly faded, leaving the pair of us standing quiet and still, too reticent to speak. I reached for my moon and his fingers brushed against my palm. The feeling gave us both pause. Our eyes lingered on one another. So many longing thoughts were in my head. I almost said them all aloud. But his eyes drifted from me, for they found the sight of Pella, of Jayce, and of Celine.

I turned and spotted them nearing us. They looked like strangers who had happened to find themselves walking together. I wondered how Jayce was faring with his drop. Then I remembered I did not have to merely wonder.

When they approached, I drew Celine to my side and pressed the orb into her palm. I explained to her what it was, and she giggled with wide eyes.

It told her she was embarrassed, and I knew at once it was Jayce's doing. I tried hard not to laugh.

"Here, hold this," Celine said to Jayce, foisting it into his hand before he could object. At her touch he became flustered. Varyn and I exchanged knowing glances and hid our expressions as Celine stood watching him. "You are nervous?" asked Celine as she matched the orb's color on the square. Her tone bore incredulity and a hint of something else I could not name. Understanding perhaps, for she retrieved the orb from him with a certain grace she had not bothered to employ in her initial handling. Jayce refuted the orb's assertion and mumbled something under his breath about Haneshi swindlers and their peddling of useless implements.

Pella gave it a turn, and when it claimed she was amused, I felt I had the pieces of a story but lacked a scribe to spin the tale.

"I could do with a bit of mead. No. I could do with a pitcher of it actually," said Celine. She sighed and looped her arm through mine. Jayce looked as if he might strangle me at any moment.

"Let's find a tavern then," he said. "Mead for everyone. I've got crescents enough for a whole barrel."

Celine raised her brow. "Lead the way," she said.

Jayce walked ahead, glaring at me, and fell in with Varyn and Pella while I trailed behind with Celine.

"Why were you embarrassed?" I asked her. She chuckled and shook her head.

"*Jayce.* At first it was for the way he behaved and spoke. He keeps telling me of my beauty in the oddest manner. I have never heard anyone make such comparisons in an attempt to flatter."

I could not help laughing. "And now?"

"Now it is shame. He's not at all the sort I like, all lumbering and brawny, and oh, you should have heard some of those comparisons. But despite myself, I'm charmed by him."

"I suppose we cannot help who it is we like," I said.

We shared a quiet laugh at the absurdity. As we walked, she told me of her studies. She had managed to obtain full control over her Nerosi abilities and could shield herself from the forms and voices of the dead at will if she did not care to correspond with them. Now her instructors were nurturing other capabilities in her, for she could traverse the veil and summon its energies if she so desired.

"What will you do with your skills when you have mastered everything?" I asked.

"I'm not sure. I want to bring solace to people. I know that much. Not only in Ethelia but all over. My father, the one of the body, still sends me letters. He lives in Karlindé now and says there's a need for my talents there. Perhaps I'll visit for a time when I'm older."

I wanted to suggest an alternative but Jayce appeared by her side as I made to speak and offered his hand to help her inside the tavern. She accepted and untangled herself from the coil of our arms.

The sun had dipped under the horizon during our journey, and only the dim light of a few lanterns lit the tavern. It was lively and bustling with the sound and song of many instruments. Mortals sloshed their drinks as they danced with one another—their voices and chatter carrying over the melodies.

I glanced out the window and spotted the Magician, shuddering at the likeness of the headdress as it disappeared from my view. Jayce found us a vacant corner after he had acquired the mead he promised us. I did not care for the taste but sipped on it as a courtesy. Varyn, however, drank deeply, golden skin becoming brighter with each mouthful. We sat across from one another, and I watched as he and Pella conversed in hushed tones. She leaned toward him as he spoke, pulling away every so often to giggle at something he had said.

It soon grew too loud to hear much of anything over the high sound of song and the clatter of dancing feet. All around us, pairs of mortals twirled and swayed to the beat of many instruments. After drinking a fair amount of mead, Jayce somehow persuaded Celine to join him in the center of the floor for a dance.

He moved clumsily and the sight of him reminded me why I so hated dancing. Celine, however, spun airly about, inhibitions dulled from the mead. Jayce, too, had loosened. Whether it be from Mistress Dalmaa's drop or the drink, I did not know. But he was smiling at Celine, and she was smiling back. He lifted her once in the air and swirled her round. She seemed delighted by this, laughing hysterically when he planted her down again. After that, wherever she went on the floor, he followed, all of his attentions fixed on her and only her.

So immersed I had been in their courting that I did not realize I was alone at the table till I turned and found Varyn gone. I searched the crowd for him and saw his face among the many—saw Pella's arms hung round his neck like a pendant as they danced together. He held her by the waist, grinning down at her. I had not noticed how much smaller she was by comparison till now. My mouth, as I watched, felt dry. I turned from them and wet it with some of my mead, wincing at the unpleasant taste. A lump formed in my throat, and I chased it away with more sour drink.

Outside the window, I spotted mortals huddled around a burning offering and rose to get a better look. They were venerating Arcana.

I stared at the billowing smoke wafting up from their crafted effigy to be swallowed by the night sky. I wondered what they asked of her. Prosperity? Healing? Fertility? Protection? There might have once been a time, long ago when she would have Granted these things to them. I began to miss her but then remembered the harsh words she spat at me, the callousness. I reflected on them often, twisted them round till their thorns fell away—imagined it was some other Celestial who wielded the blade that cut me so deeply. I watched the smoke till it dwindled and let my bitterness dissipate along with it.

"Come and join me on the floor." I felt a large hand pressing against my shoulder, the abrupt pressure jolting me from the trance of musing. It was Varyn, tugging at me with that urgent fervor he sometimes had when we raced or practiced for the games.

"You are drunk," I said.

"Yes," he admitted, nodding his drunken head and flashing his drunken smile. "Slightly. But not nearly enough to stomach the sight of Jayce fawning over my sister. I don't know how much more of that I can take." He laughed, eyes waning like winking half-moons. I laughed too. "Come on, this song is my favorite. It is one for friends and brothers." He tugged at me again.

"I do not like dancing," I said.

"That is because you have never danced with me."

There was a fluttering within me. I shook my head to quell it. Varyn persisted, placing both hands upon my shoulders. "Come, it's poor luck not to dance at a festival when asked, especially when the song is so fitting."

His eyes were pleading. I nodded and let him drag me by the hand to the center of the floor. I looked about and saw others, groups of three or four, dancing together in harmony, their movements so fluid they appeared rehearsed. I watched them with the envy of the untutored.

"I do not know the steps," I said.

"Just follow me. Do as I do."

I tried to mimic the motion of his hands and feet but in so doing, stumbled over myself. No one except Varyn saw me fall, and he laughed as he helped me off the floor. "Put your hands on my waist then. We'll do the simple version for children." He pressed his palm against the small of my back to guide me and drew me closer. We swayed together, feet taking short steps—left right left.

"You're dancing," said Varyn, the warmth of his breath brushing against my cheek. I felt his hand shift, sliding further up to steady me.

"Not very well, I am sure." He smiled at this, and I leaned closer, like a flower bending toward the sun. More of his breath swept across my face, grazing the bow of my lips. I became aware of his—pink and full. He wet them, and the sight gave rise to that familiar fluttering inside.

"It is well enough."

We were closer now than we were before—I could feel the heat of his body on mine. With his free hand, he reached for the hollow of my neck and fingered the crescent moon that hung there. The pad of his thumb skimmed across my bare skin as he withdrew, and I shuddered. "You still have this?"

"I thought you said you knew of how us Cancerians were about our sentiments," I teased, hoping he could not hear the quiver in my voice or the harsh drumming inside my chest.

"And is it still the best gift you have ever been given?"

I parted my lips to answer but became distracted by a jarring silence as the song ended. A new one began quickly thereafter. I liked its melody more than the one before it. As I listened, I forgot what it was he had asked me.

"This song," I said, "is it also for friends?"

"No, it is meant for lovers." He chuckled at me, for I could not help the widening of my eyes upon hearing it.

"Perhaps we should retire then?"

"What for?"

"This is a song for lovers." I do not know why I repeated it.

He shrugged. "So what if it is? Is there really such a difference between the two? Are lovers not also friends?"

I could not speak. We stared at one another. I could see nothing save for him—the golden glow of his skin, the bright fall of his hair, the honeyed hazel of his eyes. Together, they undid me.

Our dancing slowed to match the quiet rhythm of the song.

More of his warm breaths came wafting across my face. I leaned, and his hand drifted down my back, pulled me closer. More breaths. Again I leaned, desperate for the feel of them on me.

Our lips were—

"My turn!" Pella's voice, shrill and giddy from too much mead. Varyn's gaze slid away from mine. I longed to have it resting on me again. We broke apart from one another, and the loss of his heat made me feel bare. A moment ago, I had been swathed in the cloth of his arms. Now they wreathed Pella. I watched them dance together the rest of the evening.

Chapter 30

THE SEASONS PASSED SLOWLY, ONE DRAGGING AFTER THE OTHER. They plodded along this way till I turned seventeen. Then, they seemed to race by as if being chased. In a blink I found myself in the Virgo season—one season away from Varyn's Quartz Games. His lessons had ended, and we spent nearly every waking moment preparing for them. I had grown firmer, I think, and broader, too, from the relentless exertion of our drills.

Varyn seemed convinced he needed always be engaged in some sort of movement, or else he considered himself lacking or somehow falling behind the other competitors, none of whom we knew, I reminded him. He ignored this and pushed on day after day but I was becoming weary of it. To appease my complaints, he told me we could rest till the end of time after the games concluded. I did not care to wait that long. We fought on this, and I do not know how I managed it, but I persuaded him to take a day of respite.

I spent the majority of it surrounded by the walls inside the quarters of my little inn. The matron had given me a few chores, and I tended to them.

My light had remained steady over the years. I wondered about this often, for I was not a venerated deity. Save for the events in which it moved through me involuntarily, I could perform no great feats with my divinity, but always, I could rely on it. Those great bursts of godhead had not happened again in the years since the temple. Divinity in me was like a muscle—if over-exerted, it grew weary but with rest was replenished.

I was feeling the tiring effects of it now as I sat eating a bit of roasted meat on bread the matron had prepared for me. I had mended some splintering wood on a door earlier, then went about performing other small tasks with my light. It was rather late in the day, and I had not yet called upon Varyn. I intended to after having slept. We spent our nights about the village, sometimes in taverns, others strolling in conversation. Our talks now were different than they were when we were children. They carried with them the weight of our future. I had never given much thought to mine till Varyn. As I went to rest, I saw his glowing face behind my eyes.

When I woke, it was to the light of a new day. I had meant to sleep for only a short while and rushed to leave the inn. It was past the time Varyn and I usually met in the forest. I imagined him glaring at me for the enormity of being made to wait and laughed to myself at the conjured sight of him. But when I arrived at the forest, it was I who waited. I thought perhaps I had mistaken the sun's position in the sky. I waited and waited for him to arrive, but he did not come.

It was near evening when I left in search of him. I arrived at the manor and looked through his window but found the room empty, though others were inside. I knew, for I saw the light of many lanterns from outside and crossed paths with the serving boys and girls who bustled in and out. I noted a frantic sort of energy in them as they went about their duties.

I heard one of them make mention of Varyn's name to another and listened hard, but caught only pieces of what was said. Something to do with refusing a meal in the carriages. I could not make sense of it and endeavored to go and explore the area where the carriages were kept.

When I entered, I heard sniffling, and followed the sound of it till I saw him. He sat upon the ground, slumped against the back wall, and was partially obscured by one of the carriages. His knees were drawn up to his chest, and his head rested against them. He shuddered, taking shallow breaths and whimpering in between. I did not wish to stand there watching him like a spectator. But I also did not wish to call out to him simply to make my presence known—it seemed a crude thing. Taking quiet steps, I approached him and sank to the ground beside him. Cautiously, I reached.

"Varyn," I whispered, placing a hand on his back. "What is the matter?"

He lifted his head slowly, wiping away tears with the back of his hand. Fresh ones poured from his red-rimmed eyes, and again, he wiped them away. Heat rose in my eyes at the sight of his distress. I struggled to fight back tears of my own. He stared at me a moment, gathering his words and his strength as more of them rolled down his face. I swept them away with my thumb and prepared myself to hear the sound of his voice—to hear what had caused him this pain so that I might set about a course to destroy whatever vile thing that dared to hurt him this way.

"It's my mother. She is dead." The revelation stunned me. I had been expecting to learn of a slight someone made or of a quarrel. I could mend those for him. I could approach whoever was responsible and have revenge—could curse or blast them with my light.

But the grief and sorrow reflecting across his features were intangible things. I could not cure death. I could do nothing but watch his heart break.

"I-I am…" I did not know what to say. The sight of him filled every corner of my mind—there existed room for nothing else. Words escaped me. Feelings overwhelmed me.

"I hate the gods. I wish their realm would fall from the sky. I wish them all dead," cried Varyn. His eyes blazed, fierce with contempt. My heart felt as though it had stopped beating. *Please, do not hate me. Please.* I wanted to say these words aloud—to plead for his grace. But that would have been selfish and unfair. I had not lost a loving mother. As much as it pained me, he was entitled to his hatred of gods—of my kind…of *me*.

I rose to my feet, staggering as if wounded.

"I am sorry," I muttered. It was the only thing I could think to say. I turned to leave, and he seized me by the arm.

"I did not mean you. You are not like them. You are my friend." I had not even spoken my fears aloud. I did not need to. He knew the shape of my mind. I do not know why I ever thought he could hate me. He pulled me down, and I went with relief. I put my arms round him, grateful to give him this comfort at least. The sobs racked through him. I held him to me—and smelled the sunlight on his hair.

I had never given any thought to death. It was something only mortals did. I had not realized how terrible a burden such a thing was till this day. Lady Elayne was kind to me, always. And now I would not see or speak to her ever again.

When I come to the end of this testimony—when every detail has been laid bare, I hope it will be clear to all why I have chosen to walk the path that led me here. I ask not for forgiveness or mercy but only understanding—only that my perspective be honored and taken into consideration for once.

The feel of Varyn's chest, his beating heart pressed close against mine as he wept, was what brought me to the pivotal realization that he, too, would one day meet the same end as Lady Elayne.

Varyn falling ill or growing old. The mere thought of it was too much to bear. To lose my only friend to the cruelty of time. I held him tighter, clutching him like treasure, willing the reality of a life without him into non-existence. He will never leave my side. He will be here always. He must. Tighter, I held him, as if I thought he might slip away from me at any moment. It was a long while before I loosened my hold on him. He had stopped crying by then.

"Did you go to the forest today? I'm sorry I wasn't there. I did not have the strength to come." His voice was hoarse and thin. I broke from him and stared into his sad eyes.

"Do not apologize. Of course you did not come. I would have thought you mad if you did."

His lips quivered. I think he was attempting a smile. "Tomorrow we will go. And work twice as hard."

"Would it not be better to leave it?"

"And fall behind? No. I cannot miss another day if I want to win."

"But—"

"She would not want me weeping for all my days. She would see me win." His eyes drifted from mine. He stared past me, looking out into the empty air. "Every day, I talked to her of the games. It was our secret from Father, from Celine too. She could not wait for me to compete—to tell her all about them."

"You are still going to play?" I asked. He focused his attention back on me.

"Yes. It's what she wanted for me. When I was little, I used to race against her. Each time I won she would lift me in the air and call me *nilröze*, greatest gift. I would practice running all day just to have my lift, just to hear her say it." He smiled as if reliving these races.

I slipped my hand over his. "Tomorrow we will go. But now you must rest. Have you eaten?"

"Not since last night."

"That will not do. Come and have supper. You need strength if you are to win."

He let me pull him to his feet. "Will you stay with me tonight—sleep in my room again like when we were children?" he asked.

I nodded and led him inside.

He ate slowly, nibbling on his crust of bread and ignoring the rest. Every so often I would say things like, "Have you tried this yet? It is very good", or "This is meant to increase endurance" in an effort to make him eat more. It worked, and his plate was nearly empty by the end of the meal.

After supper, we washed, and I watched him pen a letter to Celine at the institute so that she might come back for a time to mourn. Lord Vedlan had not left his chamber since the morning, Varyn said, and that is why he took it upon himself to send correspondence.

He rubbed at his eyes as he wrote. The delicate skin around them had reddened from a combination of friction and too many tears. Once he had finished writing, Varyn took the letter out to be sent. He said there was time still before the carriers closed their doors to patrons. Celine's institute was half a day's journey by carriage and she would receive it the morning after next. The mortals had a clever way of expedient transport with their carriages and Luminary Lumes. I hoped Celine would be alright.

I had been lying on my side, atop the cot I made for myself on the floor across from Varyn's bed, when he returned from the carrier. He looked as if he had done more crying on both the way there and back. His bed was still unmade from the morning. He crawled into it without a word and pulled the covers half over himself. The sight of him lying under them seemed unusual to me. Something about it was wrong. I peered up at him from the floor through narrowed eyes, trying to place what it was about him I found so peculiar.

At first, I thought it might be his morose temperament, but that was not it. I kept on looking at him till I realized I could hardly see any of his features. Most of them were partly covered by a curtain of long curls. He shifted under his blanket, and more of them fell into his face, more disheveled than I had ever seen them. It dawned on me then.

"Varyn," I said softly.

"Hhmm?"

"You have forgotten to braid your hair."

He smoothed a hand over it, sweeping it away from his face. "Oh, right. I haven't strength enough to deal with it tonight." He yawned.

"Let me," I said.

"You do not have to."

"I want to."

Slowly, he sat up.

I went to him and gathered his thick mane of auburn hair behind his back. I had seen him perform the task a dozen or more times. I needed no instruction. I knew the pattern by heart. Gently I began, weaving and tucking each piece. Left right left right left, always over the center.

Varyn sighed. "It feels nice to have someone else do it, actually," he said.

I felt proud to hear him say it. I cannot name the reason why but my chest swelled with the feeling. I kept on, smiling absentmindedly to myself, till I finished.

I secured the end and he ran his hand down the length of it, pulling it over his shoulder to check the weave. It was the first smile I saw from him all day. Small and tired but still his, still warm, still pretty as the sun.

"You did it well," he said. "Thank you."

I nodded and returned to my threadbare cot on the floor, then lay awake, watching him, waiting. Till he fell asleep.

Chapter 31

THE REMAINDER OF THE SEASON WAS HARD FOR VARYN. He and Lord Vedlan quarreled often about the smallest of things. They held a ceremony in honor of Lady Elayne, and it was one of the few days in which there was peace between them, for Celine had told them of a vision she had on the night of her death. Till then, they had believed she had learned news of her mother's death through the letter Varyn had sent. But she had known it from the moment Lady Elayne drew her last breath. Such was the immensity of her capabilities. Till now, I do not know what message Celine brought them from beyond the veil. I had not asked. It was not my place. But whatever she said had eased the tension between them.

Of the three, Celine had fared the best in her grief. She had been closer to her mother than both Varyn and Lord Vedlan, yet I had not seen her weeping or being sullen.

Later, when I asked if she was getting on well, she smiled, then showed me one of her mother's possessions—a pendant, and told me that with her gift, she could hear Lady Elayne's sweet voice through it.

·········>·) ✹ (·(·········

The Quartz Games happened to fall on a dreary day at the end of the Libra season. Varyn could hardly contain his excitement the night before them, though some of it had drained from him by the time we arrived at the arena. I had expected something more resplendent. It was merely a vast, open field with spectator seats and obstacles strewn about. But there was mortal charm in it. The games had drawn hordes of them from neighboring villages and regions. I had never seen so many in one place. Not even the festival had carried such quantities of them. I could scarcely make out the sight of anything from the seat I had taken, for bodies were crowded all around me. Were it not for Varyn's bright-colored hair, I might not have been able to spot him among the many.

It was satisfying to watch someone other than myself lose to Varyn. The heads of his competition hung low as he left them behind in the trail of his dust, kicked up by his swift heels during races. Tall, slight, large, short—it did not matter. They were all the same to him. I felt pleased, smiling after each victory, as if I had been the one to beat them.

Though I began to fear for him when it came time for jostling. I did not understand the rules or why he had been paired with an opponent larger than him by half. I even heard others grumbling around me that it seemed unfair. They had wagered crescents on Varyn based upon his earlier performances and now they feared the loss of them.

They shouted curses from their seats as the match began. My heart quickened at the sight of Varyn being struck. I winced at the repeated blows and harsh maneuvering. During some parts, I closed my eyes and only opened them again when I heard cheering. Somehow, Varyn had overtaken the boy. I should have known he would not lose.

Later, when the games had finally concluded, men and women swarmed him. I watched from a distance as he accepted their praise and gifts. A major draw of the competition, I learned, was an inflation of status. They were meant to pluck the best of the competitors from obscurity and shine upon them the light of repute. Varyn had come away the victor in each of his categories, and for this, wealthy suitors flanked him, offering the hands of their sons and daughters, some offering themselves. The exertion of the contest had left him disheveled but despite his appearance, he looked a deity as he stood encircled by them, staring proudly down as though he were propped upon an altar. When the throngs of mortals and their congratulatory fawning had dwindled, I went to him.

"How does it feel to be a winner?" I asked.

"Exhausting." He grimaced. "And painful." He lifted his muddy smock and revealed his bruised abdomen. "But worth it."

Now it was I who grimaced, regarding the discolored flesh with a mixture of sympathy and revulsion. "Come, it is time to leave," I said.

He did not object, even when more curious mortals approached him, inviting him to attend this occasion and that. He declined them all politely, and we made our way back to the manor.

It was hard to watch him limp about his room after he had washed himself. Every movement looked to be an arduous chore.

"Let me try and heal you with my light."

He shook his head. "No, I need to feel this."

"What for?"

"It serves as a reminder of what I have accomplished."

"Can you not simply call upon your recollection for that? It is senseless to endure discomfort. Like torture, really."

The chortle he had attempted devolved into a whimper and he clutched at the various aches upon his body.

"You are being ridiculous," I said.

"Perhaps," he replied, taunting me with a smirk. "But do you want to know something I've just realized?"

I nodded, and he sat beside me on his bed, moving as though he were an aged man instead of a spry youth of seventeen. "You are not as reluctant to use your light as you once were. You command it now. It has become stronger as you've grown."

"Yes, I suppose. But I still do not have shades."

He looked as if he meant to shrug his shoulders but found himself too stiff with injury to manage it. "What does it matter? And anyway, they may yet come."

"They are not coming. Soon it will be time again for my trials. Without them, they will be just the same as the last. I only wish I could forgo them."

"Can't you?"

"No, it is a requirement."

He nodded. "Well, there is time. As I said, they may come." He suppressed a yawn. His eyes began to water from the effort. I think letting it out would have caused his stiff joints too much pain. I rose from the bed with a sigh.

"It is late. You should rest. I am going back to the inn since you are not going to accept my healing you."

Again that maddening, taunting smirk. "Your nostrils flare a little when you're angry. It's rather charming," he said.

He was right, I was irate with his stubbornness. But I chuckled despite myself and left him.

Chapter 32

MY QUARTERS AT THE INN ARE QUIET AND STILL when our Moon is highest. She hangs like a lantern in the dark expanse of her sky. I have been staring at her for a long while, restless. These bleak nights were made for longing, it seems. And for thoughts of him. They come, unbidden, and consume me, torment me. I think of hands pulling me near, of warmth against me. I seek to rid myself of these impossible feelings, to release them and see them live someplace else, somewhere outside of me. I fetch the journals I keep. There are so many words and passions swimming round the ocean of my mind. Yet when I press my quill against the yellowing page, all I can think to write, *is his name.*

Chapter 33

WE RETURNED TO CRESCENT FOREST on the warmest day of the Cancerian season.

After the games, I was in no great rush to see it again. I only came at Varyn's insistence.

"Come, I want a swim. I have not had one since I was seventeen," he had pleaded.

He was eighteen now, we both were. I sat on the riverbank, after having lost many races in the water, and watched him swim. Even without a match to win, he was swift as the river itself. His arms appeared and disappeared, taut upper frame gliding through the ripples as the sun gleamed on him.

"Will you come back in?" he asked, shouting somewhat to be heard from the distance between us. I stretched, leaning backward on my hands and tossing my head back, eyes closed to shield them from the beaming sun.

"No, I am dry and comfortable and tired of losing."

I heard him chuckle. A low, deep sound. The high and bright laughter he owned in boyhood had been replaced by richer tones.

"But I will not make you race. Just swim with me."

"*No*. Has the water filled your ears and stopped your hearing?"

Another chuckle, deeper, longer. I smiled, bathed in the light of the sun, content to not be lured in for another race. He would have to try one of his other tricks—for I knew he had many. I thought he might use them. Any moment I expected him to call out to me again, try once more with a subtler persuasion. I had my counter ready for him and waited to use it, but he said nothing.

My limbs had grown stiff from too long in one position. I rose and walked about. As I stretched them, he swam toward me, closer and closer, till he reached the riverbank. He pulled himself from the water, glistening like a crystal. I willed myself not to study him for too long—not to idle there, watching the way the drops trickled down his golden skin. He was always more beautiful in the forest, under the rays of the sun. I had learned how to guard my gaze from him when we leisured here—how to steal glances without him noticing.

The carved muscle of his abdomen caught my eye as he stood drawing the water from his hair, twisting with both hands, head down as he worked. I let my gaze linger on him a little longer as he distracted himself with this, let it drift across his broad chest. My eyes swept over the whole of his taut, lean upper body. I could not help their slow descent as they trailed the fine hairs that led down his lower half. I knew I should not chance looking there but temptation fought against better reason and won. I allowed myself a glance. Then, as I pried my attention from that forbidden area, he lifted his head.

"What are you looking at?" he asked.

"Nothing," I lied, ignoring the roar of my pulse. He had never caught me staring before. I did not know what he might have seen. Did not know what sort of expression had overtaken me as I stood gawking at him.

"No, it was not nothing." His tone was accusatory. He took a step forward. I wanted to disappear. "What were you staring at? Tell me."

"I did tell you. It was nothing. Just..." I waved my hand through the air, stalling, searching for another lie. I could not find one. He became impatient.

"Just what?" The distance between us had shortened. The silence grew. I searched again for a lie to break it.

"I thought I saw something, a marking on your flesh. I was mistaken."

"You're lying." He nudged me on the shoulder. It felt like a threat.

I nudged back, indignant. There was chirping in the distance. And the sound of the river as it flowed. Neither of us said a word. Despite this, some of the tension eased, and he raised a brow. "Let us jostle it out in a match then. That should settle it. When I have won, for my prize, I will have the truth from you."

A knot twisted in my stomach. "That is not fair."

"Few things are in life." With this, he shoved me.

"Stop provoking me," I said.

"Why don't you make me?" He shoved me again, and this time, I pushed him back, weary of his goading. A startled grin pulled at his lips. "Yes, come on, that's it," he said.

Before I knew it, his hands were on me, and mine on him, both crashing together like waves in the sea. I fought against his strength, struggling to stand my ground. We tussled this way a moment, each using their weight against the other. But we were no longer children, no longer scrawny equals. Varyn was larger than me and far more muscled. With little effort, he knocked my feet from under me, and I landed on my back. Quickly he covered my body with his.

I was pinned beneath him, could see and smell nothing but him. All around me was his hair, falling on my skin like rain. Our bodies were pressed so near we were sharing breath. My instincts blared at me to writhe myself free from his grip... but he was not gripping me. All the force he used to get me in this position had left him, and now he merely stared down at me.

Our gazes held.

"What are you doing?" I whispered. There was something different in him—in the way he regarded me.

"I..." he paused. His lips were a hairsbreadth from mine. I felt each breath on me. "I know what you were staring at—I know *why* you were staring. If you do not want this, then tell me. Turn me away, and I will never...I will never again..." Once more, he paused, and his hands roamed over my shoulders.

Yes. I wanted it. So badly it burned—and to know that he too...that I was not alone in this yearning. For so long, I had been quietly drowning in it, and now, I had been given air. Yet I did not have words with which to speak, could not find them in this moment as I lay pinned beneath his watchful gaze.

And so I let my body speak for me, let it react to him.

At first we only stare at one another, panting, timorous. Then, Varyn kisses me, breathing his honeyed warmth down my throat. I am dizzied by it. A revelation springs forth, flooding my head as his tongue seeks mine: all along, it had not been godhead that I lacked, nor divinity—it was him, it was *this*.

He kissed me breathless, hands exploring every part of me. They slid across my chest, over my stomach, down down down.

I gasped into his mouth as he slipped his hand into my undergarment. Gently, he stroked. I fell to pieces under the delicate movement. It drew breath from me, ragged mewls and whimpers. I could not control them. I did not want to. He kissed my neck, my chest, captured my lips with his, and swallowed the sharp cries and moans that escaped them. Faster, he stroked. Harder. On and on. I was so loud. He did not care—nor did I.

My breaths were shallow as puddles after rain by the time I arrived at the pinnacle of my pleasure. I reached and reached and reached for him till it burst forth, rippling through me. I trembled beneath him in the throes of it, still wanting and sticky with rapture. It covered me. I did not mind—he had given me this. It was evidence of my slaking, I thought, intoxicated from the high of him.

Above me, Varyn was panting. I had softened, yet he was still rigid with desire. For so long, I had craved the feel of him against me. I took my time exploring him, drawing out his pleasure with deliberate care. I traced every part of him with my mouth, lingering where I knew he wanted me most. He guided me, my hair between his fingers as I worked him to his peak. He could not stop saying my name. The one that he had given me. I loved to hear it. Over and over, it left his lips.

Afterward, I lay in his arms and listened to the soft thrum of his heart. He held me firm against him, with his chin resting on my head. I used to dream of this moment. Yet the reality of it was far sweeter than anything I had imagined. There were so many things I wished to say, but I did not want to break from this feeling, this bliss. It was too perfect. Words would only muddle it. And there were none which could impart the absolute joy within me. Every hardship I had ever endured was worth it, for it led me here—to this.

He is my divinity.

I was born to know him, to share sun and breath and life with him. This is what I think as his chest rises and falls beneath me.

"Why did you never say anything?" he asked, breaking the spell. His voice after pleasure was heavy with rasp and the sound of it sent a quiver through me.

"I thought you would not like it. That you would not want me. That there were others that you desired."

"There were. But I was waiting for *you*." He shifted, and drew my face up to meet his, handling me gently by the chin. His lips were soft as petals against mine, his kiss tender. "All I want is you," he whispered, kissing me deeply. He held me closer, tighter, cradling me in his arms. There was more passion in this embrace, it poured from us both. Afterward, we panted against one another. He smoothed his fingers along the fine hairs of my temple. "I'm sorry for shoving you. I should not have done it. I was angry with you. And with myself."

"Angry with me? Why?"

"You swore there would be no more secrets between us. But you hid this from me."

I had. I grew hot with shame. "I am sorry. I did not know how to be honest with you." I laced my fingers in his, kissed them. He smiled at me with only his eyes. They sparkled like stars in the night sky. "Are you still angry with me?"

"No, not anymore."

"And with yourself?"

He shook his head. "I did not know how to be honest with you either. Or with myself."

"And now?" I asked.

"Now I want to tell you every secret. Every thought." He chuckled. "It's embarrassing, really."

"What is?"

"How often I think of you."

After much coaxing, he told me of all the ways he thought of me. Hearing them stirred me and made me want to pleasure him again. I did.

Over and over and over.

Chapter 34

AFTER THAT, WE WERE SELDOM AWAY FROM ONE ANOTHER. We came to the forest nearly every day. I did not have to steal glances any longer. I marveled at him openly. Now when we swam or wrestled or raced, it ended in our coupling, with our bodies tangled up like vines. I learned everything there was to know of his.

I thought I knew happiness. Nothing now could compare to this, to him. To the two of us together. The days were made for him and me. At night he held me, and I slept listening to the sound of his breaths.

One evening at the manor, as I sat behind him weaving his braid, he turned to me.

"Your trials," he said. "When do you have to go back for them?"

I had not thought of them much at all. And many seasons had passed. Varyn was nineteen now. In three more seasons, I would be too.

"Oh, right. Soon. I will go back soon for them. Next season."

"How long will you be away?"

"Not very long. I will come back straight after."

"And later? Will you ever return there? To live again?"

I secured the end of his braid, and he faced me. "I do not think so. I do not like it there. Why do you ask?"

"I want to leave Ethelia."

"Leave Ethelia? And go where?"

"I don't know, somewhere, anywhere. Father wants me to begin an Aurora apprenticeship soon. I don't yet know what I want in life but that is not it. There is much beyond Ethelia. I want to explore it. I want to cross the Piscean Sea. I want you by my side when I do. I want you there always, for as long as I live."

Something dawned on me then. His words sparked a thought, a memory. In it, we are underwater. I beat him in a game. It is the only time I have ever won against him. I cannot lose this game. It is impossible. My divinity will not allow it.

My divinity. Mine alone. He does not have it.

"What's the matter?" he asked. I think I must have been gazing off at nothing or wearing a strange expression. I collected myself.

"Nothing."

He frowned. "Ambroz, we talked of this. Don't lie. Don't hold your thoughts from me. Is it talk of leaving that bothers you? You don't wish to come along with me?"

I shook my head forcefully. "No, of course that is not it. I will follow you anywhere. You know I will."

"Then what is it? What is bothering you? I can tell when you are unsettled. You get a wrinkle just here." He rubbed a circle in the center of my forehead playfully, then leaned forward and kissed it. When he pulled back, I managed a strained smile.

How could I tell him I feared the day I would lose him? That I would rather we never knew one another than to live an eternity without him. He stared at me, seeking the answers I withheld. I stared back, taking him in, trying to memorize his features. Etching them upon the canvas of my mind—every freckle, every hair and curve, every part of him.

"I cannot protect you," I whispered. The words escaped me before I knew I had spoken them.

He drew his brows together. "Protect me from what?"

"Time. What it makes of things, what it takes."

"I don't understand."

"I am not like you, Varyn. I am not a mortal. Your lives are...one day, you will not be here. Yet I will. Always."

He parted his lips. No words left them. He sat like that a while, half-gaping, wide eyes looking beyond me. His body might have been near me, but he was not in it. His mind had run off someplace else. I placed my hand over his and brought him back to me. "I should not have told you," I said.

He did not say anything. Perhaps he thought there was nothing to be said. I reached for him and smoothed my hand over his head, running my fingers along the braid I made for him. I loved being able to touch him this way—to show him these affections. I thought of all the time I spent quietly longing for him. Now I could love him out loud.

I fingered the neat braid a while longer, then let it slip from my hand. As I drew back, he caught my wrist, pulled me near. The silence that hung between us was no more. Heavy breaths and the soft sound of our moans replaced it. He took me slowly that night, lingering long and pressing his kisses into my nape. He worshiped my body—worshiped *me*. Not because I was a god…but because I was *his*.

Later, he lay in my arms, spent and dozing.

"I wish I could live forever with you," he mumbled this into the hollow of my neck, where his face rested. I do not remember what I said in answer to him. It did not matter. Half of his awareness had gone by then, chasing the equanimity of repose. He drifted to sleep, and I followed him.

· · · · · · · · ·)·) ● (·(· · · · · · · · ·

In the morning, I woke to him rubbing his nose against mine. I was still nestled beneath the covers, naked in his bed. But he had already washed and dressed. He was usually not so full of energy in the early light of the day.

"I had the strangest dream," said Varyn.

I squinted, eyes struggling to adjust to the beams of sunlight flooding in. "What did you dream of?"

"I dreamt I was a fish, swimming underwater without needing to breathe. Then you came and kissed me. I turned into myself again, and then we both swam deep below the surface. Neither of us needed air. I think you made me divine, like you. I woke up gasping for air. Isn't that funny?" He giggled, shaking his head.

"Yes, it rather is, and very absurd. I would never kiss a fish."

He pouted. "You would not kiss me if I were a fish?"

"No, but I might eat you. I am sure you would be delicious."

"By the stars, you're cruel." He shook his head again, laughing.

"Is that why you are in such a pleasant mood? Because you dreamt yourself a fish? It is no surprise—you are already fast as one in the river. You are not so different from one, really," I teased.

"No, no, That's not why. It's because I received a letter from the east, from Hanesh. An invitation for a temporary post," he said.

I rubbed my eyes and sat up. "What sort of post? And who sent it?"

"I made an acquaintance back when I won the games—a wealthy merchant and his wife were visiting and chanced upon the competition. He wanted me for his daughter, but I refused. We kept in correspondence anyway. I sent him some of my drawings, and he showed them around. Apparently, my talents are wanted there. One of my illustrations has become popular. I've been offered compensation in exchange for a portrait of one of their famed dancers."

"Oh," I said, lifting a brow. "And will you go?"

"I haven't decided." He sighed and began twisting one of his bright curls round his finger. "Do you think I should?"

"It depends. Is it worth it? The compensation they are offering, is it adequate?"

His eyes became bright as stars. "Haneshi crescents are worth more than Ethelian ones. It's the most I've ever been presented with at once."

"It sounds as though you want to go."

"I would be lying if I said I wasn't tempted. But there is Father to worry about. I don't know how I would explain it. He is so rigid in his thinking. We're already arguing so much about my delaying starting an apprenticeship."

"Perhaps you need to think on it a while. Give it some days. If, after them, the temptation for it is still strong. Well then, you have your answer."

He traced his finger along my collarbone. "And if I go, you will come with me?"

"That is like asking if the rain is wet or the night is dark. You know I will."

He leaned to kiss me, but a knock at the door pulled him from me, and I was left wanting.

I hid from view and quickly dressed as he went to answer. It was Lord Vedlan—he had come to collect him for Aurora duties in the temples. I knew Varyn had come to loathe that work. He was no longer the boy who once revered Celestials. The one who ran through forests chasing after sparkling Emros, putting his life in the way of danger for mere hopes. He no longer bothered about offerings. His deference for them had ebbed away, season after season, till it altogether dispersed like a cloud of smoke caught in strong winds. He did not love the gods. I did not blame him.

I listened as his father bade him to depart from the other side of the door where I could not see him. Varyn went with reluctance and cast me a furtive glance of farewell before stepping over the threshold, leaving me. I lingered there and made the bed that still held the shape of him.

Shortly after, I returned to my inn and found a number of chores waiting. My thoughts drifted as I went about performing them, a stream of mundane musings flickering in and out.

I mended a hole in the ceiling where water had pooled and begun leaking down. I found myself thinking now of Varyn's dream. Of the water he swam in. Of the fish he had become. My mind had still been cloudy with sleep when he recounted it to me, but now, as I did my work, a new clarity had come over me. Something he mentioned had stuck in my head. It blared at me, and I broke from my tasks to listen to it.

A kiss, he had said. *I think you made me divine, like you.* The words came to me again from the cellar of reflection. I heard them spoken in the rich tone of his voice as if he were near.

More words came. The ones he uttered against me in the night before sleep had claimed him. A wish. One where he and I lived together. Lived forever. The two of us, always as we are now.

I could not put this out of my mind. I tried to drown it out with other thoughts and labor, but it persisted, returning stronger each time, its details more vivid. At first, I merely fantasized for days and days. Dreaming him an eternal being, like me. It was a comfort to envision it. I would become lost in my imaginings.

Soon I began wondering about it, positing as though it were truly possible. I would make up conversations of it between Varyn and me in my head, living out my little delusions. It was a childish and silly thing, I knew, for it was impossible. But I could not let it go.

On one occasion, near the middle of the Taurus season, Varyn grew impatient with me. I had been deep in one of these fantasies as we sat across from one another in our favorite tavern. So immersed that I did not hear him speaking to me. I was too embarrassed to tell him what I had been thinking of when he asked, and this merely served to agitate him further. Eventually, at his insistence, I confessed. I thought he would laugh at me or find me absurd for letting such a notion overtake me to the point of my sundering from awareness. But he did not laugh or even smirk. Instead he rested his chin on his fist and leaned forward.

"I've been thinking of that too. Since the night you spoke of it, it's haunted me. I cannot forget what you said. That I will change and grow old and you. You will—"

"Yes. I know. You do not have to repeat it."

"Sorry," he said, reaching for my hand. He covered mine with his, running his thumb across the back of it. "But it's not possible, right? It's not something which can be Granted?"

I made to respond but paused upon realizing I had no answer for this. It was not something I had ever considered. "I...I do not know. I have never thought of that."

"I assumed it was obvious—that the progression of your thoughts would inevitably lead you there. Never? Not once since you began thinking of it?"

I shook my head, feeling somewhat chided, though he spoke with tenderness.

"It did not occur to me," I said. "Would you even want it? I know little of mortals, of what happens when they leave this realm. Is there not something beyond it for you? A place where you might see those you have cherished again?"

"I would not see you. What want would I have to find myself there if it is absent of what I cherish the most?"

I wanted to take him up in my arms, kiss him till he was panting. But there were many others around, and so I merely brought his hand to my lips and pressed them against his soft skin. We did not speak. Between us lingered a quiet regard, along with the chatter and instruments of the tavern. But it was not an uneasy silence. It was soon broken when Varyn let out a small gasp.

"What is the matter?" I asked.

"I just thought of something."

"Tell me."

"What if I asked it of you? If I made an offering or prayer to you? Would that work? Could you Grant me an eternity?"

Chapter 35

I SAT GAPING AT HIM, MIND TURNING IN A THOUSAND directions as it searched for an answer to his clever question. Could it work? I had not Granted since we were children, and even then, it had not been by intention. The use of my light came forth in middling bursts when I called upon it. I could not fathom Granting something so remarkable. Nor was I certain it was at all possible.

"I do not know if that can be done," I said. "And if it can, it is not within my power."

"Not yet."

This child-like optimism was something I adored about him. I could not help smiling. "Not ever."

"You cannot know that."

"I know what I am capable of. There are limits to what my light can achieve. You have seen it for yourself."

"Yes, I have. I've seen you do impossible things with it. Mend crushed limbs, thwart an attempt on my life. Time again, you've healed me when we were boys. If death is the most fatal of injuries, would this not be just another healing in the end?"

"Well, yes, but—you are making it sound far more simple than it is. Assuming I can do it, which I assure you, I cannot, how are we to know it actually worked? How would you know if you were invulnerable?"

"Remember when you cut yourself in the forest, hanging from that tree?"

I nodded. "Yes, what of it?"

"Well, it would be like that for me, right? I could wound myself intentionally, just a small cut, and see if it heals."

"I-I suppose, but…"

"It's worth a try."

"But I have never Granted. Not of my own volition."

"Perhaps this will be the first time."

"Varyn, you are impossible."

"A reasonable assessment." He smirked. "Come on, let's see if it works."

"What, now?" I asked, gaping at him as he rose. Before I knew it, I was on my feet, following him.

·········>·) ● (·«·········

From the window of my inn, the last morsels of sunlight glinted off Varyn's head as he kneeled, igniting his shimmering spirals of auburn. I did not like to see him prostrating at my feet. It made me feel as though we were not equals.

Though I suppose in a way we were not. He was always the better of us.

"How much longer?" I asked.

"Shhh. You're breaking my concentration. I need to make certain the reverence is strong and earnest before asking in prayer. You know that," he clipped.

I did not know it, in fact. What would the Fool know of veneration when no mortal save for Varyn had ever revered me? I thought of my effigy. And of the time I first heard the faint sound of his whispers as I knelt before my marble. I wondered what it looked like now.

For a moment, I saw it in the eye of my mind, bare and dim as it always had been. I conjured the others and contrasted mine against them. Arcana's by now must be twice or more what it was when last I gazed upon it. I thought of the twelve courts, of their sprawling palaces, inlaid with jewels forged of stardust. Of their gardens and splendid structures. The moonlit archways with their flowery illusions. I did not miss any of it.

I left those thoughts and looked down at Varyn. He began reciting a prayer. I rested my hand atop his head. It made the ordeal more bearable. Why could I not have been born like him? I would have made the perfect mortal. Their realm and all its hardships suited me far better than anything I had inherited. Here I was not lesser.

I sighed as I listened to the pleas of his orison. When he had finished, I sighed again in relief. He looked at me, expectant and curious. I did not feel any different than I had a moment ago.

"I do not think it worked," I said.

"You haven't tried anything. Set your intention on me, like you did with the parchment when we were twelve. Begin imagining I am invulnerable. Come on. Try."

I was hesitant and backed away from him as a precaution. Slowly, I did as he had suggested. I was not prepared for how quickly my light came forward. Or how forcefully it left me. It nearly blinded me. And there was pain. There had never been pain before. It seared like a raging fire behind my eyes. My legs buckled beneath me.

Before I fainted, I saw faces flashing into my view. Familiar and disapproving. My father and mother. The Oracle. It was a memory, I think, or a dream. It felt like neither.

When my awareness returned, I found Varyn hovering over me, wide-eyed and frantic. He threw his arms round me.

"Stars, I thought I would never see your eyes open again." His embrace was tight and crushing. The pain in my head had gone, but I felt feeble and drained. I sat upright, slowly.

"What happened?" I asked. "Did I hurt you with my light? There was so much of it." He loosened his hold and drew back from me, shaking his head.

"You collapsed before it reached me. I ran and caught you as you fell, then carried you onto the bed. Does anything hurt? Are you in pain?"

"No, it has passed. How long have I been unconscious?"

"A while." He pulled me close again, pressing a kiss against my cheek. He held me at length. When we broke apart, I noticed a fresh cut on the back of his hand. He tried to hide it from my gaze, but I seized his arm, gently, and mended the wound with a small quantity of my light. If I could do nothing else, at least I could do this. He rubbed the healed flesh and stared at me sheepishly.

"I just wanted to make certain it hadn't worked. For all the effort it cost you, I was hoping—"

"I am sorry I could not do it," I said. My voice was a thin half-whisper.

"You have nothing to be sorry for." The words were out of him quickly. All at once.

His eyes, as they searched mine, were tender. I reached for him and tucked some of his hair behind his ear. It had grown nearly past his chest since he last cut it. The sun had gone to rest under the horizon during my loss of awareness, and he had lit the small lantern while I was absent. But I did not need its light. My Varyn was bright as any star. I let him wrap his arms round me again—let myself be enveloped by his golden warmth. It was like a drug, being held by him. I should not have allowed my overwhelming want to linger within me for so many years, gathering like rainwater in a pail. I should have confessed it to him sooner. I have missed out on so many of these embraces for it.

Our attempt to circumvent our dilemma and all its tragedy had failed—we will have so little time with one another. Why had I wasted so much of it? Each day with him now was numbered.

This is what I think as he holds me. As he draws me nearer to him, cloaking me in his tight embrace. I have never known a home. I have never felt I belonged in any place or realm.

But I belong in his arms.

"Varyn," I whispered, resting against him. "I love you." I do not know where I found those words. But they flowed from my lips with the familiarity of an assured truth, as if they were known to me, like the seasons or the names of our planets. He did not reply when he leaned back to look at me, fingers buried in my hair. He did not need to. It was there in his silence, staring out at me. Living within the honeyed hazel of his eyes and in the depth of his kiss. I was breathless by the time he withdrew his mouth from me. He pressed his forehead against mine and brushed the pad of his thumb across my bottom lip.

"My soul knows yours as waves and tides know the sea—is drawn to it as water by the Moon," he said. "If in another life, you are born again as Crescent Forest, then I long to be its trees and its river, for I cannot be without you."

He is my divinity.

Again he kissed me. I never tired of having his lips on mine. And like being in his arms, they, too, were an intoxicant. I lost myself under their influence, drifting on the high of him.

"You speak of rebirth, but I wish we could stay here, like this, for all eternity," I said.

He sighed and slipped his hand in mine—entwined our fingers. "Is there no other way? Is there not somewhere you could look for answers…somewhere to find an alternative method if there is one? Or someone you might go to for help?"

"Someone like who?"

"From your realm, a Celestial."

Desperation poured from his gaze and filled mine. I thought of all the callous gods I knew. Thought of Father and Mother. Of Uncle and all the other major divinities who never so much as acknowledged my existence save to mock it. I thought of my distant cousins, those lesser divinities of the Cups and Swords, Wands and Pentacles. I drew to mind a former Arcana, the one who did not hate me. She might have aided me once—before her father's venom took hold of her. But she was lost to me now. Our alliance had vanished like a palmful of sand in the wind. No deity would abet me.

"No," I said, deflating. "There is no one."

I saw Varyn turning this answer round and round in his head. He sat hunched, eyes roaming over the bare walls of my quarters. His brow was set as if concentrating or drawing. I knew all of his expressions, and this was my favorite of them. I watched it deepen and waited while he worked to arrive at the conclusion of his contemplation.

"In lessons, we were made to memorize the attributes of the major Celestials," he said, "like the Hanged Man and his trials, the Devil and his tricks. I was taught Mercury of the High Nine imparted the Hermit with boundless wisdom—all the knowledge that will ever exist. Mercury, with all his wit, made her a god of great wisdom. I know you must return soon. Will you see her? Is she as cold as the rest?"

At this, memories of my encounter with her came rushing back. How could I have forgotten it? I heard her voice echoing from the past, bestowing upon me some of my future while I stood beside her in the Hall of Effigies, watching as she collected her venerations. *A day will come when you will seek me out for guidance.* That is what she had said. My breath became trapped in my throat, and I made a strangled sound. Varyn thought I was coughing and clapped me hard on the back.

"Are you alright?" he asked.

"You are brilliant, Varyn. The wisest man I know."

He stared at me, bemused yet smirking. "Really?"

"She will help me. I must go to her. She will not refuse me."

"Where is she?" he asked, brows raised and eyes wide.

"I—I do not know. I have only seen her once in our realm."

"Then we must search for her. We must—"

"Wait. I think I know how I will find her."

"How?"

"With my divinity."

Chapter 36

IT TOOK SOME DAYS BEFORE I COULD ATTEMPT IT. Trying to Grant Varyn's orison had left me in somewhat of a weakened state. The first time I endeavored to transport myself to her was mere moments after coming to, between the short interval trailing my bout of fainting. Varyn had urged me to wait, but I was eager and did not heed any of his warnings. I should have listened. It was too soon. With me, all use of divinity need be followed by a period of recuperation. But the waiting and anticipation while I rested was agony. I felt as though there existed an invisible being hanging over me, keeping record of the time, silently urging me to seek her out before it was too late. But I was prone to unease and kept reminding myself this was nothing more than an irrational and self-imposed foreboding. With a fair amount of difficulty, I quieted these fears and gave attention to my recovery.

When I had regained enough of my strength, I tried again to go to her. I did not know if it would work. It was yearning and ambition and delusion, some might argue, that convinced me to stretch the bounds of my divinity.

I sat in my quarters and readied myself with a quantity of deep breaths. Traveling somewhere I had never been proved an arduous undertaking. I could not draw upon past experience to guide me, for those had been destinations of which I was already familiar. Now I had only memory to serve as my direction.

I called to mind every detail of her I could conjure. The sound of her voice, the glow of her skin. Her eyes and their wise hue, golden as the rising sun. I cleared my thoughts of all else but her qualities and willed my godhead to find her, wherever she might be.

Time passed and the walls of my quarters began to fall away, but I remained within the confines of them as they waned. I rose to stand in the center of the floor, and once on my feet, the bed vanished.

More of my chattels faded into obscurity, one after another. Where they previously rested, little peaks of jagged rock took form in their place.

The transfer from one state to the next had never been so gradual. I was half in one place and half in another. I could not say for how long I had been standing caught between them like this. Time seemed to have stopped moving things forward.

My thoughts became muddled, and I shut my eyes, using the loss of sight and surroundings to concentrate once more on those mysterious features I saw so long ago as a boy, seeking refuge from my troubles in the Hall of Effigies.

In this arrested condition, there came the sound of rustling wind. Of water. Of birdsong. I opened my eyes, and before me was the view of an island, of which I appeared to be the sole occupant. My feet rested atop pale sands. I walked along the warm stretch of them till I came upon a large structure comprised of many tall columns, all white as clouds. I slipped through them and found a door nestled on the other side. It stood ajar.

"Hello," I said, pushing softly against it. I waited but heard no greeting or welcome.

Inside I was met with more silence. More emptiness.

"Is anyone here?"

Still, there came no answer. I spotted a hearth, its embers dwindling. I moved to stand near it and found remnants of a meal.

"No Celestial has ever stepped foot in here other than myself. I am curious. How did you find me?"

I whipped around and there she stood, drink in hand, as if she had been there since the dawn of time. She brought the cup to her lips and drank, peering at me all the while.

"I—it was—my divinity managed it for me," I stammered over every word. In her presence, I felt like a boy again. "With it, I sought you out. I was not certain it would find you. I am glad it did. Though I hope you will forgive my intrusion."

"You needn't seek my pardon. Come. Sit."

She poured me a cup of what she had been drinking as I sat beside her hearth. I sipped and was delighted to find the sweet taste of Stars Brew on my tongue. I drank deeper and took in the dwelling, eyeing its opulent furnishings.

"Your home. It is magnificent," I said.

She sank into a chair of cushions opposite me. "Thank you. But I'm sure you did not journey here merely to pay me compliments."

My cheeks warmed. "No," I whispered. "I came for something else."

"On behalf of your mortal love, yes?"

I narrowly avoided choking on my Stars Brew. "You know of him?" I asked.

"You should have come to me sooner."

"What else do you know?"

"That you tried to Grant this mortal that which is forbidden to him."

I half shrieked and leaned forward. "Forbidden?"

"You did not know?"

I shook my head, numb. "How did you know that I tried to Grant?"

"It is known to all in the realm by now. To them, immortality is the right of the divine only. The Oracle's seeing water safeguards against any attempts to Grant a mortal with an eternal life through Celestial light. Did you not feel her spell upon you?"

"That is why I collapsed," I said, feeling the cloak of comprehension settling over me.

"Yes. If you return to the realm, they will shackle your light, cast you into an enchanted chasm so that you may never leave. That is why you must be careful not to be seen when you go back."

"I am not going back then!"

"You must if you are to retrieve what you have come for."

I thought at once of Varyn. "You mean there is a way? To keep him with me for my eternity?"

She sank deeper into her cushions with a sigh. "Yes and no. Eternity is but an illusion. You and I, we are only immortal insofar as the starlight which courses through our veins is. We Celestials wane and will one day, eons from now, be as the constellations are—incorporeal."

"We are...not immortal?"

"We are descendants of the Sun, and so have his starlight. So long as it remains within us, we go on."

"You mean it can be taken from us?"

She did not answer, merely drank and stared at me. I asked a different question. "Can it be given to another?" To a mortal? Please, if there is a way—"

"Yes. But to do so will be placing him in the way of great danger."

"Danger? What danger?"

"You have learned of the prophecy, I assume?"

Slowly, I recalled that vague prediction that had once circulated among the twelve courts. "Yes, and I think it is absurd. I have done from the moment I heard it."

"But there are many who do not. Already speculations are abound—rumors of what will become of the realm if mortals are seeking immortality, if there are Celestials willing to Grant it. Many of them believe this is how it will begin—the destruction the prophecy warned of. That your love for that mortal is heralding it."

"But that is ridiculous, he cannot possibly..." I paused and pinched the bridge of my nose, squinting. "Do you share their beliefs?"

"It does not matter what I think. Only what you think, what you choose."

"Him! I choose him. I choose Varyn. He is the only light I have ever known in my life. To lose him, to walk the earth without him...I cannot. I *will* not."

"Then it is settled. Your mortal is safe as of now. Though after I have imparted you with the knowledge you came here in search of, he will no longer be."

"No one is going to hurt him," I said, with a fierceness that shocked even me.

"Some will try. And will stop at nothing to prevent you during the harvest."

"What harvest?"

She rose and poured herself more Stars Brew, offering some to me as she filled her cup. My stomach was in knots, I did not want to drink anything. I could scarcely breathe the air around me. But I thought it impolite to refuse her in her own home and accepted another, cradling it with perspiring hands.

She took a long sip once she had settled back into her plush chair, sighing heavily after swallowing it.

"Moonsoil. You will need a great quantity of it, enough to fill this urn." She used her light to manifest a small, silver vessel upon the table which rested between us. I set my cup down and reached for it, turning it over in my hand. "It's enchanted so that when you store it in your breast pocket, it will be weightless and invisible and impervious to the elements."

I tested this claim and shoved it inside my garments. It disappeared inside them. I looked down and could not see it, could not feel it.

"It will reappear upon your touch and yours only."

I plunged my hand inside, searching for it, and felt it at once, whole and cool against my fingers.

"Moonsoil," I said. "That is in the Nebula Gardens, the floating stardust petals blossom from it."

"Yes, that is what you will gather inside the urn. From it, you shall reap the element needed for your mortal's elixir."

"An elixir? That is what will make him like you and I? That is all?"

She nodded. "But it will be a great labor to procure it. Listen closely for what all must be done."

I leaned forward as though our proximity would induce retention.

"The stardust which is infused within the Moonsoil is what everything in the Nebula Gardens thrives on. Itself, it is the seed of many flowers, trees, plants, and so on. But in the mortal realm, it will be different. The only thing that can be derived from it is a single flower. It will bloom wherever the Moonsoil is planted and watered. It will take twelve mortal years to grow it."

She paused and let this settle over me—let it suffocate me.

"Twelve years," I repeated, my tongue numb to the words as they spilled from it. I thought of all the things which could go awry, of the misfortune which could fall upon Varyn in that ocean of time.

"Once it has grown and bloomed, you must pluck it carefully. Then an extraction. Within the flower, there is nectar. This is what you have grown it for. It is the essence that will bestow continuous life and vitality. Mix it with water and give it to your mortal. There will be pain as he sheds his mortality. It shall pass—you'll know it's worked then. Wait a day, and it will be done."

I sat envisioning the years and years of waiting that Varyn and I would endure to reap the reward of our efforts. The Hermit watched me as I spun it round and round on my tired wheel of musing.

"The Moonsoil," she said after some moments, breaking me from my thoughts. "Do not plant it all in one place. Some grounds may fail to cultivate its effects through no fault of yours. A palmful of it yields enough for one flower to bloom. Spread it around the many regions of their realm. It will leave you more room for blunders that way. And with your gift of travel, you can tend to them all easily."

I did not know it then, but this was crucial advice. "Thank you," I said, and then, all at once wary of her altruism, asked, "Why are you helping me to do this? What will you gain from it?"

The sound of waves and birdsong filled the silence that preceded her answer. "Peace of mind in the knowledge that I did all I could for you—for one who has never known fairness." She leaned back, sinking deeper into her chair. "Do you know that your gift of travel is astounding? To move between realms by thought is...most need a spell or wings. You were meant to be greater. You may yet be if this does not..." she let the remainder of her words wither and die, waving her hand through the air as if dispersing a cloud of smoke.

"If this does not what?"

"Nothing, it is nothing, too much Stars Brew. I have said enough. Go to your mortal, he has been long without you. Time on my island is different."

"No, please, tell me what you meant. You said I may yet be greater. Did you mean my shades? I have never had them. Will they come? When we were children, Varyn told me of Celestial natures and what shades are to them. I have longed to know of mine ever since he told me. Do you know which of them I have inherited?"

"I cannot say, but what I believe is that you have neither."

"Neither?" I sounded incredulous. "But why?"

She looked past me, toward the tall windows, and out into the view of her island. "Why indeed?"

"But...I...will I ever—"

She held up her hand. "It's best you make your return, and hastily, your mortal may begin to worry. I cannot be certain, but many seasons may have passed there. Better to be off in case he is in distress or in need of you."

There were more answers I wished to pursue, but at this, I sprang to my feet. *Please*, I thought, *let him be alright.*

I worked to clear my head and to see within it nothing but the sight of him and his quarters, but a fear, abruptly sprouting, pressed upon me and prevented the scene.

"Does the realm know what I mean to do?" I asked.

"They will, eventually."

I could not spare another moment on inquiry, and would have to accept this, however vague. With a nod, I closed my eyes and once again evoked his dwelling, drawing to mind his bed and dressing table, his window, the sweet, lingering scent of him.

"Wherever you leave it, bring it water every six seasons." Her voice lured me from my impression, and now I was half-imagining my inn. I opened my eyes to re-gather my attention and found the setting of her home had fallen away. The Hermit and her island were fading. "It is resilient and will thrive so long as there is sunlight," said her disembodied voice. I forced my eyes shut once more and tried to envision everything anew.

I discovered I had returned when I heard a shrill cry. It belonged to an aged man who I found nestled beneath the covers of the bed in my quarters. He looked as if he had seconds ago rolled over and spotted me. I had come back to the inn—was led to it by distraction. I huffed.

"Who are you? How did you get in here?" asked the man.

"I am the porter," I said, pretending to busy myself with the door's frame while I formed the rest of my lie. "I have a key, pardon my use of it. I thought this room to be vacant."

"Oh, right, so you've come back then? Good. The matron will be happy. She seemed sad to have lost you. Said you had abandoned your post for nearly a season. She was reluctant to give the room away."

A gasp became trapped in my throat. Nearly a season?

I gave the man a hollow apology and rushed off to find Varyn. Outside, the sun was slowly sinking to its rest. I sprinted till I was away from the eyes of the villagers. From behind the cover of a large tree, I transported myself to him.

But his chamber was empty and mussed. I had been ready to race from room to room, calling out to him, but paused midway through starting and reminded myself such an action was unsuitable, as this was *his* home, not mine. I left by way of thought, then reappeared at the front door, rapping on it frantically.

A serving boy swung it half-open. He jolted when his eyes fell on me.

"Where is Varyn?" I asked.

A strange expression flitted across his features, there and gone in a blink.

"He is not to be let inside by order of Lord Vedlan. He does not live here anymore."

I BECAME AS INANIMATE AS THE LARGE DOOR—held open by the serving boy, gaping.

Varyn does not live here?

The words did not fit together. The sentence was nonsensical.

Of course he lives here. This is his home, and he must always live here. He must always live.

"That cannot be right," I muttered. "Please, go and get him."

The serving boy cleared his throat. "He is not here. He is gone."

"Gone where?" I think I shouted this. I did not mean to. He flinched and reasserted himself. I asked again, trying hard to mask the tremble in my voice. "You are certain of this?"

He nodded and narrowed the gap in the door, leaving a sliver of opening. Poking his face through it he said, "He had a row with Lord Vedlan. He ran off with his things not long ago." He shut it and left me standing there, staring at the blank slate of dark wood.

Long moments passed before I could move again. I wanted to kick the door in. To scream and shout and cry and beg. But that would not bring me to Varyn. I turned away as the heat threatened to build. Threatened to pool, to stream down my face in hot streaks. Stiff legs carried me from the manor and down the village streets.

The aged man's words blared in my head: *a season.* That is how long he has been without me, left to wonder where I have gone.

I raked my hands through my hair as if this would dispel the thought, staggering along the path to...where? I did not know.

I walked aimlessly, thinking now of Lord Vedlan, cursing him. Whatever happened, Varyn did not deserve to be turned out of his home. I had a mind to tell him this—to make my way back to the manor and defend Varyn like I had when he spoke so tersely of Lady Elayne. I thought again of that day and saw myself running after him, desperately following him through the streets till, at last, he stopped for a rest and...

My breath caught. Might he have gone there again in hopes of revisiting the same solace he found the last time his father had driven him out? I did not spare even a moment's contemplation for doubt or likelihood. I broke into a run, tearing down the path as though I were racing, and headed there.

Night would soon fall, and villagers were abound, present on every stretch of my charge. I bumped shoulders with them and ignored their indignant grumbling. A few shouted threats at my back, accusing me of being a careless youth who lacked manners. I did not care what they called me. I would not have stopped.

I felt I had been running for ages when, finally, the fountain came into view. I ran even faster then, rushing as though it would disappear at any moment, and take with it all my hopes. By the time I reached it my eyes were blurry with tears and stinging from the wind. I wiped at them till they were clear again, then searched for him.

He was not there.

I walked further along, pacing the length of the square and still I did not see him.

There were shops and taverns near, I thought. Perhaps I would find him taking refuge in one of them. I looked inside a number of them, studying the faces of each patron, hoping to find familiar features staring back at me. But instead, I saw only strangers.

When I had seen every corner of every shop and tavern, I wandered back to the fountain, circling it like a leaf caught inside a winding breeze. Would I never find him? I sank to the ground, crumbling under the weight of that despairing thought, and leaned my back against the fountain. The sound of its trickling waters reminded me of him. I sat there till my mind went blank. I might have stayed there all my days, I think, but a passing mortal tossed a few crescents at my feet and offered a tight-lipped smile. Many others were around now, too, and I rose so as not to be taken as a beggar again by any of them. That is when I saw him in the distance, hand flying to his chest.

He stands there, in the bustling center of everything, honey-eyed and golden-skinned. He is color itself. A burst of it among a sea of dull, breaking through the mortal monotony like shining rays between gray clouds. My Varyn, I think, grinning through the steps it takes to reach him, to settle into the warmth of his arms. To hold him and be held.

I did not want to let him go. He broke from me to press kisses upon my cheeks, onto my forehead, over the whole of me. I told him I was sorry, that I had not meant to leave him for so long. He brushed away my apologies.

"It doesn't matter," he said. "I'm just glad you came back to me."

When I had regained enough of my composure, I asked him what all happened with his father. He shook his head.

"We have been arguing so much. Since Mother died he has become unreasonable, even Celine agrees. We fought today about my starting an Aurora apprenticeship. He demanded I begin in the coming season. I refused. We were both yelling. One thing led to another, and I mentioned Hanesh and the Quartz Games—"

My mouth fell half-open. "You told him?" I asked.

"It just slipped out. I wasn't thinking clearly with all that shouting. He got so angry. I thought he would hit me. He told me to leave. Said I was not a nobleman's son any longer but a commoner. Told me now I could live like one, too, on the streets. Celine was crying. She helped me pack my things." He tapped his foot against a brown chest resting beside him. I had not noticed it till then. "It's not everything but we managed to gather up enough to start over. She gave me half the allowance she's saved. Together with mine, it's plenty to sustain me for a while until I can find steady work out there."

"Out where?"

"In the east, in Hanesh," he said, placing his hands upon my shoulders. "Come with me. There is a ship leaving the day after tomorrow. I was going to find an inn and wait for you for as long as I could. But now that you're back, there's nothing holding me here."

His eyes were wide and pleading. He did not have to ask. I would follow him across oceans, across the world. I would follow him anywhere. "I will come," I said. "But there is something I must do first."

I took his hands in mine and told him of everything I had learned on the Hermit's island. The tale seemed to knock all the breath out of him. He lowered himself onto his chest of belongings and stared up at me.

"By the stars. Twelve years for one flower?"

I nodded and reached inside my person for the urn. "I think the hardest part will be filling it," I said.

Varyn took it from me, tracing his fingers round it. "Take me with you. I can help."

I snatched it back. "No," I said, heart jumping. "I will not put you in the way of danger. I will never let them near you."

"But you will walk in the way of it yourself? All on your own?" He paused and seemed to swell with something. Fear? Resentment? I could not tell. "This season without you—it was unbearable. Waking every day not knowing where you were or if I would see you again. You're asking me to let you go a second time and live through that torment even longer right after having gotten you back? You can't go on your own. I need to know you'll be safe. I can protect you."

"I am the one who must protect *you*. They are gods, Varyn. You can no more guard yourself against them than an insect can escape being swatted."

He flinched at this, and I knelt before him so that his knees were pressed against my chest. "Please. I wish more than you that I could stay, but I must go. I must do this. Alone."

He clenched his fists, his jaw. Turned his face away from mine. I had never seen him so upset. I placed my hand on his chin, but he brushed it off without looking at me. Again I reached and made him see me. There were tears forming, glistening like diamonds in his eyes. "Promise me you will be careful then," he said finally. "Promise you'll come back to me."

I think his tears were not for me alone—but for what all he had lost in the short span of an evening. His father, Celine, his home, where he had spent the whole of his life. I could not fathom the loss of such sanctuary. He was the only home I knew.

"Nothing will keep me from you," I said. "I will come back. I promise."

He fought back his tears. If they had fallen, I would have wiped them for him.

········)·) ◉ (·((········

We went back to my inn. I found the matron and apologized profusely to her, naming an unforeseen crisis as the cause of what stole me away from our agreement. She seemed understanding, and herself offered apologies for giving up my quarters. I told her it was alright and that I would no longer be in need of them, for in two days' time, I planned to sail off to the east with Varyn. She was sad to lose my assistance round the inn, she said and gave us her only vacancy—a cramped corner space with a single bed. She had kept the meager quantity of my belongings and gave me that as well. I had thought they were lost to me and was happy to have them back. When Varyn offered her the crescents for our stay, she refused and said it was a parting gift to me.

The inside of our narrow dwelling was dim and carried in the air an odor of damp scouring cloths. Varyn sank onto the bed and scowled, recoiling from the piercing creak it made upon receiving his weight.

"Pity," he said.

I furrowed my brow. "What is?"

"That we cannot couple on it without making a racket."

I was smirking now. "Who says?" I asked. "I can be quiet."

He snorted, shaking his head. "You won't have to on this scant thing. It'll make enough noise for the both of us." He lay on his side and peered at me. "I'll get us a proper space in Hanesh. All ours. We can be as loud as we want there."

I smiled as I pictured it. He and I, arriving together on another land after sailing the Scorpion Sea. It was a pleasant musing till I reached inside my garment to soothe an itch and felt the urn there. Now, instead of our joy, I thought of that slowly growing flower—of the Moonsoil I must procure to bring it to life. I set it aside atop Varyn's chest of belongings.

"What's the matter?" he asked.

"Nothing." I could tell by the nature of his gaze he did not believe me. He knew me better than anyone, better I think, than I knew myself.

Later, after we had both washed, I braided his hair and joined him on the bed. It was barely wide enough for one body, let alone two. But I settled beside him anyway. I found my favorite spot between his arm and chest, and rested my head upon it, breathing him in. He smelled like the forest and its flowers. Its river and the rain.

"You are afraid to go back, aren't you?" he asked, stroking up and down the length of my back. I had been dozing, but at this, I became alert again.

"I am only afraid of losing you."

"You will not lose me."

"Then there is nothing to fear."

With that, we slept and, in the morning, woke with stiff and aching joints.

"Curse that bed and curse these lodgings," muttered Varyn as he stood stretching before the window. The light poured over him, turning him to gold. I sat watching him undress from the bed, nibbling on a crust of bread with honey. He threw open the lid of his chest and rummaged about it in search of fresh garments. "There are some plain smocks in here if you need them. They'll be ill-fitting, but when we get to Hanesh, we can buy new ones." I nodded absently and said a word of thanks, I think, but I had scarcely been listening. My eye caught the colorful edge of something inside the chest. It had been hidden beneath his possessions, but now that he had removed a portion of them, was in full view. I finished my bread, then rose and stood over it. Varyn thought I had come to collect the garments he offered and placed them in my hands. I took them without looking, for my attention was captured by a collection of familiar features.

My own.

I reached inside and gathered up the thin stack of his drawings, most of which I was the subject. He had drawn me in the forest, naked by the river. In another, I lay resting in a bed of flowers on my back with petals in my hair, still naked.

He put a hand on his hip and, with the other, pinched the bridge of his nose. "Stars, you weren't supposed to see that."

I covered my smirk with my fingers, head lolling to the side as I studied his elegant lines and curves, marveling at the way they merged and made the whole of me. "I am glad I did. They are beautiful. I still have the one you made for me when we were children. I thought you were brilliant then but your skill is much improved."

He stopped pinching his nose and looked at me. "Do you really still have it?"

I nodded, still gazing down at his illustrations. "It is among the belongings the matron kept for me. Go and see for yourself if you do not believe me. Are you so surprised?"

"I suppose I shouldn't be. You are, after all, a Cancerian."

He was jeering, but I paid him little attention, for the majority of it was taken by the drawings. There were some of Celine, and of Lady Elayne. The forest and river, too. I found many more of myself etched during the various stages of my growth. I had forgotten how small and slight I used to be. I reached the last one when Varyn slipped them from my hands and tucked them away again.

"I brought them because I didn't want to forget. Memories fade and change, but these won't. I'll always have them just the same as they were, every detail preserved."

I raised my brow. "And to think you were a moment ago deriding me. You are as much a water sign as I am."

He shoved me for this. I deserved it and snorted as I stumbled backward onto the bed. It released a shrill creak, and then all we could do was laugh.

"When we get to Hanesh," I said, clutching the aching stitch in my side as I caught my breath, "we will make new memories for you to preserve."

Chapter 38

LATER THAT DAY, WE TOOK A CARRIAGE TO THE SEAPORT and purchased tickets for a one-way voyage to Hanesh. The journey there would take nearly a season. I had lost one already on the Hermit's island and would now lose another, in idle. But I would lose it alongside Varyn, and that alone gave me solace.

While we were there at the seaport getting our passage sorted, Varyn penned a letter to Celine. Though she had completed her education at the institute, he addressed it to be sent there so as not to have it intercepted or disregarded by his father. It was Celine's idea, he said, and once we settled in Hanesh, he would send another.

I wondered what sort of place Hanesh would be. I thought of the merchant at the festival and of the prize Varyn had won me. From those fine exemplars it seemed a charming region, one of liveliness and color perhaps. Each time I was reminded of the looming undertaking I was set to embark on, I would fill my head with the prospects of a new life there and be comforted by their whimsy till my dread was forgotten.

⋅⋅⋅⋅⋅⋅⋅⋅⋅)⋅) ● (⋅(⋅⋅⋅⋅⋅⋅⋅⋅⋅

The Moon turned and the night was running from the early light of dawn. I had not slept but instead listened to Varyn's breaths as he slumbered. Our ship would be sailing off this day shortly after the sunset. There was something I needed to see done before then. I crept from the crying bed and made efforts not to wake Varyn. He knew that when he woke, he would not find me sleeping beside him. We agreed I was to meet him at the seaport once it was done. I sidled toward the urn and took it up—stowed it in my garment.

"Tell me again what I must do if I do not find you waiting on the ship."

I loved his raspy sleeping voice, but I winced upon hearing it. I thought I had been careful in my movements and that they would not stir him. I turned, sighing as I knelt by the bed.

"You must sail with the other passengers, as we planned. If I miss it, I will find my own way there. I will find my way to you."

We had talked all day of the plan. Over and over, I repeated it to him. Each time, he found a new reason to distrust it. He sat up in bed and propped himself up on an elbow, resting his head in his hand. I thumbed the braid I made for him as he stared at me.

"You are sure you will be safe?" he asked.

"I cannot say. I do not know what they will do. But I am coming back here. They cannot stop me. They cannot keep me from you."

"Use your light if anything happens." He shifted, ill at ease. "There have been times in the past where it was strong. So strong. I'll never forget that day in the lower villages. What you did to that vagrant—do it to them if they try to hurt you. Promise me you will."

"You do not have to worry, Varyn."

"Promise."

He put his hand over mine. I brought my lips to his, melted into his warmth.

"I promise." He gave me a gentle push and I stepped back. We were both reluctant to take our eyes off one another. "Turn around, go back to sleep. I will meet you on the ship," I said.

He hesitated, then sighed and turned away from me.

I lingered, watching his breaths rise and fall till I satisfied myself he was fine. I thought of the Nebula Gardens. Their floating petals, the shimmering stardust. I imagined the taste of sweet sap on my tongue and the feel of Moonsoil running through my fingers. It took only a moment of this before the magnificent tapestry of the realm wove into existence around me. I stood under a familiar sky, teeming with bright stars—they lay scattered across the expanse like jewels. The night was in full bloom here, the gardens bathed in moonlight. There was beauty in this realm, but so too was there beauty in the deadly Emros.

I studied my surroundings. Some cousins were abound, lofting and licking sap from their fingers. With quiet steps I ambled about, feigning intoxication till I was away from their eyes. It was as it had always been, my presence went unacknowledged. I thought there would be peril, that my arrival would be received with rancor. But they behaved as apathetically as if I were an insentient petal falling from the enchanted skies.

Discreetly I gathered a palm of Moonsoil and brought it to my chest, dropping it in my urn. I looked to see if anyone had noticed me, then scooped another fistful to add with the other. I reached again and the action caught the eye of a cousin from the Suit of Pentacles, Stellaria. Once, when I was a boy, she tossed a crystal at my feet in mockery.

"What are you doing down there?" she asked. "All these perfectly good petals floating around and you choose what has fallen in the dirt?" Her laughter drew the attention of other Celestials. I do not think she recognized me. I was taller, broader, older. But I saw among them one who would know me no matter how much I had changed. Tiberias had nearly laid eyes on me, but I was quick in my retreat.

I let the Moonsoil slip through my fingers as I dashed behind the ivory column of an archway.

"Who were you talking to?" asked Tiberias. The years had not improved the grating and unpleasant timbre of his voice.

"One of the other Pentacles, he's just there, crouched in the dirt like a fool."

"Lay off the sap, Stellaria, there isn't anyone there." I imagined her face, its features twisting into the mask of bemusement as they regarded my vacated spot. I did not wait to hear her response. I fled by way of thought to the only place I knew would be empty, and safe.

Time had touched nothing in my lofty chamber. I had not seen the inside of it in long seasons. I had been a boy when last I was here, now I stood surrounded, as a man of nearly nineteen, by unfamiliar familiarity. So many moons I had spent enclosed in the walls of this palace and yet it all seemed so foreign to me. Even my reflection bore strangeness. I had given up mirrors in the mortal realm. I had given up searching within them for my shades. I thought I knew it well, my dark amber. But as I stared, I found the prominent presence of that hollow youth who lived within my gaze had lessened. Varyn had drawn me once with these eyes. All along he had seen me as I am now, even when I could not see it myself.

I sank onto my bed and thought of him. His skilled hands, his laughter, the nurturing sphere of his arms and the feeling of being wrapped in them. On and on these musings streamed, till I was filled with nothing but him. Our Moon regarded me through the window. Could she hear these whispers circling in my mind? I have said that I loved her once already and forgive me if I say it again, it is easy to fall into repetition when recounting a tale that spans so long a course. But I know now that she has always loved me, too. I only wish I had known it sooner and…ah, there is more yet to be told before I come to that.

In the distance, I heard my mother's faint laughter, echoing through the halls of the palace. I wanted to drive my fingers in my ears. Instead, I peeked at the urn.

A thin layer of Moonsoil coated the bottom. It was as good as empty. I cursed Stellaria for taking notice of me. I might have filled it and been back already were it not for her. Upon my return to the garden, I thought, I would have to move with quicker hands.

I sat waiting for the right moment to arrive. I had been so long away from the realm, so removed from its conditions, that I did not know when it would be most suitable to go back. My fear was that I would find it teeming with Celestials. But I could not stay hiding within the confines of these palace walls for much longer. The dawn light was beginning to pour from the sky. Soon I would have no shadows or half-light to conceal me.

It was with caution that I crept from the bedchamber. I did not want to use my gift of travel, for I might take shape before another's eyes.

But the realm was a sprawling place with all its courts and halls. It was not easy to both navigate it and be furtive. Twice I had narrowly eluded the notice of passersby. The minor divinities liked to roam in groups of three or more. I did not know what edicts had been put in place since my attempt to Grant a forbidden orison. News of it had spread among the courts I was sure. Celestials delighted in that sort of talk, and they would delight in accosting me. How much did they know of what I intended to do? Had the Oracle's seeing water revealed to her this day? I could only hope it had not.

I found the gardens occupied by much the same quantity as they had been when I first arrived. Stellaria still hung about them, though her awareness had declined. Her head drooped like a limp, dying flower. Even so, I took care to avoid her. I saw no trace of Tiberias as I roamed the gardens. But there were other familiar faces present. I knew the Hanged Man from his gleaming, sun-like mane of hair. His back was to me as he sat showering in stardust. I slipped into one of the swinging beds of enchanted petals and pretended to rest there.

As it swung, I peered through slits at my surroundings. Most had fallen under the spell of intoxicants, and were merely half-alert. I let myself sway in feigned repose, side to side. Surreptitiously I reached, hand sliding into my garment as if to soothe an itch. My fingers met the lip of the urn. I paused before drawing it out, and turned my head left, then right, then left again.

In one rapid motion, I snatched the urn from my garment, plunged it to the ground, and dragged it along the soft, sinking surface. I do not know why I had not tried this method during my first attempt. Within short moments the urn was filled with Moonsoil. I sealed it and stuffed it back inside, where it rested against my pounding heart, invisible, weightless. Victory. It was done.

If my surroundings had allowed for it, I would have rejoiced with laughter and thrust my fist into the air. But my celebration took the form of other gestures: I worked to slow my beating heart, to steady my breaths. And to think of escape.

I stared up at the bright skies, still swaying in the petal bed. The visions came easily. They often did. I waited for them to transport me.

Nothing.

More waiting and more…nothing.

A quiet turmoil brewed within me like gathering storm clouds. I tried to leave once—twice—three four five times. I tried tried tried tried tried tried

"Cousin, how nice it is to see you again."

Chapter 39

I LAY TENSED, LOCKED, AND UNMOVING IN MY SWINGING cage. Arcana stood over me. She waved her hand through the air, and the enchanted petal bed went still. As still as my body. Slowly, the use of my limbs returned.

I think I muttered a word or two of contrived greeting before stumbling to my feet. She looked so much like her father. The smile plastered on her face belonged to him.

"H-how, how are you?" I asked, and as I spoke, I envisioned my departure. I saw the mortal realm, clear as morning skies. But I could not get to it.

"I am well. Better than you. You can stop trying to leave. It won't work around me."

I ignored the shiver crawling up the length of my spine. It had never been like this. Traveling by thought was like running and now I felt as though I were running in place. My thoughts, when they flowed, seemed to meet with a wall of resistance. I could not break through it.

"What do you want?" I asked.

"Right now? In this moment?"

I shrugged. She sighed.

Neither of us said a word. I used the silence to exert more effort toward shattering the barrier in my path.

"You're wasting your time on that."

"I do not know what you mean." I ceased trying in order to give credence to my lie.

She snorted. "I'm brightest burning now, did you know that? I don't suppose so. Not with your proclivity for playing at being mortal. Anyway, you've been gone a while, so you wouldn't know about my new trick. I haven't told anyone, actually, so you'll be the first. It's been the greatest amusement—my toying with the others. They don't suspect a thing."

My eyes were slits. "What are you talking about?"

"So far, I've only been able to manage it with the lesser divinities and—"

"Manage what?"

She crossed her arms. Glared at me. "I was getting to it if you would let me finish. So far, I said, it has only served me with Cups, Swords, Wands, Pentacles, oh, and Temperance as well. And now you. It's hard to put into words what I'm doing, but simply put, I can control the use of your divinity."

I struggled to stop my hand from flying to my mouth. She would not see me startled. I would not give her that.

"So what now then?" I asked. "I take it you have been watching me all the while without my noticing. Now that you have me where you want me, what will you do? Is it not enough to be the best, Arcana? You have won already. Do you need to flatten me under your heel too?"

"This is not about competition, I have no equal here, nothing even close to it. This is larger than that. I know you're practically absent of divinity, but are you so without sense that you cannot see what you've brought upon our heads? You could have played at being mortal for all eternity. No one would have so much as lifted a brow at you. But to try and give them the attributes of a god? If one pathetic mortal can be elevated to such heights, why can't they all?"

"He is not merely a mortal. He is not pathetic. He is—" I paused upon realizing I had been shouting.

"Go on, say it. Tell me of your love for that mortal, and I will tell you of its dangers. Tell you it has the power to destroy our realm. You may be content to see it fall, but I will not relinquish the glory of this dominion for that or for anything."

She took the neck of my garment in her fist, dragged me forward by it. I struggled against her as she slipped her other hand under it, sliding it up and down my chest. She must have seen me gathering the Moonsoil. Her eyes flashed sienna as she groped for it. But her hand came up against nothing. The Hermit's enchantment held, and it was all I could do not to cry out to her in thanks. Arcana kept on sweeping across my chest as though she thought the urn would reveal itself if she pressed hard enough. But she would not have this. It was mine.

I dug my heels into the soft garden and wrangled myself free of her grip. With all my might, I shoved her. She fell hard and tore open her flesh on a jutting stone. I fled through an archway.

"What's this?" asked the Hanged Man's drowsy voice as it trailed behind me, faded to mere echo by the distance between us. None of the Celestials in the garden had taken notice of either of us as we stood arguing. The trance of intoxicants held all their attention. I owed my retreat to it. On and on, I ran, all the while trying to use my gift of travel. Still, it did not work. Faster, I ran, passing wide-eyed Celestials and bumping shoulders with them. I needed to get as far away from the gardens as possible—far away from *her*. And perhaps with enough separation, my divinity would return.

The path ahead of me was wide. I knew it well. It led to an alcove. I had been darting toward it for short moments when I collided with Arcana—all three of her. How could I have forgotten she held this power? She must have been using it to watch me in the gardens.

Three pairs of sienna eyes regarded me.

"You made me bleed," said one of the Arcanas.

"Shall I do it again?" I spat. Another of the Arcanas seized me by the arm while the second sent a blast that seared daggers into the flesh of my shoulder. I had never screamed louder than I had in that moment.

"Yes, go on. Do it again. I dare you," said the same Arcana who had spoken earlier. I looked down at my shoulder, stunned to find it already healing—stunned to find the pain of it lessening despite the loss of my other divine gift. I stared first at the mended wound, then at the one who had given it to me. How could this be the same Arcana I used to admire? The little cousin who would advise me and grant me portions of her veneration. The clever girl I used to confide in. Where had she gone?

"What does it feel like, cousin, to be so cruel?" I asked. "Is it like being venerated? Is that why it comes so easily to you?"

Two of the Arcanas vanished, and I was left with a single, glaring deity. "You should know better than anyone," she said. "You would see our realm destroyed just to have what you want. That's crueler than anything I'm doing or have ever done. My father warned me about you for so long. I wouldn't listen. 'But he is my dearest cousin' I would say whenever he spoke ill of you and your deficiency. I see the reason for it now. He was right all along."

"Of course I was, Archie."

I did not need to look to know Uncle had arrived. In his presence, the air turned to smog. But eventually I glanced, and found him emerging from the cloak of his divinity. He had likely been there all the while. I wondered if there was ever a time when I had truly been alone in the realm and free from the persecution of the Magician's poisonous gaze.

Now the two of them stood on either side of me, imprisoned me with their leering.

"What's this?" It was the Hanged Man's voice again, resounding and no longer an echo waning in the distance. He stalked toward us, and my two captors were now three. His skin glistened with stardust from the gardens. Its haze still influenced him. "You're the Devil's boy, aren't you?" asked the Hanged Man. "Jupiter's spot, I would never have believed that horned, unduly exalted gloat could produce such a—"

"Where is it?" asked Arcana, pressing her palm against my chest.

"Where is what?" I asked. I should not have said anything. She seared me again with her light, singeing me across my abdomen. I nearly collapsed, but the Hanged Man broke my fall and steadied me.

"Lying to me is unwise. I saw you in the garden. You filled a little vessel with Moonsoil, then hid it. Where is it? And tell me why you took it."

"Moonsoil?" asked the Hanged Man. "You chanced coming back here for that? What for?"

I stood clutching my abdomen, head drooping. It had healed already, but I needed time to think. They did not yet know my intentions, it seemed. Did not even know what use could be made of the Moonsoil I had taken.

Arcana placed her hand under my chin, lifted my face. "Where is it?"

I said nothing. Uncle leaned. He smoothed a hand over my chest and this sent me flinching.

"He put it inside his garment? Are you certain? There's nothing here," said the Magician, peering across at Arcana.

The Hanged Man smirked. "It's obvious he's used a concealment charm. Quite an effective one, too, it seems. Here let me. Surrender is my specialty." His hand glowed with light, and he swiped it over my chest. It burned like nothing I had ever felt, worse than Arcana's light. I could do nothing but shriek. It went on for long moments till I thought my awareness would dwindle like a flame in the wind. "Ah," said the Hanged Man, withdrawing from me. "There is definitely something hidden there. I can sense it. Usually, that spell removes any veils of concealment."

"Well, has it been removed?" asked Uncle, clicking his tongue.

The Hanged Man sighed, frowned. "No," he replied. "What do you want so badly with a pile of Moonsoil anyway? What are you planning to do with it?"

I did not answer.

"It doesn't matter," said Arcana. "He's not leaving with it. He is not leaving at all."

"Perhaps the Oracle knows? Surely there's knowledge of its uses somewhere in the Cosmic Library?"

"No," said Uncle. "He is going to tell us." With this, he burned each of my thighs. I fell to the ground like a leaf during Libra season. Uncle crouched beside me, put his lips to my ear. "Each time you are asked and do not answer, I will burn you." He rose, and I sat trembling there, flesh aching as I panted. Arcana wrangled me to my feet.

"Why did you take it?" she asked.

I pressed my lips together and despite my pain, stared defiantly at her. This time, it was the Hanged Man's light that singed me—a hot sting of fire slicing silver down my arm. The moment it healed, he tore it open again. And again, and again.

Any dignity I possessed fled from me like hunted prey. I begged for their mercy, but my cries merely served to impel them to crueler torments.

"What did you take it for?" I could not tell which of them had asked. Their voices now all carried the same timbre. Or perhaps I was too delirious with agony to distinguish one from the other. When I gave no answer, a swift and needling slap knocked my head to one side. This is when I knew I had truly angered them. It was one thing to wound with light and another entirely to use one's own flesh to enact brutality. It was both humiliating and crass. Even dumb beasts were not handled this crudely.

They continued on this way with burns and blows. I do not know for how long.

"In the pit we have prepared for you, there will be no light from Moon or Sun." Uncle's voice pierced through my cloud of delirium. But as the mist cleared, I could scarcely look at him. "No food or drink for all eternity. Nothing to distract from your suffering. Deities will come and ogle you, never offering a word of kindness. They won't even waste breath to mock you. They will come only to watch, leer. Have you any idea what a miserable existence that is? You'll never escape it. Not even madness will free you from its torment." I heard these words but had not the strength to react to them. The Magician meant for them to stir me to confession, and when they did not, he drove his knee between my legs.

"I'm bored of this honestly, if it's all the same to you I'd like to get on with it. That pit is ready, you said?" asked the Hanged Man.

By now I was on my knees, every part of me shuddering. One of them grabbed a fistful of my hair, raised me by it. Brought to height I could see their shadows, stretched by sun. The noon light would soon fade to evening. They had been at me for the better part of the day.

"Your mortal. He is bright-haired, yes?" asked Arcana. "Born with hair like flames, you once told me. How hard do you think it would be to find him down there? To hunt every vibrant-headed man and fling him into that pit to rot in your place."

At this, my weariness drained and was replaced by something I cannot name. It rippled through me like water under a skipping stone. What else had I told Arcana? I could not remember. But I remembered Varyn's parting words; heard again the worry in his voice as I assured him all would be well. Had this been what he had feared would happen?

Arcana whispered more threats, and they drew to mind the blade I once saw pressed against Varyn's throat. I saw it again and again, and now it was not Arcana or the Hanged Man who stood surrounding me, but that vagrant and his blade, sinking ever deeper into the neck of the only boy I have ever loved.

My light left me with the force of flood waters barreling down a narrow path. The blast knocked Arcana off her feet—sent her skidding backward. I think it was the first time she had ever been burned by another's divinity. I knew the shade of her shock. It stared out at me as

I sent more of my light to burn her. The sound of her screams might have pained me once, but now they were a symphony of Lerawyns strummed round a tavern's table.

I turned my light on the Hanged Man. Burned him once, then again, and again, and there would have been a third were it not for the Magician's fist in my hair. He dragged me by it. I twisted round to face him and burned him too.

He did not expect it. He did not expect the back of my hand to slap across his face either. Again I burned him, and while I was burning him, I thought of the seaport. Of the ship carrying passengers across the water. I imagined wind ruffling through my hair and

…the wall had crumbled. There was no Arcana to keep it in my path. She lay shivering on the ground, trying to heal her burns. The realm around me began to fade. A hand seized me by the wrist, and still, the realm continued to dim. I struggled against the taut grip to no avail, twisting, yanking, fighting to pry myself free of it.

I should have fought harder.

But I had been concentrating on other tasks.

It took little more than a blink to be transported from one terror to another. For as I stood near the seaport, the fading sunlight of the mortal realm shone half on me…and half on the Magician.

Chapter 40

WITH AN EFFORT I HAD NOT KNOWN EXISTED IN ME, I ripped my wrist from Uncle's strangling hold and punched him. He clasped both hands around his nose. I hoped more than anything that I had broken it. Not only for the satisfaction of inflicting pain, but for the knowledge that mending bones demanded intense diligence, even for the most powerful of Celestials.

As he nursed the injury I had given him, thoughts of the sea swam into my head. I let them overcome me, and then I was no longer merely standing near the seaport. I was not standing at all but floating in the sea.

Though there was great distance now between us, I spotted Uncle among a crowd of mortals on the docks where I had left him. He whipped his head this way and that, searching for me. But I was safe in the middle of the sea, and for all his trickery, I knew he would not think to look here.

I watched his frustration grow as he glanced around for me, turning in every direction but the sea.

Keeping him in my sights, I swam further out. The waters were up to my neck. Beneath them, I massaged the flesh of my wrist, where his fingers had dug. It still bore the sting of them. Had I known I could carry others with me through use of thought, I would have been more careful. He had not managed to catch me, but he knew now the place where I had sought refuge all these years. I felt as though something precious had been taken from me.

But I had not been dispossessed of everything, at least, for I would not continue dwelling in Ethelia.

Across from me, far in the distance, I spotted the ship bound for Hanesh—the very one I meant to board. It was a towering vessel. I watched it creep along the surface of the sea as I remained afloat. My Varyn was somewhere inside. I had kept my promise to him and called forth my light to escape the fate that awaited me, just as he had asked. It had been as it was in the alley, in the temple.

Other times too, it had come out in our youth. Once to mend a bone he had broken falling from a tree in the forest. Another to stop him being hit by a passing carriage. And countless more, which time has waned into obscurity. It dawned on me then, as I treaded water in the middle of the sea, that always when Varyn was in need of aid, it was there. A burst or blast, surging forward to scorch or save. The one constant of my elusive divinity. Steady and sure, only for him.

I trailed the path of the ship, eyeing it as it advanced further from me. I felt myself growing weaker with every moment that passed. It was a small mercy that the waters were not terribly frigid and the season was mild. I could bear being submerged for as long as I needed till the Magician was gone from the seaport. A few times, he had been swallowed by the horde of busy mortals, merely to reappear shortly after. When finally he stalked out of sight and did not return, my whole being sang with relief.

The ship had traveled a long way from me by then, but at last I could imagine myself on it—could imagine sitting beside Varyn, clutching him in my arms, feeling his soft lips on mine. In quick moments, I was there, shivering before him. Upon my arrival, he flinched and began choking on something he had been drinking. With trembling hands he set it aside on a small table, which rested next to an equally small bed. His eyes as they regarded me were wide, puffy, and red-rimmed.

"Oh, thank the stars, you're back, you found me! I was so…" he pulled me to him, wrapping me in his warmth, clinging tightly despite my sea-drenched garment and skin. To hold him again was like quenching a prolonged thirst, like rest after hardship. His lips found mine and there was nothing either of us could do but sigh into each other. Our tongues, swirling and eager, spoke of their own accord—in a language only we understood.

He is my divinity.

He broke from me, breathless, and pressed his forehead against mine.

"I am sorry it took so long to—"

"Shhh. You're here with me now. That's all I care about. Nothing else matters." He held me tighter. We stood like that a while, tangled in one another's arms, swaying with the sailing ship as it rocked and heaved along. The constant motion was disorienting. But I did not lose my balance. He was there to steady me.

·········ᴗ·ᴗ ● ᴖ·ᴖ·········

When I was out of my wet garments and resting upon the small but comfortable bed of our cabin, Varyn brought me food and drink. I had expected the ship to be unpleasant and cramped. To my surprise, it was more spacious than the narrow room we had been given at the inn, and there were two beds instead of one—along with a desk and other chattels. I sat, taking in the charming compartment as I ate the meal he brought me. I could not name what all he had given me, but among the provisions, there was spiced meat and a duly scorching drink. I coughed a little as it went down.

"Oh, I forgot. You have to add this cream to it. It's a Haneshi delicacy, called Zèkhei. They have Haneshi workers aboard in the kitchens. Do you like it?"

I nodded and waited for him to stir in the bone-white mixture, then took another sip. Whatever it was, it had lessened the intense taste of the drink and enhanced its sweetness. With each bite and swallow, I felt my strength returning. As I ate, Varyn sat across from me on his bed, casting furtive glances in my direction. When he thought I was not looking, he reached for the urn and peeked inside.

"It is dry still. The Hermit made the urn impervious. It can be planted. There is nothing to fear," I said between bites. He eased at this and sealed it away with his things.

"Will you tell me what happened? Did they hurt you? Is that why you didn't come back to the inn, why you were out in the sea?"

A flash of that torment flickered back into my mind, and I shook my head. "It will only serve to upset you. I am alright now. And safe, here with you. Let us think of other things. Like how we will fill our days. We have a whole season ahead of us on the water."

"Ambroz."

He was scowling. I finished my last few bites and glared at him. I did not want him to know of my ordeal. It was over and done. The knowledge would merely weigh upon him like mountains. Burden him, as the memory of it burdened me. If he learned of my suffering, I feared he would sleep and find no rest but meet instead wretched nightmares of pits and torment. This load—it was mine to carry, not his.

"You will really keep it from me?" asked Varyn.

I sighed. "What good will it do you to know? I came through it. I am fine now. Is it not enough that I am here?"

"No!"

"No?"

"You look a weary wreck. Like you've been beaten for days. Like you've bled and cried and…and…*screamed…*" He rose and made for the narrow doorway but stopped and turned round to face me. "You promised there would be no more secrets between us. No more withholding. You're still keeping things from me. Hiding what ails you. How can you hope to be cured when you cannot even admit that you're sick?"

"I told you I am fine. Just leave well enough alone, Varyn."

I am not sure what expression my features had arranged themselves into. Perhaps they bore shock. Perhaps, to him I looked indignant. Whichever of them he saw drew out a scoff, and then he was through the door and gone.

I cried when he left. Not straight away. But later, far later, when the stuffy room grew dark and still he did not return. I went to look for him and found the passageways of the ship confusing.

We were on one of the uppermost decks, I did not realize it till then. And I did not know how many there were in all. Below, some men, women, and children were about. They offered nods of acknowledgment as I passed. The feeling of the moving ship was foreign beneath feet which were accustomed to standing upon inert surfaces. The perpetual motion was jarring. I did not do well with it. One of the other passengers took notice and asked if I was alright. I pretended all was well and inquired if she had seen a bright-haired young man pass through. She told me she had, and I followed her directions to the ship deck. But he was not there. I walked the length of it and saw many dark heads. None bright.

If I were in a better condition, I might have swept the whole of the ship searching for him. However, the meal in my stomach was in battle with the sway of the vessel, and I feared if I remained on my feet, it would all leave me.

When I returned to the cabin, it was still void of him, and this is when I broke down sobbing. Everything made itself known all at once, my fears, my unpleasant memories, the torment I had just escaped. All of it now came barreling out at me. I shook and shuddered and heaved as the tears rolled. When the worst of it passed, I lay in the bed sniffling, gazing out at Varyn's vacant spot, wishing he would come back. I stared stared stared. At some point, I found my eyes growing heavy—found that I could not resist shutting them.

I woke to the sound of clinking glass and was slow to stir. I wish I had risen more swiftly, for I caught the barest glimpse of Varyn setting down a plate of food and drink atop the bedside table. The view was of the back of his vibrant, auburn head. It was there and gone before I even had the chance to sit up.

The bright sunlight of a new day illuminated the cabin and made it appear more spacious than I knew it to be. I peered at the bedside table and saw the morning meal he had left for me. It seemed a silly thing to be at odds with me yet still maintain some level of cordiality—of thoughtful consideration. But this was Varyn.

I nibbled on the food, though lacked an appetite for it. My sampling was more a show of appreciation for the gesture. Of course it was as silly a thing as his avoidance, for he had not been in the cabin to see me eating. But this was me.

Among the selections was a warm cup of Zèkhei. It eased the scratchiness of my throat. I had cried it nearly raw in the night. He had not forgotten to add the cream to it this time, and I smiled while sipping. The half-curve faded quickly from my lips as I glanced around the cabin and was reminded of my solitude.

I stretched out my legs, sighing.

My foot met with a pile of garments. They were the sum of my possessions, neatly arranged at the foot of the bed. I finished my Zèkhei, then washed and dressed.

When I ventured out of the cabin, it was on steadier legs than the night previous. I went in search of Varyn again and saw him talking with a group of women on the deck. Our eyes met, lingered. The expression in his seemed pained. I joined them and stood beside him.

When I introduced myself to the women, they stared at me with furrowed brows as if I had many heads instead of one. The woman nearest to me flashed a thin smile and began speaking but it was in the Haneshi language which I did not understand. Varyn said something in response which sent them all giggling, then they resumed conversing as if I was not there. I felt foolish after a while, standing around them, listening to their strange tones without knowing what they meant. I sauntered off and busied myself with learning the ship.

I spent a good portion of the day exploring it and discovered that on the uppermost deck, they kept livestock. There was someone tending to them—a young boy, likely not much older than twelve. He collected what they hatched and took it away. I found their lodgings crude. The smell was also unpleasant. I followed the boy who had tended to them to escape it. Led by his trail, I was guided to the kitchens. How the workers could stand the smothering heat of the cooking fires down there was beyond my understanding. I left as soon as a sweltering wave of it enveloped me.

The air on the deck welcomed me once more, and I sucked it in like a man on the precipice of suffocating.

But with the large gulp of it came also the inhalation of smoke. The familiar sweet herbs I had smelled burning in the streets during the festival season now occluded my nose and throat. Nearby, a mortal had made a small altar to my mother and was mumbling out a stream of orisons. Even at sea, I could not escape the gods.

I moved away so as not to hear or smell the offering.

Further along the deck were many people. Some stood conversing. Others went about exercising their limbs. I sequestered myself near the bow of the ship, where the quantity of mortals had thinned and stood watching the sea ripple beneath me. I could tolerate the unending movement of the vessel far better when I had eyes on its course. There existed something soothing about the waters, and momentarily, my ills were forgotten, swallowed by the great mirror of the sea. I met such serenity that I had not noticed Varyn's presence till he cleared his throat beside me.

We stared at one another. I cannot speak to my expression, but his bore a vain stubbornness. As though his little noise had been merely to announce himself. As though it were meant to spur me to speech. I remembered how foolish I felt, being spurned in front of the women earlier. Resolutely I stared at him, waiting. We went on this way at length. It became painfully apparent he had no intention of breaking the silence and so I left him.

I did not huff or sigh or even scoff. Merely went along the path as if strolling. I felt his eyes on me as I walked away.

Chapter 41

WE CARRIED ON IGNORING ONE ANOTHER'S EXISTENCE FOR DAYS. It was maddening. Between us, a sort of routine coldness had emerged and shaped our habits. It went as such: in the morning, I would wake to an empty cabin and find a meal waiting on the bedside table. Then, during afternoon leisure, when our paths inevitably crossed, we would engage in a game of 'who can glare at the other the hardest.' He won each time. We took our evening meals in the small but adequate dining hall, and sat on opposite ends of it. When finally, the blue of the sea grew wine-dark, we would settle into our beds in the cabin, facing away from one another. And the next day, we would have it all to do again.

On the third morning, the bedside table was empty. But the remainder of the day carried on in much the same vein as the previous. The ship, having a finite number of places one could go, did little in the way of keeping us apart. In spite of this prolonged circumvention of one another, I missed him. Missed his smile and his laughter. His hands on me. More than once, I felt the whole thing a petty waste and made to end it. But his honey-eyed glare deterred me each time I tried.

On the fourth morning, I rose before him. In rest, his features—unburdened by awareness—were peaceful and pretty as jewels. They had gone days in contortion, molded by the influence of glares. It was nice to see them back as they were. I stared down at him, adopting the slow measure of his breaths. Without my noticing and as if drawn, I bent till his warmth brushed across my cheeks. I kissed his forehead. He stirred but did not rouse. His eyes remained closed, and a faint smile bloomed, tugging gently at the corners of his lips. I do not know how much longer he slept. Quickly thereafter, I left the cabin and resumed our routine.

………»·) ● (·(·………

That afternoon, there were fewer mortals than usual scattered about the deck. The previous night, there had been a storm, but now the skies were clear as the water. I stood leaning over the bow, humming a tune that I picked up from one of the other passengers. Some of them took to playing instruments after the evening meal to entertain themselves. The chords sounded unlike anything I had heard played in the taverns back in Ethelia. They carried a deeper, more melodious essence. Once heard, they were hard to forget.

"You don't know words? That one have beautiful words. Haneshi words."

I started and turned in a singular motion. Beside me, an older woman was smiling. I smiled back at her. She reminded me a little of the Alchemist from the festival—Mistress Dalmaa. She wore the same long braids and shared the same dark skin. I thought I had kept my humming low, but she was grinning as though she had been listening along for the entirety.

"No," I said, barely containing a bashful smile. "Do you know them?"

"Yes, yes, I know words."

"Will you sing them?"

She threw her head back laughing, then shook it, flailing her hands.

She pointed a finger at my lips. "This voice. Yours voice. I not have one so beautiful like that. Yours like gods. Sing more. I want keep hear."

I shook my head, shy of her flattering attentions. But she would not relent. She rummaged through her breast pocket, then snatched up my hand, foisting a few crescents into my palm to urge me along. I refused them but cleared my throat anyway and began to hum the tune. I thought it might be easier to oblige her if I pretended that her eyes were not on me, and so I closed mine as I went about the melody. There were portions of it I knew better than others, but she did not seem to notice. And if she had, she made no mention of it. Near the end, I found the courage to open my eyes again. She watched me hum the last chords with one hand pressed against her chest, swaying, grinning.

251

"I have heard it played merely a few times so forgive me if some parts were not correct," I said, averting my gaze. Even after having acquiesced, I still felt a lingering bout of diffidence hanging over me.

"I not knowing what that mean," she said and grabbed me with both hands. I thought she had intended to shove the crescents into my palm again, but instead, she clasped my hand in hers and gave it a gentle shake. "I name Oléina. Yours name?"

"I am Ambroz."

"*Ambruze?*"

I nodded, though this was the incorrect pronunciation. "Yes, right," I said.

She smiled and let go of my hand. "Where you go, in Hanesh?"

"I am—well, I am not sure. I have never been. First time." I spoke the words slowly, drawing out each one in the hopes she would find them easier to understand.

"Ah, not living in Hanesh before?"

"Yes, right. Never been."

"In Uorliék, I go."

"What?"

"Uorliék," she repeated. "Uorliék is…" she paused and began making elaborate gestures, drawing an invisible scene through the air. I followed along as best I could, somewhat bemused.

"Oh," I said after resonating with one motion in particular. "A city?"

Her brows soared like tiny birds above her eyes. "Yes! This mean Uorliék. You come in Uorliék. With me. In Hanesh?"

"You want me to come with you to Uorliék?"

She nodded. "Sing more. Learn words. I have shop. Smoke. Drink. Girls, boys who dance. You come sing there for crescents?"

I did not know what she meant by this and stumbled over my words trying to find an answer. After my third attempt at a reply, Oléina's attention began to drift. It settled somewhere off to the side of me. I followed the line of her gaze and found Varyn, peering at her over my shoulder. He was a few steps away and to my surprise, came closer upon my spotting him there. She greeted him, and he returned it in Haneshi. Oléina's brows became birds again.

A torrent of the language came tumbling from her lips. Varyn stood nodding as he listened, half-smiling. It was the first voluntary one I had seen from him in days. I watched the two of them converse till they paused, and each looked at me.

"She thinks you have a beautiful voice," said Varyn. "She wants you to come and work for her in Uorliék. It's a large merchant city. She says it's competitive and that a voice like yours would attract more patrons to her business."

"What sort of business?" I asked.

"It's hard to explain. From what she's described it's sort of like a tavern but not quite. It's a bit more formal. It's where the wealthy men and women of the area come for entertainment. And to spend crescents on…other attractions."

"Other attractions?"

"Beautiful men and women."

"Oh," I said. "I see."

"She thinks you're very beautiful and that it's rare for one with a face like yours to have a voice to go along with it. But she's offering her crescents for your voice. Just your voice. Sixty silver a night."

"Is that many?"

"Yes, it's quite a lot for what she's asking of you. All she wants is for you to sing—to learn a bit of Haneshi for the songs. She heard you humming, she said."

With this, he smirked. My skin warmed in spite of the cool breeze which rose from the sea and kissed it. "Well, I am—I have—"

Oléina began speaking again. She leaned to me, and placed her hand upon my shoulder. When she had finished, she looked expectantly at Varyn.

"She says you don't have to answer right away. You can think on it for the duration of the voyage. She's on the same deck as us. Her cabin is ten doors down from ours. When you've made your decision, she'd like for you to come and tell her."

"Very well," I said and nodded. Oléina clapped her hands together, then turned to Varyn and said a few more Haneshi words.

"She wants you to know that even if you decline, she'd still like for you to pay her a visit in Uorliék."

"Her shop. What is it called?"

He turned and asked her. "Qêl-Ceréi, it means jewel of the night."

I nodded and Oléina smiled. She said a word or two more to Varyn before taking her leave. I stared after her as she walked across the ship and watched till she disappeared below deck. Varyn remained standing beside me. We gazed awkwardly at one another, wind whipping through our hair. I had a mind to turn and go, but this urge was overcome by the desire to hear him speak to me with his own words, not Oléina's. And so I set aside my pride.

"Thank you for helping me talk to her," I said softly.

My meek outpouring of gratitude was met with a long pause. The hum of the ship treading upon the sea filled the empty air between us.

Finally, he said, "You're welcome. I had come to find you actually...I..." he sighed and tucked some of his hair behind his ear. "I suppose I have been behaving rather childishly."

These words were quietly out of him. I reached and swept more colorful hair from his face. It was wonderful to touch him again.

"Well," I said. "So too have I." He caught hold of my wrist. Rubbed circles round the inside of it with his thumb.

"It was wrong of me to make demands. If there are things you don't wish to share with me, then...then I shouldn't pressure you. I should not force it from you. Will you forgive me?"

I drew him into an embrace, relishing the feel of his body against mine, the feel of his arms around me. How could I have allowed such churlishness to steal these moments from me?

"Yes, of course I do. It was a petty thing to let it go on so long. I could have ended it at any time and yet...I will not keep it from you. If you wish to know what happened there, then I will tell you everything. I thought I was protecting you with my silence."

"Protecting me?"

"I did not want to burden you with it."

We broke from the embrace and he rested his hands upon my shoulders.

"You thought it would be better to have it all to bear yourself?"

I nodded, casting my gaze toward the sparkling sea. I could not look at him. But he made me, with a gentle nudge upon my chin. "Yes," I whispered.

"Have you learned nothing from all your losses?"

"What?"

"How many times have I beaten you jostling? You, above everyone, should know of my strength." He grinned and spun me around, twisting my arm behind my back. "See how easily I've overpowered you?"

There was nothing for me to do but chuckle. "Let me go," I said.

He obliged, and I turned to face him. "I'm stronger. There is no weight that is too heavy for me to carry," he said. "Whatever burdens you, Ambroz, from now on, let me help you carry it."

⸻⸻⸻ ◉ ⸻⸻⸻

From then on, we were back as we were. And in the evening, I told him everything. He listened with his brow set in firm consternation as he sat on the bed across from me.

"I wish you would have told me sooner. I would have held you all night," he said when I had come to the end of it. "And three against one. How did you manage that?"

"Scarcely. It was like a bout of oblivion had come over me."

"Like in the lower villages, the temple? The Emros?"

"Yes, exactly like that. I even pictured it, I think. The vagrant that is. Then the next moment, they were all burning."

"You must never go back there."

"I do not intend to."

"Your trials?"

"What of them? My life in that realm is over. I do not live by their order any longer. I will not. Trials, shades. I do not care for them. My only concern now is getting our flower to grow. And keeping you safe till it blooms."

His eyes fell on his chest of things, where he had stowed the Moonsoil after my return.

"Twelve years," he whispered, gaze lingering on the large case. "We will be men."

"We are already men."

"Proper men. Older, wiser."

"Twelve years is long, but it will be nothing in the face of eternity."

He tore his eyes from it, fixed them on me. "Do you really think it will work? That I will become an immortal?"

"Yes. I do not doubt it…wait. Do you not want it anymore? Are you having second thoughts?"

"No, not at all. I want this. More than anything. I want you. Forever. I just don't want to spend years chasing a false promise. The Hermit. Are you sure we can trust her?"

"There are not many things I am sure of, but she is one of them. I cannot say why, intuition perhaps. But I do not think we have anything to fear from her. Merely the others."

He nodded and let out a small yawn. The sight of it infected me. I let one of my own escape, stretching my limbs about the bed. "I meant to ask," I said. "What do you think of Oléina's offer? Should I go and sing for her?"

This sent him chuckling. "If I'm to tell the truth, I'm a bit jealous."

"Jealous?"

"From her descriptions, Qêl-Ceréi sounds rather nice. If you don't want to work there, I will take your place." He smirked and stroked his braid.

"So you think I should do it then?"

"I think it's good work. But it's up to you. If you want to do it, then I think you should."

"We will need crescents to help pay for things. You only have what you have saved from your sinecure."

"Yes, but I will have my own post as well. If I can garner more of an interest for my drawings aside from just the one dancer."

"Right, the merchant you were corresponding with. I forgot."

"It would do us good to have two sets of earnings though. With both of our crescents, we can afford to live in Oléina's merchant city. What's the name of it again?"

"Uorliék."

"That was a rather good pronunciation."

"Will you teach me Haneshi?"

"On one condition."

I stared across the cabin with raised brows. "Oh? And that is?"

He made me wait a while before answering, regarding me through slits. "If you are angry with me, shout. Scream at me. Curse me. Do anything but ignore me. Celine used to punish me with silence when we were younger. It drove me mad. You Cancerians are all the same. So stubborn."

I sighed. "You are one to talk. You glared at me for days!"

"Only because I was hurt!"

"You are quite handsome when you glare, actually."

He tried to glare at me but could not maintain a stoic bearing, and so the whole thing looked ridiculous and I laughed. "Tell me something," I said, settling beneath the covers. "On that first day of our row, when I came to join you on the deck—why were you laughing at me with the women?"

"We weren't laughing at you. *They* were laughing at *me*. At something I said."

"What did you say?"

"The one who spoke to you, she said you were pretty and that it was a pity you could only understand High Celestian. Then in a joking manner, I told her she was only allowed to look at you one more time because you were my lover and not hers."

Heat bloomed across my cheeks. I flung the covers off myself and beckoned him.

He came to me.

Chapter 42

HALFWAY INTO OUR JOURNEY, I RETURNED ONE EVENING to the cabin and found a letter resting in the center of my bed. I had not seen Varyn for much of the day. We were both weary of being at sea. Him more than me, I think. He was one used to variety, and going about to seek it whenever he wished. But there could be none of that on the water.

We were, in a way, captives. The most exciting thing we had done here thus far was meet the captain. She was from Ethelia—a pleasant woman of middle age. She took a liking to Varyn. Most who met him did. Out of courtesy, she showed us round her quarters and let us see her method of keeping on course. Varyn tried to hide his sulking when we learned there had been a navigation mishap which would add more days to our journey. But I could read displeasure on him easily. From the back of his head, I would know it—or from his posture or gait. He had corrected himself before she took notice however, and asked her about the workings of the ship to further distract from his petulance.

Already I was in awe of mortal carriages, but the ships were an even grander feat. Much of what she told us, I did not understand. Though Varyn listened to her explanations of industrial transport crystals and Luminary steering with the temperament of one well-versed on the subject. I struggled to see how the workings of the large vessel differed in any way from magic. Mortals were possessed of their own godhead, it seemed. It was all around me, here on this hulking carriage of the sea. Even my cabin, floating along the water without its contents toppling over, amazed me. Inside it, I unfolded the letter and took a seat upon the bed. My heart quickened at the discovery of Varyn's neat writing. I admired the shape and elegant curves of his words first before reading them, swelling with anticipation.

Dearest Ambroz,

You seem not to have noticed that your birthday has come and gone. Perhaps you are as weary of this journey as I am and have given up keeping record of the time. Can't say I fault you for it. I long to be off this ship. How great it would be to walk through the merchant cities of Hanesh. I see it vividly in my mind. I imagine you donned in Haneshi fashions more and more these days. It sounds silly, I know, but who can help the thoughts in their mind? The man who has accomplished that is a man deserving of envy. Well, when the moment we are walking on Haneshi land finally arrives, I suppose our time confined to this cabin on the water will make it that much sweeter. My father used to say things like that to lessen unpleasantness. I don't know why I just wrote that. Stars. This is my third attempt at this letter, and I'm not starting it over again, so just pretend you haven't read that bit.

Anyway. You are nineteen now. Finally, you have caught up with me (teasing). This letter is all I can give you for a gift. I was rather down about that for a while because I wanted you to have a proper celebration. You have had so few of those. Do you remember the dance we shared at the festival? I have been thinking of that quite a bit lately. I almost kissed you that night. I had so much mead. Sometimes I wish I had gone for it. For seasons I relived that moment in my head. But looking back on it, I'm glad I didn't. The forest was the best place to have kissed you for the first time. I will never forget that day. I came alive then. My thoughts are everywhere. I swear I had them better sorted than this. What I wanted to tell you is that there will be a gathering on the top deck tonight with instruments and other merriment. Some of the passengers have even brought along spirits. Come and find me on the deck after you've read this. I want to dance with you again, like we did that night.

And this time, I will kiss you.

All my love,
Varyn

I held the letter to my chest, grinning like a youth with a fistful of sweets. On my second read of it, the grin widened. My cheeks began to ache and instead of reading it a third time, I merely sat tracing my fingers along the words. It seemed such a simple thing to remember one's own birthday, yet I had forgotten it. But Varyn did not. Why should something so insignificant bring me this much joy? It was like an intoxicant from the Nebula Gardens, the effect he had on me. I loved to feel it.

I tucked the letter away with my things, remnants of a grin still painted upon my lips. Sounds of the gathering above could be heard as I made my way through the ship. The melodies greeted me long before I stepped foot on the deck. The Cancerian season was often warm and there had been many hot days on board. Though now, the night air was cool against my skin, chilled by the Scorpion Sea.

The above deck looked the liveliest I had ever seen it. Nearly every corner of it was occupied by a mortal. Some stood conversing, others eating and drinking. But most were on their feet dancing. I searched among them for Varyn. I did not have to stand seeking for very long. He was waiting for me.

"There you are. Happy birthday." His voice greeted me from behind. He stared, grinning, and stood balancing two nearly overflowing cups of Zèkhei in his hands. I relieved him of one. He pushed gently against the small of my back. His touch guided me toward a partially secluded spot near the bow. A strip of bench rested there and we each lowered ourselves onto it.

"Your letter," I said, leaning to him. "It was beautiful." He blossomed beneath the praise and sipped on his Zèkhei, peering at me from behind the rim.

"Have a sip of your Zèkhei. I put a little surprise in there for you."

"Oh? What sort of surprise?" I took a sip and was answered in taste. The usual sweetly spiced cream of the Zèkhei had been overtaken by another flavor. Strong spirits lined the back of my throat—I half-winced, half-giggled as it went down.

"Too strong? It's a Haneshi festival drink. Rather concentrated compared to anything you'd find in Ethelia."

"It is…" I swallowed down more of it, "rather intense. I like it. Is this another of my gifts?" Soft winds blew our hair about our heads, and we grinned, each smoothing the other's back into place.

"When I have sold my drawings, for your next birthday, I will lavish you in the finest Haneshi silks. Wait and see."

I glanced up at the stars, still grinning, and imagined it. He slid closer to me. I draped my arm round him, craving even more proximity.

"You said the forest was the best place to have kissed me for the first time. Why?"

"Because," he drank more of his Zèkhei, "it's home to so many of our firsts. The first time I ever saw you, raced you, swam with you."

"The first time you ever beat me in a match," I added.

He smirked. "Yes, that too."

"I will miss it there. Our Crescent Forest."

"We'll make another like it then, in Hanesh. Somewhere only for us."

I shook my head. "No, it cannot be replaced. The things we are most fond of never can be."

"A home then. Will you be fond of that?"

"Anything shared with you is a fondness to me."

He pulled me to my feet and gulped down the rest of his Zèkhei. I finished mine as I walked with him to a more inhabited area of the deck. The drink had warmed me and loosened my limbs. I had never found dancing so easy or pleasurable. I was ignorant of the steps, but I did not care. I had Varyn to guide me, to catch me when I faltered. It was a gift to be in his arms, dancing under a sea of stars. We carried on all night till the sounds of songs and instruments waned. Till there was only the melody of waves battering against the ship—the whisper of the floating breeze. We stood amidst it all, swaying together.

He drew me in and, just as he promised me in his letter, kissed me.

·······›·) ◉ (·‹·········

I had given a great deal of thought to Oléina's offer over the long course of our voyage. I think Varyn had grown tired of my asking his opinion on the matter. Over and over, I had consulted him. Each time, his answer was the same. He was too kind a person to tell me off or dismiss me. He knew of my shyness—knew that I plagued him with these unabating questions because of it. I could not envision myself singing before the eyes of strangers night after night.

Yet there was a small part of me that wanted the attention, I admit. During one of my interrogations, Varyn reminded me of a time when we were boys of twelve—of when I had sung to the melody of his

Lerawyn at the academy. He told me I beamed then. And that Qêl-Ceréi would be no different than that afternoon at his lessons. But I confessed to him it was the knowledge of him watching me that had made me beam.

"If you accept the post, I will come and watch you then," he had said that evening as I sat braiding his hair. "Every night, I will come."

This eased me, and on one of the final days of the journey, I had at last arrived at my decision.

Chapter 43

OLÉINA FLUNG THE DOOR OF HER CABIN OPEN AFTER a single knock. She pulled me inside the instant her eyes fell on me, lips splitting into a wide grin.

"You come tell me answer for singing my Qêl-Ceréi?"

I nodded. "Yes. I want to sing for you. I will do it."

She clasped her hands together and said many words which I did not understand. I assumed they were an expression of gratitude. I should have had Varyn along to accompany me but he had taken to sleeping later and later. The long days at sea were wearing on him. After hearing my decision, Oléina went rifling through her things. Her cabin was twice the size of ours, and her chests and cases were ornately made. I had not noticed it at first, but her garments, too, were of a fine quality. Her smile never left her as she sorted through her possessions. If these had been my accommodations for the length of the journey, I think I might also have worn a perpetual grin.

"I find. Look here. My Qêl-Ceréi," she said as she turned to me, thrusting a colorful leaflet into my hands. "Here you sing."

I gazed down at it. There were many symbols and words which I could not understand. They were of the same sort written on the square that accompanied my little moon—the one Varyn had won me. A large, golden illustration of an opulent, domed structure took up the majority of the space. I flipped it over and found more foreign writing.

"This is Qêl-Ceréi?" I asked.

"Yes, yes."

"It is beautiful. Very nice."

"Take to other one." I glanced up at her, unsure of what she meant. She raised a hand to her head and smoothed it over her hair, then pointed at a gold band on her finger. The fat jewel resting inside of it was a vibrant red. It took her repeating the action a few more times before I finally understood its meaning.

"Oh, you mean Varyn?"

She snapped her fingers and pointed at the leaflet. "Yes. Ethelian names, easy forget. Take to him. To *Varun*. He's knows Haneshi words."

"I will show him."

"Good, good. Come back if want know more."

With this she dismissed me, guiding me toward the door through the use of gentle pushes against my back. After having left, I wandered to the top deck and idled there. It was getting hotter by the day, and I dashed for the first spot of shade I could find. Shielded from the sun, I gazed down at the leaflet of my future post.

Qêl-Céréi, if this was what it truly looked like, seemed a charming, if not exotic, oasis. My fingers traced the shape of its dome. I sat imagining what the inside might consist of—envisioned its chattels and patrons, and for the first time, wondered about my place among the mortals there. Varyn knew their language already. But how long would it take me to learn it? It was strange that mortals had so many different ways of communicating. I had never given any thought to the nuances of their existence. No Celestial did. But every day spent drifting on this ship separated me further from those memories—the ones of courts and wings, of power and shades. I felt less and less like a god.

It surprised me how readily I welcomed the surrender.

When I had all but burned the illustration of Qêl-Céréi in my mind from prolonged staring, I turned it over and thought of Varyn.

A yearning to know what meaning that foreign writing held is what moved me from the cool shade of the deck.

Down in the cabin, Varyn was yawning himself awake, sitting in the center of his bed. I had stopped by the dining hall on the way, thinking some warm Zèkhei would sweeten the disturbance of his rest. But I did not have to disturb him. He had risen of his own accord.

"Good morning," he said as I entered. His eyes fell on the cup, and I offered it to him.

"It is afternoon now."

He grunted, then slipped the Zèkhei from my hands. As he began drinking, I took a seat beside him. Right away, his gaze settled on the leaflet.

"What's this?"

"Qêl-Ceréi. I went to visit Oléina, and she gave it to me. I was hoping you could translate it for me."

"Yes, of course. You've decided then?"

"I told her I would come and work there. She seemed pleased."

Now it was Varyn who seemed pleased. He tore his eyes from the colorful Qêl-Ceréi, fixing them on me instead. Smiling, he said, "I'm proud of you."

"Proud? What for?"

"You're so shy. It's what I love about you. But with this, you're forcing yourself from that Cancerian shell of yours." He nudged me with his shoulder, and I hid the slow growth of a grin behind my fingers, chin against chest. But I was drawn from my retreat as his lips sought mine. I let him kiss me, tasting on him the sweet warmth of Zèkhei.

"Well," I said. "What does it say?"

He took his time going over it, sipping in between glances. Anticipation simmered in my chest as I watched him studying the leaflet. "Stars, her services are expensive," he muttered, still reading through narrowed eyes.

"What sort of services?"

"She's got one for the whim and fancy of every individual that exists, it seems." He was half-grinning. "I don't fault you for your shyness now."

"Why not?" I peered down at the leaflet as though I had somehow gained the ability to understand its contents.

"These services are…something."

"Tell me what they are," I urged.

"It's interesting. Some are quite ordinary, just company and polite, flattering conversation with a pretty man or woman, they are learned of many languages it says. Apparently, she employs about fifty of them. She offers private dances from one or more. Some are trained in card reading and fortune telling. A few are possessed of Nerosi talents. Some in hypnosis. Others can read the lines of palms."

"Oh? And the not-so-ordinary services. What are those like?"

"Pleasure."

"What is so extraordinary about pleasure?"

"Well, being pleasured, I should say. And that in itself is nothing out of the way, only, the methods are…rather odd." He pointed to the first words on the leaflet. "Some of these ones are normal enough, warm oil massages and the like. You could find similar fare in Ethelia. But the list progresses onto other things—whipping, bondage. Pleasure under hypnosis. One of the most expensive options includes five or six of her prettiest workers. For the price listed, they'll strip you naked while they themselves remain covered in garments and take turns slapping you around. Then, at the end, they'll massage you to," he drew the leaflet close to his face, "satisfaction. That's what it says here, along with an option to inquire within for a more exclusive version."

The description left me speechless and gaping. "I think I might have been better off not knowing any of this."

"Oh, come, it's not so bad. You likely won't encounter any of it. All you'll be doing is singing in the main room. That's what I gather from the description."

"The main room?"

"It's where the instruments are. Says here that's where they keep company—mix with one another. It's how the selection begins. Think of it like a tavern only larger, and with more to do than just drink. From what I've read, Qêl-Ceréi is many things in one, rather convenient actually."

I plucked the leaflet from him, gazing at this supposed jewel of the night, imagining the goings on inside. I almost laughed at the absurd visions I came up with.

"You can always change your mind, you know? If this doesn't suit you," said Varyn. "Just tell her you've had me explain everything to you and now—"

"No. I want to. As you said, I need to come out of my shell. This will help."

"You're sure?"

"Yes. Certain."

He raised an eyebrow, then leaned. I thought he meant to kiss me, but instead, he took the leaflet from my hands.

"Do you know, perhaps we should try one of these together when—"

I snatched it from him and made for the door, ignoring his teasing and laughter.

············»·› ● ‹·«·········

On a hot evening, near the middle of the Leo season, Varyn and I busied ourselves with packing up the cabin. We were set to arrive in Hanesh the following afternoon. I could scarcely believe it. At times, I felt the journey would never end. It had been the longest season ever endured by either of us.

"When we dock and are on land again, I'm going to run and jump. You won't catch me sitting down for at least another season," said Varyn, stuffing his belongings into the chest. He lifted a small pile in the corner of the case to make more room, and I caught a glimpse of the urn. I kneeled—reached for it. As I opened it, he paused to watch me peer into the dark mouth.

The Moonsoil was just as I had left it that day, brown and brimming, flecked through with bits of gold. With the sight of it came a rush of remembrance—of feelings. My heart began to race. My mouth became dry as bone. Before I knew it, Varyn was at my side, lifting me by the arm. Once he seated me on the bed, he took the urn from my hands and buried it beneath his belongings where it had been.

"It's the smell," he said. "That is what's bringing it all back to you. Sometimes, our senses turn on us. Don't linger with your face so near it again. You're not yet healed enough for that. You need more time to separate yourself from what happened."

He came and sat beside me. I had not known I was trembling till he placed his hand over mine. One touch from him and I could breathe again. I tried to speak, to give a word of thanks, or at the least, acknowledgment. But my voice had left me, vanishing like the sun behind clouds of a storm. He did not need to hear it. I rested my head on his shoulder and his arms came round me, folded me into his warmth.

"You never have to touch it. Not until you're ready. When we get to Uorliék, when we find our home, I will plant it. I already have a place in mind. Your Oléina gave me a list of them that cater to foreigners. We'll see as many as we can tomorrow. Turns out Uorliék isn't too far from the port. Not even a full day's journey by carriage."

There were so many things I wanted to say, but my voice remained behind those clouds. We were already pressed near, but I held him tighter to me, burrowing my face into his neck. Breathing breathing breathing him in.

"They will never hurt you again," he whispered. "For as long as I live."

He kept on holding me there, stroking my hair, my back. I could have stayed nesting under that golden warmth for all eternity, but I forced myself from it and continued packing up the cabin alongside him.

He urged me to retire to bed mere moments into the task. I went, though I had not been weary enough for rest. But all of that changed as my head met the soft mound of cushion. From the comfort of it, I watched his back as he worked, loose curls tumbling down its length. I fought against the heavy curtains of flesh till they narrowed to slits. Through the strip, I saw a blur of his vibrant, copper hair and thought of how nice it would have been to braid it for him.

⋯⋯⊶⟩⟩ ✹ ⟨⟨⊷⋯⋯

I slept well, and later, woke to a firm hand upon my shoulder, shaking me. Bright sunlight shone through the small windows of the cabin. It would be the last morning either of us ever spent here.

"We're close to arriving," said Varyn, barely able to contain his grin. "How do you feel?"

Rest had rid me of my worries. "Better. Much better."

"Good. Come and wash. Then we can take our meal in the dining hall. The last one we'll have on this cursed ship and thank the stars for that." He had all but skipped through the cabin doors, leaving me blinking and stretching.

Though the ship had grown on me, I could not help being affected by his cheerful disposition, and became just as eager to leave it. When I had washed and dressed, I found him already eating at the table.

"I wonder what Hanesh will be like," I said between bites and sips.

Varyn smirked. "I talked to the captain earlier. I've been up for quite a while. She said the winds were favorable and that we're ahead of the course. We'll be there any moment. You won't have to wonder. You'll be walking the streets soon, breathing the hot air. I can hardly wait."

268

Nor could he sit in idle. No sooner had the last sip of Zèkhei traveled down his throat than was he on his feet, pacing the hall. When I finished my meal, he suggested we collect our things and head for the departing area of the ship.

Later, I was grateful for his enthusiasm, for I had not gone through the boarding process and was unaware how crowded the passageway leading to the gate would be. Already a horde of passengers had gathered there. Varyn and I were swallowed by the throng of eager mortals upon our approach. We moved in slow increments, pressed shoulder to shoulder as the line went along. Each of us was meant to depart during a specific time, but it seemed none of the passengers had abided by this instruction—their tolerance of cramped quarters had dwindled. The long days on board did little to engender further patience.

After shouldering through the crush of bodies, endless chatter, wailing children, and weary huffs, Varyn and I stepped off the ship that had housed us for more than a season and walked into the dry heat of Hanesh.

Chapter 44

I THOUGHT I KNEW HEAT. I THOUGHT I KNEW THE SUN. Neither of them had ever conspired to suffocate me in Ethelia. But in Hanesh, they seemed to be doing just that.

"By the stars, I think we're wearing too many garments," said Varyn. He stripped off a layer of his and used the cloth to wipe the sweat from his brow. I was tempted to do the same, but I had been wearing less than him, and would be left partially naked if I had done. Instead, I took up the handle of Varyn's case and helped him carry it through the busy seaport. Eventually, the dense crowd thinned and we found ourselves stepping into the center of a bustling street, lined on either side with merchants.

Several of them approached us, rattling off in Haneshi, offering what I could only assume were the goods they had for sale. Along the narrow streets hung woven tapestries, herbs, ornaments of gold and silver.

Sweet-smelling smoke hung heavy in the air. Men and women dashed out of the way of quickly moving carriages, which themselves bore intricate, jeweled designs. Varyn stood beside me, conversing in a rapid flow of Haneshi with one of the merchants, each tossing animated gestures at the other. I would have believed them to be engaging in a heated argument were it not for their pleasant expressions. Swiftly my awareness of their interaction drifted to explore the sights around me. In the distance, resting at the far end of the street, sat a structure with many domes and pillars. Thin towers of ivory speared from some portions—their gold tips stretching up to meet the sky.

Somewhere nearby, a crate had toppled over, spilling its contents onto the streets. I watched as both fruits and jars tumbled down the way, till my attention was drawn to the smooth, rounded obsidian they rolled atop. The whole path was inlaid with the flat, rich stone. The surrounding beauty did much in the way of distracting me from the sweltering climate. I had been so beguiled by it that I failed to hear Varyn as he spoke beside me. He spun me gently by the shoulder till I faced him. I think I had been gaping, for he chuckled upon meeting my eyes.

"Sorry, what?" I asked.

"I've found someone with a carriage. He's agreed to take us into Uorliék for a few crescents. It's not far from here. There's an inn we can settle into for the night. We'll get there by sundown, maybe a bit sooner."

I nodded and followed him down the busy streets, pausing every so often to admire a merchant's display. So many things drew my eye, I would have liked to have crescents of my own to trade for them. Perhaps it was merely the novelty of being in a foreign land, but everything I encountered charmed me. Even the transport, of which I had already been familiar.

Haneshi carriages were loftier than the ones I had ridden in Ethelia. We loaded our belongings first and had plenty of room to sit comfortably beside one another. As soon as I climbed inside, a wave of relief swept over me. The choking heat had gone, and in its place, cool air caressed my skin. A perpetual flurry of it flowed about the carriage like a breeze. I thought perhaps I had imagined these pleasant conditions but when I looked over at Varyn, his bright curls stirred as if caught in mild winds.

"Ah, that's better," said Varyn, sighing and tilting his head back. "Thank the stars for these clever Haneshi inventions."

"Is that where all the cool air is coming from, an invention?" I asked. "Where is it? I cannot see anything."

Varyn leaned forward and began conversing with the owner of the carriage. The man pointed at something that a partition had obstructed from my view. Then he motioned a finger upward at the low ceiling. Strange bars like minuscule pillars were scattered about it in sections.

"How brilliant," said Varyn, placing a hand over them. "They call it a cooling crystal. It's the same sort mined for running the carriage. Except they've found a way to use the sun's light to power it, then that power is harnessed to distribute energy around the carriage, it comes out as air through these small blowers built into the carriage walls. He claims there are larger ones for use in homes and taverns—says that Leo and Cancer season are an absolute torture without them."

He had told me once when we were younger about crystals and their uses. I had failed to understand it then, and I did not understand it now. But the cool air was a pleasure against my hot skin, and like Varyn, I thanked the stars for it.

Along our ride, the comfortable temperature of the carriage, coupled with its progression down flat, cobbled roads, evoked drowsiness in me. It crept, silent as still water. Before I knew it, I had been lulled into a state of near tranquility. Several times, the slumber-seeking, forward nod of my head was jolted backward, thrusting me into full awareness. I fought against the draw of rest through sheer impetus of will, till finally, I surrendered to the pull of equanimity and drifted.

⋯⋯⋯≫⋅❁⋅≪⋯⋯⋯

Gentle fingers ruffling through my hair is what woke me. When I peeled my eyes open, I discovered the scorching yellow rays of the Haneshi sun had greatly diminished. The sky was as colorful as one of Varyn's drawings, streaked through with an amalgam of soft, scarlet hues.

"We're nearly there," said Varyn, still stroking my temple. "We've arrived in Uorliék already, just a bit further to the inn."

I covered my mouth to trap the yawn which threatened to escape. "If you keep kneading your fingers through my hair like that, I am going to fall back asleep."

He did not stop but merely found a more pleasurable pattern to smooth into the back of my scalp. I seized his hand in the end to stop his teasing and tickled the inside of his palm. Just as I was beginning to enjoy this torment, the carriage stopped. I swept the short curtain aside to peer at our new city. The light of many ornate lanterns competed with one another, suspended by drawn ropes all about the tall structures of Uorliék. In spite of its vast landscape, many of the roads were narrow, and so too were its buildings, all densely packed together like trees in a forest. I stepped out of the carriage, and under my feet, the smooth obsidian gave way to dirt, though in some stretches it remained.

Varyn paid the escort his crescents while I unloaded our things. The sun had nearly disappeared, and the beginnings of a lively night took shape before me.

Spirited sounds of taverns spilled out of entryways in brief waves as patrons came and went. Above the door of our inn hung Father's likeness. I half-shuddered as I walked over the threshold.

But as far as inns went, this one carried about it an elegance. Ribbons of sweet-smelling smoke danced beneath my nose while warm light glowed from embellished lanterns. Inside, Varyn conversed with the matron, each of them escalating in volume with every word exchanged. When they ascended to what sounded like the pinnacle of their voices, I leaned to him.

"Is there trouble?" I whispered.

"I'm trying to make certain our room has one of those cooling crystals. She thinks we'll be able to manage without one, and I told her I'd sooner sleep on the roof than in this heat."

I nodded, all too aware of his frustration. Nights were cooler than days but I had a feeling that in Hanesh, the air would be stifling, no matter if Moon or Sun reigned the skies. They continued on with their loud negotiation. I had never seen Varyn fail to obtain his desires, and tonight was no different. He came away with a key, wearing a satisfied smirk.

"The room will be cool, but there's only one bed," he said as we walked down the corridors. "The other two vacancies had more space and *two* beds, but neither had crystals. This one cost a fraction of the crescents she wanted for those other hot graves. I think she was counting on my Ethelian ignorance. No Haneshi citizen of sound mind would choose an inferno with two beds over an oasis with one."

"She was trying to turn a profit."

"At the expense of my sanity."

"Our sanity."

He flashed another of his wily smirks at me and shoved the key into the lock. The chilled air greeted us as soon as the door swung open. Varyn met it with outstretched arms, tossing his head back. He flung himself onto the bed and sighed up at the ceiling. I shut the door and stood near him, taking in the space. After so long confined to the small quarters of the cabin, the Uorliék inn was like a palace. Varyn stretched his limbs about the bed, back arching off it.

"It's large enough to accommodate both of us, so long as you sleep holding me."

"Perhaps I do not want to merely sleep."

He sat up, grinning, then took hold of my wrist, dragging me down onto the bed with him. I went without protest. Once I lay beside him, his fingers crept along my neck. He tickled the sensitive column of my throat, and any attempts at retaliation were thwarted by his lips enveloping mine. I took my fill and pulled away, leaving him panting. He murmured something against my neck, his mouth open and hot.

"Later," I said. "First, I want to have a wash and scour this journey and all its heat off my skin."

"We can always wash together."

I smirked, and we did as he suggested, among many other things.

Afterward, I sat upon the bed, drowsy, clean, and sated, watching him braid his damp hair. He perched himself on the jutting ledge of the window and looked out at the sights below. For a moment, it felt like we were twelve again, sharing a room—me admiring him from my cot of blankets and him, far, so far away from me. But that breadth stood crossed now. He was here. He was mine. Always he would be.

I stared at his hands as they worked to knit his braid, already dreaming them on me again, despite the pleasure they had moments ago granted. When he had come to the end of it, he turned and walked from the window, twirling his finger round the curling tail. At the opposite end of our room was a desk and chair. He sat behind it, pulling out a drawer and retrieving from the compartment some writing materials.

"What are you doing?" I asked.

"I promised Celine I'd write to her once we'd arrived in my last letter. She's already gone a season without correspondence. She couldn't send a reply to your inn since we wouldn't have been there to receive it."

"But we have no permanent residence here. Not yet."

"I know. That's why we must find one as soon as possible, so that she'll have an address to send her responses to. I just want to get my thoughts out while they're still ripe. I'll wait until we've settled somewhere to actually send it."

I nodded, though his back was to me as he wrote. "Give her my regards. Tell her she is sorely missed."

"Of course. She'll be happy to hear it. She's always been fond of you."

"And I her." I rose and went to gaze out of the window, peering down at the scenery of Uorliék's night. "Perhaps you should send one to your father as well. I think a season away might have been long enough for him to see that his treatment of you was unjust."

"No."

"You are still angry with him then?"

"Why shouldn't I be? He's behaved like a proper ass. Throwing his own son—his own *blood* out into the streets like waste, all because I did something he didn't like. Mother would never have allowed that. She was right to leave him that first time. I hope Celine leaves him, too. Let him rot in that manor all alone."

I said nothing. He had a right to his anger. It would be a lie to say that I had not harbored some of my own toward Lord Vedlan after what he had done. And though I felt Varyn was justified in his ire, I still hoped one day there might be a reconciliation between them. Varyn had lost a mother already. It pained me to see him lose a father, too. I saw a great deal of my own father in Lord Vedlan, but unlike the Devil, there were better qualities hidden within him—ones I knew Varyn cherished and that cherished him in turn. But I set these thoughts aside as I stood opposite the window, for its view offered a distraction from them, and I welcomed it.

Below, it was the bright-colored garments of wandering Haneshi men and women that caught my attention. They were a winsome people, thick-haired and deep-skinned. The sounds of their language and laughter floated up to meet me. I only wish I knew what they were saying. Briefly, I considered asking Varyn for a lesson on basic words but decided to leave him to his letter.

Far beneath me, some vibrant flowers drew my eye as I made to turn away from the window. We were in a corner room, and a dense bed of them rested to the furthermost line of my vision. I followed the sight of their fanning petals, craning my neck till I could no longer see them. Mourning the loss, I opened the window and shoved my head through the aperture. At once, the smug heat assaulted me, but I ignored it, leaning as far as the gap would allow. I saw more flowers poking up from their bed of brown. They covered a path along the inn, reaching its outermost edge. I was half out of the window by now and it took that for me to realize that what I beheld was merely a small portion of a much larger garden.

"Will you close that cursed window? You're letting all the cool air out. What are you doing hanging out of it like that anyway?"

At this scolding, I abandoned my view. "Sorry," I muttered, drawing the window shut.

"What were you doing?" asked Varyn. He was on his feet now, folding the letter.

"Nothing, something pretty caught my eye. I was trying to get a better look."

He nodded with divided attention, still putting creases in his letter. "Do you want to go out? Are you hungry?"

"No, are you?"

"A bit. And I could do with a little walking after so long on the ship."

"I might have shared those sentiments earlier, then I arrived here and felt myself cooking in that heat. Now all I want is to stay indoors, where the air is cool."

His shoulders rose and fell in alignment with his chuckle. "Can't say I fault you for it. Do you mind if I go out?"

"No, go on."

"You're sure?"

"I will be fine."

He pressed a kiss onto my cheek, stashed his letter, then pocketed the room key and left. I went to the window again, watching him make his way through the city crowds till he vanished from my view. I returned my sights to the garden, wondering what it was that had captivated me so. My thoughts strayed, ambling along aimlessly. Soon, they found their way to the urn. I glanced over at Varyn's chest on the floor and knew at once why I had been so drawn to those bright flowers.

Chapter 45

I SAT UPON THE EDGE OF THE BED, CLUTCHING THE urn in my hands. After what happened on the ship, I was wary of removing the seal. Why this sudden aversion? I had made my escape. They could not hurt me. Not here. But this knowledge did not stop my hand from trembling as it hovered over the opening. I closed my eyes and steadied it, along with my breaths.

If Varyn were here, he would come and hold me—tell me that I am safe. A part of me wished he would burst through the door and rescue me from this torment. But another was glad of his absence—grateful that he could not witness my coming apart at the hands of something inanimate. I glared at the urn, hating to feel this humiliation wrapping hands around my throat, choking me, taunting me.

I clutched it tighter, feeling a quickening of my pulse and the harsh beating of blood. It pounded in my ears like a drum. To know that sight alone had caused this panicked turmoil infuriated me. But I would not sit here and let it brew—let it build. I tore the seal from the urn and flung it to the floor. Wary, downcast eyes met its contents, challenging the pile of rich, brown earth. Varyn had warned me not to smell it. But who were my senses to betray me? Was I without both divinity *and* self-sovereignty? Could I not even control this?

Yes, I could. *I would.* This much, I decided as I fought down the mounting frenzy within me, bringing the urn up till it was level with my chin. The scents of our realm, of that day, came pouring out at me. To ward it off, I turned my head, stared down at the ornate rug on the floor, and clenched my eyes shut. But behind them, I saw Uncle, Arcana, the Hanged Man—saw all their light flooding out at once to singe my flesh. I peeled them open and heard now the sound of their voices. Their threats and taunts echoed in my ears. With shallow breaths I rose and looked about the room. Found it empty. My unrest grew talons—hooked me through.

"Enough!" I shouted. I had not meant to yell. But as I shrieked, the voices quieted, my breaths evened. The talons withdrew. Sight and sound plagued me no longer. A ruse it had been. A phantom of my own making. All of it in my head. None of it real. Emboldened, I seized a fistful of Moonsoil from the urn, brought it to my nose. It still carried the scent of my realm. But my breaths remained steady. My heart did not quicken. A triumph.

I thought of the garden outdoors as the Moonsoil rested in my palm. To drift there would be so simple, so effortless. Like breathing. Impulse led me. I followed it. The inn dissolved, and I stood gazing at those pretty flowers I had seen from above.

Outside, the smothering heat of Haneshi air was more oppressive than I had anticipated. But I did not care. I had stumbled upon the perfect spot. It was naked of flowers as if it had been waiting there for me all along.

I returned my palmful to its urn, then knelt and patted the bare earth. Quickly, I bore into it with my fingers, parting the soft dirt, on and on, till I made a hollow. Inside, I filled it with a small amount of Moonsoil.

Resting against the wall of the garden was a pail of water. I remembered the Hermit's instruction. *Water every six seasons.* I reached for it, pouring onto the bed of earth a mere splash. Before me, the dirt shimmered gold—a brief, bright flash flared within it. I whipped my head in every direction to make certain no mortals had been lingering to witness the spell take root. They had not. It was done. With the distraction of excitement gone, the stifling heat made its presence known again. A longing for the coolness of the inn took hold of me. I imagined myself there, feeling the chill of relief. My return was swift, and I sighed as the breeze of our quarters surrounded me.

Varyn's chest sat upon the floor, thrown open as I had left it. I tucked the urn back inside it and lay sprawled across the bed. The exertion of reliving my attack came pummeling down on me. My body felt as though I had raced through Hanesh's hot night without pause.

I do not know when I drifted or for how long I slept. Only that an arm slipping round my waist is what stirred me. I turned, still half-asleep, and breathed in the scent of Varyn. The Uorliék air and heat had clung to his skin, his hair—it radiated off him. Remnants of my dreams swirled in my head as I burrowed my face into his neck, seeking its comfort.

"I didn't mean to wake you," whispered Varyn.

I lingered, inhaling. "You did not—not entirely, anyway." Reluctantly, I left the warmth of his neck and squinted through the dim light of a single lantern. It shone on his vibrant, auburn hair, turning him into a beacon of the night. "No, actually, that was a lie. Now that I have seen your bright head, I fear full awareness has come back to me. It is like a sun in this room."

He flashed a wolfish grin. "Then I will shield it from you at once and bury it between your legs." With a sleepy smile, I lifted an arm to swat at him, but he caught my hand, brought it to his lips.

"How did you find the city? Did you enjoy walking about it?" I asked.

He nodded, staring at my hand as he fondled it. "Yes. I acquainted myself with the area, ate and drank a bit, then took a carriage to Qêl-Ceréi. It's not far. I think you will like it there, from what I saw of it anyway. I didn't go in, but the outside is a grand sight—that parchment didn't do it proper justice," he turned the corners of his mouth down as he studied my hand, still stroking it. "Why is there so much dirt beneath your fingernails?"

I stared at the thick layers under each of them. "That garden out there," I said. "It called to me. After you went out, I had this urge to plant the Moonsoil. It was like it had been on the ship—at first, I felt nothing but terror as I looked inside it, but then, my fears fell away, almost as if by magic. Once that happened, I went and...I did it. It took only moments. Of course we will have to plant more elsewhere, but this night, that garden. It felt fitting. I cannot say why."

Each of us now was staring at the state of my nails. Varyn kept quiet as he lay beside me and gently began plucking the brown layers from underneath them.

"Tomorrow," he said, "we will leave the inn early and go in search of quarters of our own. I picked up something tonight that will help us. It won't be difficult to find lodgings, not in a city this large. Then we can plant more of it there. The sooner, the better."

"I was thinking, once we find somewhere permanent, I want to go back to Ethelia and leave some there as well."

He grimaced. "You want to get back on a ship?"

"No, no. Not at all," I said, placing two fingers upon my temple. "Now that I have seen Hanesh, well, I can move between here and Ethelia easily."

His scowl faded. "Oh, right. But why go there at all?"

"The Hermit said it would be wise to disperse the harvests. I think it wiser to scatter them diversly, across vast distances of the mortal realm."

"I hadn't thought of that. Where in Ethelia will you leave it?"

"Crescent Forest. It will have plenty of sunlight there."

He smiled, and I found it hard to resist mirroring him. I let one of my own spread. "I suppose that's the perfect place to grow an eternity," said Varyn.

In the half-light of our room, his eyes shone like bright stars. Their honeyed hazel gleamed. I gazed into those golden pools of warmth and imagined forever with him.

"What will you miss about being mortal?"

"What is there to miss? Death? It's a mercy to avoid it."

"But others will not avoid it. Celine, your father. All those you meet and befriend will not be spared from mortality. Only you."

"And you," he said. "You will be spared from it. If I have you, then I have everything."

My smile widened. I loved to hear him say such things. He laced his fingers through mine and kissed them. "But you are sure you want this, Varyn? The mortals you love. You will not see them again."

"Who says I will not? I have seen my mother. When I go to rest every night, I see her. Beyond the veil, she is well and happy. They say that's what it means when you dream auspiciously about those who have passed through it. And Celine—she has spoken to Mother many times with her Nerosi. Her pain is gone. You don't need to worry about my seeing anyone again. If I was to stay mortal, it is *you* I would never see again. There's no veil to reunite gods and mortals. I know what I want, Ambroz. And this is it. I have made my choice. I choose you, forever."

He had told me this once already.

280

He will tell me again. So many times, he will tell me. He will never tire of reminding me. He knows I need to hear it. He is patient with me, always so very patient. It is why I love him so fiercely. It is why I have done what all I stand accused of. But many more events need be told before I give testimony of those atrocities.

·······«»)·) ● (·(«»······

The night passed quickly. Varyn held me for the whole of it. When it ended, we woke to Hanesh's blazing sun against our skin. I did not want to leave the bed and face Uorliék's heat but Varyn forced me from it, urging me to wash and dress so that we might begin our search. He bought us each Haneshi garments while he was out the previous night and I could not help but grin to see him wearing them. Their colorful way of dress was in stark contrast with what I had been accustomed to in Ethelia. With his golden skin and copper hair, already Varyn was a man of many vivid shades. Now he was a walking ornament.

"What are you smirking at?" he asked as he stood before the mirror, adjusting himself.

"Nothing," I said, pretending to look elsewhere. He came to me and began fixing my garment in the same manner he had tended to himself in the glass. Haneshi fashions were loose-fitting and left little skin exposed as a protection from sunlight.

Outside, I was grateful for the thin, forgiving cloth. We went about much of our search on foot and I complained for most of it. After viewing three unsatisfactory Uorliék quarters in succession, Varyn grew weary of my whining and traded a few crescents at a merchant's stand for some chilled Zèkhei to quiet me.

"If we see another place which is absent of that cooling crystal I will lose all sense of decency," I said between sips as we walked down the path leading to our next destination. Varyn had his face buried in a map—he came by it during his outing on the night previous. It held a list of vacant Uorliék dwellings.

"I'm not sure you were possessed of much to begin with."

I scoffed and swallowed down more cool drink, then offered it to him. He drank without breaking from the map.

"How much further till we get there? Can we not take a carriage?" I asked.

"Carriages cost crescents. I'm trying to preserve them as best I can. As it stands, we only have enough to get us through for about seven seasons."

"So we are to traverse through the Haneshi heat on foot then, how delightful."

He ignored this, and we kept on in silence till turning down a narrow pathway. At the end of it sat one of the charming structures I had seen upon our arrival. It was smaller but featured the same golden dome and thin ivory pillars.

"That place looks rather charming," I said, pointing over at it. "Is it one of the lodgings on your map?"

Varyn squinted down the path. "No, we haven't reached the next one marked here yet. We've still got a ways to go before we get there."

I huffed. "But I want to go and have a look at that one instead."

"We probably can't afford it."

"How would you know? You have not even gone and asked anyone."

He glared at me before tucking the map away. "Fine then, we can go and have a look. And spend even more time out here roasting in the heat while we're at it. Have it your way."

I snatched the Zèkhei from him and finished it. "I am certain that place has one of those cooling crystals. If nothing else, we can at least be granted a moment of reprieve from this scorching Haneshi sun. Stop your bickering, and come on."

"You know Ambroz, if you weren't so handsome and dear to me, I'd have long had my hands wrapped around your—"

"Quiet and hurry along, will you," I said, shoving the empty bottle of Zèkhei in his hands for him to discard.

It did not take long for us to reach it. From a distance, the structure seemed a grand, hulking thing, but as we neared the entrance, I found it short and far less imposing. It sat hanging on the corner—an island compared to the surrounding frameworks.

I stepped through the archway and peered between the spaces of its gate, which barred us further entry. There was not much I could see through the slivers, save for some sunlight reflecting off the marble floor. I called out for someone, using a Haneshi word of greeting I heard spoken several times by locals, but there came no answer. I turned to Varyn, ready to hear whatever aggrieved comment he had waiting on the tip of his tongue. Beside me, however, he was still and quiet, eyes narrowed as he gripped the bars. I tried to follow the line of his gaze but saw nothing from the angle in which I stood staring.

"What is it?" I asked. "What are you looking at?" He did not respond but instead reached for me without tearing his attention from the sight. I slipped between his body and the gate, gripping it as he had done.

"Just there, do you see it?"

"I do not see anything. Merely the light and a few chattels. That chair is quite elegant. Is that what you were looking at? Do you like it?"

He placed his hands on either side of my head and gently guided it in the direction he wished for me to look. "Right there, up on the wall. Do you see it?"

Finally I took notice of a colorful drawing. "Ah, yes. How pretty. Reminds me of one of yours, actually."

"That's because it *is* one of mine."

Chapter 46

THE LONGER I STARED, THE MORE OF HIS LINES AND curves made themselves known to me. I peered more intensely, squinting through the bars as I pressed my nose against them. A smile took hold of my lips, spreading till the whole of me beamed. I slipped from under Varyn and turned to him. Found him also beaming.

"You mentioned before that one of your works had gained favor here, but I think this is some sort of sign."

He fiddled with the lock, thumbing it as though it were a pendant hung round the neck of someone he adored. "I think you're right. But it looks empty in there. Like someone's abandoned it," he said.

"Should we go in search of the owner then? Perhaps one of the merchants can tell us who they are. We passed a few on the way."

He took me by the arm and led me through the archway. When I stepped out from it, his hand slid round the back of my neck. He drew me forward. Kissed me on the forehead.

"Sorry for being cross with you earlier," he whispered.

My smile carried with it an air of smugness. He noticed this and smirked.

"You are forgiven," I said.

The heat seemed not so overbearing as we walked from merchant to merchant in search of the owner. Perhaps our mirth distracted us from it. We had asked almost every nearby shop and establishment to no avail. I stood waiting as Varyn spoke to the last one in the area. He gave her some crescents in exchange for another chilled Zèkhei.

"She knows him—says he might have gone to a tavern he often visits," he said. "We have to find a carriage to get us there. It'll take too long on foot. I think I saw one back the other way."

We turned and headed for the path which led to it.

"Wait!" yelled the merchant. She put a hand on Varyn's arm. "You say need carriage? I have. Can use for crescents."

Varyn nodded, and the woman shouted again. Moments later, a girl who looked to be a few years younger than us appeared. We followed her to the carriage.

"How will we know who to look for?" I asked as we went along. There was cool air inside, and I tipped my head back to let it rain on me.

"He stopped by her shop earlier. She said as best she could remember, he was wearing green."

"But there are many wearing that color. Even you."

"His eyes are also green, and he is dark-haired. She said that we would know him by his laugh.That he is always laughing. And that the sound of it is irritating."

I half-snorted. "I see. Did you ask her if it was his? If he lives there?"

"No, he lives elsewhere. He has many places and an inn as well. It's how he earns his crescents."

"Do you think he will want many for it?"

"I can't say. It's the nicest place we've seen thus far. At least it appears to be from the outside. Surely it will cost more than any of the others."

"I will go to Qêl-Ceréi and start my nights then. As soon as Oléina will let me. Take whatever crescents I earn to help cover the cost for it."

He put a hand on my thigh. "You won't have to work there long. I promise."

"I think it will be good for me to stay a while, actually. The longer, the better. This way, I will have no choice but to learn Haneshi."

"You can learn it from me. I said I'd teach you, remember? And when you start going for your nights, I'll accompany you to translate. Then you won't be the only one there who is fluent in High Celestian."

I nodded, smiling, and we went the remainder of our journey in silence, each of us lolling under the splendid feel of cool air brushing against our skin. Soon the carriage stopped.

Stepping out into the heat again was like being saved from a fire, only to find the flames had sprouted legs after being doused and once more engulfed the surroundings. But to my pleasure, the inside of the tavern had an agreeable temperature. Its interior also was something to behold. Deep, crimson cushions embroidered with gold trimming lined the walls. Piles of them formed a plush array of seating for the patrons. Many sat blowing smoke, drinking, and conversing while servers dressed in elegant garments tended to each group of three or more. They lit pipes, poured spirits, and offered meal selections from silver trays.

It took very few moments to spot our man among the patrons. His raucous laughter was what alerted us to his presence. He sat craning his neck toward a group of women two seats over, conversing with them through shouts and giggles—though he alone seemed to be doing the majority of both. The women wore strained smiles as he spoke at them.

He was quite a bit younger than I had imagined him and a fair amount more attractive. Though his riotous temperament greatly diminished this. However, the sight of Varyn and I nearing him curtailed it somewhat. He tore his keen, unwanted attentions from the women, then fixed them curiously on us. Varyn stepped ahead of me, giving him the formal Haneshi greeting, along with other words I could not understand. I was taken aback to hear the man answer in High Celestian, with the barest trace of a Haneshi accent.

"And what does a foreigner from Ethelia want from me?" he asked before draining his cup. Another full drink sat waiting beside it.

"How did you know we were Ethelian?" I asked.

He pointed at Varyn. "Vowels. But barring elocution, he walks like the lords there, chin up, looking down his nose at everything, back stiff and straight as a board." He swallowed some of his drink and shook his finger at me. "But you, I'm not sure what you are. A lowland prince from Dorst, perhaps. Or a minor god, you're pretty as one." He grinned at me, revealing a set of yellowing teeth. Or I thought they were yellow—upon a second glance, I saw a reflection in them. Rows of gold rested in his mouth, some with sparkling jewels inlaid. His grin stretched further along, the corners of his lips curling up. "You looking to make a few crescents tonight?" he asked. "I've got an inn up near

Ennéi with the most exquisite bed. You'd look nice in it. Look even better under me."

I did not like the way he leered at my body as he spoke. Neither did Varyn. He drew me near and ushered me into the seat furthest from the man, then took the cushion beside me.

"We've not come here for that sort of business," said Varyn. "We'd like to discuss other affairs."

"What sort of affairs?" And who told you I was here anyway? They ought to mind their own. Giving my whereabouts to perfect strangers. Tell me who it was so I can wring their neck."

"Nevermind that. I've an inquiry about one of your properties."

"Is that right? And what does an Ethelian lord want with one of those?"

"To live there. I'm not a lord."

"And I'm not a gambling or drinking man, please. You're as noble as the night is dark. I know a lord when I see one."

"And if I was? What would my foreign titles matter here anyway?"

"They don't. Who said they did? I just don't like being told I'm wrong when I'm right."

I leaned closer and cleared my throat. "We want the place at the end of the merchant street. With the gold dome and locked gate."

"And I want to bed every beauty I lay eyes on. Can't always have the things we want." His eyes leaped from mine and fell on Varyn. "Besides, that place is what we call a Nékhourí—little palace. It's not suited for friends. The last two I made the mistake of doing business with fled to the north and left all their useless articles strewn everywhere. Well, one of them did anyway. And as I understand it, it was all over some piffling disagreement they had. The other couldn't keep up with the crescents. Which left me in a less-than-favorable position. So you see, I don't deal in fickle friendships any longer, young lord."

"What about lovers? Do you do business with them?" I asked.

He raked a hand through his thick hair. "I tend to prefer it, yes. But it depends. Are you married?"

"Yes," said Varyn without pause. "We are husbands. I am Varyn Carnelian. And this is Ambroz. And you are?"

He sat squinting at us in turn. "Gùidan El-Fourêi. Merchant, owner of many things, and overall visionary."

"Well, sir Gùidan, it's a pleasure," said Varyn, extending his hand. Gùidan took it hesitantly, giving it a listless shake.

"Is that why you've come to Hanesh then? To flee from an unpleasant arrangement with some other nobility in order to be with this pretty one instead?"

Neither of us said a word. Gùidan drank deep, keeping his gaze fixed on Varyn. It flickered to me, and I nearly flinched. I have told my fair share of untruths in times past, but I was not as confident a liar as Varyn. And moreover, I knew nothing of marriage—had not the language for the answers to any questions this sordid Gùidan might ask in reference to it.

I shifted uneasily atop the cushions while Gùidan's unwavering gaze burned the air from my chest. The longer the charged silence stretched between us, the more it tightened. I nudged Varyn furtively, begging him to break it.

"I've not fled from any arrangement. I'm not bound to any obligations across the sea. Ambroz and I are tethered to no duty—to no one but the other. We are husbands, as I stated earlier."

"I don't believe you."

"What would it take to convince you?" asked Varyn.

Gùidan looked at me. "Where is your marriage contract?"

I knew that if I made to answer, all would be lost. My tongue and lips were not to be trusted. I did not want to flounder there like a fallen leaf caught in a current, and so I waved a hand through the air in some silly gesture, as if conjuring that which had been forgotten to mind.

"Transport," said Varyn, taking my wayward hand in his, "Remember?"

"Ah yes," I replied, grateful to have been spared from the horror of improvising wit of my own. "That was the word I was looking for."

"Some of our things are still in transport. We're waiting for them to arrive. The contract is among the possessions. Quite the inconvenience," said Varyn.

Gùidan glared. "How long before it's returned to you?"

"It'll likely take a full season to get here."

"Well, come back to me in a season then."

"Oh, come, sir Gùidan. You're a reasonable man, I can tell. Surely you wouldn't turn away two fine, stable tenants. Think of the crescents you'd be losing by letting that Nékhourí sit vacant at the end of the street."

"That's just it. How do I know of your stability? You've not even a contract of your commitment to one another to substantiate your claims. What do either of you do for your crescents anyway? How am I to know you aren't vagrants aiming to swindle me?"

Varyn opened his mouth, readying to give his reply. But a passing server came and stood over us. She reminded me a bit of Celine, but older and with dark hair. "The crescents for your smoke and drink are owed now, Gùidan. I'll not have you scurrying off like last time and have my wages deducted for it."

Gùidan grunted. "Put it on my dues with the other charges."

"No," said the server, snatching up the empty glasses and rolling her eyes. Varyn reached inside his garment and took from within it a few crescents. He placed them in the server's palm. "Will that cover it?"

She looked down at her hand with wide eyes and gave two of the crescents back to him. "Yes, that will do, many thanks," she said, grinning as she walked away.

The furrow in Gùidan's brow smoothed. Varyn leaned forward. "Each of us are skilled artists. Our crescents are earned through our respective talents. Mine are made with my hands, and Ambroz with his voice. We are not vagrants."

"I've never heard of Ethelians who are fond of the arts, much less ones who earn their keep with it. Hanesh is, without question, a haven for the artist. But Ethelia, they pluck it all out of you in boyhood there. What with all your lessons, apprenticeships, and such. What would Ethelians know of anything to do with artistry? With painting, with dance, with instruments. Your lot have not made a single notable contribution to it. You've no culture. Everyone knows the best artists are Haneshi."

"I do not doubt it," said Varyn. "But you've asked where we got our crescents, and that is the answer. I trust you know how handsomely Haneshi employers pay their artists. Look, if you will not let us have the Nékhourí, then fine, it's clear you've some prejudice against Ethelia. Unjustified, might I add. I'm sure there are other *overall visionaries* with a place up for offer who'll be glad to take our crescents for it, no matter how Ethelian." Varyn rose, lifting me by the arm. "We will leave you to your leisure. Come, Ambroz."

He stormed off, and I trailed after him, somewhat dismayed by our inability to sway Gùidan. Outside the tavern, Varyn fumed, though it was evident to none but me. He had a way of clenching his jaw in place of words or gestures. I put a hand on his shoulder.

"We will find another. It was probably not worth it anyway," I said. Though the latter was a lie, I knew the inside of his Nékhourí would have been all I had hoped it would be.

"I should have boxed his head in. Just who in the stars did he think he was talking to anyway? With all those insults about Ethelia."

Now I wrapped my other hand round his waist, guiding him away from the tavern. Together we walked down the path. "Forget him. Take out your map. Let us go and have a look at the other places." He took it from his breast pocket and unfurled it. I slipped it from his hands, curious of the foreign writing.

"Do I really look down my nose at everything?" asked Varyn.

"Ignore him, he was a buffoon. Why do you care what he thinks?"

"You're right. It just irritated me, I suppose. No one's ever spoken to me like that in Ethelia."

"That is because you are a lord there, dear husband." The use of this title drew out his sparkling smile, the one I loved to see. It grew into laughter, and soon, each of us was seized by it, so intense was our fit that we were made to halt as it rippled through us. It was the sort of giggling that left no room for breaths, and we struggled to catch them after the bout had ended. I gathered mine slowly, but the sight of Varyn wiping tears from his cheeks nearly set me off again.

"Lies come to you too easily. What made you think to say that anyway?" I asked.

"Say what? That we are husbands?"

"Yes."

He shrugged. "I thought he might have taken my word. I didn't expect to be interrogated further about contracts and what have you."

"Nor did I. You would think a man flaunting a mouth full of gold and jewels would be eager to do business with a lord. I meant to ask—why did you deny your being one? Would it not have aided our credibility if he believed you to be a nobleman?"

"I didn't want him to think I came from wealth. Men like him are always looking for means to exploit circumstances in any way they can. If he'd known and been willing to let us have his precious Nékhourí, the amount of crescents he'd want for it would be twice that of his normal asking."

I often found myself in awe of Varyn. He was so much more clever than me.

"That would have never crossed my mind," I said.

"It didn't need to." He took the map from me and peered at it. "That's what I'm here for."

I pulled him near to me, hand gliding round his waist. Together we studied the map, each bending our necks to it like withered flowers. Surely there would be one among the areas which would suit both our tastes.

Above us, the sun was still brightly burning, and I pointed to a course nearest our current orientation so that we might find some reprieve from its scorching rays. We agreed it best to embark on foot there and set off down the path. Though halfway to the end of it, the sound of shouting called our attention from advancing further on.

I turned in search of the cause of such racket and found Gùidan baying in the distance near the tavern, beckoning for us.

Chapter 17

VARYN AND I STOOD SQUINTING THROUGH THE HARSH sunlight at Gùidan as he waved us forward.

"I'm not moving from this spot," said Varyn. "If he has something more to say to us, he can come down here and make it known. Who does he think we are—children that will go running at his call?"

The three of us stood motionless as carved marble, glaring at one another from opposite ends of the street. When it became clear that Gùidan had no intention of stepping toward us, I waved a hand, gesturing for him. Beside me, Varyn chortled. After a period of waiting, in which two patrons came and left through the doors of the tavern, Gùidan begrudgingly began making his way to us.

I had not realized it inside, for we had all been sitting, but now that each of us was on our feet, Gùidan appeared quite short. I was slightly taller than most and Varyn was taller still. I mention this because it seemed a matter of contention for Gùidan. His eyes swept lengthwise over us several times, brows growing closer together with each pass. He kept grunting—all while drawing himself up and taking on various awkward poses, shifting his weight from one foot to the other in order to find which bearing gave him the most height. Of all of his positions, none afforded him much improvement. Finally, he abandoned the effort and settled on glaring with his arms crossed tight against his chest.

"How old are you?" asked Gùidan.

"Old enough to be considered men," clipped Varyn.

"Temper is as fiery red as your blazing head, then, eh?"

"Sir Gùidan," I said, stepping between them before Varyn had a chance to react to his slight. I felt the tension radiating off each of them. "Is there something you needed to tell us?" I smiled at him, remembering his earlier leering and comments on my beauty and leveraging them to cool the heat of his flame. It worked, he eased, uncrossing his arms to flash his gold teeth at me.

"I've reconsidered your offer on the Nékhourí."

Varyn smirked. "We haven't made you any offer."

I threw a sidelong glare at him and clapped him on the back. "Not yet, he means, but we would like to," I said, maintaining my contrived smile. "Perhaps you can give us a look at the inside?"

Gùidan stared first at me, then off into the distance at something behind my back. "We can take my carriage," he said.

Varyn and I followed after him as he walked toward it. His carriage was cramped but cool, at least. The ride there seemed to drag, however. I felt Gùidan and Varyn would at any moment start up arguing, and dreaded the mere thought of playing mediator in such a confined space.

Once the Nékhourí came into view, I breathed a sigh of relief.

The inside of it was palatial and white as pearls. Everything from the walls to the marble floor was bathed in the hue.

"Is there a cooling crystal?" I asked as I ambled about the space, taking it all in.

Gùidan scoffed. "Of course. What do you take me for, a depraved ruffian? It's out on the side where the sun is brightest." He disappeared for a few moments, and upon returning, cool air began descending from the ceiling. It was all I could do not to spread my arms wide and toss my head back.

Instead, I walked the length of every chamber, finding a few chattels in each. They were charming, useful pieces. Gùidan trailed behind me as I went about and said that if we chose to stay, then all that had been left behind was ours to keep. There was an ample bed, plush floor cushions that lined the walls of the main area, dressing tables, chairs—I stumbled upon a large washroom with the most splendid marble bath. All the windows were archways from which light flooded in great quantities. Looking back, I do not know why we ever thought it appeared abandoned. It truly seemed the little palace its name purported it to be.

As I explored, Gùidan remained nearby at my ear, imparting me with some pointless detail about every corner of the Nékhourí I laid eyes upon. I tuned him out for the most part and went to find Varyn once I had seen the whole of the dwelling.

He stood in the main room, hands clasped behind his back as he gazed up, admiring the drawing that hung on the white wall. I took a place beside him and stared too. Quickly Gùidan came to join us, studying the illustration whilst half-smirking.

"Ah, this one is from a very skilled Haneshi painter," said Gùidan. "The art styles which come into fashion here are always changing you see, but this one seems to have set a trend. I quite like this artist's use of color and curves. There've been lots of imitations since it's become popular, but none, in my opinion, have come close to what the creator has expressed here. This one makes you feel something when you look at it that the others don't."

Varyn blinked a number of times in quick succession. I could tell he was trying very hard not to turn and glare at Gùidan.

"This skilled Haneshi painter," said Varyn, each word leaving him in a measured tone, "what is their name?"

"I'm not sure. I believe he is a young man. Well traveled, they say. The rumor is that he sent it as a gift to a friend—a wealthy merchant who goes by the surname Dènzi. Apparently, some of Dènzi's circle liked it so much he had copies made for them. From there, a demand sprung. I even heard the great dancer Zèmrin took a liking to it, and wants a portrait drawn. Very skilled painter indeed to have aroused this level of interest from a single work." Gùidan sneered, peeling his eyes off the drawing and planting them on Varyn. "Has Ethelia such an artist?"

"Yes," I said, "they have."

"Who?" asked Gùidan.

I put my hand on Varyn's shoulder. "Him."

Gùidan chuckled. "Well, word of your greatness hasn't yet traveled here, but work hard enough at your craft, and perhaps one day you can be to Ethelia what this young painter is to Hanesh."

Varyn's hands were fists at his sides. He likely wanted nothing more than to knock Gùidan over the head with one. I could not blame him. He clenched his jaw, and I stepped between him and Gùidan just as I had done earlier on the street.

"We have at last decided. And would very much like to take up residence here," I declared. It was all I could think to say to distract Varyn from his seething.

Gùidan clapped his hands together, oblivious. "Wonderful. Let's talk crescents then," he said.

I listened as he and Varyn discussed the matter, their voices growing steadily louder. In the end they came to an agreement which suited us more than Gùidan. Varyn had switched to speaking Haneshi halfway through, and by the end of their conversation, had come back round to High Celestian. He somehow managed to convince Gùidan to reduce his asking by nearly half. Varyn gave him a portion of his crescents, acquired our key, then ushered him out of the Nékhourí and turned to me.

"He is to collect our crescents at the end of every season," said Varyn, collapsing onto one of the cerulean floor cushions. He sighed while massaging his brow, and I plopped down beside him, letting out a sigh of my own as the soft seating received my weight.

"Why did you start speaking Haneshi?"

"Did I? I hadn't noticed. Stars, he was getting on my nerves. We found the best possible place attached to the worst possible keeper. That man is insufferable and dim-witted. How he came to be a successful merchant is beyond my understanding."

"Will it cost us many crescents to stay here?"

"Yes, but it's nothing we can't manage. What with your nights singing and my," he trailed off and looked to the drawing on the wall, waving his hand in its direction, "the nerve of him, going on about working on my craft while praising something I've made in the same breath. He didn't even know what he was looking at. Calling it a painting when it's clearly a sketch. You were right to call him a buffoon."

I smirked. "Imagine how silly he will feel for belittling your talent when he discovers you are the one who has caused such a stir with your art," I said.

We shared a chortle at this, and he draped his arm round me.

"A few times when we were talking, I wanted so badly for you to use your light on him. I pictured you burning off his eyebrows to shut him up."

I snorted. "That is…shocking." With a smirk Varyn put his head in my lap, sprawling himself half over my legs and half over the cushions.

"I'll tell you what," he said, "this air feels marvelous." I smiled down at him, stroking his head and soft curls.

"Our imaginary marriage contract. Does he still want proof of it?" I asked.

"He didn't mention it. I don't think he cared either way. He merely wanted a reason to make things difficult for us, that's all. But if you'd like, we can still become husbands." He paused and grinned up at me. "Do you want to marry me, Ambroz?"

I knew he was teasing and pinched his ear for it. But I bent to kiss him anyway.

"I would love nothing more than to marry you."

"Then we will go to the capitol at the end of the season and wed." This earned him another pinch. He took it with grace, chuckling as he buried his face into my midriff. It remained there, and I twirled a finger round one of his copper ringlets, idly coiling it as I gazed blankly ahead. Outside, the ambient sounds of Uorliék whirred beyond our gate. We listened in silence, indolent and uncaring for the time as it passed.

A feeling overtook me as we lolled on the cushions, I cannot name it save to say it felt as though a pleasant swelling bloomed in my chest. It spread to other areas, my stomach, my scalp. The latter prickled, as it had done many seasons ago on that first day when I stumbled upon a bright boy in the forest—the one who lay resting in my lap. I had awakened then, I think. I had not known it before, but something was broken in me. He mended it that day, with his slow-spreading smile; with his high laughter; with his games. I sat remembering all our footraces, our matches, our nights at the manor—living them again as I cradled him. Against me, I felt his warm breaths. They were changing—slowly morphing from indistinct to the heavy pattern of one drifting into slumber. I kept on looping my spiral, smiling faintly, for this had been what eased him to rest. It would have been effortless for me to allow my eyes to fall shut—to follow him to the distant shore of dreams, but a sharp mewl interrupted my drowsing.

Fully alert, I glanced about.

Another cry resounded, somewhat softer than the last. I whipped my head in the direction of it but saw nothing. When a third squall crept along, I gently transferred Varyn's head off my lap and onto the cushions, carefully maneuvering myself from under him to ensure he remained asleep.

I heard the sound again and followed it, surprised by where it had led me. I had not noticed that our Nékhourí held a side entrance. The door of it hung half-open, and a little furry head peeked through it.

The kitten purred at my feet, its coat of sleek, orange fur gleaming in the sunlight. I scooped it up and carried it in my arms, stepping outside to place it on the ground. When I set it down, it whimpered and began circling where I stood, occasionally stopping to brush its soft body against my ankle.

"You want me to pick you up again?" I whispered. It answered with a drawling mewl. After peering into its pleading green orbs, I decided this was a declaration of assent and once more scooped it up. Upon bending, I caught sight of a brown patch of earth. It was a departure from the surrounding street and appeared to be mere remnants of what perhaps had once been a larger portion of croft. Within it, a few thin stalks had sprouted. I went to get a better look, but the kitten purred in my arms, and the intention was forgotten. "Are you hungry, little one?" I asked, gliding my hand down its back. "I am sorry, I have nothing to feed you."

"I could go and find a bowl of Zèkhei for it." I glanced up and spotted Varyn in the doorway, rubbing the sleep from his eyes.

"Would you?" I asked. He nodded, shuffling over to me and reaching for the kitten. It cried during the exchange of hands, sniffing Varyn as he held it to his chest, then quieting as it settled into his arms. He lifted its tail, along with his brow.

"I'll go and get her something." He stroked her and made for the door, pausing at its threshold. "That looks like a tiny sphere of garden," he said, pointing at the patch of dirt. I stared down at it as he disappeared with the kitten, wondering why I had not thought of it as such before.

········)·) ◉ (·(·········

Later that day, when the kitten had her Zèkhei and our things had been fetched from the inn, Varyn and I knelt at the patch of garden. The light of the sun would soon give way to our silver Moon. We sat studying the dirt as it grew darker beneath the fading rays. Beside me, Varyn had the urn tucked under his arm.

"Should you do it, or should I?" he asked.

"It does not matter. But since I did the last one, perhaps this time it should be you."

"Are you sure—what if I get it wrong?"

"You never get anything wrong. Go on," I said, nudging him. Slowly he dug into the patch, making a hole inside it. When it grew large enough, he opened the urn, looking at me with apprehension.

"How much should I plant?" he asked.

"As much as you like. Whatever feels right to you." He seized a small palmful, studying it a moment.

"I didn't expect it to feel so ordinary, from the way it shimmers," he said, peering down at his hand a while, watching it glint there before emptying it into the patch. "Now what?" he asked.

I handed him a clay pot I found lying about inside. It was filled with water I drew from the bath.

"Pour a little over it."

He held the pot, hesitant. Some of his hair fell into the water, and I held it out of the way for him as he leaned forward. Steadily he tilted it till a thin stream flowed over the patch.

"By the stars, what's happening?" Varyn asked, wide-eyed and panting as he glimpsed the brilliant flash of gold sparkle briefly beneath him.

"It is merely the spell," I said, rising and lifting him up with me. "It has taken effect."

He smiled down at it in awe, placing his hand on my waist—pulling me near.

Together we gazed upon the beginnings of an eternity.

I could not wait to spend it with him.

Chapter 48

MY FIRST NIGHT AT QÊL-CERÉI WAS PERHAPS THE most illuminating experience I had come by since my arrival in Hanesh. The heavy, smoke-filled scent of perfumed air greeted me the moment I stepped foot inside, along with the eyes of every patron. It was dim, yet I felt as though each gaze were a shining light upon me. I think I would have turned and left were it not for Varyn's hand pressing against the small of my back, urging me forward.

"What's the matter?" he whispered.

"They are all looking at me."

"Of course they are. You're the talent. Come on, let's find Oléina so we can discuss the terms of your arrangement."

But we did not have to find her. She had spotted us the moment we entered through the golden doors. The sea of ogling patrons parted for us as she called Varyn and me over with a gesture. She seized me by both shoulders and pressed her cheek against mine, a multitude of Haneshi words tumbling from her lips. The only one I understood was *Ambruze*. After releasing me from the embrace, she turned to Varyn and repeated the action, uttering more rapid Haneshi. He pulled away from her, laughing and shaking his head.

"What did she say?"

"She's down a man tonight and asked if I wanted a post. Says my hair and eyes are hypnotizing."

I frowned. "Don't worry," said Varyn, grinning. "She's only teasing. She knows I am yours. But come, we weren't supposed to enter through the main door. There's a back gate for the workers. She wants to show you how to get there. Then she'll draw up a contract for your post and discuss wages."

I followed them, still feeling eyes on me as we made our way out of what I assumed was the main room. It had been extravagantly ornamented, as opulent and stately as a palace. So, too, were the patrons, dressed in fine silks, some with large jewels hanging from their ears and necks. They loafed upon the immense cushions that garnished each corner, reveling with one another while conversing, smoking, drinking, gambling, and many more things I had no words for. I hoped to spot a portion of the selection Varyn mentioned reading about on the leaflet during our journey here, but had not yet seen any of Oléina's men and women among them from the glimpse I caught as we passed through.

Varyn and Oléina walked ahead of me, I had been keeping pace with their navigation till we came to a wide passageway. Both sides of it stood lined with a number of doors. The further along I walked, the louder the sounds from behind them grew. I heard a man screaming a Haneshi word over and over, each cry escalating. I paused, listening as they became more intense. During his loudest shriek, Varyn's hand gripped my arm and yanked my attention from it.

"Ambroz, come on. We were halfway down the other hall, talking to the air, thinking you were still behind us."

"Oh, sorry," I mumbled, embarrassed to have fallen so far behind—to have listened for as long as I had. "I thought someone was being hurt in there."

He smirked. "They probably were and paid good crescents for it, too. Get used to it."

He ushered me down the hall and into Oléina's study. It was modest in comparison with everything I had seen but still lofty and embellished. She explained to Varyn her expectations of me.

I was to sing twenty nights out of every season, starting from this night. I would have my crescents at the end of each one. I would need to learn Haneshi songs, but till then, her musicians could play melodies to the few Ethelian ones I knew. When she had finished, she gave instructions for me to ready myself in the sitting room with all the other workers.

Qêl-Ceréi had two selections per night, and the second was to be presented with the accompaniment of song and instrument, for it announced the most sought-after among her talent. It would not commence till I had taken up singing in the main room. I thought perhaps there might be a rehearsal, but she was confident in my abilities and dismissed the notion, urging us on as she left to tend to other duties.

Varyn rose before I did, looking expectantly at me. I found myself stiff with nerves. On the ship, I had imagined myself singing in isolation, but being faced with the reality of what I had agreed upon harrowed me.

"Are you alright?" asked Varyn as we made our way to the sitting room.

"My throat. There is a hard lump in it that does not go down no matter how many times I swallow."

"You're nervous. Don't be. I'll be sitting there when you come out. Just find me in the crowd. Look only at me as you sing."

I kept on trying to swallow my lump as we walked down the long corridor. Varyn embraced me once we reached the doors.

"You are not coming in with me?" I asked, chest tightening. He shook his head.

"I don't work here. It's not really appropriate for me to be in there whilst everyone's preparing. You'll be fine. Oléina says they're expecting you. Most of them can speak informal Celestian, so you won't need me to translate. Go on. I'll be waiting for you out there." He gave my shoulder an affectionate squeeze, then turned. I watched him recede down the hallway, eyes fixed on his vibrant hair till it was a mere speck of color in my view. From the other side of the door, I heard laughter and low voices. I listened a while as I fought to gather my courage.

With a deep breath, I gripped the cool, crystal lever, then twisted it.

Inside, tall mirrors framed in gold hung on the walls. Garments were strewn about, draping off the backs of chairs and covering decadent floor cushions. As I entered, a spell of silence fell over the room, in which every head turned in my direction. My breath caught. A dozen or more gazes regarded me at once. They seemed to have become statues upon my arrival, mouths hanging open, limbs stuck in the position of whatever action they had been going about prior.

My gaze swept over their faces, all of them painted with graceful yet intimidating bearings. Their features varied—and individually, each mortal was striking.

My lump became larger—my mouth dry as the Haneshi heat. Perhaps if there were only one or two of them, I could manage a few words. But to be the subject of their collective attention unnerved me.

"You the new singer then? The Ethelian?" This was a woman's voice. She had been leaning into the glass, painting her lips with some crimson paste. Now she rose from her chair, revealing her height, and stood before me, tall, slender, and dark.

"Yes," I said, fighting down the lump. "I am Ambroz."

"Gods, you're handsome. Glad you're not one of the selections. I'd hate to stand next to you out there. You'd snatch the top spenders right from under me," she said.

They all burst into laughter at this, then returned to their mirrors, no longer statues beholding me. I eased and took the hand she extended, offering her a small smile.

"I'm Zèfver, highest earning, most charming. Pleasure."

"Oh please, love, you're as ordinary as the rest of us. And about as charming as sweat-sodden undergarments," shouted a man at the end of the room. More laughter erupted. Zèfver rolled her eyes.

"I'd be jealous of me too if I were you," she said, flinging her long braids over her shoulder, then trailing her eyes along my body. "You're not going out there wearing *that*, are you?"

I found my reflection in one of the tall mirrors. "Well, yes. Is there something wrong with it?"

"No, it's painfully unremarkable, though, if you're to be in front of so many patrons with deep pockets. Boring really." She turned the corners of her mouth down. "It won't do. Come."

She pulled me by the arm, walking quickly down an aisle with half-dressed mortals on either side till we reached a particularly large mirror near the end of the room. Without consulting me, she yanked my garment over my head, hands swift as a breeze. "Gods and the High Priestess. Look at this body. You were really going to hide it under this dull smock?"

Many eyes fell upon me, and I grew warm. A pair of them belonged to a young man with rich-brown hair. He came and stood beside Zèfver.

"I'd suffer the bite of an Emros if I could have your chest and arms," he said, studying me. "It's not fair that you get to be pretty *and* broad. Who did your mother make offering to while she grew you in her belly? I hate you."

Zèfver laughed. "Well, don't curse the man Árástin. He can't help his looks. Come, let him have one of your silks."

"I'm only teasing, darling," said Árástin, touching my upper arm. He turned his head to the side and observed me, pursing his lips. "I've got a deep green that would look lovely on you. And cuffs. Gold ones to bring out that bronze skin."

Árástin went to fetch them while Zèfver preened my hair with her fingers. "You should let me put a bit of pomade in your curls, they'll sparkle like stars while you sing."

I let her apply the sweet smelling oils in my curls. She arranged them neatly about my head. When Árástin returned with the silks he gasped.

"Oh, that's really not fair," he said. "Why'd you go and do that? Who'll bother looking at us when he's up there all dark-haired and gleaming?"

"Hush. The prettier I make him, the more inspired they'll be to spend."

"How do you figure?" I asked.

"They can't have the singers. So naturally, their eyes will roam, eager to find the next best thing: me."

Árástin snorted. "If I had your confidence, I'd own this place and everyone in it. Gods, you're delusional."

"Shut up," clipped Zèfver. "Help our Ambroz put the silks on." Árástin draped them over one side of my body, fastening the bulk of the garment around my waist. He stood behind me, both of us facing the mirror, and adjusted them to fit the shape of my body.

"There," he said. "That's lovely on you."

"Is there more cloth?" I asked, taking in my reflection. "It feels as though I am naked."

"That's the point. Hold out your arms, darling." I did as he asked, and around my wrists, he clasped circlets. They were thick and nearly covered the whole of my forearm. "Marvelous," said Árástin, "now for the final gem on top." He adorned my neck with a string of heavy jewels. They glinted in the mirror. Some of the other mortals turned and glimpsed, nodding and lifting their brows in approval.

"Put something on his eyes," someone said, shouting from across the room.

Zèfver rubbed circles over her chin. "Yes, I thought something was missing. I'll go and get a fresh stick of Jêqal."

Árástin smoothed oils over my chest while she went in search of it. The workers of Qêl-Ceréi were not shy of touch it seemed. I had not expected to be tended to in this manner. Nor had I expected to find it so pleasing. Here, I was a prize. By the time Árástin had finished with me, my skin glistened like the jewels which hung round my neck. He stood appraising his work, nodding and pursing his lips.

"Buy yourself a crimson silk with the crescents you earn tonight. They won't be able to keep their eyes off you," he said.

Zèfver appeared and shoved him with her elbow. "Stop flirting, and move aside so I can concentrate." She held me by the chin and gently tipped my face upright. "Have you ever worn Jêqal?"

"No. What is it?"

"You'll see."

"Look up at the ceiling, darling. That way, your eyes won't water," said Árástin, hands on hips. I took his advice. In my periphery was a blunt splotch of black, then something firm pressed upon the delicate rim of my eye. She dragged it across the area, and I fought to keep it from fluttering closed. Again she repeated it, placing her efforts upon my other eye. When she had finished, I let out a sigh of relief, sniffling a little. Árástin and Zèfver each wore satisfied expressions as they assessed me.

"I really am glad you're not one of us," said Zèfver, urging me to have a look at myself with a flick of her wrist.

The dark Jêqal she had smudged upon my eyes made me appear fierce, almost threatening. But the silks and jewels softened me, and I could not stop myself smiling at my reflection. I wondered what Varyn would think when he saw me. It was Ambroz who had come into the sitting room—I did not recognize the menacing beauty that stood staring out at me now. Would my Varyn recognize him? Would he like what he saw? I grew warm at the thought of him and remembered—unbidden—our nights of passion, our coupling.

Still smiling, I leaned toward the mirror, admiring the winsome face within it and imagining Varyn's hands on me, undoing all of Zèfver and Árástin's work. I fell further into my vanity, still thinking of Varyn, staring at my pretty eyes—their shape, their color. That is when it happened. It was there a mere moment, then gone the next.

For the briefest flash, my eyes flickered from their dark amber…and shone a vibrant shade of green.

Chapter 49

"SOMEONE TELL THAT SINGER OLÉINA'S READY FOR him," said a disembodied voice in the distance. I did not bother to turn and look for its owner. My heart was in my throat. I had seen the barest glimpse of those elusive shades—the ones I had spent my life longing for. I tried again to see them. To retrace what had led to their sudden appearance in that glass. What had I felt as I peered into it?

"Darling, they're ready for you." This was Árástin's voice. I ignored it as I grasped at the fleeting sentiment. Desperate to identify it so that I might feel it again—so that I might see that dazzling green once more. I conjured Varyn to mind. It had been him I was thinking of when I saw it. Was it joy I felt at the thought of him? Happiness? Yes, that was it. I let that warmth fill me again and stared. *StaredstaredstaredstaredstaredstaredstaredstaredstaredstaredSTARED*

"Don't tell me you're shy, darling. I've got a rose quartz that works wonders to calm nerves if you want it." Árástin's voice again, his hand slid up my arm. I did not break from the mirror. I kept on searching for my shade, unblinking as I willed its return. But it did not come. It was gone. And so, too, was that joyous feeling which had summoned it. The one which I now purported was contrived—a mere pretense.

Árástin slid his crystal into my palm, and the coolness jolted me back to awareness, back to the soft sounds of chatter from busy, half-dressed mortals.

"Forgive me," I said, turning to him at last. I gave him back his rose quartz, I did not need it. "You and Zèfver are sorcerers, it seems. I hardly recognize myself." His rich-brown eyes had been regarding me with a concerned expression, but at this, he eased, smiling and shaking his head.

"Handsome *and* smooth of tongue, gods, keep him away from me," he said, sauntering off down the aisle.

I spared another glance at my reflection, hoping that vivid green would make a reappearance.

Dark amber sparkled in its place. I left for the main room.

Why had I gotten so excited? Had I not already assured myself of the irrelevance of shades? So what if they did come? I had not a care for Celestial things any longer. I felt a hypocrite as I made my way down the beautiful corridors of Oléina's charming Qêl-Ceréi. Shame blanketed me like smog—drained the colors around me and turned them all dull. But with every step forward, I reclaimed them, vowing to myself again that I did not need shades. I had Varyn. I had eternity.

I sank into that knowing and became so immersed in these musings that I had forgotten where my legs were carrying me—forgotten to be overcome with nerves. But they came rushing back as I stepped into the dim light of the main room, where every patron shone their gaze upon me. Oléina had been talking with a server, and she stopped and gasped when she saw me. I went to her. She took my hands in hers.

"Oh, beautiful, beautiful. Even more than voice. Go on floor, sing now. *Varun* tell them song you know." She pointed to a platform raised by three short stairs—golden drapes that hung from an intricately carved structure surrounded the area. Near it sat the musicians, waiting for me with listless expressions, instruments in their laps. My lump returned. I spun to ask Oléina for more time to gather myself, but she had taken up scolding one of the servers for sitting on a floor cushion. I watched as she pulled the young man to his feet by the arm. He rose with a huff, indignantly shuffling across the room. I trailed his course, and behind him, I spotted Varyn's bright head of hair. He sat sipping on something, most probably Zèkhei with spirits, legs propped upon a luxuriously embroidered cushion the color of deep scarlet.

Despite the enthused patrons prattling away on either side of him, his expression was blank. He raised the drink to his lips and took another sip, eyes flitting in my direction. I thought I might see his face light up at the sight of me, but his gaze did not hold and merely swept over my presence as though I were a stranger. He carried on drinking, still with that same indifferent bearing. It stung not to have been noticed by him. Already, my lump was threatening to choke me. Now I felt my legs nearly buckle beneath me at the thought of singing. Varyn had told me I must find him in the crowd to quell my tumultuous nerves. Yet here I had done so and found no remedy for them. Somehow in spite of this, I found the strength to stop lingering near the margins of the room and moved from my spot.

Placing one foot in front of the other was like lifting an insurmountable weight. Still, I carried it, trudging along past the musicians, past leering patrons. I looked out at Varyn again before ascending the dais. He was busy taking sips.

As I made to climb the little stairs, my foot became tangled in the long, flowing silks Árástin had draped over me. I was spared the ignominy of tumbling to the floor by a firm grip planted round my arm.

– "These silks. Must lift them up first, pretty one," whispered an olive-skinned woman. Informal Celestian, spoken in her accent, was soothing as moonlight. She had a Lerawyn tucked under her arm—the Haneshi sort were larger, I noted, but carried the same circular shape and color as the Ethelian ones. The woman had a deep scar running down the side of her face. I could not help staring at it, not for its harshness, but for the way it shifted as she spoke. It made her more charming.

"Thank you," I said.

"Most welcome. I am Zanthéi. Look at me once you are ready for the melody to start."

I nodded and told her my name, then climbed up the platform without incident. The golden drapes on either side of me shielded my view of most everyone. Even so, I felt the eyes of them upon me. Once more, I sought out Varyn. He sipped and sipped.

Finally, our gazes met.

His hand flew to his chest. He had noticed me at last. He hid his gaping mouth behind his fingers. The sight of this was all I needed to rid myself of that dreadful lump. I gave Zanthéi a quick glance and cleared my throat. There was much distance between us, but Varyn leaned to me, drawing himself up as the soft melody began. I flushed upon hearing it. He had taught me the verses. We were thirteen then, leisuring in the forest after his lessons, his hair damp from the river. Skin lit gold by the sun. It was the first time that strange fluttering had taken hold of my being. I still remember the high, clear sound of his voice as he sang to me.

As I stand upon the dais, I hear him again in my head and smile. I forget my nerves. The words flow. I sing.

He is my divinity.

During my performance, the selection had entered at some time or other—I cannot say when for my eyes never left Varyn as I sang. I was aware of the patrons who flocked to my dais, gathering there like birds around crumbs. But I was not shy of them and sang my verses with the clarity of the self-assured. I only noticed the arrival of Oléina's selection when the quantity of patrons below had begun to disperse, breaking off to shower their attentions upon them instead of me.

As I had come to the close of my last song, Varyn rose. He started toward me, but Árástin blocked his path. I climbed down from my height and went to them but was also barred by patrons bestowing upon me their laurels of crescents and praise. I could not understand them, of course, but nodded thanks anyway, peering over their heads in an effort to spot Varyn. Árástin had gone by the time they had cleared, and Varyn approached me, smirking.

"Stars, I looked right over you earlier," he said, tracing his fingers along my silks, my hair.

"You did not recognize me."

"Not at all."

"You have Árástin and Zèfver to thank for it."

"I don't know any Zèfver, but I think I just talked to Árástin, actually."

"Yes, I saw. What did he say to you?"

"He was after my crescents and offered himself to me. I told him I was here for you. That you were mine. He told me to keep dreaming."

I laughed, and he kissed me. Together, we watched the patrons take their picks. Zèfver had been right to boast. She held the eye of more than one. Occasionally, gazes roamed in my direction, but Varyn cloaked me with an arm, pulling me near each time. In every corner, the affluent patrons sat cooing in the ear of their selection, negotiating till they rose and disappeared down one of the many corridors. It did not take long for the room to clear. Oléina came and found me soon after, wearing a broad smile.

"Never gone so fast. Yours voice like...like..." She turned to Varyn and switched to Haneshi, then caught hold of my hand, stuffing my earnings into it with a firm shake.

"She says you've cast a spell over the room with your singing. And that it's never cleared so quickly. She's made a small fortune tonight," said Varyn.

I was shy of such direct praise. Varyn knew it and ruffled my hair, teasing me so that I did not have to wilt under it. Oléina said a word more and left smiling. As she walked away, I took Varyn's hand, planting the crescents in his palm.

"For our Nékhourí," I said. He received them with raised brows, then counted how many there were. Afterward, he placed half of the quantity back into my palm.

"Keep some for yourself. We'll share the cost for now."

The crescents were cool against my flesh. I stared at them, feeling a sense of accomplishment. Before, I had been dependent on Varyn for them. Now, I had some of my own to trade for whatever I liked. Few things compared to the rush this gave me. My head clouded over with excitement. I left Qêl-Ceréi grinning like the Fool I was.

At our Nékhourí I still wore the countenance. My cheeks aching from the stretch. I did not care. Inside I found the little orange kitten clawing the floor cushions, and even when I scolded her, I did so whilst beaming. We had taken to calling her Cress for the crescent moon-shaped patch of white fur upon her head. I swept her up and carried her into the bedroom, planting her far away from anything pretty or vulnerable to ruin by her destructive claws. Árástin's silks would need to be hidden somewhere she could not get at them. Though as I made to undress, I struggled to liberate the knots he had fastened. Varyn appeared at my side and worked them free, taking in my bare form as I stored them in a closet, along with the jewels Árástin had given me.

"You came out of your shell tonight," said Varyn, reaching for me. I went to him, aware of the suggestion hidden behind these words, simmering beneath the low tone of his voice. I loved nights like these, when he initiated. "I'm proud of you." This last he whispered, one hand buried in my hair, the other resting on my hip.

"It was only because of you. Because I knew you were there," I said. He pulled me closer. "I will always be there." Now his hand traveled from my hip, rested upon my chin. His lips were soft on mine, as soft as the silks I had worn. "I have an idea," he said, abruptly drawing back.

"Oh? Tell me."

"We have not had a match in a while, so let's play a game."

"What sort of game?"

"Do you remember when we were at that inn—suffering the sound of that cursed, creaking bed?"

I chuckled. "Yes, what of it?"

"Remember what I promised you?"

I thought back to that day, unable to stop myself grinning. "You said that we would find a proper space—that we could be as loud as we wanted there."

He grinned too. "Can you guess what sort of game I want to play then?"

Already, I knew the nature of his game—the line of his thinking, but I pretended to give it consideration anyway, then shook my head. "I cannot. You must tell me." I wanted to be the one teasing him for once. I wanted to hear him say it. He made me wait, of course, bottom lip caught between his teeth as he stood dragging his fingers along my collarbone. He planted soft kisses there. I trembled beneath each of them.

"Let's see which of us can make the other moan the loudest," he whispered.

I laughed, and his kiss deepened, traveling the length of my neck, across my chest, soon he was planting them everywhere. My laughter turned to sighs, my sighs to whimpers, my whimpers to moans.

We played Varyn's game all night.

I lost.

Chapter 50

IT HAD TAKEN ME TWENTY-FOUR SEASONS TO LEARN Haneshi and countless more to speak it with confidence. Varyn was made for teaching, it seemed. He remained patient and encouraging the whole while, only occasionally jeering at me when I stuttered through words or sentences whilst trying to communicate in the merchant cities. There had been many times I wished simply to be over and done with it, but always he rallied me to the challenge. To know him was to know the ethics of determination, and I saw now how he came to be the best at so many things. It was true that some of his brightness was innate in him, but the rest he had obtained through dedication.

Often I would come home from my nights at Qêl-Ceréi and find him still working on an illustration he had begun in the morning. It was not uncommon for him to tear it to shreds and begin anew the next day. I shrieked the first time I saw him do such a thing, collecting the pieces in disbelief. He assured me it was for the best and for all my vehement objections, he was right.

Varyn had distinguished himself as an esteemed artist here in less time than it had taken me to gain my fluency. After the famed dancer had sat for him, commission upon commission poured in—from singers and poets, lords and merchants. Gùidan could scarcely meet his eyes when he came for our crescents at the end of each season. Word of his talent had even spread to some parts of Karlindé. Celine had told us as much in her letters.

Here in Hanesh he seemed to crave art, crave the feel of the tools in his hand. Our Nékhourí was home to an array of them. Always I found myself stained with some pigment or other. Oftentimes, too, I was the subject of his practice. I did not mind sitting for him and would keep the drawings, comparing them to the ones that came before and finding myself pleased with the differences I found in each of them, for I had changed much since our arrival. Both of us had. We were men now of twenty-three and twenty-four.

Between us, Varyn had changed the most. I do not know how else to describe his transformation other than to say he became more of himself. More clever, more beautiful, more talented. He grew and grew before my eyes. So broad and capable he was that he drew the eye of many suitors here. Women wanted him for his mind, his talent, his eyes, his gentle nature. Men desired his skill, his intellect, his strength, for he was hard and muscled. He liked their attentions. I knew he did.

More than once, I told him he should entertain them if he found them pleasing. But always, he refused. "All I want is you," he would say. I would ask him to reconsider often, just to hear him repeat this. It was more comforting even than being in his arms. We spent long seasons, long nights, tangled together, entwining two hearts, falling deeper into one another. Our pleasure in those days shone full as the Moon. Nothing could dull it.

Even the slow growth of our flower did not lessen our joy. Through the seasons, many things had changed, but the patches of our gardens remained the same, flat and barren. Varyn had accused me of fostering an obsession and claimed that I lingered about them too long each day, looking for the beginnings of the harvest.

But early one morning, I woke to find him gone from our bed. I rose and went about, expecting to find him sitting in the drawing room, with Cress perched upon his lap, purring as he stroked her. It was his habit to drink Zèkhei with her while he sorted through the creative depths of his mind, searching for inspiration. On this day however, I did not find him there, only Cress, eagerly licking up a bowl of water. I knelt and thumbed the crescent moon atop her head, circling it affectionately. As I got to my feet, I spotted streaks of sunlight beaming across the marble floor. They shone through an undraped archway, the one which led to the side door Cress had emerged from all those seasons ago. I walked out of it, and there was Varyn, crouched in front of the patch of garden, still with his hair in a braid.

"How long have you been out here?" I asked.

"Come and have a look at this," he said, glancing briefly up at me. I joined him, lowering myself till I saw what he beheld. Within the dark soil, the tip of a sapphire stalk had sprouted.

"Is this it?" asked Varyn. "Is it supposed to be that color? Should it not be green?"

I assessed the bit of vivid blue stalk, mouth half-gaping. "Flowers and their stems are all sorts of shades in the Celestial realm." It was like magic to finally see evidence of the eternity we had spent season after season cultivating, nurturing. I reached for it, but Varyn seized my hand.

"Don't, it looks fragile. What if you snap it? All those seasons for nothing."

"I am not going to snap it. There is hardly anything to snap."

"No, you're wrong. There's plenty here to be harmed."

"It is barely the length of a fingernail. Cress has larger claws than that."

His eyes widened at the mention of her. "She cannot come out here ever again."

"Varyn."

"What if she tears it out and eats it?"

"Be reasonable. She would not. Come back inside. You have been too long out here staring." I tugged him by the arm. He resisted.

"No, wait."

I huffed. "And you say I am the one who lingers too long on them? Get up."

"In a moment. I swear I saw it getting taller. The soil around it moved. I know it did."

"That is merely the wind."

"Go and fill the pot with water," he said. "Bring it out to me."

"It has had water already, some seasons ago."

"That was before it sprouted. This portion needs some. It's never had any."

"*Varyn.*"

"*Ambroz.*"

I stalked off and went inside, snatching up the clay pot and fetching water for it. I knew from past experience he was impossible to argue with. From the washroom, I heard him scolding our Cress. She must have scurried out there in my absence. When I came back to the garden, he had her curled in his arms, still staring at the bit of stem. I tilted the pot but he grabbed hold of it before any water poured from the opening.

"I want to do it. Take Cress inside, close the door," he said, foisting her into my arms.

Up till this moment, I had not realized how much this flower meant to him. I thought it had only been me who longed for it so fiercely. In the past, we had spoken of it as though it were intangible, despite my acquiring the Moonsoil, despite us planting it together. Now it was real for him. For me.

Inside I sat upon the cushions with Cress in my lap, feeling her purring against me. Many seasons ago, I had journeyed through use of thought back to Ethelia, back to Crescent Forest. There I had left a harvest and now I pondered if the same sapphire stem had sprouted within the fertile soil. As I mused, considering a return, Varyn came in, sinking into the cushions beside me.

"I can't believe it's finally started to grow," he said.

"Did you give it more water?"

"Yes. I thought it would light up again like it did the first time. Nothing happened."

"It will. Soon. Before long, we will have our flower. We will have eternity. If you still want it."

"You know I do." He reached for Cress and took her gently from my lap, then closed the gap between us, resting his hand where she had been. "Do you doubt it?"

I could not find words, and so I said nothing. He leaned, placed his head upon my shoulder, his hand over my heart. My arms came round him. In them, he was brawny, broad. Mine was a muscular form too, but by comparison, I was dwarfed. I cradled him anyway.

With his face nuzzled in my neck, he tells me all the things I long to hear, dispelling my insecurities, my doubts, my fears. At times, his voice alone is as soothing as a melody. My eyes flutter shut as I listen to the low rumble of it.

He recounts a story now, one from our youth. The details paint themselves behind the dark canvas of my lids. It is a silly tale and a favorite of mine. I cannot help smiling at its absurdity. The way he tells it makes me feel as if I am living it anew, living it for the first time. He comes to the end, and I burst into laughter, my eyes flying open, my worries forgotten.

Moments later, I lifted his face from my neck and saw that we were sharing this laughter, each of us peering at one another through half-moons. After we had calmed ourselves we sat staring, recovering. Wearied, I threw one leg over his lap, slumped deeper into the cushions. A strange musing struck me. I turned to him and thought aloud.

"I am curious. What will you do about your fame when you are made immortal?" I asked.

Remnants of our fit lingered and he regarded me through crescents still. "Aren't all worthy artists immortal? Their verses, their poems, their melodies. It all lives on. It's only their body that does not."

"That is legacy, and it has no flesh—no body. But you will."

"Then I suppose I'll disappear for a century or two and emerge again a different man with a new name."

I smirked and tugged on his braid. "Clever. But you will always be Varyn to me."

He smirked too, taking my hand, cupping it between his, letting his smirk bloom, till it became a grin. He was so beautiful when he beamed this way, bright and warm as the sun.

"There it is again," he said.

"There what is again?"

"Sometimes, when you look at me, your eyes sparkle green."

I somehow managed not to gasp. "They...they do?"

"Yes, it's the most charming color. Dazzling and clear. I almost wish I could draw with it."

"H-how...when..." A thousand thoughts and words circled in my mind, but I could not make order of any of them. I stammered and stammered. He squeezed my hand to silence me.

"When did I first notice it? That's what you want to know, right?"

"Y-yes."

"The first time I saw it was that day you hurt yourself on the tree. When I helped you heal, I noticed it then. I thought at first it was a trick of the light and convinced myself of it. But it happened again sometime after. Then, more and more. But just for a moment, it would flash, never for much longer than that."

"Which moments? How many of them?"

"Like when we danced at the festival, it was there. And when I kissed you for the first time. There were more occasions—when we jostled or swam, it would glint, then fade. It wasn't constant. Some seasons I never saw it all. Just your normal amber."

"Why did you never mention this?"

"I tried once before to tell you, right after the Quartz Games, but…your shades. I made mention of them and you said they weren't ever going to come. You seemed irritated by the subject. I didn't want to upset you further. I said nothing more of them."

I remembered that day and others after it—times when I had expressed annoyance or disregard for my lack. If I were him, I would not have told me either.

"Are…are they still—"

"Yes," he said, letting go of my hand to cup my cheek. "I see it more and more the older we become. It lingers longer now than it used to." There was a little table where we took our meals, resting near the cushions. Upon it sat a jeweled hand mirror. Árástin had given it to me as a gift. Varyn snatched it up—held it in front of my face. I peered into the glass and saw what I had seen that first night at Qêl-Ceréi, only brighter, more lively. I marveled at the beauty of the shade, the fierceness it lent me. I do not deny I was pleased to see it again. But as I took it in, I maintained my former belief in regard to their irrelevance. I did not let excitement overtake me as I once had. The realm and all its standards were behind me. And in front of me were things far greater. One such thing sat beside me, peering at my reflection. He planted a tender kiss upon my cheek. The shade grew more vibrant.

"What do you feel?" he asked.

Joy, I feel so much joy.

"I am happy," I said. "I have never been more happy than I am now, in this moment—with you." He kissed me again. We stared into the glass, stared at the dazzling green. Deeper it became.

This is the shade of my joy.

∞

Chapter 51

I RETURNED AGAIN TO CRESCENT FOREST NOT long after the faint beginnings of our flower had emerged. I had visited the harvest near the Uorliék inn and found it nearly identical to the one resting at the side of our Nékhourí. It was the Taurus season and in Hanesh, already sweltering. But here in Ethelia, the breeze felt as pleasant as the air blown from a cooling crystal. I envied the mortals here for it—they would never know the choking, dry heat as intimately as I or Varyn. Never suffer the fiercely beaming sun.

By contrast, Ethelia's rays were far milder, they shone harshly on me, yet I did not shield myself from them as I would have done in Hanesh. But rather, I welcomed them—squinting a little as they broke through the high trees of the forest. A brilliant beam of light scattered its warmth over the tuft of Moonsoil I planted long ago. I knelt there and absorbed the sight of a blue stalk sprouting from within the rich brown. Varyn was not here to scold me for touching it, and so I reached. It was longer than the others, thicker. Perhaps the surroundings, full of thriving trees and flowers, had lent it better nurturing.

I pinched the stalk between two fingers, and a feeling of delight coursed through me. Soon enough, I would behold the blossom of eternity. Gone would be my worrisome thoughts of a life alone—of an existence void of Varyn. Each day passed in harvest was a day without this certainty. I longed for them to end. This peeking bit of stalk gave me solace. I ambled to the river and fetched water for it. The running stream evoked memories of Varyn and I, racing his impossible matches as children. As I plucked the small chalice I brought along from my person, I thought fondly of our days here. Everywhere I looked held some impression of our presence; the ground for our racing, the trees for our climbing, the riverbank for our respite. Even the air carried with it the reminiscence of mirth—of a youth shared reveling in it.

I filled the chalice, half-smiling. Though this countenance fell from my lips as I emptied it onto the area. A soft rustling drew me from the task. I whipped my head over my shoulder to confront the sound. My gaze met nothing but the open forest. I was alone. Above me were birds perched atop the branches of trees. Perhaps it had been their flight that had alarmed me. But with the sound had also come a feeling of unease.

"Is someone there?" I called out, voice echoing through the expanse of green like ripples in water. There came no answer but chirping, the wind, and the running river. I lingered there at length, peering about through narrowed eyes, listening for…what? I did not know. Whatever it was had gone. And so, too, had that strange discontent. With the Moonsoil watered, I had no reason to dawdle about. I glanced below at the damp spot of brown beneath my feet, admired the blue gem springing from its center, then summoned our Nékhourí to mind.

Trees morphed into archways, and Crescent Forest vanished with a blink.

Cress hissed at my ankles, for coming so abruptly into view always unnerved her. The hissing gave way to mewls as the familiar scent of me calmed her feral instincts.

"It is alright," I whispered. "It is only me." The sound of my voice dissolved the rest of her trepidation, and she rubbed her little head against my ankle. I lifted her.

Seasons of being spoiled with rich foods had made her plump. She was heavy in my arms. I kissed her crescent-marked spot of fur and went looking for Varyn. It did not take long to stumble upon him.

He had turned one of the rooms of our little palace into a study, not unlike the one in his father's manor. Gradually, over the course of many seasons, it became filled with his materials, with books and the tools of his craft. I watched him quietly from the threshold, noting traces of Lord Vedlan in his bearing and posture. It was striking how similar a son could be to his father. Little things greatly resembled the latter—such as the way Varyn held his quill or how he sat reading, chin on fist. These habits endeared me. He performed one now as he sat studying something I could not see, eyes downcast. I watched, silently adoring him, escaping his notice all the while.

Long moments in idle passed and many more would have gone by were it not for Cress. She made our presence known with a loud mewl, after which she leaped from my arms and pranced off. Varyn acknowledged me with a quick glance and even this was reminiscent of his father.

"What are you over there smirking at?" he asked without looking up from what occupied him. I was not aware I had been but realized the tugging curve of my lips upon his mentioning.

"You," I said, grinning.

"*Me?* And what have I done to be worthy of a smirk?" He still had not torn his gaze from the desk. I wanted to laugh now at these similarities.

"Plenty. What are you reading?"

"A letter."

"From whom?"

"Celine."

I stepped over the threshold and made my way to him, planting myself on the desk. "What does she say? Is she well?"

"Very well. She wants us to come and visit her."

"In Karlindé?"

"Mm, yes. Here. You can read it if you like."

He slid the letter across the desk. I admired Celine's writing. All her words were carefully chosen, tidy, and measured. In my head, I heard her voice, speaking them as though she were here before me. In her soft cadence, she told me of Karlindé's charm, of meeting the man who was her father by flesh only. She spoke of her Nerosi, of the fame and crescents it afforded her, just as Varyn had said it would. She told me of how she missed him, of how happy she was to learn that he had me for a lover now. Though I could scarcely believe it, she had taken one too—Jayce. I nearly snorted and covered my mouth upon reading of how he had followed her everywhere, begging at her heels, showering her with offers till she accepted. Her experiences came alive through the words of her letter. I read it over once more and briefly lived another life. I was smiling by the time I reached the end of it.

"I want to go and see her," I said.

"We will, one day. In time."

"When? How much time?"

"I'm not sure. I can't say with so many commissions waiting. I can hardly break in the middle of them for a season's long voyage to Karlindé. But we will go to her. I promise."

I tried not to frown as I traced my fingers along the letter. Whilst reading it, I had been dreaming of all she described. I wanted to see her life, her home, her face.

"Why don't you write to her in the meantime? I'm sure she'd love to hear from you," said Varyn. He rose and rummaged about, gathering materials. As he set up the drawing frames, I sank into his chair, feeling the lingering heat of him. There was parchment, quill, and ink before me. I took them in hand.

In the past, I had given Varyn a line or two of correspondence for Celine, and always he wrote them into his letters. It would be better to write one of my own.

"I should have done this sooner," I said. "I do not know why I never thought to."

"That is why you have me. I'm here to do your thinking for you."

The frame and canvas shielded him from view, but he poked his head from behind it to flash a jeering wink at me. I smirked and wrote. He drew.

Sometime later, I received a reply. I read it with Cress in my lap, beaming all the while.

·········◦)·) ◉ (·(◦·········

From then on, Celine and I corresponded often. I looked forward to receiving her letters—each one brought news of some exciting detail. For many moons now I had been urging Varyn to make time in his work for a visit. He would set out arranging plans for a voyage only to abandon them midway when another offer came about. I grew restless and told Celine of my eagerness for a reunion in many of my letters. She expressed the same in hers for it had been long since she extended the invitation.

The seasons bled swiftly into one another, passing like clouds across the sky. Much had changed in her life, and she wished to share it. Much had changed in ours, too. The flower was near to blooming. Varyn was a man of twenty-seven, esteemed and striking as ever. In a few days' time, I would enter my twenty-seventh year as well. But I did not want to grow even a season older without having visited Celine.

Surrounded by chattering mortals, I sat before the mirror in Qêl-Ceréi, reading her most recent letter. In an earlier one, she mentioned harboring a surprise. I wrote back, begging for revelation, but she refused to name it through correspondence and insisted that Varyn and I learn of it in person. I combed the new letter, ignoring the noise around me as I searched for hints of her surprise in it.

"Don't tell me you've taken a new lover, darling," came the voice of Árástin. From behind me, he draped his arms round my neck and peered over my shoulder at the letter. I flipped it to obscure the writing from view and glared at his reflection. His eyes were painted gold—gleaming bands of the same hue encircled his arms.

"What?" I asked.

He clicked his tongue. "Wearing a smile like that. One can only assume you're reading a lover's poem."

"I have no lover except for Varyn. It is from a friend. Anyway, mind your own affairs."

"Where's the fun in that?" He sighed and sat beside me, tilted his head. "Here, put this on," he said, reaching inside the drawer of a dressing table. A sparkling necklace dangled in his hand. I let him adorn me with it. "I earn the most crescents when you sing in jewels. Something about a man donning twinkling gems really does it for them. Oh, and I'm relieved to hear it, by the way."

"Relieved to hear what?"

"That you've not taken another lover. You'd be mad to dally about with anyone else when you've got that strapping, ruby-headed beauty to crawl into bed with every night. Then again, I suppose it would be a good thing if you had. Then I would have my chance to—"

"Enough. Is there not something else you could be doing aside from pestering me?"

"Do you know, I'm most curious. I've been wondering about it for so long."

"Wondering about what?"

"Your Varyn—is he the sort to saddle or be saddled?"

I rolled my eyes and got to my feet.

Chortling, Árástin put his hand over my arm. "Oh come darling, all these years we've known each other and you've not spared one detail. I tell you about all my dalliances—impart me with *something*. It's not fair you have him all to yourself. He saddles, right? Oh, tell me he saddles. I need this knowledge, Ambroz. You don't know how badly I need it. I'll keep it between us, gods, I swear it." He looked left, then right. "Saddler or saddled? The rider or the one ridden?" he whispered.

I swatted his hand away, leaning and lowering my voice. "Both." Árástin squealed. I left him squalling there and headed for the main room.

I walked through the dim corridors, humming. My nights at Qêl-Ceréi had become less and less since Varyn gained esteem. His crescents alone supported us. Now I sang not for need of any income but for the sake of pleasure, and courtesy to Oléina. This only served to draw more patrons in for her. Scarcity had bred demand, and on my nights, there were more bodies filling the place than on any other. I will not pretend as if I did not enjoy the way mortals adored the sound of my voice. They fawned over the sight of me while I stood upon the dais. It felt like worship to watch them cherishing me from above it—to hear their praise and descend upon the many, wading through the flock of seeking hands. They received me with smiles of admiration. It was better I think, than the veneration given to Celestials, those cold and distant beings, as aloof as stars fixed in the sky. Better for I had earned it from them.

After singing, as I sat in the main room, watching the selection gradually dwindle, I thought of the twelve courts—and of my effigy. It had been a long while since the hall of them crossed my mind. I was a boy when last I imagined the smoke and glow of offering. That is not to say I was imagining it now, for I was not. But instead, merely recalling the yearning I once harbored to see it brightly burning.

Unbidden, an image of it blazing flashed in the eye of my mind. I banished it, replacing the vision with thoughts of Varyn, of our flower, so near to the end of its harvest. My nights now were filled with dreams of plucking it from the ground. In them, I did not worry for Varyn's safety. I did not fret over the possibility of some unforeseen mishap that would take him from me. Nothing could hurt him in my dreams. And soon, nothing could hurt him at all.

"Smiling, smiling. Why this big smiling?" said Oléina. She was making her way to me, grinning. Though I had learned Haneshi, she insisted on speaking to me in broken, informal Celestian still. I had not been aware of my smiling face. Thoughts of Varyn always bid them. I let it broaden and answered Oléina in Haneshi. She had come to give me my crescents for the night. I took them and headed back to our Nékhourí.

Before going inside, I lingered around the patch of garden, staring at the half-formed flower. Much of its stem had sprouted. It seemed a resilient thing, as impervious as the urn I had transported it in. The winds did not sway it, nor was it at the mercy of any manner of winged creature. There were many in the mortal realm, always buzzing here and there, yet never did they land upon our slow-growing flower. I had become covetous of it and, perhaps, like Varyn had once accused, obsessive. A day could not pass without my laying eyes on it. I watched it a while longer, then went inside.

Now I stared down at another precious thing. In rest, his features lapsed into their boyhood innocence. I could not help treasuring them, and reached, gently brushing his cheek with the back of my fingers. His face twitched under them like the wings of butterflies. He stirred, and the thick hair of his lashes parted. Behind them, a pair of honey eyes warmly regarded me. He grunted, smiling faintly, and they fluttered closed again.

"What are you doing standing over me like a thief in the night?" he asked, groaning as he groped the air for my hand. I placed it in his, and he pulled me on top of him. "How did your singing fare tonight?"

I kissed his forehead, then rolled onto my side. "It always goes well. Before I left, I went to the post and found a letter from Celine."

"Oh? Is she well?"

"Yes. She has a surprise."

"What sort of surprise?" he asked, eyes still closed as I stroked his face, his braid.

"She will not say. She wishes for us to go to her. It has been too long. We are men now—proper ones, as you say. The last time she saw either of us, we were at the end of our being boys. We must go and visit her."

There was silence for a while, then, still with his eyes shut, he nodded. "You're right. We will go at the end of this season. That way, I can settle some accounts, and you can give Oléina notice of your absence. She will be fine with you taking leave of Qêl-Ceréi?"

"Yes, of course. I am hardly there as it is."

He nodded again, then fell silent and drifted back to sleep.

In the morning, I feared rest had clouded his head—that all we agreed upon had been merely the work of his drowsy, sleep-drenched mind. But by afternoon, instead of sketching, he left to secure our tickets for passage. I beamed when he returned with them, yet I dreaded another voyage at sea. Though even this bitterness was assuaged for now we had the crescents to afford us more spacious lodgings on board.

I turned twenty-seven soon after he arranged our transport. For it, Varyn lavished me with gifts; jewels, silks, a new carriage. A portrait too, one which depicted me with joyous, emerald eyes.

On the day before our voyage, I took Cress to stay with Árástin. She mewled and whimpered shrilly for my abandoning her there. I almost wished to turn back and take her with us, but a ship was no place for one as precious as her.

As I prepared to leave our Nékhourí for the journey, another of my darlings called to me. I went to look upon it and shrieked.

"What's the matter?" Varyn shouted from inside. But there were no words illustrative enough to describe what I beheld. "Ambroz?"

I gave no reply, merely knelt, fingers covering my mouth. Varyn came and found me—mirrored my expression. He let out a small gasp when he saw it. Upon the tip of our flower, where there was once nothing, now rested a little bud. I wanted to linger and watch it all day, but such a luxury was not possible. Our ship would soon sail.

A joy settled over me as I gazed at it, though the feeling was marred by a wave of unease. Nevertheless, I bid it an ephemeral farewell, then left.

Chapter 52

KARLINDÉ SEEMED THE YOUNGER, TEPID SISTER of Hanesh. Its heat was fierce but not choking, the sun bright but not blazing. Varyn and I stepped onto the seaport, walking circles in the open to stretch our limbs, which had yearned for more exertion than was afforded during the voyage. The unmoving deck beneath my feet was a welcome element after so long on board. We had set off at the end of the Cancerian season and arrived a few days shy of the start of Virgo.

By contrast, this journey felt leagues better than the first we shared as youths of nineteen. Wealth and status and the wisdom of many seasons had greatly improved our conditions. We teased one another at times on sea, recounting that silent, days-long confrontation engendered by the stubbornness of youth. As men, we still bickered on occasion or found ourselves at odds, though never to that extent—the respect and admiration fostered between us left no margin for such quarrels. Our lives in Hanesh, the union we shared there—few would ever know one like it.

I stood amidst the chaos of busy mortals as we waited to be received, some were frantic with arrival, others bustling about to arrange affairs. All of it I ignored whilst peering at Varyn. His curls hung loose, fanning in the breeze, shining in the sunlight. The vibrant beauty of him called to mind that peeking bud coming to life beside our Nékhourí. The slightest things evoked remembrance of it. For the whole of the journey, it ruled my thoughts. We had just arrived and already I wanted to go back and tend to it—to nurture it to blooming so that the worries which plagued me would abate. Such a yearning was futile, I reminded myself, for the flower would flourish in its own time, and there was much of it yet to abide. Notwithstanding, I mused and conjured imaginings of an eternal Varyn as I watched him, fiery hair still rustling in the soft winds. More mortals passed between us. He turned and caught me staring.

"And what are you gawking at?" he asked, chin jutting, hands on hips. It was his teasing stance. Soon he would nudge my shoulder, ruffle my hair till I gave a satisfactory answer. I pretended not to hear him. He started toward me, brow quirked.

I backed away, grinning and ready for the challenge, preparing to bolt. He was too quick, however. His long legs sealed the gap between us. Swiftly, he seized my wrist. His eyes glinted with mischief, and I knew he would torment me now. To avoid further conquering, I pecked his cheek. He released his hold on me, drew me in with his gaze alone. I loved when he looked at me this way. He bent slightly—beckoning my lips. I pushed his hair back and tasted his sweet warmth.

"Gods and Jupiter. I could have gone my entire life without seeing that." We broke apart and discovered Jayce lumbering toward us, feigning revulsion. He was even larger than I remembered and twice as irksome.

"Oh please. That's likely the best view you've had in ages," said Varyn. Jayce tossed his head back, laughing. The three of us embraced in turn, exchanging comments on changed appearances and heights.

"And where is Celine? Is it not torture enough you've attached yourself to her? Must I also suffer your company without her presence?" asked Varyn.

"Ha, I'm the one suffering. She's at home, come, the carriage isn't far. Try to keep your hands and lips to yourselves when we get in, why don't you."

I hid my smirk as Jayce led us through the swarm of mortals. We snaked our way around them to transport. As the carriage waded down the dry, sandy path, he regaled us with an account of all that had occurred in his life leading to this day. It proved a lengthy tale, and several times throughout, my thoughts drifted, returning only when the sound of Varyn's chortling snapped me back into awareness. I listened enough to learn that he had given his full devotion to Celine—expending all manner of efforts to win her in spite of her affections for other suitors.

A part of me wished she had taken one of them for a lover instead of Jayce for their descriptions seemed more tailored to Celine's deft character. Though as his tale progressed, I felt slightly ashamed of such harsh judgment. Despite her rebuffs and courting of others, he patiently pursued her, gentle in his advances. He claimed it was him who suggested she take up establishing her Nerosi talents in Karlindé.

"I bought her the shop as part of my marriage proposal. She's the jewel of it. I only help manage her clients. There's so many now," he boasted, the corners of his grin touching each ear. "You should see the inside. It's glorious."

"So that's why she agreed to marry you. I'm relieved. She's not gone out of her head after all," said Varyn.

"Shut up. Celine adores me."

Varyn sneered. "I'd adore you too if you purchased a shop for me."

I nudged Varyn. "That was kind of you, Jayce. I cannot wait to see it."

Jayce beamed. "Do you know, Varyn—I can't understand what a sensible person like him even sees in you."

"More than Celine sees in you, I'm sure."

I nudged Varyn again, harder. "What is this surprise she spoke of in her letter?" I asked.

"Ah, that," replied Jayce, beaming brighter. "I promised not to spoil it on the way. You'll have to wait until we arrive. We're nearly there. You'll find out soon enough."

"Give us a hint," said Varyn.

"Can't, I'm afraid. Anything I say could ruin it. Celine would have my head. She wants to see the looks on your faces."

Varyn grunted. "Oh, come on. Just one won't hurt."

"Still as stubborn as you've always been, eh? Stop asking," clipped Jayce.

"I've figured it out already anyway," said Varyn.

"You have?" I asked, brows raised. He nodded and leaned, cupping his hand over my ear. Jayce glared as Varyn whispered. I pulled away grinning, feeling somewhat daft for not arriving at the conclusion on my own. It was so obvious now.

"You had better keep up your pretenses, Varyn, or I swear by the gods I'll box your head in. If Celine looks even the slightest bit disappointed, I'll—"

"Oh, save it. She was my sister before she was your lover, I know better than anyone how to fool her, and as far as you boxing my head in, I'd like to see you try."

They carried on bickering back and forth, but I paid them little heed. All I could think of was our arrival. The journey seemed to drag on, and for the whole of it, my heart leaped in my chest, excitement surging through me. When the carriage finally stopped I helped Varyn unload our belongings, each of us glancing over our shoulder whilst discussing the surprise in hushed tones.

We took our things toward the door of Jayce and Celine's quaint home. The former trudged behind us while I waited with held breath for the latter to swing it open. Halfway along, she held it ajar, sticking her head through the gap. Her eyes fell on me, and she squealed, giggling as I dashed to her. Time had hardly touched her features. She appeared much the same as she had always been, only slightly taller and with wiser eyes. They widened as I drew nearer to the entrance.

"Gods, why didn't you tell me you'd gotten so handsome," she said, gasping, "and you too, Vary. I hardly recognized you. Here I thought *I* would be the one surprising *you*. Speaking of." She threw the door open. I prepared myself to feign shock but it was not at all necessary. The precious sight of Celine's plump little daughter sucked the air from my chest. She was a mirror of her mother, smaller and rounder but just as bright. Pretenses aside, Varyn appeared veritably stunned. He reached for the small girl, who clung to her mother's side, chewing on her tiny fingers. She cooed, hesitated, curiously blinked her large, gemstone-like eyes, then went to him.

"That's it, you know your Uncle Vary, don't you, dear one," he said, bouncing her. "Stars, she's beautiful, looks nothing like Jayce and thank every planet above for it." Celine smirked.

"I heard that," said Jayce as he neared us.

"Good," said Varyn. He kissed the girl's fat cheeks, and she grinned. They beamed at one another, transfixed. "Who knew a toothless smile could be so pretty—what's her name?"

"Elayne," said Celine.

I did not think it was possible for Varyn's smile to grow any wider, but it did. "After mother, how fitting," he said softly. I looked fondly on as he swayed her in his arms, watching him sweetly stroke the short, auburn curls atop her head.

"Did I hear you call Ambroz handsome earlier? You never call me handsome," said Jayce.

Celine waved her hand through the air dismissively. "Quiet, that's not true. Help them take their things inside, then go and set the table." Jayce huffed. She ignored his indignant grumblings as he took up our possessions. I helped and hauled them over the threshold, leaving Varyn, Elayne, and Celine to their reunion. Her home reminded me somewhat of the manor in Ethelia. Though less grand, there was space enough for five or six to live comfortably. I spotted the drawing which had gained Varyn acclaim in Hanesh hanging upon a wall and welled with pride as I passed by it.

Jayce led me to the room which had been prepared for Varyn and me. After he left, I busied myself with laying out some garments. As I plucked one of Varyn's silks from the chest, the sweet scent of him flowed out at me. I breathed it in—let it transport me to our bed, to Hanesh, where everything carried the scent of him, the essence. My eyes closed of their own accord as I took it in. Slowly, I opened them and in so doing, found my reflection. For being so long at sea, I was not terribly disheveled. Though my dark hair was windblown. I went to the mirror to tame it and met in my gaze that elusive, sparkling shade of emerald. I felt tempted to linger there as I used to in my lonely chamber of the twelve courts. That Fool would have stared and stared—would have commanded other shades to come forth. He would have chanted for his glow, cried out for his light.

Comeoutcomeoutcomeoutcomeoutcomeoutcomeoutcomeoutcomeout OUT OUT OUT

I had no such urges now to beg for what I did not have. What a strange journey. From lack to abundance, yearning to contentment. Despite never having attained a full grasp on my divinity, I felt in this moment whole. Worthy and complete. Tears might have formed if I had allowed myself to succumb to them, for I was a creature of sentiment, a child of the Moon. I was water. From my reflection, I flowed and drifted back like the tide to carry on with my task.

As I worked, Varyn called out to me, and I left the chamber, followed the sound of his voice.

"There you are," he said as I came into the drawing room. Elayne had her head pressed against his chest now. I cherished the sight.

"Where'd you disappear to for so long?" I pointed in the direction I had come, parting my lips in answer. Celine's tongue was quicker.

"It doesn't matter. He's here now," she said, pecking me on the cheek. She turned and gently peeled a dozing Elayne from Varyn's arms, "And that means I can show you my second surprise."

"Another surprise? You never mentioned this in any of your letters," I said.

"I know, I know, shame on me. But let me put little Elly here down for a nap, and I'll show it to you in the dining room. Then we can all eat something. Karlindé has the most decadent foods. You'll love everything you try, I promise."

Celine left with Elayne's sleepy, limp form slung over her shoulder.

While she walked away, Varyn came to stand by my side. He smoothed my wind-tousled hair down as he spoke adoringly of his niece. I listened to his endearing descriptions, beaming while he told me of the smiles she had given him or the noises she had made—one of which he claimed sounded like an attempt at his name. He performed a reenactment of this sound to the best of his ability and I nearly cried laughing. As I mocked him for it, he chased me across the room. In the end, it was Celine who put a stop to his pursuit, chiding Varyn instead of me for such immature behavior. His retreat was momentary, and I let myself be captured by him, enduring his punishing tickles as Celine led us to the dining quarters for an afternoon meal. We reached the doorway, and she turned to us, glancing from me to Varyn.

"He's waiting for you," she said.

"Who is?"

Celine nudged him over the threshold. He took a few steps and halted, growing stiff as a tree.

I knew what shock looked like on Varyn. Even from behind, I knew it. I did not need to see his face to know his lips were parted and his brows were raised.

A tension as thick as morning fog permeated the air surrounding us.

I hurried to Varyn's side to learn the nature of Celine's surprise, pausing after a few steps just as he had done. Now I, too, had become a tree, and each of us stood rooted there in a forest of our own making. Celine went inside first, body brushing against mine, rustling my leaves. Her movements broke me from my trance, and I followed behind her, but not without slipping my hand in Varyn's, giving him the support I knew he needed. I took slow steps, and reluctantly, he did the same. We were trees before the table now, the three of us wordlessly regarding one another while Celine occupied herself with arranging the placement of dishes. I extended my hand across the wood which separated us.

"Hello," I said, "it is nice to see you again, Lord Vedlan."

Chapter 53

VARYN'S FATHER ROSE AND TOOK THE HAND I OFFERED, shaking it with less force than I had anticipated. He seemed smaller than I remembered, frail even. His hair had gone white, and many more lines than before were carved into the weathered skin of his face. Familiar, brown eyes rested on mine, lingering for a moment, then traveling beyond to settle upon the honeyed hazel ones beside me.

"Are you well Father?" I was taken aback by the sound of Varyn's voice, by the absence of bitterness or hostility in it. For so long he had refused my suggestions of initiating correspondence with Lord Vedlan. Now he had been the one to break their years-long silence. All of his former shock had fallen away, and he stood firm, chin jutting, looking down his nose as that insufferable Gùidan had once accused. Though it was not a stance born of arrogance as he had so crudely implied, but one of due regard.

Lord Vedlan moved from behind the table and closed the distance between him and Varyn. They rested a hairsbreadth from one another, each motionless. It was Lord Vedlan who broke the stillness, taking one of Varyn's hands and enveloping it between his two.

"I...hear you are an artist," said Lord Vedlan, a slight tremble in his cadence.

Varyn nodded. "Yes, I am."

"It is not what I wanted for you, but...your mother...she would be proud."

"Not would be," said Celine. "She *is*. Very proud."

Lord Vedlan clapped Varyn gently on the back, beckoning him into an embrace. I noted a change in the measure of Varyn's breaths and hooked my arm through Celine's, bidding her. Varyn did not like for others to see his tears. I am sure his father was the same. We left them alone to shed their silent drops in each other's arms.

I sat with Celine in the drawing-room, where we fell deep into conversation, exchanging stories, filling in the gaps of all the seasons spent apart. I told her of my life in Hanesh, of Qêl-Ceréi. She told me of her hobbies, of her love for Elayne, of her Nerosi, which she had feared the loss of during her pregnancy. The life that grew inside of her had occluded her ability to traverse the veil and hear those beyond it.

"I couldn't make out a single thing for nine seasons, not even a whisper. I was afraid it would never return, and the shop would close, but Mother assured me it would come back."

"You can still talk to your mother? After all this time? I thought mortals must pass on—that your guidance helped them make the transition." I said.

"It's not normal, and it takes a strong spirit to manage it. But she's got one foot in this realm still, and the other in what is beyond. I've urged her to leave so many times, but she wanted to be there for me, see me become a woman. Even when all the other voices and visions stopped, hers was still there. It was the only one I could communicate with."

"How did she know your Nerosi would come back?"

"She says time is different on the other side. That everything is happening all at once and so she knew. I don't understand it."

"And straight after you had Elayne, it returned?"

She shook her head. "It took three seasons. I almost shrieked the first time I saw a vision again. They're stronger than ever now after having her. I just wish other things I've lost would come back too."

"What other things?"

"My hair."

I wrinkled my brow as I peered up at her tight coils of copper. "But you have plenty of hair."

Her shoulders slumped, head drooping slightly as she lifted each side of her thick mane, pulling it back to reveal patches of bare scalp.

"I'm told it's normal to lose some after a birth," she mumbled, eyes downcast. She smoothed her coils into place again. "But it feels awful."

I took one of her hands in mine.

"You are still beautiful," I said. At this, she gave a shy half-smile.

"The most beautiful," said Jayce. He had been listening from the doorway. Smirking, he waltzed into the drawing room and planted a kiss atop Celine's head. "I'm starving. Let's go and eat," he said.

I wondered if we had been away from the dining quarters long enough for Varyn and his father to have come to a proper reconciliation. As we entered, however, it became clear they had. Varyn's eyes were puffy and red-rimmed, but behind them lived no sadness. He smiled when he saw me, and as I took a seat beside him at the table, began stroking his finger along my collarbone. Of all the ways Varyn showed his affections, this was my favorite one. Though I was shy now, of receiving it in front of Lord Vedlan. I may have been a man, but my boyish diffidence had not left me.

Varyn kept on dragging his finger delicately across my neck. It stirred me, and I seized his hand to stop him. Instead of ending it there as I had hoped, he brought it to his lips, kissed it. Heat flushed across my face, kindled like a small flame in my chest.

I tore my hand from Varyn's grip.

Lord Vedlan's gaze briefly met mine. I thought there might be disapproval or contrition in it, for Varyn was his only son, a luminous star deserving of a light equal to his, but I found warmth in his regard of me, not scorn. I eased and sipped the drink I had been given. Soon, the sound of chatter and laughter filled the room.

As we ate, I felt I had been transported back to the manor in Ethelia. Many times as a boy I shared meals in the company of Varyn and his family. This reminded me of our youth, our lies and games. Halfway through the meal, little Elayne came crawling in, face streaked with evidence of her nap. Lord Vedlan doted on her. She loved being spoiled, I think, and allowed herself to be passed from hand to hand without protest, enduring pats upon the head and pinches on the cheeks from most everyone.

When my turn arrived, I spared her this and merely held her. She felt like Cress in my arms, plump and soft. I kissed her on the forehead, and she grinned her precious, toothless grin. She could not speak, but we conversed nonetheless through gestures and smiles. Varyn grew envious of our secret language and stole her from me. She went happily to him. I watched the two of them together, feeling an elation I had never known welling within me. It lingered all throughout the day, and later that night, as Varyn climbed into bed beside me, it reached its pinnacle.

I lay there and breathed in the clean scent of him, twirling his braid round my finger. It was still damp from his bath.

"You should have let me," I said.

"Let you what?"

"Braid your hair. I would have dried it first—properly, with a cloth."

"But then I would not have my favorite thing."

"What do you mean?" I asked. "What *favorite thing*?"

"Your eyes on me, watching me as I braid it."

There was a sliver of space between us in the bed. I dragged myself forward and narrowed it so that the tips of our noses touched. His breaths on me were sweeter than honey, warmer than sunlight. We were so near, and yet I yearned to be closer still. I reached across, held him by the chin, tilted his face, and aligned his lips with mine. I parted my own, readying them to be enveloped by his warmth. But he pulled away from me.

"You are tired?" I asked.

"No."

"Then what is the matter?"

He chewed on the inside of his cheek. "Why did you shy away from me earlier at the table? Are you embarrassed of our union?"

"What? No, of course not, I—"

"Why then?"

I opened my mouth, then closed it. Opened it again. "The best part of me is you," I said, cupping his face in my palm. "Your father...I...feared he would...not approve of my being with you. You are his son. You are Varyn. Who am I? I have no titles, no merit. These things are what started your feud in the first place. I thought he would be disappointed to learn that you had not chosen someone better."

He scoffed. "Someone better?" Now he was glaring at me. "That voice in your head, the one that told you that. It's the Devil's, the Magician's. Not yours. I thought you had stopped listening to it. Was I wrong to think this, Ambroz?"

"No, you—I..." I stopped myself from lying to him. What he said of the voices, it was true. I had not realized it till now, but their hooks were still in me. I had ascribed qualities of my own father onto Lord Vedlan—shrunk myself into the disappointment he had always believed me to be. The Devil had never approved of me—would never approve of me. "You were not wrong," I whispered. "I lapsed into old ways I...simply...needed reminding."

"Good. Look at me," said Varyn. I stared through the dim light. "This *someone better* you speak of. If they existed, I wouldn't want them. They are not you."

I beamed. We embraced.

So much of my life has faded to blur. It is all a vague obscurity now. These tender moments with my Varyn, however

    they remain

    as clear as quartz

    they will never leave me.

Chapter 54

I FEEL MYSELF GROWING WEARY, THE DETAILS slipping from memory like grains of sand through fingers. These years I have recounted, they are held dearest to me, sparkling bright as jewels in the watery eye of my mind. I cherish their simplicity, those uneventful seasons we shared, passing passing passing on.

I have not said all I care to say on this, there is more, so much more joy. But I am weary of shedding my shell. I will give it now, my vital, remaining testimony.

Hear the impetus of my atrocities.

Chapter 55

ON A SWELTERING DAY IN UORLIÉK, I LEFT the blissful cool of our Nékhourí and went outside to find the flower had bloomed. Varyn and I were thirty-two. The years were wonderful to us, each of them filled with nothing but mirth, love. On this day, he and I had nothing to do and the whole day to do it. We had returned a week prior from another voyage to Karlindé. It was our routine now, to go and visit Celine and her dear Elayne at least once in every twelve seasons. I had come out into the heat merely to glance upon the flower. It was a habit of mine. On each occasion however, I found no changes, no bloom. But as I stood shying from the furious rays of Hanesh's sun, brilliant sapphire petals bent toward it.

I had waited so long for this moment. Even so, its arrival left me breathless. My hands shook as I reached for the delicate stem of eternity. It came out of the ground with little effort—a single tug, and it was free. I felt as if I held a living thing in my hands. Nothing else existed but its color. That vibrant blue made everything around me seem dull and lifeless. I carried it inside, walking slowly, feeling as if any swift movement might tear it from my gentle grip.

In the drawing-room, I pried my gaze from it and saw Varyn standing at the gate. Gùidan's grating voice floated beyond it, the volume assaulting my ears. He had come to collect his crescents and was now asking for more of them than what was agreed upon.

Varyn spewed curses, gave him what was owed and nothing more, then slammed the gate. He strode toward me, infuriated. But all the anger bled from his expression when he took notice of me, clutching our flower. He became as still and solid as the ground beneath our feet.

"It…it is done." He was panting as the words left him.

"Nearly," I said. "We must get the nectar from it. Then it will truly be done."

"Now, I want to do it now."

I had never seen him so eager. His eyes nearly glowed as they beheld the flower.

"We need water then. And something to—"

"I know. I have a needle to help with getting out the drops. I'll go and get the water."

The clanking of fists against the gate tore our attention from one another. Cress appeared by my feet suddenly and hissed at the entrance, back arching.

In the distance, Gùidan yelled muffled, indiscernible threats from behind the door, prompting Varyn to turn and shout more curses at him.

"What is he on about?" I asked.

"I've sold a drawing to the wealthiest merchant in Uorliék. He got word of the cost she paid for it somehow, and now he feels like he's owed something—that it's within his rights to charge us more crescents for our living here."

"But that is absurd," I said.

"Try telling that to him."

More loud banging from Gùidan erupted. Now Cress was circling the small table near the floor cushions. She leaped atop it, knocking things over, and delivered more hisses toward the gate.

"Perhaps we should give him the crescents he wants," I said. "So that he might leave us be."

Varyn scowled. "I'd sooner abandon this place than agree to that nonsense." He stormed to the door and threw it open. Gùidan stood behind the gate, wagging his finger as a deluge of rapid Haneshi poured from his lips. Varyn reached into his pocket and, in a blur of movement, flung a few crescents through the bars at Gùidan's head. Varyn spouted more curses at him and slammed it shut again. As it closed, I saw Gùidan kneeling to gather the crescents from the ground, muttering under his breath.

"You should not have done that," I said.

He waved this off. "I know. It felt good though. Sit down. I'll go and fetch the water."

I wandered to the table near the floor cushions, looking over my shoulder at Varyn, already the tension within him had eased. Cress still had not calmed and idled about the area, fur standing on end. I sank behind the table, making room on its surface for the flower as I crossed my legs. I placed it down, staring. It seemed larger than it had outside, where it was merely a coveted treasure jutting from the dirt. I stroked the soft petals in awe of what they represented. I knew the nectar lay deep within it and felt a sting of sadness that all else of this beautiful thing would be discarded after so many seasons spent waiting for it to take form.

Whilst I mused, Varyn came in with a glass of water and sat opposite me. He slowly lifted our bright bloom from the marble. Right away, his nimble artist's hands worked to liberate the nectar from inside it. He was patient with it, sweat beading on his forehead in spite of the cooling crystal's air. As he toiled, I wiped it with a bit of cloth. He continued on without pause. Drop after drop fell into the water. I do not know where he learned such a skill. I would not have been able to manage it.

The trickling orbs of amber nectar held me in a trance. He coaxed them free with care, each one twinkling as it cascaded into the glass. More sweat formed on his brow. Again I wiped it away, leaping at the chance to be of some use.

"Thank you," he mumbled, eyes never leaving the task.

It dawned on me then that after he drank this elixir, he would need more heedful tending, for the tonic would render him ill. The Hermit's instruction—those pivotal words spoken in haste more than a decade ago—came flooding back. She had warned there would be pain, a full day of it.

Dismayed, I drank in the sight of Varyn, brow fierce with diligent effort as he drained the flower of its essence. He had been ill only a handful of times in his life. I did not like to see him suffering. As I sat inwardly bemoaning, he broke from the task and glanced at me.

"What's the matter?" he asked.

I had not been aware of my scowling, his tone of inquiry alerted me of its presence among my features. But I eased upon taking in the even measure of his expression.

"It will bring you discomfort," I said.

He forced another sphere of amber from the flower. "You mean the nectar?"

"Yes."

"I know. I remember everything you told me that day. I'm not afraid of the pain. I've nothing to fear, so long as you're with me, I can endure it."

I touched the cloth to his forehead again, lingering affectionately. He carried on with it, concentrating as if it were one of his drawings till finally there was nothing left to be taken. The flower hung limp, petals curling in on themselves. Before us rested the glass. The once clear water was now tinted amber, like a sunset descending upon the sea. I pushed it gently toward Varyn, eager to set his eternity in motion. He sat with both hands tucked in his lap, looking down at it.

"Stars, my heart's racing. I don't know why."

"Take a deep breath," I said. "The threat of pain is making you nervous, I think."

He nodded and closed his eyes. "You're right. I just need a moment to steady myself."

I waited for his nerves to settle, picking at the drooping flower. It seemed so ordinary, now, its petals no longer vibrant. A part of me mourned the loss of such beauty. Another rejoiced. Varyn had come back to himself as these conflicted feelings wrestled within me. He reached for the glass, and elation reigned victorious.

Then a number of things occurred at once.

A cacophony arose as Gùidan hammered on the gate. The harsh clanking startled not only Varyn and me but Cress as well. She appeared suddenly and leaped upon the table, sending the elixir toppling over. The contents of the glass spilled onto the marble before it crashed to the floor, shattering.

I stared dumbfounded at Varyn as Cress hissed. A dozen or more emotions seized me—anger, grief, fury, sorrow, hate, all of them, among many others, came pouring out. I felt a pulsing heat rising in my eyes, the sort that heralds a burst of my light.

Gùidan would be the one to feel its burn.

I stalked toward the door, ignoring Varyn's pleas for reason. Normally it was he who needed calming. He clutched my arm but I shook him off as I reached for it, flinging it open.

I barreled out of the gate, head whipping in every direction, searching for Gùidan. He was halfway down the path by the time I spotted his stout form stomping away. Fury filled me, I raced after him, Varyn running close behind at my heels. I had never beaten him in any of our matches, and this day was no different. Each of us reached Gùidan at nearly the same moment. He had not realized he was being chased. I took full advantage of his lack and yanked him by his silks, spinning him round to face me. His eyes bore shock and terror, for I had always been kind to him in the past. Before he could utter a word, I raised my fist. It connected with the side of his head.

"Ambroz!" This was Varyn. I ignored him and summoned my light. Gùidan cowered there before me, clutching the spot I had thrashed my fist against, wincing. I had every intention of singeing the silks off him, but the horrified look in Varyn's eye spared him from this. He had placed his body between me and Gùidan to shield the latter from his fate.

"Out, I want you out! The both of you are mad! I've left a notice on the gate. I've had enough," yelled Gùidan, backing away from us. The street was normally quiet and empty—though now, however, curious spectators lined either side of it, for we had drawn a small crowd with our quarrel.

Varyn took me by the arm as Gùidan scurried off. "Stars, Ambroz, what's gotten into you?"

I was panting and had not breath enough to answer. He led me away from the prying eyes of mortals. I went willingly down the path alongside him, slowly regaining my composure. I had no reply to his question. I do not know what came over me. It felt as though a dormant beast had been living within me and, without warning, tried to claw itself free. I trembled as we walked.

Shame took root when we reached our Nékhourí.

The sight of a whimpering Cress circling the entrance made it all the worse.

"I am sorry," I said to Varyn, to Cress, to the entirety of Hanesh. Varyn said nothing and led me quietly inside, still by the arm. He secured the gate and door, then turned to me.

"It's fine. There's nothing to forgive. He's had it coming for ages. In all honesty, he deserved a worse beating than that. I wish it had been my fist against his thick head." He said this with divided attention, eyes roaming over a piece of letter parchment.

"What does it say?" I asked.

He swiped a hand through the air, sighing. "He's putting us out—want's us gone by the end of the season."

I plucked the letter from his hands and tore it to shreds. "We are not going anywhere," I said. He regarded me with raised brows.

"You know you're frightening me a bit. Out there, when you were getting ready to burn him—that is what you were doing, right?" I nodded. "It's like you became someone else," he continued, "I've never seen you act like that."

"I am surprised you were not the one to bolt after him. All that we have worked for is gone—because of him. It is all his fault." My hands were fists at my sides, teeth clenched. I stood over the broken shards of glass, observing the nectar-infused water pooling at my feet. Hot tears streamed down my cheeks. I wiped them away with the back of my hand—a pointless act, for more flowed and took their place. Now Varyn was beside me. He thumbed away the fresh ones as they fell, then wrapped me in his arms, stroking my back.

"We have others—at the inn and Crescent Forest, remember?"

"I know. But we were so close, and he ruined it. I am just angry," I said between sobs. He let me weep into the warmth of his neck, kneading circles across my back all the while.

"I'm angry too, believe me, I want his head for this. But it's best we keep our wits about us and stay calm if we're to do it all over again with the other flower. We'll need to be of sound mind and emotion to carry on with it."

I nodded against him, and cried a while longer. Eventually, he eased me from him and guided my body toward the cushions, lowering me onto them with gentle hands. Cress came and plopped herself down upon my lap. She was in need of soothing after that earlier fright. I caressed her coat of smooth fur, listening to the sound of her soft purring.

Varyn began scooping the broken glass from the floor. Fresh tears welled in my eyes as he tossed a cloth down to absorb the fallen elixir. He was right about Gùidan—he *did* deserve a worse beating than was received. I should have struck him harder. My jaw remained clenched the whole while I spent watching Varyn tidy the area. He kept quiet as he sopped up the hard-earned culmination of his labor. When it was done, he sank onto the cushions beside me, tempting Cress to abandon the comfort of my lap in favor of his. She went and curled herself over his legs. He stroked her with one hand, placing the other upon my thigh.

"You need to rest. Go and lay down," he said.

"But the sun has not yet disappeared."

"It will soon enough."

"I am not tired."

"No," he said. "But you are weary."

I sighed, rubbing a hand over my face. Varyn placed Cress on the floor; as she ran off somewhere, he rose and pulled me to my feet. With reverent nudges, he ushered me into our bedchamber, then drew the drapes shut.

In the half-light, he undressed me. I let him escort me to the bed. He threw the covers back, and I slipped between them. I thought he might leave, but instead, he climbed in, positioning his body behind mine. The covers were warm, but his arms were warmer. He swathed me in them, and in spite of my earlier protests, I slept.

I woke to the sound of Cress mewling softly in my ear, her whiskers tickling my cheek. My eyes flitted open, and found her plump body resting in Varyn's spot. I reached for it, expecting to feel his lingering warmth, but the bed was cool against my palm. I looked about the room for him, squinting as the sunlight of a new morning shone through the windows. Cress hopped down from the bed and nipped at my ankles—she always greeted me this way upon rising. I dressed and bent to scoop her up.

Through the crack in the door, I glimpsed a portion of Varyn's bright head. With Cress in my arms, I stepped out into the drawing room and took in the full sight of him. He did not lift his head to meet my gaze, for his attention was fixed elsewhere. I studied him more intently and saw, resting between his fingers, the familiar sapphire petals of another of our flowers.

Chapter 56

VARYN SAT EXTRACTING THE NECTAR IN MUCH THE same manner as he had done before, only with more dexterity and quicker hands. It took him a while to notice me standing there.

He cast a swift, upward glance in my direction. "Keep Cress far away from this glass," he said, smirking. "I hope you don't mind my leaving you there. You looked so peaceful sleeping—didn't want to wake you."

"I wish you had," I said.

"Sorry. It came out of the ground easily enough, though. I managed just fine on my own."

"Yes, but I could have saved you the trip—my way of travel could have spared you the ride there and back in that heat. You have already worked so hard."

"I don't mind, really. Come, sit down. Are you hungry? I bought some honey, and there's fresh bread here." He kept his eyes rooted upon the flower as he spoke. Even from the doorway, I could spot the drops steadily descending into the glass of water. I welcomed the sight, relief sluicing through me. Cress was burdensome in my arms. The fear of another mishap prompted me to set her down on the floor of our room. I sealed her inside it for good measure.

"You are nearly done then?" I asked, peering into the glass as I took a seat across from him. The water bore the same sunset hue it had the day prior. A brief vision of it spilling over the marble table flashed in my memory. I thought again of that meddlesome Gùidan and hoped to the stars his head still carried the ache of my fist pummeling against it.

"Yes, almost. There's a few more yet to be taken from it."

346

I sat in silence as he worked, envisioning the end of this years-long pursuit. We were so close. In my mind, I saw it clear as a cloudless sky—me with my dear Varyn, walking hand in hand through this strange life together for all eternity. What would the seasons not yet lived bring us? More joy? More bliss? I could hardly wait to find out.

"How much longer?" I asked.

"Stars, you're impatient," he said, a half-grin slowly unfurling whilst he concentrated, "go and eat some bread with honey. When you've swallowed the last morsel, it'll be done."

I did as he advised and went to prepare myself some. As I nibbled on it, I stared out the window and tried not to mull over Varyn and the flower. It proved a difficult thing, for with each bite, my mind wandered, estimating the passage of time based upon the remaining portion of bread. I stuffed the final piece in my mouth and turned to him. Just as I began to chew, his eyes found mine. I watched as he lifted the glass to his lips. He swallowed it down in five continuous gulps, panting afterward. I ran to him, grinning.

"Well?" I asked. "How do you feel?"

He drew in a long breath. "Same as always. I thought it would taste unpleasant or make me ill within an instant."

"There is no pain?"

He shrugged. "None at all. I feel fine."

"Perhaps it needs a moment or two more to settle in you."

"We'll give it the rest of the morning then," he said, nodding.

As he went to release Cress from confinement, I picked up the empty glass. All traces of amber had vanished. Not a single drop of water had been left behind.

I watched him intently all morning, looking for signs of infirm. He appeared as healthy as ever. By afternoon, it became apparent that no illness had revealed itself. Each of us grew concerned with the realization and busied ourselves to distract from it.

"I've just remembered something," said Varyn as he emerged dripping from the bath, donned in only a bit of cloth tied round his waist. I had been tidying our room, sipping Zèkhei between chores. Upon hearing him enter, I spun to face him, brow wrinkled.

"What is it?"

"I know why it hasn't worked."

"Tell me?"

"It didn't take—the flower. That day, you told me about everything you learned on the island. You mentioned she'd said some of them wouldn't take."

No sooner had the words left him did the recollection of her advice come pouring in, filling my mind like a stream of water in cupped hands.

"You do not think it worked?" I said, a numbness overtaking me as I stood gaping.

"I know it hasn't." He held up his hand, revealing a gash in his palm. I stumbled toward him and seized it, recounting that day at the inn when I collapsed and returned to find he had opened his flesh, with the hope that my divinity had Granted his eternity.

Without hesitating, I healed it for him with my light, just as I had done back then.

Beyond our room, the sun disappeared behind clouds. I wished to vanish along with it.

"I...I do not..." I placed a hand over my chest, feeling a tightness there. Varyn peeled it away—replaced it with his.

"Everything is going to be—"

"Fine?" I asked, breaths coming hard and fast. "No, it is not fine. We have only one more, in Crescent Forest, and then—"

"Shall I tell you something I've kept from you? A secret."

"W-what?"

He rested his hands upon each of my shoulders. They had been drawn up like a knot with worry and tension but relaxed a measure at his delicate touch.

"There's several more I haven't told you about."

"What do you mean?"

"I planted them on my own."

Outside, the clouds that had swallowed the sun parted, giving way to beams of light. My desire to vanish faded.

"When?" I asked, gasping. "Where?"

"All over, different parts of Hanesh, some in Uorliék, others in the cities I've traveled to for commissions." He paused and waited for me to say something, but words escaped me.

"Varyn, you are..." He was brilliant and more thorough than anyone I knew. Of course I should have planted more than three. Why had I not? Why had I such faith that everything would work as intended? I felt an imbecile as I stood with his hands upon my shoulders, mouth ajar as I marveled at him. "I am so foolish," I whispered.

He scowled, then planted a kiss upon my forehead. "Don't speak down on yourself that way. It's not true. And I don't like it." He kissed me again—on the lips now.

"What would I do without you?" I asked.

"You'll never have to do anything without me."

Now it was me kissing him—his lips, his neck, his chest. I planted them everywhere. He grinned as I looped my hands round his waist, placing a tender peck upon either side of his face. He was laughing.

"What are you giggling about?" I asked.

There came more laughter from him. "I know what you're thinking."

"Oh? Tell me then."

"You want to take me."

I tucked my lips away to hide my grin. "And what makes you so sure of that?" I asked.

"These past few seasons, I've noticed something—a change in you."

"What sort of change?"

He placed a finger under my eye. "It's a bright copper, a little like my hair. Whenever you are in the mood to couple, your eyes glimmer with it."

I did not know whether to feel embarrassed or delighted.

After a few moments of smirking at one another, with only the sound of our breaths between us, I decided to be delighted. He went languidly to the bed as I tugged him by the cloth tied round his waist. It came undone along the way and fell to the floor. Neither of us minded. The sun made him more golden—every part of him shone. It felt like that first time all over again. We pleasured one another as we had in the forest.

Like an ardent youth, I explored his body anew, hands roaming over uncharted grooves, lips discovering sweeter spots.

"They're the brightest I've ever seen them now," he whispered against me in the throes of rapture. He told me again and again of their glow.

Afterward, I lay facing him, entwined in his arms. "What shade are they now?" I asked.

"They are amber again."

"Good, now you cannot read my thoughts."

We smirked in unison. "Who says I can't?" His hand came up and swept away the hair which had fallen half-over my eyes. "I can simply look at you and tell what you're thinking, just by the set of your jaw alone, by the measure of your breaths, by the expressions that color your features. I don't need shades to know what's in your head. I've known you all my years. At times, I know the words you'll say before you utter them—before you even form them in your mind."

I did not refute him. It was the truth. How precious a thing, to share a bond as tightly woven as ours. This I thought, as I rested near him. He sank his fingers into my hair, smoothing circles against my scalp.

"I want to go and get one of your flowers," I said. "Where is the nearest one?"

"The ones I've planted haven't yet bloomed and likely won't be ready for another twelve seasons. It wasn't straight away that I buried the Moonsoil."

"Twelve seasons?" I repeated, frowning somewhat.

"Oh, come," said Varyn. "We've endured longer periods of waiting than that. Twelve is nothing. And anyway. Those are just there as a precaution. We still have another in Crescent Forest."

"I will go there now and get it then," I said, making to disentangle myself from the warmth of his arms. He wrapped them tighter, pulling me even closer than I had been.

"No, stay with me—I don't want you to leave. I want to lay here with you a while longer. It will still be there tomorrow."

"But I will be there and back in the blink of an eye. It is only afternoon, we have the whole day ahead of us still."

"Mmm. And I want to spend it in bed with you. I want to see that copper glow in your eyes again."

A warmth filled me as I stared across at him. I could not deny him anything. I did not want to.

And so I stayed in bed.

We did not leave it.

I remember everything about that day. I remember the scent of him, fresh and floral as a meadow. And the high, clear sound of his laughter. I remember the way his petal-soft skin felt against mine. The rush of being under him, over him, behind him. I remember the way he held me. I remember every word he whispered, every blink and breath. I remember his colorful hair between my fingers and the pattern of his curls cascading to frame his ethereal face. I remember the adoring way his honey eyes regarded me. I remember feeling at home in his arms. I remember it all. Every day I remember it.

I remember and remember.

Sometimes, it is better to forget.

Chapter 57

I STOOD WATCHING THE RIVER RUN IN CRESCENT FOREST.

Before I left our Nékhourí, Varyn bade me to indulge in a swim. He told me that he loved the lingering smell of its waters on me. I dove into them, wishing he was by my side, racing against me in another of his impossible matches. I floated there.

The sun reflected off the clear surface. I sank below it, letting the bliss of weightlessness encompass me. I stayed under and stared at the rippling distortion of rays beaming from above. It was like a dance unfolding. For a long while, the warping sparkle of movement held me in a trance. Slowly, I broke from the spell and ascended.

More of the sun's rays covered me as I leisured alongside the riverbank, hands tucked beneath my head. I lay there till the soft breeze dried my damp skin and hair. I took my time pulling my garments back on.

Once dressed, I found the spot where the flower lay…and shrieked.

It was gone.

I became as still as the branches surrounding me. If my Celestial heart could stop, it would have ceased beating within my chest. *No, it cannot be*, I thought. *Perhaps I have mistaken the strip of ground.*

I searched about the area for a space which bore similarity to the one I beheld. But it was useless. I had not mistaken it for another. This was it.

I knelt and pressed my face to the forest floor. Within the soil was a faint marking, a spot where a thing once rested. It was here once. I was certain of it.

"Looking for this?"

If I had been standing, my knees would have buckled beneath my weight. That voice. I recognized it. I *hated* it.

On trembling legs, I rose, turned. The vivid, sapphire petals hung in midair, twirling as if being spun. Gradually, the fingers that held their stem faded into view, as did the rest of his body. Uncle looked much the same as he always had. The mortal realm made him seem more imposing. I had passed easily here, but he could not be mistaken for anything other than divine.

Instinct urged me to flee, but he had my flower, my Varyn's eternity, resting in his malefic grasp. And I would have it from him. I would not leave this place without it.

His strides as they progressed were unhurried, his shades a mystery. I could glean nothing from them. Even his expression left me bemused.

"How did you find me?" I asked through clenched teeth. He paused and sneered.

"You even speak like them. Do you know—I'd have mistaken you for a mortal if I was ignorant of your features. You carry yourself in their slumped fashion even. Must be the lack of light in you."

"I am not lacking any light," I spat. "How did you find this place?"

He sighed, gaze sweeping the sky. "You know so little of us gods, our tricks, our nature. We are as distant to you as the planets are to us all. The realm and its workings are beyond your understanding—a shame, really, to have been born in it but not be of it. To not know an existence there. I suppose your benightedness is a requirement of mortal life. Though I admit, I'm surprised by how utterly naive you are. That you could really have believed you were safe from the master of illusion."

Impatience prickled within me. I clenched my fists to distract from it. "How long have you known of this forest?"

"The wiser question is: why haven't you destroyed this pathetic little sanctuary of mine? And to that, I'd say it crossed my mind a time or two. I could have set this place blazing. But then I would not have this." He brought the flower to his nose and inhaled. "That concealment charm on this was...quite impressive. I didn't know what you were doing at first, coming back here all the time, crouching and watering a barren plot of ground. Discovering the seam of the charm took me longer than I care to admit. Imagine my surprise when I peeled it away and found your treasure."

"You could have destroyed it. And saved yourself the trouble of waiting and watching from the shadows like an imp," I said.

"But then I would not have you—or the delicious look in your eyes as I crush your immortal dreams. I've come to bear witness to it."

He plucked a single petal from the flower and I raced toward him with a speed which shocked even me.

Powerful Celestials like him were used to enacting a specific sort of violence when the occasion called for it—they fought all their battles with light, with divinity, and so my thrashes and tackles were something foreign to Uncle. He did not take them well and was momentarily dazed beneath me, gasping for the wind I had knocked out of him.

The flower lay on the forest floor above his head. And I lay atop him. Quickly, I straddled his waist and took him by the throat with one hand. With the other, I restrained his arm, pinning it to the ground beside his face. His free limb, unfamiliar with the act of retaliation, remained limp, like a dead snake in the grass. But his eyes shifted through an array of shades, the mask of many hues falling away. He meant to burn me, I could tell.

Scrambling in desperation, my fist connected with his jaw, giving me the advantage of time. He would need a few moments to convalesce from a blow that forceful. My knuckles stung from the impact.

I summoned what divinity I possessed as his grimace formed and faded. It rose in me, like the sun at dawn, spreading its warmth behind my eyes.

Uncle writhed beneath me. I would not be moved.

His eyes glowed, and I braced myself for what was to come.

Our light left us in unison, almost as if orchestrated. I had tensed in preparation to burn and be burned but met no scalding. The streams of our divinity merged as one and locked so that neither could overpower the other. We sustained this odd coalescence, stretching it beyond the bounds of reason.

The scorching I had steeled myself for might not have come, but a strange force was at work in my mind. I felt as if every thought or secret within me was made known.

As we held our light, my awareness of the Magician became less and less till it waned and gave way to images of Varyn, of Hanesh, of our Nékhourí, all of it flashing before my eyes—memories. I felt him digging for more and somehow thwarted his attempts. I cannot say by what method I achieved this, but it seemed as though I had dealt him a mental kick. And then, it was his memories that filled my head.

In them, I see my father, only he is a child but even so, Uncle is no match for him. There is torment. Decades of it, at the hands of the Devil, and Uncle takes it all, falling under the agony like dead leaves from a tree. His pain is worse than anything, his humiliation greater still. There are centuries more. They pass in that same pitiful way, one after another. Father is a man now, like Uncle, and the torture is unending. Mother is there, too, jeering at him.

"You thought I loved you," she says, *"You are not as powerful as him."*

I felt Uncle's memories fading then, but more of mine took their place. Varyn and I as children, racing, laughing; the two of us at sea; me at his lessons; my nights at Qêl-Ceréi. Again I jerked myself free of his prodding and once more traversed the murky waters of his buried evocations.

"The child you beget will be strong but the one born of the Devil will be strongest in the realm, stronger even than him. But dark magic can bind his divinity—stop his shades so that he is neither Reversed nor Upright in nature, but fixed in neutrality. You can manage it. You'll have to cast the spell over her womb. When he is born, it will keep all his years, so long as he does not know love here or anywhere. So long as he is shunned as the weak should be."

This is the Oracle's voice. I see Uncle's reflection in her black eyes. He is grinning. They both are. He gives her his light for this, stores upon stores of veneration. She glows with it. The memory wanes, another takes its place. Uncle holds an infant, cradling the child in his arms. He stands with the Oracle again. They are hovering over her seeing waters.

"She is destined for greatness, it is done—her fate has been altered and elevated, she will be in no Celestial's shadow, she shall wield the power of a thousand stars and each divinity combined."

The Oracle strokes the infant that is Arcana. Uncle smiles. Again the scene changes. Now I see Arcana in all her glory—she is in the great arena of the Aquarius Court for her second trials, the ones I have forgone. The mortals in attendance bow and bow and offer and praise. All over, banquets are held in her honor. I see her effigy, and its light is almost blinding. I see her face, too, shaped as sharp as a knife's point by the divinity within her. So baleful are her features now I hardly recognize them. She gloats, and I can feel Uncle's pride even through the haze of recollection.

The vision wavered again, faltering to nothing. I tried to concentrate but struggled as if being yanked. More pieces of my life came flooding out—each of them fond to me. I fought against the intrusive pressure in my head and managed again to reel these sights from its clutches. Then I was plunged back into the abyss of Uncle's mind.

I see myself from his perspective as he watches me in the forest. I remember this day. He has come here many times, but on this occasion, his presence is felt. I turn and search the air for him. I stare at him and see nothing. I leave. He watches and watches, waiting for my return. He is here but not here in the seasons I visit. It is by some working of his godhead that he perceives me, a viewing portal of sorts. I do not like being in his head. I do not like that he has invaded my thoughts, my sacred harbor of refuge.

"Enough!" I screamed. The visions faded away, thinning like sunlight at dusk. I was left in darkness.

Normal sight returned to me, and I cast my eyes down at the Magician.

The connection was broken. Disorientation emerged in the absence of it.

Wading through the fog of this, I swiftly maneuvered his body, flipping him so that he was still beneath me but with his face shoved against the ground. I restrained his arms behind his back and dug my knees into it.

"You made me believe I was nothing! All my life, I have endured ridicule for it. I have been an outcast. You cannot know what that is like. And all along, it was because of you." I was shrieking, my throat raw and burning as I pressed his face harder against the forest floor. His reply took the form of laughter. The deep, vibrating rumble of it pulsed under my palm. I shoved harder.

"Yes," he said. "I clipped your wings and what of it? What are you going to do about it? Nothing, you can't. The bind won't be severed."

I thought of my shades, of Varyn, of our love. "It is already severed," I hissed.

"For now, perhaps. You forget I have seen inside your head, just as you've seen inside mine. He's not safe there. Neither of you are. Not anymore. What will become of your meager shades when he is gone?"

"I will tell everyone what you have done."

"And who would believe you? Who would care? Certainly not your wretched father. You've embarrassed him enough as it is."

"I will make them see. This…spell, this bind you cast upon me, I can feel it slipping, season after season. It is why you could not burn me. It is why our light merged. We are bound by it, you and I. I felt it like a cord around me when our light touched. I will make them see the truth."

He erupted with more laughter. I wanted to drive my fist through his skull. "Can you hear yourself? You sound absurd. Almost as absurd as your love for that mortal. No one in the realm would listen to you. They all want you cast in chains, have you forgotten? Nothing you do will rally them to your defense. You've put the realm in the way of peril with your little fantasy of Granting. It ends here, Fool."

I pressed his face into the dirt so hard now, I feared my wrist might snap from the pressure. "Why did you do it?" I asked, gritting out each word.

"Because I could."

I could not contain my rage and put the full weight of my body on him, leaning close so that my lips grazed his ear. "You have called me weak all my life. I am nothing of the sort. You are the feeble one. And what little power you held over me was merely your weakness masquerading as strength. You are pathetic. You needed to bind me, rob me of my divinity. That alone is proof of my might."

Abruptly he writhed under my weight, knocking me off balance. I slipped, and he wrangled one of his hands free of my grip. With it, he reached for the flower above his head, but I was quicker. I seized it and leaped to my feet. An instant later, he was on his, summoning his light.

A stream of it poured from him, searing one of my arms. I narrowly escaped the second blast, running and taking shelter behind a tree. He tried to burn me again, but the surge of light was absorbed by its trunk. He razed it to a mere stump. I found protection behind another, and then another, dashing dashing dashing.

And as I fled through the forest, I thought of Varyn. I thought of home.

"You are not safe any longer. Neither of you are. I have seen. You can run and run. I will catch you in the end."

His voice thundered at my back as I raced. I ignored my fear, pushed down the tumult of pursuit around me. On and on, I charged, as if trying to win a match against Varyn. I thought again of him, kicking up little storms of dust as I bolted. Finally, the green expanse of Crescent Forest began to dwindle. My thoughts lifted me, carried me off. The Magician appeared at my side.

But the next instant, I was gone.

Chapter 58

CRESS HISSED AT ME UPON MY RETURN, BARING her fangs. I had not time to console her. She trotted behind me as I rushed through the drawing room.

"Varyn!" I shouted. "Where are you?" There came no response. I shouted once more. The sound tore from my throat in a shrill cry.

"I'm here, in my study. Everything fine? Did you get the flower?"

Amidst the chaos, I had nearly forgotten its existence. It rested in my palm, battered and missing petals, but still vibrant. I held it delicately between two fingers as I paced down the corridor. Varyn was perched on the edge of his seat, holding up materials, head tilted to one side as he studied them. He dropped them at the sight of me.

"We must leave, now," I said through heavy breaths.

"What's happened to you?" He charged toward me, pressing his hands to my cheeks and holding me in place by them. "You look just the same as you did that day you returned to me on the ship."

I told him all that had transpired in the forest, leaving nothing out. He stood gaping at me once the tale was over. "Your power," he said softly, "he stole it from you."

"Yes. But he will not have any more of it. And he will not have you." I held the flower before him. Gently he plucked it from my grasp.

"No. He will not. Pack your things, as much as you can gather. We're leaving Hanesh, we're not safe here."

He turned and began rummaging through the drawers of his desk, collecting various materials.

"But where will we go?" I asked.

"To the docks. We'll take the next ship—sail to whatever region it carries us," he paused his frantic rifling and sighed, "seems that thick-headed Gùidan will have his way after all."

Shaking his head, he swallowed the rest of his contempt and kept on. I left the study.

My thoughts raced almost as swiftly as my feet. In the bedroom, I snatched up a chest and began filling it with as many of our belongings as possible. Silks, sandals, crescents—all of it went inside. I was indiscriminate of their arrangement within it; there was not time enough to be orderly.

Little trinkets caught my eye as I worked. A gem I had inherited from Árástin or Zèfver here. An old keepsake from Ethelia there.

I could not take everything.

There was pain in this knowledge. So much of who I was lived in this Nékhourí. The years spent here had shaped me—molded me into a man. Every part of it I would miss, and yet I could not even say a proper goodbye. Not to Uorliék or Qêl-Ceréi. Not to anyone.

This sadness gave way to anger as flashes of my encounter with Uncle took form in my mind. I found myself thrusting things into the chest as if I meant them to feel the ache of my blows—as if they could absorb my fury. Thoughts of shades and the spell that bound my divinity swirled, but there was scarcely room in my head to muse over what all had been stolen from me. I could not allow myself to sink into the despair of that loss. Already I had lingered too long in this chamber. I took up a few more possessions and slipped the crescent moon pendant Varyn had given me at twelve round my neck.

He came to find me moments later, ushering me out of the bedroom with urgent tugs by the arm. His chest of belongings seemed as full as mine, the weight of it throwing off the balance of his gait. I trailed close behind him but paused at the door as he flung it open to go and find Cress.

She was curled up near a window in the washroom, lazing and unbothered.

"You are coming along," I whispered as I scooped her up. She mewled but was otherwise unfazed as I carried her out of the Nékhourí.

In the carriage she rested in my lap and I stroked her, finding calm in the rhythm of her soft purring.

We arrived at the seaport by late afternoon and as luck would have it, secured boarding for a ship bound for the northern region of Dorst.

Had we spent a moment more lingering on filling our cases, we would have missed it. The three of us piled inside the vessel, and shortly thereafter, it set sail.

Our cabin was spacious enough for Cress to prance freely about. I fetched water for her and stared out the small window as we drifted on the sea. Hanesh faded little by little, and I watched bitterly as it shrank from view.

Whilst I stood there, Varyn came and put his hand upon my shoulder. I had been fighting back tears, but the comforting warmth of his gaze drew them out.

I wept. He held me.

"I will miss it too," he whispered, cradling my head in one hand and steadying me by the waist with the other. The tender cadence of his voice was what kept me from bursting into angry sobs as I had done when Gùidan caused the loss of our elixir. The remembrance of the bright petals I stole back coaxed me into a momentary peace.

"The flower," I said, wiping away the few tears that stained my cheeks, "you must prepare it now. I cannot rest till I know it has worked—till I am sure you are safe from harm at last. Where is it?"

"It's here." He plucked it from his person. The remaining petals were half-crumpled, and I hoped the precious, amber drops would not be compromised by the ragged state of it.

"Get out your tool and take a seat upon the bed. I will fetch you some water to catch the drops."

After I had given him the glass, I sat across from him, watching as he began the tedious work of releasing the nectar from it. My thoughts drifted and settled upon what I had seen in the Magician's head. With great effort, I managed not to be overcome by fury at the memory of the Oracle's words. So much of my past now was colored by this knowledge. In my mind, I saw old scenes playing out, all of them painted in new hues.

I stopped myself ruminating, then stared at Varyn and felt my heart swelling in my chest. *He is my divinity*. His love had sundered their ploy. My light shone through the cracks he made in it. With each kiss he had given me…with each bright-eyed smile and longing gaze, we defied destiny—one written under tainted stars long before I was born. He saw my worth when I could not see it myself. So many times, he had breathed life into me, kindling new flames when the wind blew mine to smoke and ash.

and if I am the fire, he is its ember
if I am the river, he is its current
if I am the forest, he is its shade

He came to me once he had freed the flower of its nectar. It had taken him most of the afternoon, for the waters we sailed upon were not calm; rain and harsh winds beat against the windows of our cabin, and the mingling of these elements did little to aid his concentration. I took the glass from his hands as he lowered himself to sit beside me. It looked much the same as the other two.

"Do you think it will work this time?" he asked.

"It must."

I handed it to him and held my breath as he drained the glass. A fit of coughs seized him after he had swallowed all its contents.

"My throat's burning. And it tastes awful," he croaked. I leaped up and fetched him more water.

"Here, drink this. It might help to cool it." He drank deep, then wiped his mouth with the back of his hand, panting. "I think it is a good sign. Are you in pain?" I asked, gazing intently at him.

He stroked the length of his neck. "A little. My throat is scratchy, but it feels better than it did a moment ago." I placed my hand over his and squeezed it. *Please, let it have worked.*

I repeated these words over and over in my head as we sat there. Outside, a storm brewed. The wind and rain battered against the ship. We conversed to distract ourselves from it. After too long in one position, we rose, stretched, then paced circles about our cabin.

"Are you hungry?" I asked.

"Not really. I could do with something warm for my throat, though."

"I will go and fetch you a hot drink from the dining hall then."

He gave me a strained smile, and I wondered how I would bear the sight of him suffering in more pain than this when his earlier discomfort had sent shivers down my spine. I worried if I might even be able to handle watching him endure the affliction of the elixir if it came.

But I put these fears out of my mind as I filled a meal tray in the dining hall, where concerned chatter from the passengers drew my ear. I listened as they complained of the raging winds and waves. Several struck the ship on my way back to our quarters. I nearly lost balance as the vessel righted itself.

Taking careful steps, I made it to the cabin without spilling anything. Inside, Varyn lay sprawled across the floor, groaning, pallid face contorted as he writhed.

The tray slipped from my grasp and went crashing down.

I screamed.

Chapter 59

VARYN HAD NEVER LOOKED SO COLORLESS. His once-golden skin appeared dull and ashen. He was hardly aware of me as I held him in my lap, wiping the beads of sweat from his brow. The pain seemed all-consuming. It was agony to watch him wilting under it.

"My insides…feels like they're…on fire," he wheezed, hand on chest, hair sticking to his face. I smoothed it back, revealing more of his wincing features. His curls were damp with perspiration, and as he whimpered there, sprawled half over my legs, I quickly weaved them into a braid.

"It is going to be fine," I whispered, hands massaging his aching body. "This means the elixir is working."

He was clutching his abdomen now, rocking back and forth across my lap like the tumultuous waves of the storm surrounding us. "It's to go on for a…full day…but…I don't know how much more I can take." With these words, he slipped from consciousness. This was the last coherent thing I heard from him, and by evening, the full extent of sickness seized his body.

When his awareness returned, I carried him to the bed. He tossed and writhed, thrashing about upon it. I was glad to see him faint again, for at least it meant an escape from that torment. I crouched near him with Cress by my side. His face twitched slightly, lips parting to release a faint moan.

Tears balanced upon the rim of my eyes as I knelt there. I wanted so badly for this storm to pass, both the one which raged within him and the one whirling on the sea. Its waters now were black, and I yearned to hasten the arrival of the sun so that this ordeal could end. I did not wish to see him shoulder through a moment more of such unrelenting torture.

At times during it, he reached for me, clutching my hand so tight I feared the bones beneath my flesh would splinter and crack. Others, he lay still, chest rising and falling with ragged, shallow breaths. I could not resist pressing a few kisses to his temple amidst these intervals, where a sliver of peace painted his features. To soothe myself further, I imagined this misery over and done—a thing endured and behind us. I thought of all the years we had yet to live. Each of them free of worry—unburdened by the looming threat of mortality.

I studied him as these promising joys filled my mind, and gazed down at the features I loved so dearly. His eyes shifted behind closed lids. I longed to be pierced by their warmth. He stirred briefly, squirming with the beginnings of a fit of convulsions. I braced myself for their onset but was drawn from him by a knock behind the door. I swung it open, and a crewman stood on the other side.

"The storm's not letting up," he said. "Captain wants it known that we'll be docking at the next port to ensure the safety of all on board."

"Thank you for giving notice," I said. He nodded and excused himself.

I returned to Varyn and continued nursing him through the cycles of this contemptible illness. Finally, there came a break in it, where he seemed as if he could be sleeping. I had been perched bedside for what felt like a season. My limbs were stiff and aching. As I rose, stretching, I spotted Cress curled upon my bed. I joined her there, keeping a watchful eye on Varyn. The soft cushion was a welcome reprieve under me. I had not meant to let my eyes shut. I had not meant to drift.

The swaying ship was the thing that jolted me from dozing. But an odd creaking cemented my awareness. I squinted through the dark for Varyn and, to my horror, found a shadowy figure hovering over him. It was of a height and bearing—its squared shoulders gave me pause. How long had it been standing there?

My breath became trapped in my chest.

"Get away from him," I commanded.

A sneer—half illuminated by moonlight. "Or what?" Uncle turned, and there was divinity brimming in his eyes. "I told you I would catch you."

Frenzy drove me toward him in a mad charge. My light broke free, a deluge of it, all streaming at the Magician's chest. He flew through the door as it made contact with him, ripping it off its hinges. I dashed to Varyn. He was struggling to sit upright in the throes of affliction. I flung his arm over my shoulder, drawing him up. He mumbled something indiscernible, barely able to stand.

"We must go, Varyn. It is not safe here. My uncle has—" I wailed as a blast of light slid across my back, tearing flesh. I turned and shielded Varyn, he was staggering, but even in his stupor of sickness, he acted in defense of me, hurling a drinking glass at the Magician as he loomed in the doorway. It bounced off his head, and I burned him once more, running toward him.

I knocked him out into the corridor, where we exchanged both light and blows. Mortals scurried around us, fleeing in fear from the scrimmage of Celestials. But this was not all that they fled from. Water pooled at my feet, rising up the decks. We were in the lower quarter of the ship, though soon it would travel higher.

In my observation, I neglected to maintain guard from Uncle. An instant ago, I had hooked him with a burn across the face, but it healed in swift moments. Now his hands gripped my throat. He lifted me by it. I went flying over a parapet and fell from a height. Uncle leaped down to join me, dragging me up and thrashing me against a wall. I was buried to the calves in water now.

"Do you like the storm I conjured for you?"

I struck him with my fist, but the force of the blow was weak, and he merely grinned, revealing the blood-stained silver of his teeth. I aimed another punch at him. He caught it.

"You would hurt all these mortals in pursuit of one? You would sink an entire ship full of them just to have this...this..." Words failed me, and so I poured every drop of my malice into him, glaring as he squeezed my captured fist. I wrangled it free and drug a beam of light across his neck. He stumbled back. "I despise you," I spat.

The seared flesh along his throat healed swiftly. I still bore wounds from earlier assaults and was fighting not only him but against my weariness too. It was like a fog descending upon me. He could sense this, I think, for he sneered as he brought forth his light. I readied myself to try and block it—to merge our streams as one as we did in the forest. Instead of directing his retaliation toward me, however, he turned and blasted holes across the floor of the vessel.

A rush of water flooded in through the perforations. He sent more of his light out. This time, it severed a beam that supported the ship. With its structure now compromised, parts of it came crashing down around me. Shouts and screams echoed from above as mortals scrambled. I thought of Varyn, ill and delirious and alone. I had to get to him. I had to save him.

This thought consumed me as Uncle carried on destroying the ship. I waded through the water, and the drifting chattels, chairs, and tables, till I reached a set of stairs. At the top of them was more destruction. Doors stood open, the rooms they once guarded now slanted in disarray. It took effort to keep balance as the tilt grew more severe. I climbed my way through it, trudging, and made it to our cabin.

Inside, a startled Cress peeked at me from under the bed, eyes glowing. She ran to me, and I snatched her up. Varyn was nowhere in sight. I cried out for him breathlessly as I ran down the corridors, searching as many rooms as time would allow. Cress clung to me whilst I navigated the frenzy of dashing mortals, all of them clambering to reach the topmost deck.

When finally we made it there, she leaped down from my arms. The storm raged, and rain beat harshly against my skin, piercing it like the prick of a thorn. As she fled from me, I followed the path of her scurrying body and shrieked.

Varyn had somehow managed to fight his way here in the midst of illness. But whatever will or strength the interim of its haze had afforded him was dwindling now. He sat slumped at the end of the rain-soaked deck, back propped against the parapet. The awareness he had acquired was slipping. His features were fixed in a pained grimace. I ran to him, shouting his name and shouldering mortals. Some I knocked over in my haste, and as I sprinted, he lifted a weak arm with which to receive me, a glimmer of hope flickering in his eyes.

I raced and raced and raced. Nothing around me existed save for him. Nothing at all.

And so I did not notice I was being chased.

The Magician fisted my hair as I ran, jerking me backward by it. I went skidding across the deck, tumbling and rolling. His light was on me the next instant. The blast caught me full in the face—a blinding white fury. I remember the pain of it, like the heat of a thousand flames. I remember flying back through the air from the force with which it struck me. I remember another blast upon my chest, knocking me over the parapet.

And before my consciousness abandoned me, I remember the sight of the stormy sky as I fell, descending toward the crashing waves.

I did not feel the water as I was swallowed by the sea.

I was already floating in blackness by then.

·········ᴖᴖ ● ᴖᴖ·········

When I came to again, I found myself beneath the water, at the bottom of the Scorpion Sea. My chest burned; it craved the air above surface. I swam up, slogging through the heavy cerulean, till finally, I broke free from it, gasping at the dawn sky as I took in breath after breath.

"Survivor! Over here!" I heard someone shouting in the distance and turned to find a small boat drifting toward me. Inside of it were two women and a man. They pulled me from the water and wrapped blankets around my body.

"The gods have blessed you," said the man, eyes wide, "we were near to leaving. Not many survivors on that wreck. I saw it going down from the watchtower, nasty storm that was."

"Survivors," I repeated, voice hardly above a whisper, "how many others have you saved?"

"A few. We didn't spot the ship quick enough to be of much help to the living. We've gathered a great many dead, though. They're on the shore with the others we saved. Was it Dorst you were headed for?"

I nodded, numb and dazed and drenched. A few, he said. *A few.*

The memory of Varyn, weak and reaching, blazed in my head. If there were a few who lived, then undoubtedly, he was among them. I would sail to this shore and find him there, waiting for me, reaching and smiling.

Yes.

He and Cress were there, and soon we three would reunite, and all would be well.

All would be well.

This I repeated as the boat went along, silently willing it to hasten its tread across the water. The sun began to peak over the horizon by the time a shore appeared in the distance. I rose and squinted hard, as if this alone might traverse the gap between land and sea. But I could discern nothing through my slits, merely a long stretch of pale sands. With a huff, I sat again and fingered the crescent moon pendant hung round my neck, drawing to mind memories of the day a bright and golden boy of twelve gave it to me, beaming his warmth upon me in the forest.

I was the first to leave the boat once it neared the shore. The land beneath my feet felt unnatural after so long afloat. I ran across it anyway, tripping and stumbling over myself. One of the women who plucked me from the water now lifted me by the arm.

"Easy there, you, the inn's not going anywhere," she said. I had been darting toward the small, brown abode, desperate to burst through its doors. Inside I found four mortals, their backs to me as they sat sipping from bowls, huddled together in blankets. None were copper-haired, none were Varyn. I turned to the woman at my side.

"Where are the rest of the survivors?" I asked.

"You're looking at them. This is everyone."

"No," I said, "you must be mistaken. Are there rooms here? Perhaps he is resting in one of them."

A tight-lipped smile spread thinly across her face. "Come this way," she said, taking me by the arm. I staggered behind her as she led me through a narrow passage. We came upon a little door, and before pushing it open, she turned to me. "If you're looking for someone, this is where you might find them." She twisted the handle, and I stepped over the threshold. Outside, the wind carried the salt of the sea...gently it blew as though it had never galed. The storm left no traces upon the sky; no graying clouds glided across the expanse. Though beneath it lay the evidence of its savagery: resting upon the sands were shrouds upon shrouds of white.

I forced myself to look at them.

"I'll pull back the covering for you to check their faces. We can start at the end and work our way up." I barely took in her words and moved forward on numb legs as if dazed.

I gazed upon one, two, three blank faces. On the fourth, I seized her wrist.

"Leave me," I said. She departed with hesitation. I crouched in the sand, feeling the grains against my bare knees. The curled tail of an auburn braid poked out from under the white shroud. Slowly, I peeled it back.

"Varyn," I whispered. "I am here. Wake up." He did not answer. "Please, Varyn. If you wake up. I can get another flower. We can try again. But you must wake up." I begged and begged. He did not stir.

His lips under mine were cold as marble. I wrapped him tighter in his shroud and held him to me. Always his warmth had soothed my pains. Now it was my turn to be a comfort to him.

His eyes do not see me as they stare.

His body, void of his brightness, is the cruelest sight.

They said the sound of me, my wailing, was like that of an animal. A wild beast who knows no awareness of self.

Day turned to night, night to early dawn. I held him. Mortals came and tried to take him from me. I did not let him go.

"Come inside now," someone said, "you must eat and rest."

I kissed Varyn's forehead, held him tighter. "If I leave, he will be cold."

Later, someone brought a meal. I did not eat it. I will never eat again.

Later still, they returned, found me dozing with my Varyn. I was dreaming of his warmth. Of his golden smile. Of his laughter.

We are happy in this dream. I want to stay here, but someone wakes me, and I remember and remember and remember.

Days pass. Varyn is so cold now. It does not matter that I am holding him. I cannot make him warm no matter how near I press him against me.

"We have made a pyre for him. Which deity did he serve?" That voice again. I turned and saw a group of three standing over us.

"What?" I croaked.

"His ashes, which deity's altar shall we erect, so that his life may be offered and his embers burned upon their effigy in the Celestial realm?"

Deity, effigy. I scoffed and spat. "None." They shared a gasp.

"But he must—"

"Leave us!" I screamed. Two scattered away. One lingered. A man. He leered down at Varyn and me. I saw disgust in his eyes.

"It's no wonder such misfortune befell him," he muttered.

I felt a fire burning in my chest, its heat spreading spreading spreading up. This mortal man remained there as it rose in me. I glared. "What I mean is, it should be done. Goddess Arcana is known to control the winds. She very well might have quelled that storm had she been venerated. Honor her and see your grief lessened." With this, he backed away, shuffling off to the inn.

I lay Varyn gently on the sand. My flesh prickled hot as though molten, silver blood ran beneath it. I nearly dug my nails in to tear it out. It unfurled within me, like a bird spreading its wings, wider and wider and wider and wider till

something

shattered

The mortal man did not reach the door of the inn. I seized him by the hair, dragged him through the sand.

Light.

It flowed and scorched the fingers from his hand. He clutched the mangled thing to his chest, screaming in agony.

"Please, please," he whimpered, "I didn't know you were a Celestial. I beg you. Grant me your forgiveness high one, Grant me your mercy." More whimpers. More prayers from him. They filled me, enriched me, intoxicated me. I knelt. Hovered over this sniveling mortal. Again and again, he venerated me, trembling there, gripping his charred hand. I should relieve him of the limb, sever it entirely. He does not deserve to keep it after uttering a slight upon Varyn.

As I made to scorch his vile flesh, the wind blew the shroud from Varyn's body. I ran to him, cloaking it once more.

The mortal fled.

I took Varyn up in my arms and carried him away.

I dropped my tears into the sea as we knelt by the shore together. He always loved the water. If he had been well, he could have conquered those waves. He would not have drowned.

I think of the elixir as I rip the shroud and anchor rocks to his feet with it. I think of how it had not time enough to make him eternal. Fury envelops me.

I stand over the rippling water and watch his body sink beneath the surface. It is torture to surrender him to the deep blue. My reflection dances upon it.

I gaze gaze gaze.

The hue of my eyes shift from amber, to black, to sapphire, to violet, to silver, to bronze. They shift and shift and shift, on and on and on on on on on on

I feel each color—I feel the depth of emotion that accompanies every one of them.

My eyes cycle through the vast array, and in the end, they settle upon a rich, gleaming, honeyed hazel.

How cruel a thing that

This is the shade of my rage.

I think now of the Celestial realm as I turn my back on the Scorpion Sea.

I will destroy everything.

Their prophecy has come to pass, and for what they have done, I will burn it down to cinder.

Till nothing is left but

ash, but smoke,

but mere

echoes of ember and effigy.

Chapter 60

THE FULLNESS OF MY DIVINITY HAS COME OUT. I feel it coursing through me with each breath. The bind is no more. For the whole of my life, I let others tell me who I was, tell me of my deficit. I was never weak.

They will see now what I truly am capable of.

Chapter 61

I BEGAN IN THE NEBULA GARDENS, WHERE DOZING Celestials peered at me through their haze. Some jeered at my return. Some made threats. Till I called forth my light, then all fled from the crashing of towers, the raging of flames, the path of my ire. I razed it to nothing. It was so easy.

In the Cosmic Library, I searched for that vile, fate-stealing divinity—the Oracle. But found Tiberias instead.

"I always knew you were daft, but I didn't think you would be daft enough to come back here," he said as he lumbered toward me, smirking. It fell from his lips as he came near, as he beheld me and the colorful rage which flared behind my gaze. I seared him, and the sound of his screams was a melody.

"Where is the Oracle?" My fist was in his hair. My light brimming. He struggled and shrank in the face of my divinity.

"I—she is—I think…" I burned him.

"Are you without wit?" My voice thundered, and I kicked him to the floor. The terror in his eyes…it brought me such pleasure. I clasped his face to derive more of it, dug my fingers into his cheeks. "Shall I relieve you of your tongue then? Since it seems of no use to you." He whimpered. Shook his head. "Then tell me where she is without stuttering. Last chance before I blaze the bottom of your face away."

"There is a gala in the Virgo Court. She is there. Please don't burn me again."

"I will if I do not find her there."

He sniveled and wailed beneath me as I dragged him through the realm by his dark mane. I scorched any divinity in my path. A flock of seven Pentacles tried to intervene and I sent them running off with no skin, leaking their silver about the halls, empty of their veneration stores. The thrill of ripping it from their chests had sent me buzzing all over.

In the ballroom of the Virgo Court, I held the glowing orb in my palm, balancing it there as I studied the face of every divinity present. I absorbed the sphere of stolen light and floated to the center of the festivities, still dragging Tiberias along by the hair.

"Oracle, show yourself," I said.

"What's this about?" A minor deity of the Cups peered up at me, wide-eyed. I plucked the chalice he held and drained it of its Stars Brew, then bounced it off his head.

"She must answer for her wrongdoing. Where is she?" I spat.

"She's not here," someone called out from the crowd.

At this, new light burned in my eyes. Tiberias received it as it poured from me. He screamed and pleaded. I did not stop. My hand sank into his chest, and with a yank, his stores were mine. Still, I scorched till there were no features or flesh but only muscle and sinew. It felt so good to burn him. I could not stop. By the time I pulled back, he was nothing more than a shimmering skeleton. The hall fell silent as the air. Only the sound of my crazed chortles could be heard. I stifled them behind glowing fingers, crouching as I stared down at the disintegrating pile of stardust.

"I did not know I could do that," I said, rising to my feet. The Celestials encircling me took a collective step back. A profusion of horrified expressions regarded me.

"His starlight, you b-burned it from his blood." Some trembling voice from the sea of them wailed this. The fear in their eyes. I loved it. I would have it from them all.

How I hated this realm, these deities.

My gaze roamed over their faces. I found the Star among them—she shivered. The trials I had alongside her at six came back to me. I should have another go at them; I should see how many of these deplorable beings I can scorch to dust at once, I thought, and as I did, something shimmered in my periphery. It sparkled beside me for a mere moment, then flickered from this place to that. I followed its course. It was making for the archway. It was leaving—escaping.

The blast of light I sent toward it shattered his cloaking spell. And the look on Uncle's face as it fell away felt even better than my slaying of that ugly Tiberias.

The Magician tried to flee, but I was fast on his heels. Just ahead of him stood a towering, crystal beam. I split it with a jet of light, transported myself by thought the next instant, then brought it crashing down over him. The impact crushed one of his legs. My hands were around his throat before he had the chance to free his broken limb from under it. He bore a countenance as smug as ever, even as my nails coaxed ribbons of silver from his throat.

"Was it worth it to take him from me?" I drove a fist through his chest, tore out his light with it. He shrieked and tried to writhe himself free, but his power was no match for the fullness of mine. He had never known it. "Was it not enough to steal one light? You had to have another from me?" I strangled him harder. "Answer me!"

"Pity I didn't get to see the look on your face when you pulled that mortal from the sea. How pale and shriveled your Varyn must have looked."

"Do not dare speak his name." I ripped more light from his pathetic chest, soaked it in, then expelled it back at him, across his throat, tearing it open. He gurgled and croaked, but his smug grin never left him. He tried to burn me with feeble, dwindling light. I plucked whatever remained from within his mangled form and held it out for him to see.

"It's… no…matter," he mumbled, struggling through each word. I peered inside his mind, saw his effigy and the abundance of its glow. In a flash I was there and back—the marble of him tucked under my arm. The look of horror in his eyes. I had never seen anything like it. Oh, how it fed me, filling a hunger newly created—one so violently ravenous. More, I needed more.

"'It is no matter. I am highly venerated. My effigy burns bright,' is that what you were thinking— is that what you were going to say?" His grin faltered. Effigies are said to be carved of a marble as invulnerable as the stardust coursing through our silver blood. But that means little, for stars and their light, as immortal as they may seem…can die. I have proved as much and more.

The sculpture cracked under the force of my fist. Its light was mine to keep. I ground the marble to grains, and around me, there were gasps and cries. Melodies.

I climbed atop Uncle in the midst of them and saw myself—my honey-shaded rage—reflected in his obsidian eyes. He had not the strength to cast his illusions over them. I saw his naked fear now and devoured it. "This is all your fault," I said.

All manner of deities looked on, huddled together like decaying shrubs in a garden. The sound of their screams filled the Earth Wing as I reduced the Magician to a mound of particles. But one scream above all drew me. Arcana came barreling through the courtyard. She flung herself at me, splitting into a multitude of deities, all of them piercing me with sienna glares. I cut them down with the ease of breathing and vanished, only to return a blink later with her marble, dragging it behind me as I paced languidly in her direction.

"That is right." I sneered, noting the bemusement that creased her brow. "You have no power over me. You have no power at all. You never did. It was never yours."

The sword of light she aimed at my head connected with her effigy, for swiftly, I had maneuvered it to shield myself.

She bellowed as it cracked. I shattered it further, and she charged.

"I should have shackled you when I had the chance," she cried, sending more of her light at me. It was easily deflected, like swatting away a winged pest.

"Yes, you should have."

Before her eyes, I demolished her effigy, but not without having first emptied it of its light. It belonged to me. Everything now was mine, even the sobs and tears she shed over the remnants of Uncle. I conjured some wind and blew the heap of him to nothing, cackling as it scattered like sand across this landscape of destruction. As she grieved, I destroyed one effigy after another. Growing fat on their light.

What will any of them be without their conduits? Nothing.

I graced the Court of Libra, of Gemini, of Scorpio, of Capricorn, on and on, till the Hall of Effigies stood bare in every wing. I sat amidst the decimated debris of the Aries Court, staring at the only remaining sculpture. I touched its head and gave it light. It glowed. It had never glowed. I smiled at my carved twin faintly. But smiles reminded me of him. So many he had given me. It faded as quickly as it came.

The pendant hung round my neck was all that remained of him.

I wept as I fingered it, longing to see the upward curve of his lips, to feel them once more under mine.

From my unbound light I fashioned him, chiseling into the marble those features I so loved. It was the perfect likeness of him. I held the stone to me and wept and wept and wept.

Chapter 62

I POSSESS THE LIGHT OF A THOUSAND STARS, AND I do not sleep. I only dream of him. The way he looked while braiding his hair. His stern brow whenever he drew something. His slow-spreading smile. I wanted these things all around me. And so I emptied the Hall of Effigies of its Celestials and filled it with him instead. Hundreds and hundreds of him.

I spend my days embracing him. His arms do not come round me, his eyes do not see me, but I love him.

It is said that time heals all wounds, but there is never mention of the scars left behind—those markings which years cannot fade. They brand themselves upon the flesh and shape new beings. I do not know how many seasons have passed. I do not know how old I am. Perhaps I have lived for a century. Perhaps I have lived for two. I cannot tell. The sun, they say, has given up rising. I hear their whispered orisons pleading for its return. The realms are in darkness. I do not care. For I have light.

Through the dimness, I stare and stare at his marble, bringing my hand to the hollow of my neck. The crescent has turned to ash, but I pretend it is still there. My finger remembers its shape and loops... loops... loops.

I trek through the decaying halls. The realm, once, long ago, would replenish itself after damage. But now it is fetid and oozing because of me. I am a killing god. Deity of destruction and murder. They will write songs of my wrath. Lines and verse of rage and ruin.

I have killed so many Celestials. Few remain. Arcana and the Oracle cling to their waning divinity. I keep them chained in the chasm they once prepared for me, their light shackled and inert. Mother and Father, too. And others. I take pleasure in taunting them, burning them.

They whisper and whimper as I draw near.

As I torture the Oracle, a voice calls out to me.

"My child," it says, "enough now." I turn and stare at the cloaked figure. She is silver-haired and towers over me, obsidian skin so smooth, it offers me my reflection. I do not recognize myself. But I recognize her. Her presence is mighty. The Moon has come down from her sky. She places a formless hand upon my shoulder. I faint under her cosmic touch.

When I wake, I am in the ruins of the twelve courts. Solemn faces peer at me from a distance.

"Do you know why you are here?" This is the Moon again. She hovers by my side. I shake my head. "You stand before the tribunal of the High Nine. Mercury and Mars have a fate they wish to see upheld for your transgressions. I do not desire it for you. Nor does Benefic Jupiter. The others are undecided. I have persuaded them to hear your account of things. It is only fair. Give us your testimony now, my child."

I know the others are watching, listening. But when I speak, I speak only to the Moon. I tell her everything. I tell her of how my heart swelled at his slightest touch. Of how it felt to be cloaked in his warmth. I tell her it was him who helped me know myself. I tell her I was never weak. I tell her that he gave me strength. I tell her of his wit, his laughter, his smile. I tell her I am sorry.

I tell her everything.

There is silence now that I have finished, and my face is wet with tears. I wipe them.

"You have asked me to stand trial—to tell you the story of me, of the Fool," I say, "I have told it. The whole of it. Now you must tell me, how will you judge my journey?"

The planets pass their judgment. First upon the remaining Celestials.

Saturn says, "You will be gods in this realm no more. You cannot be trusted with forms and will live only in the stars now."

"And me?" I ask. "What will become of me?"

Chapter 63

WHEN MY DEATH COMES, I DO NOT SEEK TO EVADE IT. I have earned it.

The Moon sings me to sleep so that I feel no pain. Her trance holds as the Sun takes back his stardust from me. After it is done, I float in the sable expanse of nothing. I am nowhere. I am mortal. I am dead. This is what I think as the darkness carries me.

But I am not in darkness. I *am* the dark.

I open my eyes and see a blue sky above me.

A river runs at my back. I stand and marvel at the forest which encircles me.

"You came!" a boy yells, running toward me in the distance. His curly hair is a bright shade of copper, and his laughter is high as birdsong. He is a child. I am a child again, too. "I knew you would come," he says, "I was waiting for you."

I run to him. We collide, and he lifts me, spins me.

Round and round.

He plants me on my feet and we are men again. His lips meet mine. He holds me so tight in his arms.

At long last, I am home.

Ambroz

Varyn

······›·) ● (·(·········

Acknowledgments

Thank you to Kelly Gaines for being the best friend anyone could ask for. Your unwavering support has given me the strength and courage to follow my dreams. Thank you to Lauren Greene for all your wisdom and guidance—for helping me find my voice and being a bright star during my darkest night. To Kauthar Rahman, thank you for your unending encouragement, and for lending me water from your overflowing well of wit. And lastly, thank you to Simone Smith for always believing in my vision and shaping it into something tangible with your invaluable advice.

THE FOOL

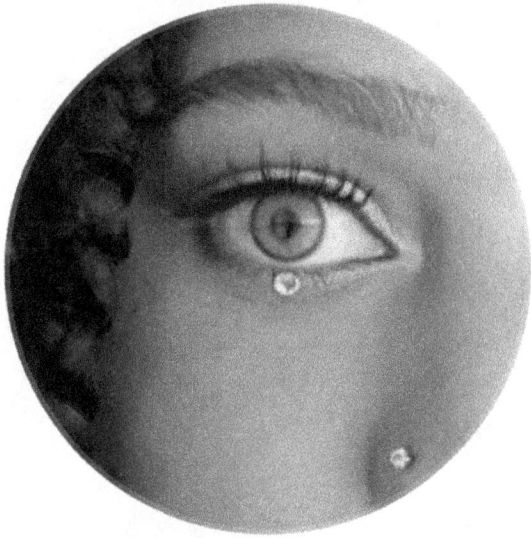

Vana Elaire is an introvert, an Infj, and a hermit. She lives a child-free life in North America. When not lost in the realms of imagination, she enjoys exploring new languages, discovering hidden bookshops, and indulging in endless cups of coffee. Echoes of Ember & Effigy is her debut novel. Find her on Instagram @veiled.by.ink